Bokeh

By

Matthew F. Winn

Matthew F. Winn

Other Books by Matthew F. Winn

The Sandman
Bring Me a Dream
Circle of Friends
Every Picture Tells a Story
Stealing Rembrandt
Chasing Shadows in the Dark
The Legacy
Shadowman
The Watcher (YA)

Coming soon

Mishipeshu: The Legend of Grand Island
Jack Kerouac Can Kiss My Ass
King of Hearts
Driven
You Are Not Supposed to be Here

Cover photography by the author
See more photographic works at www.splashofsunset.com
Published by Artist's Point Press

For

Amber Lynn Taylor for being a constant motivational force and an ever-present ray of sunshine illuminating a sometimes dark and dismal world with her effervescent enthusiasm.

One

Beauty is in the eye of the beholder, or so the time worn adage tells us. But what if the beholder is not certain what it is that they are looking at? What if the reflection staring back in the mirror's shimmering surface is a completely foreign entity? Is a monster even aware of the fact they are indeed a monster?

Our entire lives are nothing more than a series of snapshots of the world in which we live. Each photograph freezes a specific moment in our lives while the rest of time marches onward. In the mere minutes it takes for us to examine the image just captured it has already become old and outdated trapping a piece of our essence within a diminutive sliver of Kodachrome.

"Rebecca. Rebecca," a woman said aloud for a second time.

The name still rolled awkwardly off her tongue even after more than a year after adopting the nom de plume. She lightly traced the scar under her right eye. It was no longer visible in the mirror, but it was a flashing neon sign to her just the same. The miniscule line of scar tissue was nothing more than a ridge beneath her fingertip but to her it felt like a welt freshly laid by a bullwhip. A whisper of a memory invaded her taste buds and caused a shudder to ripple through her. For one brief moment she tasted earthworms and wet dirt.

She stood with her back to the Mission Hill cemetery gazing out over Spectacle Lake and beyond that, the shimmering surface of Lake Superior. In the pre-dawn hour, she could see the beacon from Point Iroquois Lighthouse warning passing freighters of the shallows. Across from that lie the Goulais Bay Indian Reserve in Canada. She envied the freedom of the passengers as she watched airplanes arcing through the air on their final approach to Sault Sainte Marie airport. For a lumbering beast of steel, they glided effortlessly across the sky with grace and precision.

When her horrors began Rebecca had thought long and hard about fleeing to Canada to escape the brutality of her life, but in the end, she could not leave her homeland. So, she settled on the next best thing, she had fled north from Troll Land below the Mackinac bridge into Michigan's Hiawatha National Forest where she assumed a new identity and disappeared into the wilderness. And still, less than two months later she ended up buried in a shallow grave.

Even though more than a year had passed after she had been left for dead, she was still too frightened to venture out in the daylight away from the safety of the small tribal community where she resided in anonymity. And even though she knew it was a prison of her own making, she couldn't shake the feeling of being unjustly confined.

The sunrise had completed its daily mission, so she began her trek back to her hidden cabin as the sun painted the horizon with a golden glow. Winter's chill was still hanging in the air, but the robin's tweet and the eagle's screech signaled spring's return was not far off. She took a long, last look over the world before retreating into her own world of forced solitude.

She mounted her horse Buttercup, a gorgeous two-year-old Akhal-Teke. The mare had been quite pricey, but Rebecca knew she would not be needing much money to support her new lifestyle, so she splurged on herself. And in all honesty, how much should one pay for their one true friend in the world. The sun broke free of a few hazy clouds and illuminated the two of them as they sauntered down the beach. Buttercup's golden coat shimmered as if she were cast from the precious metal and not a flesh and blood beast.

Pancake ice floated in the bay even though the majority of the ice and snow on land had already melted. Rebecca dismounted and walked to the water's edge where she crouched to listen to the hissing ice. The lake was calm and there were no waves, just a gentle rising and lowering of the surface as if the lake were breathing. When the waters receded, they caused the pancake ice to emit a gentle hiss. Buttercup took a long drink and gave a snort in protest to the icy glacial water.

Rebecca heard footsteps crunching the sand and shell mélange behind her and tensed. She dropped a hand into her pocket and clutched her berretta. Buttercup snorted so she used the horse's warning to cover the click of the safety being turned off. She spun on her heels in the soft sand and raised her hand holding the gun without ever pulling it from her pocket.

"Whoa, easy killer. It's just me," an older man in a forest green police uniform said while raising his hands.

"Shit! I'm sorry Chief," she said, relaxing her grip on the pistol and engaging the safety.

"I told you to call me Uncle Joe," the man said with a smile creasing his leathered face.

"But that is not your name, and you are not my uncle."

"And Rebecca is not your name either. But this is something we both need to get used to, given your rather unique circumstances."

Joe LeBlanc served the tribal community of Bay Mills as the head law enforcement officer. The little village was nestled on the shores of Lake Superior just west of Brimley and was about as boring a place as one could ever imagine, and Joe wanted to keep it precisely the way it was.

The pair walked silently down the lakeshore away from the town and toward Point Iroquois lighthouse. Joe ran his fingers through his thick black hair streaked with the ever-present silver signs of age. He was certain he didn't have as much gray when Rebecca first materialized in his world a little more than a year ago.

"Chief, it has been more than a year and I have been thinking."

"Absolutely not."

"You didn't even know what I was going to say," she said, offering him a weak smile. The sun was fully up on the horizon and the golden glow reflected off her shimmering blonde hair.

"Some of your roots are starting to show, maybe you should concentrate on that," Joe said, a little sterner than he had intended.

"You are not supposed to point out those sorts of things to a woman."

"Maybe not if she is cheating her age, but when she is trying to cheat death then I think it is perfectly acceptable."

"Don't you think you are overreacting? So, a few roots are showing."

They arrived at the Point Iroquois lighthouse, but it was still closed to tourists for the season. The edifice was a standing work of art, the lighthouse was white with gray trim and a deep, crimson roof. A beautiful, knee-high fieldstone fence surrounded the lighthouse adding an inviting spice to the structure.

Rebecca tied Buttercup to a hitching rail while she and Joe continued down the boardwalk encircling Point Iroquois. Forsythia bushes were starting to bud and would soon be exploding with delicate yellow flowers. There was just a hint of lilac drifting across the open field signaling spring was reticently making an entrance. The wind started to pick up the more the sun made its presence known bringing with it a chill that settled across the beach.

"Need I remind you that you were shot in the head, buried alive and then damned near frozen to death. And your ex-husband, the person who did that to you believes they succeeded in killing you. You are only safe from them as long as they continue to believe that you are dead."

"You are right about one thing Joe. Bryant genuinely believes I'm dead which also means he isn't looking for me."

"He may not be looking for you, but he knows quite a few folks around these parts who might just pass along information to him."

"These parts? Meaning the Upper Peninsula, not just Bay Mills correct?" she said, unable to tame the contempt in her voice.

"The entire Upper Peninsula itself is like a small town, you would be wise to remember that. Everybody knows everyone's business up here. If Milton Skunda backs into his mailbox over in Trenary while leaving for his morning errands we hear about it here in Bay Mills within the hour," he said with a reserved smile.

Rebecca stifled a shudder as a cold wind blew down the back of her collar. The smell of dirt and worms invaded her senses forcing her to gag a little and she admitted to herself that Joe was right. Her ex-husband wanted her dead and she was only safe if Bryant believed she was in fact dead.

"Are you alright?" Joe asked.

"I'm fine. Now back to how this whole conversation started," Rebecca said, brushing off the heebee jeebees.

"Absolutely not," Joe said without hesitation.

"You don't even know what I'm going to say."

"Yes, I do because you have been asking me every single week for the past six months. I thought you were just having a rough patch of cabin fever and would get over it as soon as winter passed. I guess I was wrong."

"You do know what they say about assuming," Rebecca smiled. "I have got to get away from this hell hole, even if it's just for a day. No offense."

"A lot of offense taken. This hell hole is my home and I have grown kind of partial to it. And it has been a fairly good home to you for the past year I might add. Our community welcomed you with open arms and with no questions asked if you would recall."

"Yes, I know, and I'm eternally grateful. But you are an old man, boring suits you. A young woman needs something more than just fishing, gambling, and bingo. One more bingo night spent arguing with the blue hairs and I will go nuts."

"There is a lot more to do here and you know it."

"Yeah, unending chores and pizza on Friday nights. I need to get out of this town before I go any more stir crazy than I already am."

"Don't forget about the spring arts and crafts sale at Saint Kateri's this afternoon. That is sure to be loads of fun."

"You're a real hoot Joe," she said as she mounted her horse.

Rebecca trotted off across the street where she picked up a trail running parallel to the forest road that led to her cabin in the woods. While this time of year was gray and dreary it did offer her the comfort of being able to see through the trees for a great distance. Again, she was invaded by a round of shudders brought on by the chilled breeze and her own memories coming back to haunt her. She had not thought about lying in that shallow grave for what seemed like months. Why all the sudden was the memory tormenting her now?

As clear as a bell she heard the hammer of the pistol click back and felt the cold steel pressing against the back of her ear. She felt the cold, hard stones and roots digging into her knees as she awaited her final moment on earth while praying she would awaken from the nightmare. She vividly recalled the punch to the back of her head coupled with the roar of a cannon. The metallic ching, ching sound of the shovel digging scoop after scoop of dirt. Rebecca succumbed to her memories, jumped from Buttercup's back, and ran to the edge of the woods where she vomited violently.

Maybe Chief LeBlanc was right, she was not ready to meet the world again just yet. But how long must she remain a prisoner of fate? How long must she suffer for simply marrying the wrong man. The very wrong man. The absolute worst man possible.

Buttercup clip clopped up behind her and gave her a gentle nudge with her muzzle. Rebecca stroked her best friend's nose and pulled a piece of carrot from her pocket. She pulled a curry comb from her backpack and began brushing the comely creature. She shared a few more carrots and eventually the therapeutic nature of bonding with her horse drove away her debilitating memories.

The trail leading to her cabin was narrow and winding by design. People in this part of the country were not unlike those from the mountains of Appalachia, the bayous of Louisiana or the remote wilderness of the Pacific Northwest, they insisted upon their privacy. She stopped to sniff at the purple lilac buds on bushes planted into a hedgerow. Lily of the Valley had begun to sprout broad green leaves but there were no aromatic white bells dangling from sliver thin stalks yet. Soon her kitchen table would be adorned with fragrant bouquets which she hoped would lighten her mood.

Rebecca brewed a cup of cinnamon tea and watched robins searching for worms in the tall grass while it steeped. She absentmindedly traced the scar beneath her eye, the one Bryant had given her on *accident.* That was the first warning sign she had ignored and in time, there were many others. Too many others.

She tired of the thoughts scurrying about in her head and needed a distraction, so she rinsed her cup in the sink and gathered a few things before heading out the door for Saint Kateri's.

The parking lot was a bustle of energy with tables spread out between the yellow painted lines instead of parked cars and tourists milling about. There were handmade birdhouses, yard ornaments, and wildflowers in ornate hand painted pots all signaling the arrival of spring. She bought a couple pots of trillium and pink lady slippers which she set aside for Joe to pick up when she ran into him which she knew would be sooner than later.

Inside the shrine there were tables of hand painted landscapes, handmade jewelry, beautifully crafted and painted wooden birdhouses, and several tables with photographs. Handmade soaps and candles permeated the air with tantalizing aromas of lavender and lilac.

One of the photography displays caught her eye and she meandered over through the crowd passing off smiles and head nods to the few people she recognized. Some of the festival goers looked at her with indifference, with no more thought than they gave to tourists passing through their town. Others gave her empathic glances with a certain sadness in their eyes. Those were the few who knew her story. Rebecca was looking over a series of photographs taken at Pictured Rocks National Lakeshore when Joe came up behind her.

"What is that monstrosity?" she asked, pointing at a painting tucked under his arm that looked as though the artist sneezed with fifteen different colors of paint in their mouth.

"It's colorful."

"So is a full dumpster on trash day."

"You just have no taste in art."

"That is where you are wrong, Joe. I have taste in art, just good taste," she laughed. "Where was this photograph taken?"

"That is an older photograph of Miner's Castle in Pictured Rocks near Munising. Back when it still had two parapets."

"It's gorgeous. And Munising is not too far from here is it?" Rebecca hinted.

"Absolutely not. It gets a lot of traffic especially in the spring when the waterfalls are running, and the water is high."

"Waterfalls? What waterfalls?"

Joe ignored her comment, so Rebecca put the photographs back in their display and walked away without another word. She kept her back to the man, not wanting him to see the tears forming pools in her eyes.

"I feel like a prisoner here," she blurted, spinning around on her heels.

"I'm just trying to keep you safe."

"Damn it, Joe. This is the Upper Peninsula, not Chicago or New York."

"You are right about that. In Chicago or New York, you might be able to disappear into the sea of people but up here there is nowhere to hide unless you make the effort. Bryant is a very cunning killer who wanted you dead and he thinks he succeeded. But I would like to remind you that he is still a free man."

"That is why I should have gone to the police and told them about him."

"You did go to the police; you came to me."

"No offense Joe, I didn't come to you, you found me frozen on the side of the road. And you're not the real police."

"I'm the only police around here. I have said my piece," he said as he walked away from her.

"Joe, I'm sorry, I didn't mean to offend you. Come on, come back here," Rebecca called after him, but he disappeared out of the double glass doors at the front of the building.

She wandered from table to table looking over the artisan crafts on display while formulating an apology for Joe.

Maybe an artisan pie baked with her own hand. She stopped by a woman selling fruits in glass jars and bought some thimbleberry jam as well as a few jars of the delicate fruit. She had heard about thimbleberries but had never seen one up close. They looked like raspberries to her so they should be perfect for a small torte.

A wiry little man with wispy black hair caught her attention. Not because he was trying to, but because he was just so odd looking. He wore a black leather vest over a red flannel shirt with the sleeves cut off and frayed showing off his skinny arms. His face was leathered and dark, much darker than the buckskin leggings he wore. His table had by far the largest assortment of hodge podge of any of the tables. Less artisan and much more flea market. There were odd looking totems strategically placed across the table as if they were the guardians of his merchandise. She had to smile to herself when she recalled one of the blue hairs who would set troll dolls around all her bingo cards and realized how similar the rituals were. It did not help matters that the spry little elf resembled one of the wild haired troll dolls himself.

"Good morning," Rebecca greeted while looking over the man's wares trying to avoid looking him over as well.

"They call me skunk," he offered his hand.

As she drew in closer to shake the man's hand her olfactory senses were immediately assaulted, and she understood where he had gotten the nickname. Her nose twitched a few times and he laughed.

"I don't even smoke the stuff myself, but I handle it so often the oils get imbedded into my skin. I work for a big grower just outside of the town."

"That certainly does explain the smell. I feel happier just standing next to you," she said with a smile.

"Are you looking for something in particular?" he asked, his dark eyes contradicting his warm smile.

"No, not really. Just killing time more than anything else. The days are getting longer, but around here that only means more hours with nothing to do."

"So, then you are bored? Are you telling me that the hustle and bustle of this place doesn't keep you on your toes both day and night?"

"The only hustle and bustle I've seen since I got here is when Old Lady Crenshaw yells BINGO when there have only been three numbers called. Damned near starts a riot every Friday night."

The odd little man laughed while scanning over his wares with a compassionate eye. He looked over an old metal detector, what looked to be a HAM radio set, and quickly passed over a bunch of fishing gear. A crooked smile creased his lips, and he began rummaging around under the table.

"This should be a perfect way for you to spend an afternoon or two," he said, pulling an old Canon camera out of a dingy, water-stained cardboard box. Déjà vu washed over her like a cold shower.

Rebecca laughed nervously. "I have a camera, on my phone."

"That's no camera, that is a toy. This beauty here takes skill, talent and a lot of practice to use," he said.

"Yeah, and it takes film, something I could never find outside of a big city or online."

"You're in luck, I have cases of film too."

"Do you develop it as well," she said, the sarcasm thick in her voice.

"For your information miss naysayer, there is a very competent photo lab in the Sault."

"Is that so? I must say that I'm a little intrigued, but a lot more lost. I have no idea how to use a real camera let alone an old school film camera like this."

"That is why this particular package you see here also comes with instruction manuals."

Rebecca wasn't sure why, but this fascinated her. Maybe it was the sheer boredom she had been subjected to throughout the long, dreary winter, or maybe this is something she had been wondering about subconsciously for some time. She picked the camera up and found it quite heavy and cumbersome, yet comfortable in her hands. But once she looked through the lens and zoomed in on a freighter out the window on Lake Superior close enough she could read the name on the hull she was hooked.

"What do all these different lenses do? And what are these colored glass things? And how do I load the film?" she asked in rapid succession.

Skunk laughed and said, "Slow down little lady. I'll make you a deal, share some of that thimbleberry pie with me and I'll come over tonight and teach you the basics."

Rebecca agreed and they spent the next fifteen minutes loading camera lenses, filters, film, tripods, and various other pieces of photography equipment as well as a few wildflowers she had purchased into Skunk's beat-up army jeep. She loaded her other purchases into Buttercup's saddlebags and started the journey back through the woods.

Suddenly her world was alive. Everything she looked at brought a fresh perspective. A monarch fluttering aimlessly through the air was now an elegant portrait subject. Little lilac buds required their being captured for posterity. Maybe it was finally time for Rebecca to actually live instead of just survive.

Two

Three thimbleberry tortes sat cooling on the windowsill awaiting a dollop of homemade whipped cream as Skunk and Joe came ambling up the driveway. Seeing them, Rebecca poured three tall tumblers of ice-cold milk and set the tortes in front of each table setting. She couldn't help but think it would have been a scene Norman Rockwell would have painted had he been dysfunctional.

"Joe, what are you doing here?" she asked while opening the front door.

"The fat bastard wouldn't let me come out here by myself. He stopped me at the trail leading in," Skunk said with a crooked eye in Joe's direction.

"I wasn't about to let this freeloader get my serving of pie," Joe said.

"Do you two know each other?" she asked.

"Of course, honey. Like I told you, everybody knows everybody up here," Joe said.

"Don't let him bullshit you, we go way back," Skunk said.

"Don't let him bullshit you, everybody goes way back up here."

Rebecca shook her head with a smile and finished setting the table with little dessert plates, each one bearing a different songbird. She took the plate with a goldfinch because that was her favorite bird, the cardinal went to Skunk and of course the Blue Jay to Joe because it was the bird who squawked the loudest. The two men made short work of their tortes and polished off their milk all within five minutes.

"What brings you out this way, Skunk?" Joe asked.

"I'm going to give Rebecca a crash course in photography."

"A crash course in what?" he asked with an inquisitive glance shot back and forth between the two co-conspirators.

"She bought a vintage camera from me and I'm going to show her how to use it."

"What in the hell do you want with an old, junk camera?" Joe asked.

"Vintage. And it's not junk," Skunk said.

"I just wanted something to do other than my normal puttering around. I'm a young woman and can't be cooped up like this all the time."

"What in the world are you going to take pictures of?"

"I don't know, the garden, the lake, freighters heading for the Soo Locks. Whatever strikes my fancy."

"Does it even work?" Joe asked.

"Of course, it works," Skunk said as he got up from the table and pushed his chair in.

Rebecca cleared the dishes from the kitchen table and washed them in the porcelain sink while Joe half-assed rinsed and then attempted to dry them before putting them away. She was still upset from earlier, but she knew it was wrong of her to be upset with Joe. Not only had he saved her life, but he continued to keep her safe and he gave her a place to live free of charge until she sorted her life out. He was a kind-hearted, caring man and she owed him her respect.

"You never told me who lived here before me," Rebecca said, fingering the floral pattern drapes on the kitchen window that were obviously a woman's touch.

"This was my daughter's house, but that was a long time ago," he said, averting his eyes to the hardwood floor.

Rebecca sensed it was a painful memory and chose not to push him. Skunk returned from the driveway with all the subtlety of a bull in a china shop and set a box of camera gear on the kitchen table. He started pulling the gear out of the boxes and arranged it in piles according to its purpose. There were three lenses, a dozen different lens filters, lens cloths, a couple of release cables and a dozen or so film canisters.

"Chief," the radio on Joe's belt squawked and when he did not respond immediately it squawked again. "Joe?"

"This is the chief, is there a problem?"

"There's an emergency back here at the station," a young, bubbly voice crackled over the radio.

"Thanks Cali, I'll be right there," he said. Joe tipped his hat and headed out the door.

"I hope it's nothing serious," Rebecca said.

"Nothing is more serious than cold fried chicken. That's code for dinner is on the table," Skunk said.

Rebecca laughed while looking over the materials Skunk had laid out on the table. She poured them each a glass of Traverse City cherry wine and took a long sniff of the aromatic nectar before taking a sip. Thank God for wine, it was the only bright spot to a long and brutal winter.

"What are these for? And why are they all different colors?"

"Those are lens filters. They screw onto the end of the lens. The clear one basically doesn't do much other than protect the more expensive lens glass, but it does block some harmful UV rays from hitting the film and cuts through the haze. This one is a polarizer, and it cuts down on reflections, especially when shooting scenes with calm water and it also helps cut the suns glare. It can also make the sky pop out from the clouds by deepening the shades of blue in the right conditions. You spin it around while looking through the viewfinder until you find the desired effect," he said, turning the glass disk which was housed inside of two metal rings.

"What are the really dark ones for? It doesn't seem like the camera would be able to see through them," she asked, holding one of the filters up to her eye and looking through it.

"Those are neutral density filters. They are used for shooting in bright conditions especially if you want long exposures. The pictures of waterfalls where the water looks silky smooth are shot using long exposures and these filters can help with that."

"I see, very interesting."

"And the red one?"

"That is a red enhancer, it helps to make fall colors pop."

"So, cheating?" she smiled.

"Enhancing," Skunk defended.

She poured them another glass of wine and put some juustoa and soda crackers out as well. They nibbled at the Finnish squeaky cheese while Skunk explained more about the camera filters.

"Why are the film canisters different colors?"

"That signifies the ISO, or light sensitivity of the film. On bright days you use the one hundred ISO, on cloudy or overcast days two hundred ISO and if it is gloomy or raining you use the four hundred ISO. The higher the ISO the faster exposure you can shoot, which is quite useful when photographing fast moving subjects like birds, or sporting events. The book explains all that. Bring that camera phone of yours out here in the yard and I will show you."

They went out in the yard and Skunk explained ISO, aperture, shutter speed and the use of filters as best he could with the limited resources. Her phone camera had a lot more features than he would have imagined so he was able to give her some in depth lessons. She practiced with the camera changing lenses and dry shooting to get a feel for each lens.

"You're technically savvy for an old guy," she said with a wink.

"Growing weed is a technical business," Skunk winked back.

They went back inside, stowed all the camera gear back into the box and sat down for one last glass of cherry wine. The winds were blowing in off the lake and the temperature took a sudden drop so Skunk lit a fire in the fireplace and the two of them talked about nothing for a while.

"Since Joe is not here to argue, what do you think about Pictured Rocks?" she asked.

"It's absolutely gorgeous. It would be a perfect place to practice your photography. There are at least a dozen waterfalls between Grand Marais and Munising, most of them accessible too. I think I have a few touristy kinds of books in my mountain of crap."

"Would it be safe for a young, single woman?"

"Safe from what?"

"People."

"The biggest threat out there are ticks and black flies. You might run into a black bear, but they are harmless unless they are wounded or hungry. They keep their distance from people as do the cougars and bobcats."

"Great, now I'm even more scared to go out there by myself."

"Why go by yourself? Make Joe take you. That old codger doesn't have shit to do around here anyway."

"Don't get me wrong, I like the man, and I'm grateful for everything he has done for me, but I'm sick and tired of him right now. I need to get away by myself and just clear my head."

Skunk laughed long and hard in part because of the three glasses of wine had him floating but also because he knew exactly how she was feeling. Joe was best consumed in small bites and this poor woman had been force fed the whole enchilada at one time.

"To say he is overbearing would be putting it mildly. I know I shouldn't think like that because for the most part, he is right, I'm in real danger if Bryant were to find out I am still alive. But I really do need to get out of this place even if for only a day."

"I'll tell you what, I have a cousin who owns a motel in Grand Marais, it's the off season and I'm sure I can talk her into letting you have a room. She knows the area well and can point you in the right direction. Grand Marais is close enough to Pictured Rocks that you can head out there, do some hiking, rent a kayak and still be back to the motel before dark."

"That sounds fantastic," Rebecca said.

"Don't go getting too excited, you still have to get Joe to agree to this."

"Like hell I do. I'm a grown woman for Pete's sake, I won't be dictated to."

"He is only looking out for your best interest."

"Sometimes I wonder," she said, the wine untangling her mind enough to loosen her tongue.

"I find it a little perplexing that you seem to have gotten over your ordeal a lot easier than any of us have," Skunk said.

"I guess I just got used to knocking on heaven's door, this wasn't the first time Bryant almost killed me. Besides, I was the one who was shot, buried in a shallow grave, and left for dead, not any of you. So, if I have gotten over it, you sure as hell should be able to move past it," Rebecca said, a little angrier than she had intended.

"You have to understand, before you came along the worst crime this town witnessed was poaching and Hector's kid stealing Slim Jim's from the Holiday. When Joe first spotted you, covered in mud and lying in that ditch he was certain you were dead," Skunk said.

"Believe me when I say this, I'm eternally in your debt, each and every one of you who knows my situation and who has taken me in as one of your own. But I want to, no, I need to just spend some time alone away from this place. I need some time to think," Rebecca said, a small tear forming in her eye.

"Why do you think you need this so much?"

"Because, I have yet to come to terms what happened to me. I have yet to allow myself the time to grieve for the loss of my old life. I can't begin to heal and move on until I make sense of it all."

"I'll talk to Joe for you. Maybe you could compromise and let him drop you off at my cousin's motel in Grand Marais," Skunk offered.

"I can live with that. But make certain he knows I'll be going with or without his blessing."

Three

Rebecca was well aware that Joe was still angry with her when he dropped her off at the Harbor View Motel in Grand Marais. He had not said a word to her the entire two-hour drive which suited her just fine. This was something she was determined to do and did not relish having to endure lectures from an "uncle" who was not even close to being related to her. She began to wonder if she was not suffering from a mild form of Stockholm syndrome given the circumstances.

Margaruethe, Skunk's cousin, met her at the door and helped her with her bags. She got Rebecca checked into her room and gave her several maps and brochures of the area, filled her in on the best places to eat and made sure the heater was turned on. Rebecca tried not to stare, but Skunk's cousin was damned near a spitting image of him. Bless her heart.

Margie, as she told Rebecca to call her, also gave her the keys to a beat-up Chevy truck and offered it for her to use to go to Munising but warned her it was shitty on gas and was more cantankerous than Joe. She also let it slip that her cousin's real name was Elmer which is why he didn't mind being called Skunk. Joe had sat in the parking lot for nearly an hour before driving away and leaving her on her own for the first time in over a year.

The motel room was basic, but quaint, charming and had a view of the small harbor. There were only a dozen rooms and only three of those were occupied at the time. She was pleased to find it was a no smoking facility and there were no residual lingering odors of stale smoke in her room. The view of the bay was gorgeous. She watched a kayaker in a hand-crafted boat navigate through mini icebergs floating in the bay until he was out into open water and out of sight. These were a hale and hearty bunch that was for certain.

Having shed the yoke of confinement Rebecca grabbed her jacket and headed out the door. Joe's words echoed in her brain causing her to see demons lurking in every shadow, so she simply avoided them.

Grand Marais, Michigan is a small town, tiny in fact, but it still has plenty of flavor. First and foremost, she just had to visit a place she saw on the way in, an enormous brown barrel trimmed in forest green. Its first life was as the home of a writer and cartoonist named William Donahey. Later it saw duty as an ice cream parlor, information kiosk and eventually a museum dedicated to the Teenie Weenies, Donahey's creations which appeared in comic strips, books, and advertising. The unique barrel house had grown into an iconic landmark in the region and beyond.

Rebecca's belly began to argue so she followed her nose to the local tavern which was not too difficult as the pickle barrel house was right next door. After looking at the menu for less than a minute she ordered herself a burger with onion rings. The place was crowded which made her nervous, so she switched seats several times. She finally settled a corner booth away from the large front windows and tucked in with her back into the corner and a ball cap pull down over her face. She listened to the locals talk about this and that while picking up little tidbits of information, mostly inane gossip.

She finished her burger and left the tavern to walk the beach around the bay to savor her newfound freedom. She pulled the Canon out of her backpack and zoomed in on the lighthouse across the small harbor. It was nondescript and stark white, not much of a wow factor as a photography subject. She used her phone camera to get an idea of the settings needed, then set the camera and fired off a couple of shots.

She walked for another hour, went back to the motel to put on some heavier clothes and headed for the trail to Sable Falls which was only a couple of miles away. According to Margaruethe she was to follow the beach for a little over a mile until she reached Soo Creek. She turned south and followed the river until she caught the distinctive sound of the water cascading over the sandstone cliffs.

Soo Creek snaked through a narrow canyon of sandstone and sand dunes while running parallel to the North Country Trail, a trail that was barely large enough for a deer to travel let alone a person lugging camera gear. The third time she slid into the knee deep, freezing cold water was the last time. She took off her wet shoes and socks and stuffed them into her backpack. Her feet and ankles were numb from the cold by the time she rounded the last bend and came face to face with the gorgeous waterfall spilling over the rocks and plunging seventy-five feet over the sandstone cliff face in a silvery ribbon.

Rebecca found a nice sized chunk of flat shale seated above water, so she made it her home. She cursed herself for not learning the mechanics of the tripod before venturing out into the woods and spent a good ten minutes figuring out how to work the contraption. She had, however, been smart enough to download a light meter app to her phone. It was free so it was limited in functionality, but it did provide her with the basic essential knowledge she needed.

She mounted the camera on the tripod and began to play with the lenses until she settled on a wide-angle zoom. After setting the focal point, aperture, and shutter speed she took the release cable in hand. The camera was older, but not ancient so it did have an auto focus function she decided to use until she became more adept at choosing the right settings.

She shot an entire roll of film before she knew it and decided that was enough for the day. She hiked back along the beach with her wet bare feet in the sun warmed sand. The trip back to the motel took a lot less time than the hike out as she was almost running by the time she got back into town. She immediately started to run a hot bath and put her wet boots and socks over the heater register to dry.

Rebecca laid down after a long hot bath and absorbed the day. It had been so hectic and go, go, go she never once had the opportunity to dwell on her past life. After leaving the town of Bay Mills, not once did those spindly talons of fear invade her psyche. Sleep overcame her within ten minutes, and it turned out to be the best night's sleep she had enjoyed in years. She felt rejuvenated both physically and emotionally.

In the morning her calf muscles ached from hiking, so she took a long hot shower before getting dressed. She packed the truck with extra clothes and the camera gear before changing the film in the camera. She read the manual several times before attempting the feat as to not ruin the roll she had already exposed. The film canister was cleverly designed with a lid that was different on either side to indicate whether the roll of film in the canister had been exposed or not.

The drive along H-fifty-eight was lined with dense forest on either side of her and the depth of trees was almost overwhelming, causing her to feel a sense of apprehension. The road was long and winding as it cut a swath through the Hiawatha National Forest in some of the most rugged wilderness in the country. Even though the morning air was still quite chilly she drove with the truck window open for the fresh air. It was a gesture good in theory, but the Chevy chugged more exhaust fumes into the cab than she could handle so she rolled the window back up within just a few miles.

Rebecca saw a sign and decided on a slight detour. She hiked out to a place called the Log Slide Overlook which was an impressive three-hundred-foot-tall sand dune overlooking Lake Superior. From interpretive placards placed strategically along the trail she learned of the history of logging in the area and how the timber men would cut and haul logs when they were easier to pull on the frozen ground. The lumbermen would stack them up all winter long and then send them down a wooden chute built into the sand dune into the lake below where they would be loaded onto boats. Legend has it that the logs would sometimes catch on fire due to friction earning it the nickname the Devil's Slide. It didn't help that reputation any when errant logs crushed the life out of unsuspecting loggers on more than one occasion.

Once Rebecca had her fill of the log slide, she got back out onto the road and followed the signs to Twelvemile Beach campground where she picked up the trail to the Au Sable Lighthouse. Having learned her lesson already she took off her shoes and socks before rolling up her pants legs. The place was deserted which offered her both comfort and a certain level of anxiety at the same time. Every slasher movie she had ever watched came back to her in bits and pieces until every shadow, every small tree waving in the breeze and every chipmunk scurrying through the underbrush set her tiny hairs on end. Eventually she left the trail and waded out into the lake, so she didn't have to worry about anything sneaking up behind her. Lucky for her Joe had never told her the Ojibwe legend of water panther, Mishipeshu.

She took a half dozen shots of the lighthouse before wandering down the beach and firing off a few of the wreck of the Mary Jarecki, which was half beached, half submerged and was not much more than waterlogged timbers and rusted steel rods. She wandered a little further down the Hurricane Coast and received her first taste of what she was about to explore. While not very tall at this juncture, the shoreline turned into flat rock that swooped upward from the water's edge. Striations of color painted the rocks as far as she could see. Again, she fired off a few shots for posterity. Walking back to the truck she once again felt the hairs on her neck stiffen and got the feeling she was being watched.

Once Rebecca was back in the truck with her boots on the sensation of being watched subsided. Passing through a particularly dark section of the forest triggered a vivid memory and she had to pull off to the side of the road. She was suddenly overcome with a sensation of darkness, of helplessness and she began to cry. Her skin tingled with the recollection of beetles and worms crawling all over her skin looking for their next meal as she laid powerless against them in her grave. Rebecca jumped out of the truck and wretched violently. It was a solid half an hour before she was done crying enough to forge ahead.

To distract herself from her own toxic thoughts she looked over her maps where she saw a place named Big Star Cove that seemed close to another campground further down the state highway. The road to the campground narrowed down to one lane in several places overlooking steep drop-offs. She coasted the Chevy down the steep hills and rode the brakes with both feet and a prayer on her tongue. Once at the bottom she loaded her camera gear into her backpack and started off down the trail. It was past noon already, so she had to put a move on.

After a bit of searching, she found the trail and started hiking to the north. The trail from the campground intersected with the North Country Trail which she started taking to the west but not before tying a piece of pink plastic ribbon she had found in the glovebox to a tree to mark the trail. Because of the lack of greenery, she was able to see the cliff's edge on occasion. After about half an hour she came upon a small, almost invisible, trail to the north. She bushwhacked her way through the patch of scrub until she was on a large, flat outcropping overlooking Lake Superior. The stunning view took her breath away.

She used the light meter on her phone and found that the settings were not jiving with the camera lens, so she sat down, pulled out the manual while nibbling on a peanut butter sandwich. She learned the neutral density filter would cut two stops worth of light which would be dark enough to get a good exposure. She was finding this to be more challenging than she had originally anticipated and made a mental note to go shopping for a digital camera.

"Beautiful, isn't it?" a woman's voice startled her from behind. She had been so focused on her camera that she did not hear her approach.

"It's absolutely stunning. I never imagined Lake Superior would have this many different variants of color."

"We took a trip to the Bahamas once, this place reminds me of the water there, except for the freezing ass cold part of course. My name is Amber, and this is my husband Todd," she said as she offered her hand.

"Nice to meet you, my name is Rebecca," she said after a slight pause she hoped they had not noticed. She had never practiced introducing herself with her newly assumed name, so it didn't roll naturally off her tongue.

"How far are you hiking?"

"Not far. In fact, I'll probably turn back after getting a few more shots."

"Oh, you can't do that. Spray falls is not much farther from here, maybe two miles. It's a must see. The water cascades over the cliff into the lake."

"That sounds interesting," she said.

"If you're not too scared of heights there's a small rock outcropping just west of the campground. If you scoot out there to the edge you might be able to get some nice shots of the falls,"

Todd said with a nod of his head toward her camera gear. "But be very mindful of the edge, it's a long way down."

They made small talk for several minutes in which they told her all about Miner's Castle, Bridalveil Falls, Mosquito Beach and Chapel Rock. By the time the conversation was over the couple had convinced Rebecca that this was going to be more than just a day trip. She made her way down the trail and got a few poorly angled shots of Spray Falls as she was not about to take Todd's advice about nudging out to the edge of a seventy-foot drop.

The roar of the water cascading over the cliff, the raw power and beauty convinced her that the couple was right, she needed a lot more than one day to explore. She gathered up her gear and headed back to the trail where she was stopped dead in her tracks. There was a burning cigarette on the ground on the trail right where she had been set up with her tripod. Someone had been watching her.

Four

After fifteen minutes of cruising the small coastal town Rebecca found a small motel overlooking Munising Bay on the city's outskirts and settled in for the night. She was running low on cash and thumbed through the phone book to find the nearest bank. Rebecca knew that Joe would blow a gasket if he caught her using her ATM card, but she thought he was just overreacting. He watched too many cop shows and way too many true crime exposés. Besides, it was issued in her new name, a name Bryant would have no way of knowing.

While thumbing through the phone book she ran across a place called The Dogpatch that served steaks and after the day's hike she was definitely in the mood for some red meat. There was an ATM at the Holiday station so she would fill up on gas, grab some snacks and water before heading over for a steak. But first, a long hot shower was in order.

Her mind tended to wander and today was no different. She couldn't help but think about the cigarette lying next to the hiking trail. After several minutes of mulling it over she laughed at herself for concocting such drama. She simply missed someone walking down the trail who just happened to be an inconsiderate asshole who threw their cigarette butt on the ground without any concern for littering or forest fires. She was blow drying her hair when she caught just a hint of smoke in the air. She turned off the hair dryer and sniffed the business end. No smoke.

An icy chill invaded her, and she slammed the bathroom door closed. She sat down on the toilet and tried to get her hands to stop shaking. She had smelled cigarette smoke, fresh cigarette smoke in her motel room. Someone had been in there while she was taking a shower.

"Rebecca, get a grip," she said aloud to herself. "There was no one in here, someone just walked by the window with a lit cigarette."

She finished getting dressed and headed out for a nice T-bone steak. She looked over her shoulder while filling up the gas tank on the old Chevy. She looked over her shoulder while picking out snacks and she could not shake the feeling of being watched while seated in The Dogpatch waiting for her dinner. That part of the evening she could understand her sense of being watched as she was the only young, single woman in a place filled with spring hunters.

Back at the motel she started feeling guilty about disappearing from Grand Marais without a word, so she tried to call Joe, but he didn't answer. She assumed he was pissed at her and wouldn't answer the phone. She texted Skunk and told him what was going on and asked if he would contact his cousin Margaruethe as well so the woman wouldn't be concerned when Rebecca didn't show up that evening.

She took a long, hot shower before she laid down in bed. Out of habit she turned on a television show dealing with cold case files, most of which were about young women being abducted while out on their own. She quickly turned the channel to PBS and found an old rerun of Bob Ross which proved to be the perfect ambiance to clear her mind enough to sleep.

She awakened before the sun even winked and tried to sleep in for another hour but found it useless, so she got up to take a shower. She almost fell flat on her face because her legs were wholly sore and not as awake as her brain. For breakfast she nibbled at microwaved left-over steak and half a baked potato.

She had picked up some maps of the Munising area in the office of the motel and spent some time going over the brochures. She formulated a plan that would start out catching the sunrise over the bay at Sand Point, then move on to Wagner Falls on the outskirts of town before heading for Miner's Castle. After that she planned to catch the North Country Trail at Elliot Falls on the beach and take the trail east toward Bridalveil Falls. On the way out the door she grabbed a few pieces of Trenary toast, wrapped them in napkins and put them in her pocket. Their crunchy, cinnamon goodness would be perfect to nibble on during the day.

It was still early in the morning when she hit the North Country Trail at Elliot Falls, a small, quaint waterfall that spilled from the trees, over a small rock and poured into Lake Superior. The trail wound through the forest away from the cliff's edge and into the interior of the timberland. Every so often there would be a small foot trail that would take her out onto the cliff top where the world would open into an awe-inspiring view. The water at the base of the cliffs was littered with sunken boulders and chunks of sandstone that had sheared off throughout the years. Seeing the debris below the depths of the green hued water did nothing to ease her fear of heights in the least.

Once her ear picked up the sound of the water cascading over the cliff to the north, she turned in the direction of the sound and baby stepped through the trees. Methodically she shuffled through the woods until the daylight began to get more intense and she knew she was nearing the edge. She was disappointed to find that this vantage point of the falls was useless to get a photo. A stark white passenger ferry glided by and stopped to allow passengers to get shots of the waterfall from the platform roof, so she got shots of them instead. They waved back and forth to each other like they were old friends and neighbors. It made her feel good. It made her feel normal.

She checked her phone and saw that she was making fairly good time, so she decided to push on toward Mosquito Beach and eventually hoped to see the Chapel Rock formation. It was about six miles away so she estimated she could make it there and then back to the truck before dark. Rebecca sat on a fallen tree, pulled out a piece of Trenary toast and a bottle of water. She nibbled at the dry toast coated with just a hint of cinnamon and sugar before hitting the trail again.

The day was unseasonably warm for early spring which made the hike quite a pleasant experience. Birds had begun to fill the forest with song while the squirrels and chipmunks foraged through the dead underbrush. Rebecca had never realized how much noise a small rodent could make; at times she swore she was being shadowed by a family of bears.

Once on the beach she found it was a lot windier and almost completely devoid of people. She negotiated a set of stairs in the sand that was more like a rope ladder made of cables and utilized logs for rungs. The spacing was so far apart that her short stride put her mostly in the sand. She had to dump her boots of cold, damp sand more than once. The sounds of gulls crying accompanied the harmony of the waves lapping at the shore. Rebecca checked her maps and noticed a place named Lover's Leap which seemed a bit morbid to her as she was certain no one could survive the leap from these cliffs to the rock-strewn bottom.

Along the trail were many places where she could leave the shelter of the woodland and slip out onto the flat cliff tops. Her boots shuffled through the sand strewn open areas as she eased herself toward the edge. It was a good thing she was only a touch acrophobic and didn't suffer from vertigo, but both of those afflictions were ever closer to becoming a reality at the moment. Once out on the edge she was able to look back at where she had been and take what she hoped would be spectacular shots of the multicolored cliff faces.

Rebecca focused in on the striations of color streaking horizontally across the cliff face. From yellows, to golds, to browns and rust colored streaks the rocks were painted with the brush strokes of nature. That coupled with the multi-hued water below made for a breath-taking scene worthy of gracing the pages of a photography magazine.

Further down the trail she came to Lover's Leap and snapped off a few shots. It was after she had gone a couple hundred yards down the trail and looked back that she was in complete veneration. The rock outcropping jutted out into the lake several hundred feet and erosion from the lake's constant movement had worn a large hole all the way through the cliff formation. To her it looked like a gargantuan horse bending to take a drink from the lake. There was even a smaller hole worn out for the horse's eye and a groove where the horse's mouth would be. She tried to imagine what the place would look like with the trees in full bloom, or better yet, during the emblazoned colors of autumn lending the horse a fiery mane.

Out of the blue the camera around her neck began to take pictures without her depressing the shutter button. Rebecca gave the camera a couple of gentle thumps on the side, but it continued to shoot photos. And then she heard a loud splash echo from down below and stepped back thinking it must have been a chunk of the cliff falling into the water. She realized there were no noticeable chunks missing from the cliff side, so she scanned the water below. There was something, or more specifically, someone down at the bottom on the rocks.

She quickly dug though her backpack and dug out the zoom lens and switched it out on the camera. Using the longer distance lens, she scanned the water below. There was a woman floating in the water below, a halo of long dark hair floating in the water around her head. The camera was still firing off shots without her doing anything to cause the mechanical action, so she zoomed in on the woman's face to see if she was conscious or even alive. Rebecca gasped in horror, she realized she was looking at herself in the water. She double checked to make sure it was not just her own reflection. No, the person, the body in the water looked exactly like her, but with her natural hair color.

Rebecca started to turn to grab her phone to call for help but someone gripped her tightly at her shoulders. Her feet slid on the sandy cliff top as her assailant shoved her closer and closer to the edge. She could smell smoke, cigarette smoke over her left shoulder.

"Please, stop! You're going to push me over the edge," she pleaded. "Why are you doing this?"

Her attacker managed to move her within inches of the edge before they gave her one last hard shove, forcing Rebecca over the edge of the cliff. She twisted to try and grip the edge and a look of recognition passed over her face. Time slowed to a crawl as she plummeted toward the cold lake. She couldn't help but think how beautiful the view was from this angle.

"Why?" was the only thing she was able to say as she fell backwards over the cliff. The camera around her neck continued to snap off shot after shot as she plunged into the rock-bound water below.

Five

"Hey, Sid, there's a call for you on line two," Maury, the ancient desk sergeant announced by opening the locker room door and yelling inside for his boss. His gravelly voice grated on her nerves as it resounded off the stark white tile walls.

Sydney, or Sid as she was called by her friends nodded even though the man couldn't see her and headed for her office. She pinned her long blonde hair up onto the top of her head as she walked to her office while buttoning up her merlot blouse. It was much too early in the morning for a phone call.

"This is Sydney Lamppinen, how may I help you?"

"Sid, it's Morgan over in Munising."

"Morgan, do you know how early it is?"

"Yes."

"Then you know I haven't even had a chance to have my coffee and Trenary yet," she said, applying a touch of eyeliner, just enough to accentuate her baby blue eyes.

"I know, but this is kind of important," Morgan Murray said, her voice whiney and shrill. A product of her youthfulness.

"Isn't it always?" Sydney asked, pouring a cup of coffee from the carafe even though the pot was only half finished with the brew cycle. This was already presenting itself to be a three-cup day. "What have you got? Is Heikala cooking meth again?"

"No ma'am. A kayaker found a camera on the rocks at the bottom of Lover's Leap."

"Then put it in the lost and found. Why are you calling me with something so trivial?" Sydney said, a little more than annoyed the park ranger was bothering her over a lost camera.

Morgan sensed the tension in Sid's voice and paused.

"It has blood on it."

"Has anyone touched it?"

"Only by the strap. The person who brought it in protected it by putting it inside of a box. They said they watch a lot of crime TV and wanted to preserve the evidence was the way they put it," Morgan said, her voice laced with nervous laughter.

"For once that might turn out to be a good thing. What do you think, could it simply be blood from an animal?"

"Sure, it could be, but the camera didn't show any signs of an animal having touched it. There are no chew marks, no scratches and the person who brought it in said it was obscured by the rocks. The only reason they even noticed it was from the sound it was making," Morgan said, her voice trailing off as she related the last piece of information.

"What kind of sound was it making?" Sydney sighed and rubbed her temples.

"They didn't say, but I can safely assume it's the same sound it's making right now."

"And what sound might that be?" Sydney asked.

She hated speaking with the young NPS officer, she was always forced to pry information out of her. It was not that the young woman was incompetent or lacking intelligence, she was just unsure of herself. Sydney made a mental note that one day soon they needed to take a girl's night out together so she could get the woman soused on tequila and turn a mouse into a lioness.

"I'm sorry. It's just quite odd. It keeps taking pictures."

"Take the battery out and put it back in but don't touch it with your bare hands. That should stop it from taking photos and also allow you to see what is stored on the memory card which may help to identify the owner," Sydney instructed.

"That isn't possible, Sid, it's not a digital camera."

"Put it in the office and I'll be there as soon as I can," she said, hanging up the phone before she had to answer any more questions.

She poured another cup of coffee, put two teaspoons of coffee creamer in the mug and sat back down to enjoy the only cup of coffee she would probably get for a while. The coffee was already getting cold, so she chugged it down and picked up the phone.

"Sheriff's Office," Sheriff Colby Patino, the sheriff of Luce County answered.

"Morning Sheriff," Sydney said.

"Hey, Sid, how's it hanging?"

"Toward the floor, Colby, everything is toward the floor."

"Gravity, it's the only law you can't break and get away with it. What can I do you for?" he asked, running his hand over his burr cut black hair that had just a hint of saltiness on the sides.

"Morgan just called me from the Ranger's Office in Munising. I haven't seen anything in our briefings. Have you had any recent reports of a fall from the cliffs?"

"Not that I have heard anything about, and I usually get the call even if the Coast Guard responds. Why, what did she hear?"

"It's not what she heard. A kayaker found a camera out on the rocks under Lover's Leap and turned it in at the station. Morgan claims there is blood on the camera."

"Would you like me to go take a look?" he asked.

"If you wouldn't mind. How about meeting me there in a couple of hours I'm still at my office in Negaunee."

"Hell no I wouldn't mind just as long as you stop at Ralph's and grab me a cudighi. Oh, and a pepperoni stick. No, two. And some garlic toast."

"Anything else?" She chuckled at his boyish enthusiasm.

"Yeah, some of that tuna salad, the kind made with the macaroni seashells. It is by far the best I've ever had, but don't tell my mother I said that, or I will deny it and call you a bold-faced liar."

"You know, Ralph's is not that far from the county line, you might be able to sneak over out of your jurisdiction once in a while."

Sydney absent-mindedly took a drink of her ice-cold coffee and gagged. She never understood how something could taste so good hot, but also so shitty cold. Just the opposite of tea which tasted like crap hot but great cold. One of the great unsolved mysteries of the universe she imagined. She put that on the list of questions to ask when she ascended into the great unknown.

"Colby, do you still have that tech geek working for you? That artsy type?"

"You mean Shane? Yes, he's still with us, though how, I don't know. Why do you ask?"

"Isn't he the one with all those photos for sale at the Marquette Welcome Center?"

"I think so."

"Bring him along with you. I think I'll have some questions for him."

"Should I tell him he's got a new fan? A secret admirer maybe?"

Sydney didn't give Colby the satisfaction of responding and hung up the phone before the sheriff could needle her anymore. She jotted down Colby's list of things to get at Ralph's and stuck it in her pocket. She went into the bathroom to check herself and was going to put on a little makeup until she got angry with herself. If he didn't like the way she looked then screw him.

Truth be told, she had a crush on Colby and had since their time in high school in Marquette. They spent years apart, more than a decade in fact until she was able to get reassigned to the Upper Peninsula. He had blossomed into a portly man, but portly like a grizzly bear and not like a beer guzzler. She shook the thoughts from her head and went into Ralph's.

Immediately she was assaulted by the tantalizing aroma of garlic bread fresh from the oven. She could hear cudighi sausage sizzling on the griddle from behind a set of small saloon doors at the ordering window. A bubbly high school aged girl wearing braces popped her head out between the doors with a smile that made Sydney cringe. It was much too early to be that happy. She returned the smile, exchanged pleasantries, and gave the young girl her order.

She wandered around the small store which consisted of two short aisles loaded with imported Italian and Greek products. Everything from olive oil to halva, whatever the hell that was. Sydney loaded up on all the deli order stuff from the deli counter while the kitchen staff made her sandwiches. A mild cudighi for Colby and a spicy one for her. She got another mild for Morgan as it was the right thing to do. She threw three packages of Mallowmars on the counter as well.

"What brings you out this way, Coach," the young girl behind the counter asked. Sydney thought her name was Lindsey. She was one of the girls on the hockey team she coached during the season.

"I'm heading to Munising. Out to Pictured Rocks in fact."

"Business or pleasure?"

"Business, I'm afraid," she said, hoping her shortness would move the girl along.

"Awe, that's a shame," Lindsey said, sucking air in through her teeth.

"What in the world do you mean by that?"

"Well, if you're going out there on business either Peter Heikala is back to cooking meth again or another woman fell off the cliffs."

Sydney paused, confused by the girl's morbid comment. "Why on earth would you say such a thing?"

The girl shrugged. "I don't know, from what my parents have told me that tragedy happens every ten years or so doesn't it?"

"I guess you might be right about that," she said after giving it some thought.

By the time she got back to her cruiser she had already sluffed off the young girl's comments as nothing more than an overactive imagination. It was simply the ramblings of a bored local in a small town with nothing better to do than to gossip. Sydney thought about what the girl had said and realized the reason it had gotten under her craw was that Lindsey was right about those cliffs. But she was also wrong, over the years most of them had been deemed either accidental deaths or suicide so there was nothing nefarious about the deaths at Pictured Rocks, it could be a very dangerous place.

The drive along M-twenty-eight was calming. There was little traffic, the ice was all gone from the lake and the trees were almost all filled with the greenery of summer. She stopped by Scott Falls for a therapeutic five minutes, taking comfort in the echoing sounds of spring run-off in the grotto behind the small, picturesque roadside waterfall. The earthen smell was strong and inviting, ashes to ashes and dust to dust.

The casino in the little town of Christmas was already hopping, filled with tourists and locals alike. There were a few dog walkers and even a few joggers at Au Train beach. She gave a nod and a wink to the twenty-foot-tall Santa sitting outside of Santa's Workshop, it was a shame the iconic landmark had not seen a fresh coat of paint in decades.

Being such a nice day, she almost stopped to breathe in the beach ambiance but the smell of fresh, hot cudighis permeated the air in the patrol car and her stomach was protesting in earnest.

Sheriff Colby Patino was already in the parking lot of the Munising Ranger District Office when she pulled in. All six foot two inches of him leaned across the roof of his patrol car. She could see Shane in the back seat of the car, his attention locked on a tablet.

"Is he solving world hunger? Hot on the trail of Jimmy Hoffa?"

"Nope. He's playing a game. The sounds the damned thing was making were annoying the shit out of me, so I made him ride in the back."

"He's a vegan, right?"

"Another reason I make him ride in the back, they are some kind of stinky," Colby said with a grin.

"I got him a vegan cudighi whatever the hell that is. Bun and sauce, I presume."

Colby rapped his meaty knuckle on the window, but Shane just shrugged. He walked back around to the driver's side and popped the lock to the back seat. The bean pole of a man had to stoop getting out and Sydney was a bit shocked to see that he was nearly a full head taller than Colby.

"Good morning, Shane, glad you could make it," she said while glancing at his name tag. "Deputy Crane? Shane Crane?"

"Good morning ma'am. I'd say the same, but the sheriff didn't tell me why he brought me along," he said, ignoring her dig.

"I'm not sure what we've got so I just wanted to make sure we had the right personnel involved. We got lucky, there's a forensics specialist teaching a seminar in Marquette, so I enlisted her help. She will be here shortly," she said to Colby and handed him his bag of deli goodies.

They went inside the ranger station. Seeing the bag of food Sydney set on the counter Morgan passed out paper plates and plastic forks turning the meeting into an impromptu picnic. Sydney had to admit Colby was right about Ralph's tuna salad with seashells, it was fantastic. Morgan put a fresh pot of coffee on to brew for which Sydney was eternally grateful.

"Okay, show me what you have found," she said to Morgan who darted back to the office and returned with the camera which was snapping a photo every couple of seconds.

"It looks to be a Canon AE-1, 1977 model I believe," Shane said. "But it shouldn't be doing that."

"It didn't seem right to me either," Morgan said, taking off her ranger's hat. Her long brown hair spilled out down past her shoulders. Her chestnut eyes shone with the enthusiasm of her youth.

Shane reached for the camera, but Colby swatted his hand before he could touch it.

"Hands off for now, that could be evidence."

The four of them leaned over the camera sitting on the hardwood countertop, each of them analyzing the piece of equipment as it snapped its own shutter repeatedly.

"See there, around the inside of the lens, doesn't that look like blood? And on the strap here and then again here where the rubber body meets the metal frame of the camera," Morgan said, pointing her finger each time at the affected spot.

"There seems to be more that has seeped in around the lens mount. If we are lucky some has pooled inside," Shane said. "These samples are bound to be pretty degraded. No telling how long the camera has been down on the rocks."

"I agree," Joyce Tammi said as she entered the ranger's station. Joyce was a diminutive woman, truly short and very petite. She had fair skin with red hair and a boyish face. So boyish in fact it was difficult to tell whether she was a child or an adult, man, or a woman at first glance.

Joyce spent the next hour fingerprinting, photographing, and cataloging all the evidence found on the camera. She opened the back of the camera and carefully removed the film cartridge and fingerprinted that as well.

"What do you think?" Sydney asked.

"It's definitely blood, and definitely human," Joyce said. "Sadly, your man here was correct in his assumption, the blood is far too degraded to get a useful DNA sample."

Shane took off his hat to get a better look through the camera's view finder revealing a man bun. Sydney shot Colby a genuine *what the hell* look. He just shrugged and returned a shit-eating grin.

"Do you know of any place we can get that film developed in a hurry? I'd hate to have to send it all the way to headquarters in Lansing to have it processed," Sydney asked.

"I'm pretty sure I can do it at my place," Shane spoke up. "I have all the equipment and I'm sure I still have enough chemicals to process one roll of film. I'm just going to have to remember where I stored the gear."

"Fantastic. It might turn out to be nothing, but maybe there are some shots on the film that would help us determine who the camera belongs to. Morgan, do you have a couple of volunteers you could send up to close off the section of trail half mile on either side of Lover's Leap?"

"Sure. They're all out on the trails on litter patrol. I'll give them a call the on the radio."

"What are you thinking, Sid?" Colby asked.

"I'm thinking we have to at least look into this. It could be nothing more than someone fell on the trails and the camera went over the edge. But I'd rather be safe than sorry."

"Fair enough. I'll send a couple of my deputies up on the trails to do a sweep, maybe they will find something that explains how the camera got down on those rocks."

Colby didn't argue with Sid even though he thought it was a wild goose chase. She had some history with those cliffs and knew she was reacting emotionally, even if only subconsciously. But he had also known her most of her life and worked with her for a good portion of that. Her gut instinct was good, and rarely wrong.

Six

Sidney spent a restless night haunted by old memories. She sat on her back deck with a fire going in her brazier, a medieval looking wrought iron contraption she had been given as a gag gift by her coworkers after a strange case involving cosplay. But the joke was on them, she loved it. Currently it was filled with birch that snapped and popped in the quiet morning air. She was on her third cup of coffee when the phone rang.

"Hello?" she answered, half expecting a telemarketer at that time of the morning.

"Sidney?"

"This is she. And, Shane, call me Sid."

"Yes ma'am."

"Sid," she emphasized. "Why are you calling at this time of the morning?"

"I've got something you're really going to want to see. I think it's highly possible there was a homicide at the cliffs."

"Have you told Sheriff Patino yet?"

"No ma'am, I mean Sid. I thought you should be the first to know."

"Bring whatever you have to the sheriff's office in Newberry, I'll meet you there after I jump in the shower."

Sydney jumped into the shower and spent the entire time dreading the two-hour drive to Newberry. She would be driving through deer, bear, and moose country in the wee hours of the morning just when the beasts were most active. By the time she got to Newberry her mind was a jumbled mess from going over every possible scenario of what Shane may have uncovered. And most of those thoughts settled on a young girl's broken body at the bottom of the cliffs.

By the time she arrived in Newberry the sun had started to brushstroke purple-orange hues on the horizon. It was not an angry red so traversing the cliffs might not be too bad weatherwise. Colby was waiting outside the office with a carrier of Holiday coffee which was palatable considering it was gas station coffee. She could smell the hazelnut as she approached.

"Morning, Sid," the sheriff greeted with a tip of his hat.

"I notice you didn't put a *good* in front of that. Does that mean you've already been briefed on Shane's big discovery?"

He just nodded his head and reached for the door. He waved Sid in first, not out of chivalry, but because he loved checking out her assets. She knew what he was up to and while it annoyed her to some degree, it also flattered her, so she left it alone. There was no reason to bust his balls just yet.

"Did you miss a spot this morning?" she asked.

"Miss what?" he replied while checking over the front of his uniform.

"Your hair, I see some gray showing."

"I thought you weren't supposed to point out things of that nature," he said while bending in to look at her hair closer. "Just remember I can see places on you that you can't see on me."

"You just think I can't see them. I can see that thinning spot on top of your head just fine. It's a dime today, a nickel tomorrow and a whole quarter by Friday," she laughed, knowing he would be checking his hair in the bathroom mirror in less than five minutes.

Like clockwork Colby headed for the men's locker room just as soon as they were inside the Sheriff's Department. Sydney and Shane were still laughing about it when he walked into the conference room.

"You are just plain rude," he said to her with a smile.

Reading the look on his boss's face Shane decided to change the subject and started his presentation. He laid out the developed prints on the conference table in what he best deduced was their chronological order. Both Colby and Sid scanned the twenty-four-photo array on the table. The first series of them were nothing more than typical, innocuous vacation photos. But the last batch, and especially the last five were clear evidence of a crime.

"It looks like the woman was pushed," Colby offered.

"And the bastard took photos while pushing her over the edge," Sid added. "What are all those colored balls on the right side of the photograph?"

"It's called bokeh, but quite frankly, it shouldn't be in these photos. It's quite baffling," Shane said.

"Consider me a complete idiot when it comes to photography, mainly because I really am completely clueless. Explain why they shouldn't be there," Sydney said.

Shane nodded. "Bokeh is simply a Japanese term meaning blur. Photographers use bokeh all the time for artistic effect, using varying degrees of blur to highlight their subjects. But there are two things very wrong here."

"Which are?" Colby prodded, thinking himself even more of an idiot than Sid when it came to artistic stuff, he was a jock not a painter.

"First, the aperture of the lens on the camera at the time the last photos were taken would not allow for this degree of bokeh at the focal length the shots were taken."

"Couldn't someone have simply switched the lens for a lens with a different aperture before taking the photos and then swapped them back?"

"Highly unlikely just because there would be no need, and no, because of the photos themselves. See, she has the camera around her neck with the same lens on the camera as she is falling and the bokeh is in the photo she took. The killer would have had to change the lens out after she fell."

"But the last two photos were taken of her down below, on the rocks. Are you trying to tell me our killer climbed down, got the camera, returned to the top of the cliffs, shot photos of her dead at the bottom and then dropped the camera back down?" Sydney asked, more for her own benefit.

"I can't answer that ma'am. But look at the photograph of her floating in the water."

"What about it?" Colby asked.

Sydney jumped in. "Her hair is a different color. She is a blonde while falling but a brunette in the water. What in the hell? Is this two different women? Could this have been staged?"

"I'm afraid not, it's the same face in both photos and since these aren't digital photos any alteration would have been impossible under the circumstances."

"Can you explain this?" Sydney asked.

"Sorry, no, no I can't," Shane responded.

"And what did you mean by first? What else is wrong?"

Shane pointed at the photograph. "See these orbs in the bokeh. These could only be there if there was a light source in the background in front of the lens. I could explain away one or two, maybe even three as being the sun and some reflections, but not this many. It would be impossible without there being a lot of light sources in front of the lens. Have you ever seen photos of a busy street at night, like in New York? All those blurred orbs of the taillights and streetlamps are known as bokeh circles or bokeh balls."

"What about camera flash reflecting directly off her clothing, jewelry, anything reflective?"

"The flash would have been pointed in the opposite direction, so no."

"How is any of this possible?"

Shane shrugged. "Your guess is as good as mine."

They took a break for a few minutes while Sydney called the state police post to get a list of recent missing persons in the area. Colby made another pot of coffee while Shane continued to look over the photos.

"Hey, Sid," Shane called out while she was still on the phone.

"Yeah, what is it?"

"Have them expand that missing persons search out a year or so," he said.

She shot him a sideways glance but ordered them to expand their search.

"A year?" she asked when she came back into the room.

Colby followed with three cups of fresh coffee. The department was up and running so he shut the door to drown out the noise.

"Actually, more like fourteen months or so. Look at the trees, they are bare, but there are buds on them," he said and handed Sid a magnifying glass.

"Okay, that puts it back around mid-March to mid-April," Colby said after taking the glass from Sid.

"Actually, it puts is around mid-March to mid-April of last year. Look at the side of the cliffs over there. See the brighter yellowish area with no striations?" Shane said while pointing to different areas of the photograph.

"Yes, but what does that mean?" Sydney asked?

"It means that this area here," Shane answered while drawing a circle around an area on the photograph with his finger. "Was recently calved?"

"Calved?"

"Yes, sheriff. Calving is usually a term used for icebergs or glaciers, but it applies here as well. It's when a smaller chunk of ice or rock breaks away from the larger mass. Remember those kayakers that were nearly hit by falling rocks last spring? This was the area where the cliff face broke away and there are no striations meaning it was a fresh calving when this photo was taken."

"So that camera has been down there on the rocks for over a year? That would be impossible, right?" Sydney asked.

"I would have to say no, it would not be possible for the camera to have been on those rocks for an entire year," Colby said. "The lake levels rise in winter, that camera would have been submerged all winter long and it just doesn't show any signs of being out in the elements for an entire year."

"So, whoever pushed this woman over the edge of the cliff came back a year later to leave evidence of their crime? That just doesn't make any sense at all. Not that I don't believe you, Shane, but please go show those photos to Morgan to confirm your theory about when that photo was taken."

"Yes ma'am. I'll get right on that."

"And Shane, if you ever want to get laid, lose that damned man bun."

Seven

It had been two days since the camera had been turned into Morgan and they had yet to come up with any leads on the woman in the photographs or who the camera may belong to if not her. Sydney uploaded the woman's photograph into the statewide database for missing persons hoping for a lead as to who she might be. Morgan agreed with Shane's assessment, the photographs had not been taken recently which baffled her. Sydney was sitting in the drive thru at the Beef-a-Roo waiting on a roast beef sandwich when her radio startled her.

"Sid, are you there?"

"Yeah, what is it Colby?" she asked, motioning to the fast-food clerk to toss more horseradish sauce into the bag.

"I think we may have caught a break. There is a Jane Doe in a coma at the hospital in Marquette. According to the administrator I spoke with she has been there for quite some time, though they were unsure of just how long it has been. I'm heading there to meet with them now."

"Great, I'll meet you there," Sydney said as she grabbed her paper sack from the clerk and gave a hearty thumbs up when she saw there were at least ten sauce packets in the bag.

The UP Health System is situated on a large urban style campus in contrast to the surrounding untamed wilderness. While the main building is relatively narrow it is quite long. An artistically designed building with a lot of blue-green tinted glass facing the road. Sydney found the lobby to be open and inviting. Colby was already there waiting for her. She hoped her breath didn't smell like horseradish and onions.

Colby and Sydney both showed their credentials to the receptionist and were directed to the fourth floor where they met up with the head nurse on the floor. She walked them down to the long, polished corridor to Jane Doe's room.

"I'll go let the doctor know you are here," the nurse said and left them in the room with the patient.

"Huh. That's odd." Sid remarked the moment she looked at the woman.

"What is odd?"

"Even though I noticed the difference in her hair color in the photos I still thought it was just something screwy like a lighting glitch or something."

"Please explain."

"In the series of photographs, we saw her both on the rocks below and falling. We both saw that she was a blonde in the photos of her being pushed, but do you remember the photo of her floating face up in the water?"

"Unfortunately, I can't say that I paid that much attention to her hair. I was more concerned with trying to identify her," Colby said.

"Remember, the woman in the photo at the bottom of the cliffs was a brunette."

"Are you saying there were two different women?"

"At first, I thought that might be a possibility, but look at her hair. She's a blonde except for the first seven or eight inches of new growth. That's about a year's worth of growth,"

"What the hell, Sid. How could she possibly have been a blonde on the cliffs and a brunette on the rocks below seconds later? It just doesn't make sense," the sheriff said.

"None of this is making sense right now. How do we have a camera in our possession that takes photos on its own?"

Colby and Sydney walked down to the vending machines to get some shitty coffee before returning to the room. When they got back to the room the doctor was tending to his patient.

"Good morning, doctor. My name is Sydney Lamppinen, I'm an investigator for the Michigan State Police. This is Sheriff Colby Patino," she said.

"I know Colby really well, we played against each other in high school. I was a Mustang. But that was eons ago," he said with a smile. Even with the slight patches of gray at his temples the man looked ten years younger than the sheriff. "I take it you are here because of our Jane Doe?"

"Yes. We had hoped you might know who she is or even better, have contact information for her next of kin."

"Unfortunately, no. In fact, she wouldn't even be here in the hospital if we could notify a next of kin."

"Why wouldn't she be in the hospital, she's in a coma?" Sid questioned.

"She is not on any kind of life support, she is just, in layman's terms, sleeping. She could be cared for at home. It would be a lot of work and her family would probably have to hire a care giver, but there is nothing keeping her in a hospital except we have nowhere else to send her," the doctor explained.

"Mike, did anyone from the hospital contact my office, or the state police?" Colby asked.

"Not to blow you off with a lame response, but I'm just her doctor. Beyond her immediate health concerns, I don't handle much. I'm sure someone in the hospital contacted the authorities though. Check with administration. Look, I'd love to stay and chat, but I have to prep a patient for surgery."

"Thank you, doctor," Sid said.

"Mike, Mike Parkkila."

"Ah, a fellow Finn, I knew there was something about you I liked the moment I saw you." They shot each other a smile and the doctor left the room in a flurry of white.

Sydney walked down the buffed white corridor to the even starker white bathroom. The LED lighting was threating to give her a headache so she put on her sunglasses while on the toilet and prayed no one would find here there like that. Fifty-three years old was turning out to be a bitch of an age to make it to. Five more years was all she had to put up with this shit and then she was moving to Tahiti. She laughed, the closest she would ever get to Tahiti was slathering on her coconut body lotion and slamming back a few pina coladas in her backyard.

Sydney looked in the mirror and was taken aback for a moment. Her mother was staring back at her through the reflection. She wiped her tears, splashed water on her face, and straightened herself up before she made her way back to the hospital room almost forgetting to take her sunglasses off.

"Shane, what are you doing here?" she asked as she entered Jane Doe's room.

"One of the volunteers found this thrown into the bushes about fifty feet off the marked trail. Don't worry, they didn't touch anything. They went and got a deputy who preserved the chain of evidence," he said, showing her a backpack in a paper sack marked with evidence tape.

"Good, then my typing up that bulletin wasn't a waste of time, someone actually read it. Did you find anything new about that thing?" Sid asked, pointing to the camera hanging from its strap over his shoulder.

"No, not much else I'm afraid. There's nothing to tell us who it might belong to."

"Well it either belonged to her, or to whomever tried to kill her," Colby said.

"Have you found what was making the camera malfunction?"

"Sorry, Sid, there is nothing wrong with the camera as far as I can tell. In fact, it's in perfect working condition which is amazing considering the camera's age and where it was found," Shane said.

"What's in the backpack?" Colby asked.

"Lenses, lens wipes, some lens filters and other assorted camera gear. Nothing to identify the owner though. I was going to send it to the lab for processing, but I thought you would want to look it over first," Shane said.

"We might be able to pull a print or two here locally and run it. But yes, the lab should process the whole thing. What in the hell is that noise?" Sydney asked.

"It's the camera, it's shooting pictures again," Shane said.

"Is the shutter button stuck?" Colby asked.

"No, I don't think so. It just started doing that a minute ago."

Suddenly there was movement in Jane Doe's bed. It was not much but it was enough to catch Sydney's attention. She moved over to where the woman's head was and saw that her eyes were moving rapidly back and forth.

"Is there some film in that camera?" she asked.

"No, I took out the roll when I developed the photographs and didn't have another roll to put back in. I never even thought about it."

"Is there film in that backpack?"

"I think there were a few rolls."

"Humor my bat shit crazy hunches and load film into the camera," Sydney said.

Shane nodded and carefully removed a roll of unexposed film from the backpack. He opened the package and put the film in the camera. The machine continued to fire off shot after shot until the whole roll was used and then it stopped.

"That is some weird shit," Colby said.

"Get those developed as quickly as you can, please," Sid said as she left the room to try and find a nurse.

Eight

The sun beat down on Rebecca's face coaxing her back to reality. She felt odd, weak, like she was coming down with a cold or something. Sparrows and chickadees zipped passed her as a jay called from up high. The summer sun was getting hot even though it had barely crested the horizon. She scanned her memory long and hard but couldn't remember where she was or how she got there.

She rubbed her head and found there were no bumps or bruises to indicate she had been knocked out. She had no broken bones, no cuts, no scrapes, not even so much as a hangnail. And then she smelled smoke. More precisely, cigarette smoke.

Rebecca grabbed her backpack from a deadfall tree she had been resting on and continued up the dense forest path. The drone of a fisherman's boat could be heard far off in the distance as gulls sang along in harmony. After quite some time on the trail she broke through a clump of brush and out onto a rock outcropping overlooking the big lake.

She was overlooking Lake Superior. She recognized where she was now, this was Pictured Rocks. Her memory began coming back to her like a jigsaw puzzle with only the center pieces filled in and nothing around the edges. She had been out hiking and taking photographs. But wasn't that in the spring, not the summer?

Camera in hand she focused on a section of the cliffs with a topping of green trees and fired off a shot. She was getting better at this. She looked around for her phone and couldn't find it in any of her pockets or on the ground around her. She spent fifteen minutes digging through her backpack, but her phone wasn't there either. She was about to double back but then she smelled the cigarette smoke again.

Rebecca crouched low in the bushes and listened intently to the wind. At first, she thought she was being followed, but she was downwind from the odor so whoever it was couldn't be following her, they had to be ahead of her.

"Rebecca, get a grip," she said aloud to herself and started down the trail toward Miner's Castle.

As she came off the cliffs and down onto the flat land of Miner's Beach, she spotted a couple walking hand in hand along the beach several hundred yards in front of her. The woman's light white blouse flapped in the gentle breeze while her free hand kept her sun hat from flying off her head. The pair were walking slow, enjoying the day and their time together so Rebecca slowed down to take a few photos of the waves crashing against the rocks as to not disturb their privacy.

Miner's Beach was flanked at either end by towering sandstone cliffs as they rose upward from the sandy beach. The western end, where she now stood, dead ended into the cliffs. The rocks were painted with striations of reds and oranges from the iron, shades of blues and greens from the copper and various other colors from the abundance of minerals in the soils. Because of the way the cliff base jutted out into Lake Superior the waves rolled rhythmically across the rocks before they descended upon the beach in an awesome show of force.

While the rest of the beach was rather calm, this section was loud and thunderous, yet she could still hear the couple laughing and talking as they climbed the cliffs above her. The couple was far enough ahead of her that she felt she wouldn't be intruding on their moment and began hiking the trail upward toward Miner's Castle which was just over on the other side of the cliff face. She paused to take a few shots of the rolling waves which took on brown and amber hues from the tannins in the water as well as the dark stones they picked up from the bottom of the lake.

It took her several minutes to locate the trail, but she was soon on an upward climb. Her legs burned from walking through the loose sand in her bare feet. Why was she in bare feet and where were her shoes? She couldn't remember leaving them on the beach. Lucky for her the trail was soft sand covered in soft, white pine needles. She paused to rub her feet and caught a whiff of cigarette smoke once more. An ominous sensation washed over Rebecca, and she knew something was wrong, very, very wrong.

The sounds of laughter caught her ears as she crested the top of the cliffside trail. The couple were sitting out on an outcropping which overlooked the lake while enjoying a picnic lunch. They were close to the edge, but not so dangerously close she feared for their safety. The man stood up, bent to kiss what Rebecca assumed was his wife and headed off in the opposite direction.

She glanced around and saw the man was headed toward a wooden structure beyond the edge of the trees. Using her camera, she zoomed in and saw that the rustic building was a welcome center outfitted with bathrooms. The man disappeared behind the wooden partitions.

Rebecca trained her camera on the woman as she stood gazing out over Lake Superior. Her loose-fitting white shirt flapped in the breeze as sunlight highlighted her blonde hair. She wore a genuine smile of happiness which spread to her own face as well.

A shadow moved within the trees and the hairs on the back of her neck stood on end in protest to the breeze suddenly turning ice cold. Rebecca's heart beat faster, and a lump formed in her throat.

She tried to call out as the shadowy figure crept ever closer to the unsuspecting woman. His cigarette smoke hung thickly in the air causing her to gag and choke. The figure grabbed the woman from behind by her shoulders and started pushing her toward the edge. Rebecca broke into a run to try and save the woman.

The man turned to face Rebecca and smiled before shoving the woman over the edge of the cliff. And then he vanished just as quickly as he had appeared. The woman was no longer screaming by the time Rebecca reached the edge of the cliff and peered over. Her camera shot frame after frame even after the film had been used up. Rebecca dropped to her knees and wept.

Nine

"Is she crying?" Sydney asked the nurse who was looking after Jane Doe.

"No, her eyes are just tearing up to lubricate and protect themselves. They are dry from the harsh fluorescent lighting. Even though her eyes are shut, they are not completely closed, and some light does get in. It's a normal occurrence with comatose patients. I'll bring some lubricating eye drops when I make my next rounds."

"Are you sure, they certainly look like tears."

"Essentially, they are, but trust me, the tears are not due to any emotional response," the nurse said coldly and left the room.

"Shane, can you do anything about that camera, the sound is making it hard to think?"

"Sorry, Sid. I've tried everything but it won't stop," he replied.

Shane fumbled around with the camera while Sydney continued to look the woman over. She swore she saw the woman's eyes moving rapidly back and forth as with REM sleep which, as far as she knew, shouldn't happen with a comatose patient.

"How many more rolls of film are in that backpack?" Colby asked.

"I think there were still a few empty rolls."

"Then put one in and see what happens."

"Do you think the camera is hungry, Colby?" Sydney asked with a smile.

"Hey, it was your hunch. This shit seems pretty strange to me so far, so why not try something outside of the box, even if it is your box," he said.

Shane shrugged and carefully went through the backpack making sure he didn't touch anything he didn't need to. He opened the back of the camera which stopped it from taking photos as if the machine somehow knew what he was doing. He loaded a twenty-four-exposure roll of film into the carriage and closed the back. Immediately the camera sprung to life and fired off all twenty-four exposures in rapid succession and then stopped as abruptly as it began.

"Shane, how long will it take you to get those developed?" Sydney asked.

"A few hours. But I'm almost out of the chemicals needed to process film. I won't have enough to process both rolls."

"Where can you get more?"

"I'm sure I could track some down through some online photography supply warehouses."

"Here," Sydney said, handing Shane a credit card. "Order as much materials as you think you'll need, and have it shipped priority overnight."

Shane stood there with the card still in his extended hand for several moments before realizing she expected him to be going immediately. Colby sealed the backpack up in the evidence bag and picked it up while leading Sydney out of the hospital room.

"Is it just me or was that shit weird as hell?" Colby asked.

"I'm not sure if weird is the proper word for it. Besides, maybe we're reading too much into this. Could be Shane develops a bunch of photos of the hospital room floor. But either way I think I'm stuck in Newberry for a day or two. I'll head down to Zeller's and see if they have a room," she said.

"No way in hell are you staying at Zellers."

"Why not? It's clean, the beds are comfortable and continental breakfast is fantastic."

"No way are you staying in town and not with me. If Katie finds out you were here and didn't come over to say hello, I will never hear the end of it."

"How the hell would Katie know I was in town?"

"Trust me, she would smell you on me. Now let's head down to Timber Charlie's for a burger and then out to my place."

"Great, I'll be spending the night out in BFE where all the serial killers and prison escapees hide out," she laughed and got into her car to follow Colby.

Timber Charlie's was a nondescript building with a façade that was half brick and half sided with white clapboard on one side and then a wooden slat front on the other side facing the other street. It appeared as if it were three different buildings when in fact it was only one. Their logo was a man who looked more like a Bavarian brewmeister than a lumberjack.

"Why do you do that?" Sydney asked.

"Do what?"

"Spend twenty minutes looking at the menu when we both know you are going to order the whitefish basket with extra tartar sauce to dip your fries in."

"You don't know that, I might be in the mood for something different," Colby said defensively as the waitress walked up.

"Have you decided?" she asked, pulling a number two from behind her ear.

"I'll have the Reuben, onion rings instead of fries and an iced tea with lemon please. He will have the whitefish basket, extra fries, extra tartar, with a Mountain Dew," Sydney said.

"He'll say he wants diet but then I'll have to listen to him complain about the taste the entire meal so no diet."

Colby nodded in defeat and the waitress darted off with a smile. Within ten minutes they were digging into their scrumptious fare, each of them lost in their own thoughts. Colby was admiring the sports memorabilia from the Lions, Tigers and Red Wings, until he got to the Green Bay Packers wall. Sydney on the other hand was a little creeped out by the variety of critters watching her eat with glassy eyes. The stuffed bobcat poised to pounce above them made her do a double take on more than one occasion.

With their bellies full they headed for Colby's cabin which sat on a two track just outside of Fourmile Corner with a great fishing pond in his backyard. He called it a pond; Sydney called it a swamp. About once a week he shared his morning with a wandering moose or two. Just beyond the edge of his property was some of the densest, most uninhabited forest in the world.

"You wait out here and I'll prove it to you."

"Prove what to me?"

"That Katie can smell you on me."

Colby disappeared into the front door of the rustic log cabin. Sid leaned against the bumper guard on her patrol car listening to the woods as they transitioned from the sounds of the day into nighttime serenades. And then Katie started in. She bayed and howled while throwing herself against the door. Colby opened the front door, and seventy-five pounds of Alaskan malamute came charging at her, making sure not to miss any of the puddles in the driveway. A wet, muddy, extremely happy malamute.

Colby laughed. "Sorry about that. We can wash your clothes overnight and your room has fresh linens so you can turn in whenever you want."

"I smell like dog. Wet, loveable, adorable dog," she said, grabbing Katie by the neck and giving her a big bear hug. "She's getting huge."

"Yeah, well, she keeps learning how to get into her food bin. I've started locking it up in the truck."

They went inside the roughhewn, hand-built log cabin that Colby and his father had built before his father had passed. It was in fact two separate cabins connected perpendicular to each other at the kitchen. While the outside was raw and rustic the inside was adorned with highly lacquered saplings and small trees that had been cleared from the property. This gave the interior a unique look as the living room and one bedroom were mostly maple, the kitchen was all pine, and the back bedroom was all dark walnut. Little by little he had changed out his store-bought furniture for pieces he made himself out of wood from his property once his skill level rose above that of a three-legged chair craftsman. Homey did not even come close to how comforting the cabin felt, especially when there was a fire going in the stone fireplace.

Colby brewed some coffee and set out cups, creamer, milk, and sugar. Once it was done brewing, he poured them two cups and put out a plate of Trenary toast.

"Ugh, yuck, how old is this Trenary? I didn't think it was possible for it to go stale," Sydney said, dropping the piece of toast back onto the plate. "This is harder than zwieback."

"I don't know, I don't eat the stuff. You must have left it the last time you were here. Or maybe the time before that."

She checked the date on the bag. "Colby, this is over six months old."

"How am I supposed to know? That crap starts out stale."

They both had another cup of coffee while picking at their takeout trays from Charlie's. Her onion rings were cold and disgusting but since Colby had yet to leave the nineteen seventies, he didn't have a microwave.

"Do you have any beer?" Sydney asked.

"I've got a few KBC's in the fridge."

"Any Widowmaker?"

"I should have known," he said and went to the kitchen to pour them both a beer. He brought back a dark glass of Widowmaker for her and a Pick Axe Blonde for himself.

"And I should have known," she said, pointing at his glass of light ale.

They chit chatted about nothing much for the next hour until there was an awkward silence in the room, so Colby turned on the television. It was a Zenith twenty-seven-inch console from the early nineteen eighties with a layer of dust on the screen. He only received the local news channels and once in a great while a station from Canada if the winds were calm. The national news was on.

"How can you watch this drivel?"

"As you can see from the dust on the screen, I don't."

"No, all that tells me is that you don't bother to dust," she said, slammed the rest of her beer and handed Colby the empty glass. While he was pouring her another, she sat in the other room spewing hatred at the television.

"Tell him how you really feel about him."

"Wipe that smile of your face. And don't you dare defend these lying sacks of shit."

"That was over two years ago, and you're still this angry?"

"I'm angry about all the incidents not just that one. But we both know that was a blatant lie and they did it on purpose just to get ratings."

Two years earlier Colby had arrested a local drug manufacturer who was the son of a prominent tribal elder. While transporting the suspect to the jail the man tripped and fell, honestly tripped, and fell. Although Colby was able to catch the man and break his fall for the most part, he still took a big hit to his eye on the hand railing. A reporter happened to be on hand and snapped a photo that could be misinterpreted that the sheriff had slammed the man's face into the railing, especially when the press intentionally led the story in that direction. Knowing the truth, the reporter still captioned the photo, "Was this an excessive display of force by the sheriff?"

"I got over it so should you. I might have lost a total of ten votes over the incident, and his father's vote wasn't one of them."

"It's not just that one incident, Colby. That just happened to be close to home and I knew the facts as they were so there was no gray area. These damned reporters, especially the closer they are to Washington, go around calling themselves the Fourth Estate as if they are on a pedestal above the rest of us. They give themselves awards and puff out their chests like they are doing some noble cause for mankind. When in fact all they are is that little kid on the street corner a century ago hawking newspapers for a nickel a piece. It's just a job and a job they are pretty shitty at," Sydney said and slammed her beer. "How many of these do you have?"

Colby laughed. "Enough. If you chug one more down like that you'll sleep past sunrise."

After taking care of their glasses and making sure the lights were turned off Colby sat down on the couch with Sid. There was a little chill in the air, so he grabbed a dark brown quilt with a gorgeous twelve-point whitetail buck in the center panel and pulled it up over the both of them. Sydney slid next to him and lost herself deep in thought while rubbing Colby's hand. Katie stayed on the floor curled into a ball whimpering quietly every few seconds while readjusting herself. This continued for several minutes until Sydney softly patted her hip and the malamute joined them for a cuddle session.

Feeling a tear trickle down Sydney's face and drop onto his forearm, Colby asked, "Are you thinking about her?"

"Of course. I'm always thinking about my mother."

"I meant, in light of recent events," he started.

"Just shut up and let me sleep," she said, patting the back of his hand. He didn't see her warm smile nor the cold, empty void in the center of her heart.

Ten

Katie continued to stick her cold nose against Colby's exposed leg until he started to rouse before returning to guard duty. When he didn't get up, she repeated the process, adding a little nip with her front incisors after he repeatedly ignored her attempts to wake him up.

"What the hell, Katie," he said and jumped off the couch while rubbing a tender spot on the back of his thigh.

Within seconds he was on high alert. She only stared at the door when there was someone coming down the trail. He threw on his pants and gun belt before peeking out of the curtain.

"Still paranoid I see," Sydney said. "You talk to the Jehovah's Witnesses while I jump in the shower."

By the time Sydney climbed out of the shower the house smelled of fresh coffee and bacon causing her stomach to protest. The Widowmaker effects were lingering in her gullet and a greasy breakfast was not palatable. She burped and the taste of stale, black beer invaded her mouth. She dashed for the bathroom to brush her teeth for a third time. Katie was squat on her haunches protesting in a semi growl at the morning's visitor.

"Shane, why did you drive all the way out here?" she asked when she returned from the bathroom.

"Show her," Colby said, moving away from the kitchen table to allow her some room.

There was an array of twenty-four photos spread across the table placed in chronological order. Colby handed Sydney a cup of coffee as she leaned over the table. Shane fidgeted nervously while she looked over the photographs.

"How in the hell did that camera take these photos while in our possession in a hospital room?"

"It's even stranger than that, Sid," Shane said. "Look closer."

Sydney picked each photo up from the table and looked at it closer. She even grabbed her cheaters from her pocket and looked them over again.

"Is that where I think it is?" she asked, her voice nervous and weak.

"Not just where, but when," Shane added.

"What do you mean by when?"

"Look closely at Miner's Castle."

She looked at the photograph but then back at the two men not understanding why they were so animated about the picture. Truth be told, even being from the area she did not go out to Miner's Castle very often.

"The turret is still there, Sid," Colby said.

"What turret?"

"The sand formations," he pointed at the photograph where two oblong columns rose from the rock formation side by side.

"Call me blonde, but I'm still lost."

"That tower on the right, it fell off into the lake back in April two thousand and six."

"This is bullshit. What kind of a prank are you two trying to pull? I knew something was fishy about Shane driving all the way out here before the sun even came up," Sydney said red faced.

"Sid, think about it for a minute, do you really think I'm smart enough to come up with a prank this elaborate? Live catfish in your bubble bath, sure. Putting your toothbrush in the habaneros overnight, yep, all me. This, I don't even believe it myself so I could have never concocted this."

"So, are you trying to tell me that not only was this camera able to take photos from a hospital room in Marquette all the way out to Miner's Castle in Munising, but it was also able to transport itself back in time?"

"It would seem that way," Shane said.

Knowing he was the weak link of the dynamic duo Sydney turned on him, "Where in the hell is the hidden camera? I'm not going to be some silly ass blonde in an internet video prank. If you are fucking with me Shane, so help me God you will pay dearly."

"Sid, I swear, we are not fucking with you," Colby came to the young deputy's defense.

She looked over the photos with even more scrutiny while Colby got her another cup of coffee. She took a long swallow and put the cup down.

"And what is this all over the last few photos? What did you call it?"

"Bokeh."

"And I suppose it shouldn't be in these photos either?"

"No, it shouldn't."

"Shane, really, what the fuck. How is this even possible?"

"It's not. At least not by any stretch of my imagination."

Sydney started gathering up all the photographs and tucked them under her arm. "I think you had better make another pot of coffee," she said.

"Where are you going?" Colby asked.

"To look at these in peace and quiet while I take a shit. Don't get your man bun wound up too tight, Shane, women shit too."

Once she was out of earshot Shane asked, "Why is she always busting my balls?"

"Maybe she has the hots for you."

"Oh great, so now you're going to bust my balls too?"

"What do you think I keep you around for?" Colby said with a smile and punch to the deputy's shoulder.

Colby went about the task of putting another pot of coffee on to brew while Shane tried to make friends with Katie who was having none of it. She didn't fall for his condescending baby talk nor did she fall for trading pats on the head for treats.

"Holy shit," Sydney called from the bathroom.

"Are you okay, Sid? Want me to send Shane in to help?" Colby joked.

"Good idea, I could really use a hand, mine are full and it's time to wipe."

Colby laughed so hard at Shane's reaction that white stars exploded in his eyes. Sydney strolled out of the bathroom, grabbed her cup of coffee, and shot Shane a wink complete with a blown kiss. She set two of the photos on the table.

"Do you recognize her?" she asked.

"No, should we?" Shane answered.

"Not you, young blood, I doubt you were even born yet."

"Wait a minute, yeah, I do remember her. Jane Whitely or something like that," Colby said.

"Janet Whitenaur."

"That's right. Her husband was convicted of pushing her off the cliff."

"Maybe he was innocent. The evidence was nothing more than circumstantial. He was a troll and really didn't have a jury of his peers, they were all locals," Sydney said.

"Troll?" Shane asked.

"Where did you get this guy? A troll is someone who lives downstate, under the bridge, like in old children's stories."

"Would a jury really convict a man for just being from downstate?"

"No, but they wouldn't trust him as much as they would a local. And from what I remember his story changed a lot during the investigation and then again during his testimony in court."

"Maybe he was guilty all along and we can prove it," Colby said.

"I don't think we are going to get that lucky. Shane, even with this bokeh stuff obscuring the assailant can you do some of your computer magic and get an approximate height on this guy in the photograph?"

"I think I can get you in the ballpark. It probably wouldn't withstand a court proceeding, but at least it would give us an idea."

"That is good enough for me. Why don't you go work on that and Colby and I will take a road trip?"

"Where are we going?"

"It's a beautiful day to visit MBP."

"You know I hate that place," Colby protested.

"When we're done, I'll buy you lunch at the Smokehouse," she said while batting her eyes at him. "But first, we should stop by your office."

"For?"

"This is looking more and more like our Jane Doe may be the victim of an attempted murder. We should probably put an officer watching her around the clock. At least for now, until we know more. And get her fingerprints into the system if they have not already done that," Sydney said.

"Excuse me, ma'am. That won't be possible. That was one of the first things I thought to check. She doesn't have any," Shane said.

"What do you mean she doesn't have any?"

"They were burned off, we're not sure how yet. But honestly, her fingertips look like they never had any to begin with."

"How is that even possible?" Sydney asked.

"There is an exceedingly rare condition known as adermatoglyphia where a person is born without fingerprints. But when I say rare, I mean the rarest, so I doubt that is the case here," Shane explained.

"They why impart useless trivia on us? Fingerprints would be nice but I'm sure Judge Hawkins will sign off on taking a sample of her DNA," Colby said.

Sydney walked into the other room, grabbed her phone, and dialed a familiar number. Colby went about the chores of feeding and watering Katie while locking the place up. Normally he didn't bother, but they might be gone for a day or two. Shane said his goodbyes, though Katie was having none of them, and headed out the door. Within ten minutes they were on the road to Marquette.

Eleven

"Thanks, Jim," Sydney said to the gate guard as he let them into the prison compound.

Marquette Branch Prison is well secluded from the main highway even though the gate is only a stone's throw away. The prison is known only to the locals, the inmates and anyone visiting those inmates. The average vacation traveler has no idea the darkness that lie just beyond the ornamental hedgerow.

Once inside the gate the visitor is greeted by a gothic building that more resembled a European castle than it did a prison. The grounds are ornately landscaped with a beautiful fountain surrounded by colorful flowers that could be considered a tourist attraction to some. Even brightened with an array of flora a shadow of gloom spread across the prison grounds.

Sydney wanted Bradley Whitenaur to feel comfortable, so she talked the warden into lending them a comfortable office to use for their chat session. The warden had insisted on leaving a guard in the room, but Colby convinced him that he was more than capable of handling the inmate, so the warden eventually capitulated.

"Mister Whitenaur, please have a seat," Sydney said while indicating to the guard to take the man's shackles off.

"I'll be right outside," the guard said and stepped outside into the hallway.

The office the warden had let them use was the child psychologist's office who used it for supervised visits with incarcerated fathers. The room was obviously a child's sanctuary as it was filled with puppies, kittens, and clowns. There were books and puzzles and game galore as well as stuffed animals in every corner of the room. Sydney hated clowns.

"Mister Whitenaur, my name is Sydney Lamppinen, and I'm with the Michigan State Police, this is Sheriff Patino from Luce County. We'd like to ask you a few questions if we may," Sydney said, trying not to be creeped out by the clown paintings staring at her.

"Call me Brad. Questions about what?"

The man looked tired and defeated. Three days' worth of deep brown stubble was interspersed with gray. He slumped in his chair as if this were routine and he was already bored.

"Okay, Brad. I would like to ask you a few questions about your wife if I may."

"What about my wife? I have already been convicted of her murder, what more do you people want from me?" he asked. He sat there mulling over the situation for a minute or two. "You found the evidence, didn't you?" He bolted straight up in his chair and his eyes took on a certain shine that did not go unnoticed.

"What evidence are you talking about, Brad?"

"The evidence I told that cop about. Evidence that there was another person on that cliff with my wife."

"I'm afraid we didn't find any evidence," Sydney said.

"Then why are you here?"

"We want to hear your story."

"That's all in the police reports and trial records, why would you want to hear it all again from me?"

"Satisfy our curiosity. Just run us through that day again if you can. I know it has been a long time," Colby said, finding himself somewhat sympathetic to the man's plight.

"You and your wife are from downstate correct?" Sydney asked.

"Yes, near Grand Rapids."

"What made you decide to take a trip to Pictured Rocks?"

"Janet and I were just rekindling our marriage after a long separation. We decided to try to recapture our romance, our love, hell maybe we were trying to recapture our youth. It was where we first fell in love on a senior class trip. We had been friends, but never really dated until coming up here on that trip."

"You mentioned a long separation. How long, and was this the first time you had seen her since the separation?"

"Just under two years. We had been fighting a little, the usual stuff, money mostly. But we still talked almost daily and were trying to work things out. But then out of the blue she became distant and stopped answering my calls or texts. And that was the last time I saw or heard from her until two weeks before we went north," Brad Whitenaur explained with tears in his eyes. "Regardless of what you all think, I loved my wife. I loved her so much there was no way I could kill her. There was not one single domestic charge in my file which was never brought up in court."

"Why did your story change so much during your interviews with the police?"

"I was scared, confused, and they wore me down."

"First you said she fell, then you claimed she committed suicide. How do you explain that, especially when you initially claimed you hadn't seen anything because you were in the bathroom?" Colby asked.

"My story didn't change, the context they put it in did. I was so confused as to what had actually happened that I was grasping at straws for an explanation to satisfy myself. I didn't say she fell, and I didn't say she committed suicide. I said maybe she fell and then they asked me if she could have committed suicide and I said it was possible, but I didn't believe she would do such a thing. They misconstrued everything I said."

"But why were you still confused and altering your story during your trial months later?"

"Because the doctors put me on anti-anxiety meds. I was easily swayed into saying what the police and prosecutor wanted me to say."

"So, in your mind there was a conspiracy to railroad you?" Colby asked, his voice thick with disdain.

"No, I don't believe that, at least not on purpose. I don't think there was a joint effort or a conspiracy, but the prosecutor was young and ambitious, the judge old and tired and my court appointed attorney just plain ignorant," Brad explained.

"There had to be something else going on, I read the transcripts of your interviews, you were all over the place," Colby said.

Brad Whitenaur sat silent for several minutes with tears streaming down his face before he softly said, "I was high. That's what I went to the bathroom for."

"High on what?" Sydney asked.

"A speedball."

"So why didn't you tell that to the police?"

"At first everything was so surreal. I thought it was all one big misunderstanding and I didn't want Janet to find out I was still using. I was trying really hard to quit but I needed a small bump once in a while to take the edge off. And when I finally did tell one of the cops, I was sick he got me my kit."

"A police officer gave you drugs during your interview?"

"Everything that happened that day is still kind of foggy, but I do remember that I wasn't given the drugs during my interview. I was out in the hallway for some reason that I can't recall, and a cop came by and asked if I needed anything. I was sort of being a smart ass and told him I needed my drugs, so I was surprised when he brought my kit and took me to the bathroom."

Sydney shook her head in disgust. She did not like the way this thing was headed.

"Are you sure he was a police officer? Do you remember anything about his uniform?" Colby asked.

"He wasn't wearing a uniform, I just assumed he was a cop because he was in a cop shop. Like I said, I was hurting by this time and had been interrogated for more than twenty-four hours," Brad Whitenaur said. Sydney knew one thing, he was right about one thing, his lawyer was an idiot.

"You mentioned something about evidence when we first started talking. What did you mean by that?" she asked.

"Like I said, everything was really foggy. I had just bumped in the bathroom so I was trying to get my shit together so Janet wouldn't notice. I was walking slowly to give myself a little time to adjust to the high when I saw her white shirt just kind of disappear. Then I saw someone leaving the area through the woods and they dropped something near the trail."

"What do you think they dropped?"

"I think it was a cigarette, I think they flicked it away into the woods. I remember thinking what a jerk, he could start a forest fire that way. Then some woman at the Miner's Castle platform screamed and all hell broke loose. I tried to show the cops where I had seen the man in the woods, but they were only focused on me."

"Are you sure it was a man?"

"Not one hundred percent, but could a woman have shoved my wife off a cliff? I wasn't seeing anyone else so there wasn't any woman I know who would have had any reason to push Janet off a cliff."

"Thank you for your time Mister Whitenaur, that is all we have for now," Sydney said, getting up from her chair and letting the guard back into the room. He put the wrist shackles back on the prisoner.

"Is that it?"

"I'm afraid so for now, but if we have more questions we know where to find you," Colby said.

"There is one thing that has always nagged me," Brad said.

"What might that be?" Sydney asked.

"Just before I left to go to the bathroom Janet became nervous about something. When I asked her what was bothering her she started to say something but then she stopped. I was more interested in getting high, so I didn't push her on the issue. She might still be alive today if I had," he said and turned his back on them to leave with the guard.

Once they were out in the hallway and out of earshot Colby asked, "You believe him, don't you?"

"I believe that something just isn't right about his story. More than ten years in prison and his insistence on being innocent still seems genuine," she replied. "What do you think?"

"The same. Now what? Any evidence of a one-armed man in the woods is long gone by now."

"The only thing we can do. We find out who Jane Doe is and see if there is anything in either hers or Janet Whitenaur's backgrounds that link the two of them together."

📷   📷   📷

"What are you doing?"

"Pulling over."

"I can see that," Sydney said. "But why?"

"A little relaxation," Colby said as he began rummaging behind the seat of his truck.

"You had better have some wine, cheese and chocolate behind your seat."

"Better than that, I have fishing poles."

"Fishing poles? What in the hell am I going to do with a fishing pole?"

"Oh, I don't know, fish maybe."

"I hate fishing."

"No, you don't, we used to go fishing all the time."

"I went with you, that didn't mean I liked it. There was beer, whiskey, good country music and boys, what more could a girl want. What is this place? I must have driven by here a hundred times and never paid much attention."

"It's the Chocolay Bayou," Colby said while turning over rocks and large fallen limbs.

"What on earth are you doing?"

"Getting bait," he said and held up a wriggling, fat earthworm.

"Oh, hell no, I'm not skewering that poor creature with a hook," Sydney said.

Colby baited her hook and then baited it again a few minutes later as they trolled the slow-moving water meandering out to Lake Superior. Sydney had already given up, reeled in her fishing pole, and was stowing it in the truck when Colby let out a war whoop. His pole was bent over, and he was working the reel in dramatic fashion. Ten minutes later he hoisted a six-and-a-half-pound brook trout from the waters.

"What in the hell is that?" Sydney asked.

"It's a fish. A brook trout to be exact."

"I know that's a fish smart ass, but what is that?" she asked, pointing to a snakelike creature about a foot-long hanging from the side of the fish with a thin spindle of blood flowing down its body.

"Oh, damn," he said and nearly dropped the wriggling fish. "It's a lamprey, and a pretty good sized one too."

"God, I hate those things. They scare the living shit out of me."

"Why would they scare you? You acted like you had never seen one before."

"I was teased mercilessly with them. Not real ones, the boys would put rubber fishing lures in my locker, in my pockets and in my lunch sack."

"Why would they," he started and then the light bulb went off. "Ah, Lamppinen, lamprey, I see the connection.

"Quit laughing, or I'll kick you in the ass. Kill that damned thing and let the poor fish go."

Colby rummaged around in the glove box for several minutes until he found what he was looking for. He pushed in the cigarette lighter in his truck and waited. Once it popped back out, he held the glowing red tip closer and closer to the eel-like fish until it wriggled and let go of its grip on the trout. He ground the lamprey under his boot and let the fish go back about its business, free from its deadly hitchhiker.

Twelve

Sydney had Colby drop her off at the department to grab her car before heading up to the hospital. The forensics technicians having gathered all the evidence they could from the comatose woman packed up and left Jane Doe in the room alone. She felt a certain sense of melancholy wash over her. The poor woman was suffering a fate worse than death without anyone by her side, no family, no friends and probably not even in her own hometown. It was heartrending indeed.

Sydney felt compelled to sit with Jane Doe for a while. There were so many questions running through her head and not one single answer. She stayed at the hospital for a little over an hour, but the situation began to weigh too heavily on her, and she too eventually left the poor woman alone.

She grabbed a salad and a diet Dr. Pepper from the store and headed for home. It had been a dreary day weather wise, but it was starting to clear up, so she pulled into the scenic overlook at Au Train Beach to watch the sun set over the lake. She rolled her window down to listen to the rhythmic sounds of the waves rolling across Au Train Bay as she picked through her dinner.

Brush strokes of magenta painted a backdrop behind Au Train Island as the sun disappeared behind the horizon. A lone seagull let loose a long, lonely cry that echoed across the beach.

Sydney knew the feeling. Without realizing it she had drifted off to sleep to their eerie song.

Sydney bolted awake and was disoriented for a few moments. She reached for her phone to check the time. She couldn't believe it was almost midnight. She had four missed texts from Colby and one from Shane.

She was getting her bearings back after a rude awakening in the car when she caught a faint whisper of cigarette smoke. She scanned the beach out of each window of her car and didn't see anyone, nor did she see a red-hot cherry glowing in the darkness from where the picnic tables sat on top of the dunes. She brushed it off as just her imagination and got out of the car to go to the bathroom before driving the rest of the way home. Aware of just how small the portable toilet was she undid her gun belt and locked it away in the trunk of her patrol car.

She made her way to the Porta-Potty that sat alone at the top of a small sand dune across from a set of weathered picnic tables. Sydney looked around but didn't see any evidence that anyone had been smoking and no longer smelled the odor. She shrugged it off as her overactive imagination.

The toilet was a tight squeeze even with her gun belt off. She had barely sat down when a large shadow rapidly crossed the walls of the plastic cubicle causing her stomach to lurch. She was about to laugh it off as nothing more than a gull passing overhead when she smelled smoke wafting through the still night air. Distinct cigarette smoke.

Suddenly she was terrified. Was she going to be jumped the moment she opened the door and stepped outside? Was someone planning to rob her, or worse? She remembered she was in her patrol car and doubted anyone would be foolish to attack a cop, even a female cop.

Sydney sat in the dark outhouse watching as a black shadow circled the plastic structure. Her hands trembled with fear. She was stunned by the intensity of emotion running through her. She was rarely afraid of anything and even in those rare cases when she was afraid, she was not prone to showing her fear, and never once had she let it get the better of her.

"Michigan State Police show me your hands," Sydney called out as she burst from the Porta-Potty. Her voice echoed across the empty beach. There was no one around, not a living soul.

She chastised herself for allowing her fear to dictate her actions. She went back to the patrol car and put her utility belt back on. She pulled the flashlight from its holster, unclipped her pistol and went back over to the outhouse. She shined the light all around the structure but there were no footprints in the loose sand. She searched the area using grid search tactics and still found nothing. Whoever had been outside the portable toilet was quite adept at hiding their tracks.

As she got back into her patrol car, she caught a feint whiff of something familiar. She breathed in through her nose several time, each time smell the aroma, but she just could not place it. Sydney did not recall much of the ride home; her mind was wandering all over the place. From the strange case, the even stranger incident in Au Train and the strangest of all, the possessed camera.

She pulled into her place, a small one-bedroom cabin on a remote point situated on Deer Lake in Ishpeming. Sydney managed to get two whole hours of sleep before she was wide awake. She made a thermos of coffee and headed out to Al Quaal for a run before heading into the office.

The large recreational area bordered Teal lake and Deer Lake with rigorous cross-country ski trails that doubled as hiking trails during the off season. The off season being summer in the Upper Peninsula. Sydney chose to run the longer Deer Lake loop in hopes of clearing her head.

Her run was cathartic, the rhythmic pounding of her feet on the hard-packed earth drummed in harmony with the songbirds. Occasionally a pileated woodpecker would join in to play percussion with her. She had run five miles before she realized she couldn't remember a single thought that coursed through her brain in those five miles, which was exactly what the doctor ordered.

Sydney showered at home and headed into the office to make sure there was nothing pressing that needed her attention before heading back to the hospital in Marquette. She met up with Colby in the lobby and fought the urge to tell him about the incident in Au Train the previous evening.

"Any luck with her DNA yet?" Sydney asked Shane as he came into the lobby to meet up with them.

"Unfortunately, nothing yet. But we may have caught a little break," he said and handed her a stack of photos.

"Where did you get these?"

"The camera took them last night."

"Is this the same truck in all of the photographs?" Sydney asked.

"Believe it or not, I think so."

"How is that even possible? This is like a montage of the truck's life cycle."

"Almost from start to what looks to be the end of its life cycle," he said, pointing to the last photo of a rusted back Chevy pickup truck with a burgundy tailgate partially obscured by trees.

"Are we sure it's the same truck?" Colby asked.

"No, it could just be photos of the same model year, make and color of Chevy."

"Because this case has been anything but normal, let us assume that these photos are real and of the same truck throughout its lifespan. What does that tell us?" Sydney asked.

"It tells us that whoever is responsible for Janet Whitenaur and our Jane Doe has been doing this a long time."

"And there are probably a lot more victims we don't know about. Shane, whatever you do, always keep fresh film in that damned camera. This has happened too many times for it to be coincidental. Colby, any clue where this last photo was taken?" she asked.

"Sid, that could be a million places up here. It looks like nowhere and everywhere at the same time."

"I was afraid you were going to say something like that."

"I'll show the photograph around to some of the old trappers, they get wandering about in places no one else ever goes. I had Morgan send some of her interns up to Miner's Castle to comb the woods. Maybe they will turn up something."

The three of them took the elevator up to Jane Doe's room stopping for some vending machine coffee on the way. Sid found herself grinning, Shane had lost the man bun overnight. The doctor was in the room when they walked in.

"How is she, doctor?"

"Not much change. Have you had any luck finding any next of kin?"

"No, I'm afraid not, we still haven't been able to determine her identity yet. The other day I saw her eyes moving back and forth, like she was in REM sleep. Is that possible for a coma patient?"

"Yes. In fact, she may even be conscious, though that is highly unlikely. We can do another brain scan to see if there is any activity, though I highly doubt it," the doctor explained.

"I feared I was just grasping at straws," she smiled. He nodded and left the room.

Shane headed back to the station while Colby went and got some more coffee. Sydney took the young woman's hand in hers and a hollowness invaded her. No one should die alone, especially not a woman as young as Jane Doe. It was imperative that she find out who this poor woman was.

An image invaded her mind, not so much a tangible image rather than a sensation. She felt the woman's terror as she plummeted to the rocks below. But she also felt something else, something foreign to her, but so strong it was undeniable. A mother's love. She pulled her hand away from the comatose patient's and wiped her sweaty palms against the legs of her pants. And then she realized she had caught the faintest odor of cigarette smoke.

Rebecca found herself lost within a forest of darkness, so dark in fact, she couldn't even see the trees. But there was another presence there, something warm and inviting. A simple touch.

A shooting pain invaded her brain, a headache so intense she could not even see. And although she could sense a comforting presence with her in the darkness, she also felt a boundless malevolence. She sensed a struggle between one entity who wanted to save her, and another who wanted to destroy everything that was her, even the very memory of her.

How could anyone ever hope to find her in this all-consuming darkness? Was anyone even looking for her? And if they were, was it only to finish the job they started.

She listened to the gentle hum of an engine and the slapping of waves against the hull. She was on a boat. But where was the boat? And where was she going to? She tried to roll over but found she was bound tightly to the deck. But it was not her on the deck, it was someone else. Another woman.

Rebecca could see that the woman was hurt so she tried to get up and help her but found she couldn't move. She looked to her left wrist, and then her right and did not see anything holding her in place, and yet, she couldn't move no matter how hard she tried.

The woman's red hair splayed out like a halo encircling her head. Her face was battered and bloody and it did not appear the woman was even alive. Rebecca held her own breath to see if she could hear the woman breathing but the sound of the boat's engine drowned out any subtle sounds.

The engine shut off and the boat began to drift. Rebecca craned her neck and could make out a dark shadow creeping closer and closer the boat. The shadow loomed over her, casting her into a cold darkness that terrified her to the bone.

She heard mumbled voices coming from below and then a splash. The two figures continue to argue as they rowed a smaller boat into the shadows. Rebecca noticed the woman was gone and she could move again. She picked up her camera and leaned over the upper railing of the boat. There were two men in a rowboat rowing toward the cliffs. The woman's long, flowing red hair trailed in the water behind the boat.

They shoved the woman's body into one of the smaller caves in the face of the cliffs. She zoomed in on the soles of woman's shoes and took several photographs until she found she could no longer move. The men were back on board and the boat was underway once more. Rebecca drifted off to sleep.

When she awoke, she found herself back in the ebony forest. Moonlight shone through the trees and glistened across the top of the water. She put her aching hands in the moonglow and saw they were filthy and bleeding. Every fingernail was torn and split. Why had she been digging in the dirt? The pain from the ice-cold water was intense, but she forced herself to endure it. She had to clean herself. She always cleaned herself when it was over.

Thirteen

Sydney decided to sleep in the next morning as it was Sunday, a day of rest for some, yet somehow, she was still up before the sun. She hit the trails at Al Quaal just before sunrise and was treated to a beautiful sunrise over Deer Lake. She was just getting out of the shower when her phone rang. It was Colby.

"Good Morning, sunshine," he greeted much too enthusiastically for her tastes.

"Just because I'm awake doesn't mean you can be all rainbows and roses."

"I spoke with Eno this morning."

"The captain of the cruise boats in Munising?"

"One in the same. He said the maintenance crew did some work on the engine on one of the boats and he was taking her out for a test run this morning. He invited us to go along," Colby said.

"He invited or you begged?"

"Just shut up and meet me at the Munising dock at nine."

"Is there a point to this little exercise?" she asked.

"It might give us a different perspective. Besides, he has been on these waters for more than fifty years, he's bound to know things that have been lost to history."

Eno was waiting at the dock with the engine running and his patience wearing thin. The man was well leathered from spending nearly his entire life on the water in the harsh environment of Lake Superior. The man's interior was far more chiseled than his exterior. A long burned-out stub of cigar was clenched in his teeth and his face was sporting a four-day old salt and pepper beard. He adjusted his grease covered Carhartt Stormy Kromer several times while watching the two cops converse on the gangplank rather than board his vessel.

Colby handed Sid a cup of coffee and a chocolate scone. At nearly seventy feet long and double decker the boat was able to carry one hundred and fifty passengers. Although today there would be only two. She had a fresh coat of white paint and gleamed in the sunlight.

"Good morning, Eno," Sydney greeted dryly as she boarded the vessel.

"Oh, is it still morning? I guess I must have lost track of time," he huffed and eased the boat out into open water as soon as the lines were cleared by the young deckhand who by his boyish looks was probably still in high school.

As they eased out of the channel Eno ran through his routine dialogue as though they were paying customers who had never taken the tour before. He told them all about the lighthouse at Grand Island, the history of the island itself and made sure to plug the bike rentals and campgrounds because he owned those concessions as well.

The first stop on the tour was Miner's Castle. Though not a normal part of the tour, at Colby's prodding Eno eased into the cove where Janet Whitenaur had met her fate. Sydney recognized the look on the old captain's face and had an odd feeling; it reminded her of a man filled with remorse.

"You brought the camera with you?" Colby asked as Sydney shot a few shots of Miner's Castle.

"Of course, I wanted to see if it would magically produce a suspect for us so we could catch us a serial killer."

"Whoa, easy Sherlock. Sid, we have no evidence this is the work of a serial killer."

"And we have no evidence that it isn't either."

Eno ignored the arguing couple as he had done for more than forty years driving his boat and eased them through the painted coves where striations of mineral stains reflected off the water. As soon as they came to the formations known as the Caves of Many Colors the camera fired off shots on its own until it was out of film.

"Did you do that?" Colby asked.

Sydney simply shook her head and changed film in the camera. "Eno, has anything ever happened here?"

"Happened? The kids and kayakers alike love to throw parties here. I've been flashed more than my fair share of times and my crew has spent a lot of hours cleaning up after the bastards who leave their trash in the caves."

"Not quite what I was asking. Have there been any incidents here?"

"You mean like at Miner's Castle?"

"Yes."

"Not that I've ever heard of, but I spend most of my time on the water and away from local gossip," Eno replied.

They passed by Lover's Leap where Sydney expected the camera to go wild, but it didn't fire off a single shot, so she snapped a few herself. They passed by Rainbow Cave without much fanfare. Eno seemed to have traded in his tour guide persona for that of an engine mechanic and was revving the engine and then reversing, causing the boat to lurch and Sydney's stomach to protest.

"Hey, Eno, do you have any bread up there?"

"Yeah, but it's probably stale has hell."

"Can't be any worse than Trenary," Colby said and they both laughed.

"Shut up or you are going overboard," Sydney said between gags.

Eno bypassed Indian Head, the Gull Rookery and Grand Portal due to the engine giving him fits. He made a few adjustments, and she was back to purring like a kitten, a ferociously hungry jaguar kitten.

"Just what is it you are trying to stir up here?" Eno asked.

"What do you mean by stir up, Eno?" Sydney asked.

"The dead need to stay dead. It don't do nobody any good to go digging up the past," he said, keeping his back to her.

Sydney started to get to her feet, but Colby grabbed her belt and pulled her back into her seat. Against his better judgment he shook his head no at her. He could almost feel the heat radiating from her red cheeks.

They passed by Battleship Rocks, the Flower Vase and Indian Drum formations without so much as a word from Eno let alone his customary narrative. Sydney tried to get some shots, but the captain had accelerated to a point it was impossible to focus. He sped past Chapel Cove and made a quick turn at Chapel Rock before heading back to the Munising docks.

"I never much liked that guy," Sydney whispered under her breath as they were getting off the boat.

"Never much liked you either," Eno said from below deck.

Colby jerked at Sydney's arm and tugged her down the pier. She resisted at first but quickly cooled off. Shane was waiting for them by their cars with a manila folder tucked under his arm.

"What have you got there?" Sydney asked.

"The latest round of photos from that spooky ass camera. Why am I the one who gets custody of it?" Shane said.

"You think I want that creepy thing in my house?" Colby laughed. "Besides, Sid took it off your hands today for a couple of hours."

Sydney took the folder from Shane and flipped through the photographs. They seemed to be in sequential order of a woman freeing herself from a shallow grave. The first photograph depicted a woman's fingers, bloody and raw poking through the dirt. A sensation of dread washed over her, and Sydney nearly buckled to her knees.

"Oh my God, is this who I think it is?"

"It's hard to tell, the victim is covered in mud, but I'm having the technicians run them through a facial recognition program along with photos of her now. If we get enough points of similarity, we can safely assume that it's her.

"What do you think is in the area, here where the bokeh is concentrated?" Colby asked.

Looking at the ground behind the bokeh it appears like there are tire marks in the grass. I think it's a vehicle of some sort."

"Our truck maybe?"

"I know one shouldn't assume, but in this case, I think it would be more of an educated guess than an assumption," Shane said.

"Shane, I really need you to find a way to remove these bokeh balls from all of these photos. We need to see what is being obscured."

"I'm one step ahead of you. I'm in the process of digitizing the prints which I'm hoping will give me more ability to edit the bokeh. But I can't guarantee that it will work."

"Just make it happen, Shane. And get the film in the camera processed ASAP," Sydney said, handing him the camera and then putting the photographs back into the manila folder before jumping in her patrol car. She didn't even so much as wave before driving away. She couldn't.

Sydney drove down the coast a few minutes and headed up the ramp to a small wooded rest area that overlooked Grand Island Harbor. She slammed the car into park and dashed into the woods where she dropped to her knees. It took everything she had to keep from vomiting. She leaned against a tree with her back to the parking area and cried.

Fourteen

Shane followed the sheriff across H-fifty-eight back toward the little town of Grand Marais. They stopped at the tavern for a beer and a bite to eat while devising a plan of attack.

"Is it just me, or does Sid seem to be wound pretty tight as of late," Shane said.

"She has every right to be. This case is proving to be very close to her."

"Does she know either of the victims?"

"No, not that I'm aware of. It's a lot more complicated than that, and it will be even more complicated if this strange sequence of events continues down this disturbing path."

Shane put his menu down and gave the waitress his order. She set two waters and two coffees on the table and disappeared with a less than enthusiastic smile. The place was crowded when they first arrived but seemed to be emptying out rather quickly.

He took a sip of his coffee and said, "I'm completely lost. If Sid didn't know either victim how could this be close to her?"

"Listen, I shouldn't be telling you this and I'm sure I'm going to regret it. You must promise me, not a word of what I tell you leaves this room. Got it?" Colby said.

"You sound pretty serious."

"As serious as it gets. Back when Sid was young, very young, long before we ever met. Let us just say that her mother had an incident at the cliffs to avoid going into detail."

"Incident? Like a fall? Oh, that is just tragic," Shane said.

"No, she didn't fall, or at least there was no evidence of that."

"Are you saying her mother was murdered? Pushed off the cliffs like these other women?"

"No, I wish it were that simple. She just vanished. No goodbye note. She didn't take the car. She left all her belongings at home. I have investigated the case a dozen times since meeting Sid, and I have come up with nothing every single time. In fact, it may have been what pushed me into police work in the first place, and I know it was the catalyst for her not only becoming a cop, but an investigator. Not a single thing about her mother's disappearance makes any sense," Colby explained.

"Was it a result of marital problems maybe?"

"Not as far as I could tell. There were no reports of her fighting with Sid's father. Not one single incident. No police reports for domestics, no strange hospital visits. You know how those things go, no matter how slick the abuser thinks they are, there is always some kind of a paper trail."

"What about Sid's father? What did he have to say about all of it?"

"They looked at him hard for her disappearance. The detectives assigned to the case interrogated him intensely for hours. Back then it was a lot easier with little to no accountability and an overzealous cop could get away with things we wouldn't dare do today. Eventually Sid's father succumbed to the constant pressure and hung himself. The case was closed as being a murder-suicide."

"Murder? Without a body?" Shane asked.

"Things were a lot different forty years ago, Shane. Funding was short so corners got cut. I'm sure the detectives were convinced they had the right man with or without a body. The courts were glad to see it go away, so away it went."

"And what happened to Sid?"

"Her Aunt and Uncle raised her until they disappeared when she was a teenager."

"Disappeared?" Shane asked.

"Without a trace. No note, no nothing. Sid acted like it didn't affect her, but I knew differently. She was emancipated later that year and then joined the marines as soon as she turned eighteen. She joined the police academy right after her stint in the corps was over."

The waitress dropped off their food, replenished their drinks and disappeared as quickly as she had appeared. Shane took a long drink of his water and opened a manila folder he had brought in with them. He mindlessly thumbed through some of the photos while eating his fries.

"So, what about the two of you?" he asked.

"The two of who?" Colby said, trying to deflect the conversation even before it began.

"You and Sid, I can tell there is something there."

"Yeah, well it's even more complicated than the rest of the story."

"You guys aren't a couple?" he asked, flipping through the photos one more time.

Colby ignored the question and instead focused his attention on his whitefish. Truth be told, he didn't have an answer to give the man because he didn't know himself. It was complicated. Sid was complicated.

"Pardon my nosiness, but why do you boys have a photo of that young woman? Is she in any trouble?" the waitress asked on her rounds to refill drinks.

"Why, do you happen to know who she is?" Colby asked as he sat upright in his seat.

"No, sheriff, I'm sorry. I don't know who she is, but she does look awfully familiar. Let me get our resident busybody for you, she remembers everyone who comes through that door. Hey, Franny, come here for a minute," she called out. "Remember this girl?" she asked once the grandmotherly woman showed up at the table.

"Oh my, I sure do. Frightened little thing. Like a little fawn after momma ran away," Franny said, her hazel eyes showing genuine concern for the missing woman.

"Does she live in the area? Did she come here often?"

"No, she definitely wasn't a local and I doubt she was even a Yooper. She was only in here once or twice that I can remember. Must have been more than a year ago now," Franny said, tipping her head back and putting a finger to her temple.

"If you only saw her once or twice, and she wasn't from around here, how is it that you remember her? I mean, you must see thousands of people," Colby asked.

"Not that time of year we don't. Besides, we get a lot of locals in here or groups of snowmobilers who are here so often they might as well be locals, but rarely do we get a pretty, young girl in here all by herself," the waitress said. "And she was always looking around. She got up and moved seats two or three times, finally she settled on the booth in the corner away from the windows."

"Do you recognize this truck?" Shane asked, pulling one of the photos of the Chevy from his stack.

"I think so. But I'm afraid I don't know much about trucks," Franny said.

"It looked a lot like that truck she was driving, only older and had a red tailgate," the waitress added. "You boys want dessert?"

Both Colby and Shane ignored her question, gathered their things, and went to the register to pay. The waitress disregarded their rudeness as she pocketed the fifteen-dollar tip.

"Where are the photos of Jane Doe?" Colby asked.

"In my darkroom at home."

"Do you have a printer at home?"

"Yes, but I will have to dig it out of mothballs."

"Head home and print up about fifty flyers with Jane Doe's photo and our department phone numbers. Put Sid's number on there as well. We will distribute them in the morning. We just may have caught a break," Colby said.

Shane poured himself a glass of Chateau Grand Traverse Whole Cluster Riesling and went to work on the flyers. He cropped the hospital bed out the best he could and tried to make Jane Doe look to be in as natural a setting as he possibly could considering the circumstances. He used a photo editing software to open her eyes and realized he didn't know what color her eyes were, so he used his best educated guess and hoped for the best. He would make most of the flyers with black ink so it shouldn't matter too much.

He navigated through the linens and shelves piled in the middle of his living room, a result of him having created a makeshift darkroom using his linen closet. It was cramped, but effective. He processed the roll of film Sid had taken on their excursion around Pictured Rocks.

The first several photos were of Miner's Castle and were innocuous, a little out of focus and nothing sinister about them at all. The next five or six were the same way. But then Shane developed the shots taken at Caves of Many Colors and the evening took a macabre turn.

The next photos on the roll had a different appearance as the others. They looked dated, almost as if they were from another time, but not historic in appearance. Just dingy. He dipped each print in the wash and hung them to dry, looking them over as they developed further.

Shane scanned them carefully and didn't see anything disturbing in any of the photos. There was the tell-tale bokeh in the shots of Caves of All Colors but not in any of the photographs Sid had taken. He found the photographs of the pocked marked sandstone cliffs reminded him of an old movie about an armada laying siege to a Caribbean fort, punching holes through the mortar walls with cannon balls. He was about to put them all into a folder when he noticed something. He took the photo out into the other room and scanned it into his computer.

Once the photograph was digitized, he used the cropping tool to zoom in on one of the smaller, more rounded caves. In reality it was more of a hole in the rock than a cave. There was a shoe, the bottom of a woman's shoe. He zoomed in closer until he could see a woman's ankle. It was clearly a woman's ankle with some sort of tattoo.

Shane got up from his computer and stormed over to his kitchen window.

"Damn it, Brandon. I have asked you nicely to not smoke on this side of the house. It blows right in through my kitchen window."

"It wasn't me, Mr. Crane. I quit smoking two weeks ago. I haven't had one since."

"Don't you smell cigarette smoke out there?"

"Nothing out here. Maybe it's coming from the other side of the house."

"Sorry for jumping your ass, Brandon. I'm a little on edge lately."

Shane went to the other side of the house, there was nothing. He went back and slammed his kitchen window. He checked the time and saw that it was late, too late to call Sid, so he laid down to get a few hours of sleep before heading back to Grand Marais with the flyers. Something was nagging at him, but he just couldn't put his finger on what. Before he realized it, he had drifted off to sleep.

Sydney walked the shores of Lake Superior by the Marquette Harbor Lighthouse. Even though there wasn't much of a wind and the temperature was quite mild, she was iced to the bone. The lights of a freighter shone on the horizon; sailors just as lonely as she, embracing the dark of night.

She felt a sadness welling up inside her, she had grown much too old to be alone. Life had passed her by as she searched for a life that never was. Her mother was gone, plain and simple, there was no getting her back. Even the memory of her had faded until the events of late began to unfold. And even though she had reconciled with her mother's disappearance, her need to know what happened to her never diminished.

Sydney took off her shoes and waded through the clear waters of Lake Superior. The world was asleep except for a few late-night joggers and of course the ever-present chatty seagulls. During the lulls she could hear the drone of the freighter's engines way off in the distance.

She found herself thinking about Colby and their relationship. If one could call it a relationship. They had casual sex, but only with each other and when it started to be more than once or twice a week she pulled away. The minute she realized she had left something at his place, she pulled away. Whenever he suggested staying at her place, she pulled away. She was alone because that was the way she had designed it.

"I'm sorry, mother, I fear I have grown much too old to be chasing ghosts," she said to the shadows.

Fifteen

Three days later the flyers Colby and Shane put up paid off. A local fisherman called to tell them he remembered seeing the girl. He remembered her because she was a looker even though she was plain Jane with no make-up, her hair a mess and hiding herself for the most part. She had not even seen the fisherman on the banks of the lake at first, but once he said hello, she seemed to panic and made a beeline for the motel in Grand Marais. They headed straight for the motel as soon as Colby hung up the phone.

"Hello, is anyone home?" Colby called out after ringing the bell in the motel lobby for several minutes without any response.

"The place looks deserted," Shane added.

Colby and Shane went room to room knocking on the doors without so much as rousting a single soul. They searched the three small rooms attached to the motel office with no luck. There were no cars in the parking lot, not even a beat-up Chevy pickup truck with a burgundy tailgate.

"Look at this, the last time a room was rented was more than a year ago according to the register," Shane said.

"Let me see that. That's impossible, I know I have seen this place open not that long ago."

"Maybe someone was just trying to give the place the appearance of being open."

Colby got on the radio and called for a crime scene unit and additional men. After setting the wheels in motion he walked over to the local brewery and started asking questions.

"How long have you worked here?" he asked the bartender who was busy polishing glasses and soaking beer taps.

"A little more than two years."

"Have you noticed any guests at the motel recently?"

"Sorry, our windows face the other direction and by the time I leave here it's usually dark and I'm pretty beat. I usually drive home on auto pilot. Besides, I leave in the opposite direction, out by Green Haven."

"I didn't realize there was anything in Green Haven,"

The bartender laughed. "There isn't, that's why I like it. I have a place I built on Nawakwa Lake."

"It's quite desolate out there isn't it?"

"Like I said, it's just how I like it. No electricity, no internet, and definitely no bullshit, not necessarily in that order," he said with a smile and started stocking the coolers with cans of beer.

Colby walked around the brewery to get a feel for the place. The bartender was telling the truth, unless he was looking at the motel on purpose, it was highly unlikely he would have noticed anything, even something out of the ordinary. He nodded for Shane and they started to leave.

"She pulled out of there about a year ago," an old man in a corner booth said, his voice gravelly from years of tobacco use and cheap whisky.

"Who pulled out of where?"

"The lady at the motel. But people have been staying there a few times. They leave before sunup."

"The owner was a lady?"

"Not sure if she was the owner, but she ran the place," he said and eyeballed his near empty glass. Colby waved for the bartender to bring him another and the old man bobbed his head in gratitude.

"Did she quit? Did something happen to her?" Colby asked.

He shrugged. "Don't know. Just one day she weren't there anymore."

"Did you ever see this woman at the motel?" Shane asked, showing him the photograph of Jane Doe.

He nodded.

"Do you know where she went?"

"Nope. She left the very next morning in that truck there," he said, indicating the black Chevy with the burgundy tailgate in one of the photographs. "The motel lady left shortly after that."

"Thank you," Colby said. He stopped at the counter and slipped the bartender a twenty and told him to keep the old man from getting too thirsty.

They sat in the parking lot waiting on the other deputies to arrive with the search warrant. Colby called Sid and told her the latest break in the case, and even though it was slim, it was something.

First, they tore apart the office, but it had been sanitized of any useful information on who Jane Doe might be. Nor who the "motel lady" was either. Colby sent a deputy back to Newberry to check with the deeds office to locate the owner of the motel property.

"Find anything yet?" Sydney asked, walking in with three coffees.

"Not much of anything which in itself is odd."

"Why do you say that?" she asked.

"I'm no big city detective but this place is much too clean to have just been abandoned. There is literally nothing here. It's more like a Hollywood set than an operational motel open to the public."

They cleared a few more rooms and only had two left to search. The deputies taped off each of the rooms with crime scene tape as soon as they were cleared. Their activity was starting to draw a gathering of onlookers and Colby couldn't help but chuckle. He resisted the urge to draw out a couple of chalk lines in the parking lot.

"You know you're going to have to tell them something eventually," Sydney said with a smile.

"Like hell I do. I'll have the guys pull the tape down in the wee hours, so no one sees them. Let this town wonder what the hell happened for the rest of all eternity. Someone will write a book eventually," Colby replied.

"Hey, take a look at this," Deputy Simms called out directing them to a pad of motel stationary that had slipped down behind the radiator.

Colby felt himself go flush. He was excited to find a clue, no matter how small it may turn out to be.

"Never mind, it's just blank. Sorry, Sheriff," the deputy said and tossed the small pad of paper with the motel logo across the header onto the small dresser.

Colby picked it up and turned it over in his hands a few times. He was setting it back down when the light hit it just right.

"Someone grab me a pencil," he called out.

Shane handed him a pencil from the motel desk drawer and Colby started rubbing the lead sideways across the page.

"What are you doing?" Shane asked.

"A little trick I learned from Dan August."

"Who?"

"Dan August, it was a detective show with Burt Reynolds."

"Who?"

"Get away from me Shane," Colby said and continued his rubbing while Sydney roared with laughter.

"What does it say?" Sydney asked once she had caught her breath.

"I don't want to be Rebecca. Over and over again. She wrote the same thing over and over again," he said as he handed the notepad to her.

The officers continued to scour the small room. Shane picked up the Gideon's from the small dresser and fanned the pages until he got to the end. He fanned them again and this time a white substance fell out onto the dresser top. He went back through carefully until stopping at a page in Genesis.

"What is that?" Sydney asked.

"It's the section of the Bible that mentions Rebecca. Her name has been erased," he said and showed the book to them.

"Look through that carefully, she may have left us something else. What do you make of this Colby?"

"I don't know. Self-loathing maybe. She hated her name or even hated who she was?"

"Or maybe it was an alias. Maybe she was hiding out using an assumed name. Remember what the woman said at the tavern," Sydney said.

"You're probably right. Maybe if we can find out who Rebecca was it will lead us to who she really is and then to her next of kin," Colby said.

"I'm afraid we're running out of time. She doesn't show any signs of improvement."

"I know, Sid. I know."

"It's not much to go on, but one thing is for certain, our Jane Doe was in this motel room before she wound up at the bottom of the cliffs. Shane, I want the pillows, pillowcases and mattresses sent to the lab."

"Sure thing. What should I tell them to test for?"

"Test everything for DNA. And send the bible too. It's just a hunch but if Jane was so upset she tried to erase herself from the Bible text, then maybe she was upset enough to cry. Mark the mattress with a Sharpie to indicate the head from the foot and top from bottom. Dry bag the pillow and pillowcase," Sydney instructed.

📷   📷   📷

The drive to Grand Rapids was long and tedious. For all of the beauty of the Upper Peninsula and northern Michigan the rest of the state was flat and boring. Farmland and open grasslands chewed up most of the landscape of the interior. Now, further west the coastal drive along Lake Michigan was a picturesque journey, but it was also a much longer drive.

"Mr. Musgrave. How are you this evening?"

Bryant Musgrave wore the mask of a man quite familiar with law enforcement. He crossed his arms across his chest and flexed his large biceps in a show of bravado. Sydney recognized him as a rather good-looking man who wore a tarnish of anger.

"I'm fine, but I'm wondering why the hell I'm in a police station," Bryant Musgrave replied while sitting up straighter in his chair. "And just who in the hell are you and where the fuck is Luce County?" he asked, looking Colby up and down as if to size him up.

"We'll be the ones asking questions."

"Ask away."

"Funny thing about domestic assault, especially with a conviction, the aggressor's DNA is kept on file," Sydney said, not doing a very good job of hiding her contempt for the man sitting across from her.

Musgrave got quiet and his posture deflated. "Listen, that was a long time ago and is all in the past. I've changed. I've gone through extensive therapy and it's not who I am anymore.

Why are you even bringing that up right now? You dragged me all the way in here because I missed a payment on my restitution somewhere along the line?"

"This is not about restitution Mr. Musgrave," Colby said.

"Then what in the hell is this? I've done my time, I'm off probation, so there's no reason for you to be hassling me."

An uncomfortable silence enveloped the room for several minutes. Bryant Musgrave mulled over the conversation thus far until it finally dawned on him.

"What has happened to Abigail?" he asked.

"Abigail?"

"Abigail Musgrove, I mean Walters. Abby, my ex-wife."

"Why would you ask that? What makes you think something happened to your ex-wife?"

"Don't play games with me, lady. The abusive ex-husband is always the first place people like you look. Has something happened to Abby or not?" Musgrave demanded and rose from his chair.

"Sit back down," Colby said while placing a firm hand on the man's shoulder. There was something off, this was not the reaction of a guilty man trying to hide something, this man's demeanor was genuine. He might be a grade a, number one asshole, but he had no clue about their Jane Doe, Abigail Walters.

"It looks like you used Abigail for a punching bag, why the sudden concern for her well-being?"

Musgrave looked down at his hands while thinking about what to say. "Listen, there are no words to express how deeply I regret ever hurting Abby, or the women before her. And I'm not trying to use this as an excuse, but I was, I am sick. The doctor has me taking medication and I go to anger counseling at least three times a week. Please, tell me that Abby is okay," he said, tears streaming down his face.

"Unfortunately, I can't do that because she is not okay," Sydney said. She knew what she was seeing was true remorse, but she was in no way going to let this prick off the hook just yet.

"Is she dead?" he asked, never raising his eyes from the table.

"No, but her outlook is pretty grim," Colby said and put a tender hand on the man's shoulder as Bryant burst into tears.

"Listen, I want to believe you, I really do, but your track record is less than stellar," Sydney said.

"I'll help you in any way I can and will answer all your questions. I've got nothing to hide. I didn't do anything to Abby, hell, I haven't even seen her in nearly two years," Musgrave explained.

"Then how do you explain this?" Sydney asked, pulling a pillowcase with a distinctive floral design from a paper evidence bag.

"Do you recognize it?" Colby added.

"I think so. It does look familiar. It might have been ours. Where did you get it? Did Abby move back to our old house? I thought she sold it," he said.

"We didn't find this at your old house, two years ago or even a year ago. It was in a motel room in Grand Marais just last week," Sydney said.

"No offense, but where the hell is Grand Marais?"

"It's a small town in the Upper Peninsula. We found this pillowcase there with your DNA all over it."

"Well, I didn't put it there. I've never been across the bridge in my life," Bryant said.

The interrogation lasted another hour during which Bryant Musgrove offered as much help as he could. He explained that Abigail had finally pressed charges against him after his last assault and even testified against him at his trial. While he was in jail, she divorced him, sold the house, and vanished.

"So, after your wife sent you to jail and vanished you never tried to look for her? Didn't you want revenge?"

"Hell yes I did, at first. But then after doing my year I tried to find her, but not for revenge. I wanted to tell her how sorry I was and beg for her forgiveness. But a cop warned me off, said he would make sure I went back to jail if I continued to look for her," Musgrave explained.

"A cop? What jurisdiction?" Colby asked.

"I don't know, he wasn't wearing a uniform."

"Then how do you know he was a cop?"

"I don't really know for certain, he could have been lying, I guess. But he sure knew a lot of things about the case and about me, so I just assumed."

"A lot of that information is public domain, available on the internet," Colby said.

"Hell, Abigail could have told him all that information. When was this that the police officer spoke to you?" Sydney asked.

"I don't remember exactly, maybe three months after I got out. He made it very clear that she didn't want anything to do with me. After I struck out trying to find her phone number, address, anything I just gave up. She just disappeared," Bryant explained.

"And you harbor no ill will against her for sending you to prison?"

"Jail, she sent me to jail. I was out in less than a year and I used my time productively. Like I said, I sought counseling, got my GED, I even managed to land a good job before I got out. I had no reason to harbor any ill will toward Abby. And especially not enough to do her any harm. I loved her, hell I still do. Can I see her?"

"I'm afraid that wouldn't be possible right now," Sydney said. The look on the man's face nearly broke her heart. "Tell you what I'll do, and I'm not making any promises here. You give us her next of kin information and if and when they come to see her, I'll ask them if you are allowed to see her."

"Oly Walters."

"Who is that?"

"Her father. Her mother disappeared when she was real young."

Sydney felt a knot in her stomach forming. "Oly? A Finn?"

"I don't know, maybe."

"Did her father ever talk about the Upper Peninsula?"

"You know, to be honest with you, he hated me, and I can understand why. Because of that we didn't talk too much. He did mention a deer camp up north once when Abby and I first started dating. We had planned to go hunting once deer seasons rolled around but once he realized what a prick I was being to his daughter he never came around or spoke to me anymore."

"Okay, Bryant, you're free to go. But you know the drill. Until we can check out your alibis you are still on the hook so do not leave the state and keep in contact with the Kent County sheriff's office. Here's my card in case you think of anything else," Sydney said as she tapped on the door to get the officer's attention.

A uniformed officer came in and led Bryant Musgrave up to the front desk. Sydney sighed and walked over to the water cooler for a long, cold drink. Colby shot an inquisitive glance her direction.

"What?"

"You don't think he's involved do you?"

"I'd say the chances were slim to none. I'm not sure about the validity of his alibis, but he was honestly stunned and had no clue of his ex-wife's condition. I would bet dollars to donuts he had absolutely nothing to do with what has happened to Abigail, at least not her recent trauma."

"And the pillowcase?"

"Obviously a very elaborate frame job, but by whom and for what purpose is a mystery to me," Sydney replied.

"My thoughts exactly. I'll get someone at the office to make notification to Oly Walters. I'm going to grab a bite, what are you up to? Want to stay at my place tonight? It's a long drive back across the bridge and even further to Negaunee."

"No. Thanks for the offer. I'm going to try to make it to the hospital tonight so I can meet with Shane in the morning. He seemed a bit excited in his last text before I had to block him."

"Sid, that's a seven-hour drive."

"Not with my siren and lights on it isn't."

Sixteen

It was well after midnight by the time Sydney finally made it to the hospital in Marquette, in fact it was nearly dawn. She grabbed a comfortable chair from the visitor's lobby and sat down next to Abigail Walters. And while her heart still ached for the young woman, she was able to take a small comfort in knowing she would not leave this world an unknown.

"It sure is nice to put a name to a face, Miss Walters," she said as she took the woman's hand in hers. "I have so many questions and I'm almost certain you have so few answers."

A nurse came into the room to check on her patient. She changed out the woman's pillow, fiddled with the electronic monitoring equipment and jotted notes on the patient's chart. She gave Sydney a tired smile and dimmed the lights in the room.

"Excuse me, why is this woman strapped to the bed? She is not in our custody," Sydney asked.

"That is for her own protection. She has had a few violent episodes as of late."

"Is it possible to remove her restraints while I'm here? I just learned a few things about her, and I'm sure if she were awake these restraints would do some psychological damage."

The nurse's smile turned up a bit and she undid her patient's restraints. She pulled a fresh pillow from a closet and handed it to Sydney before leaving the room.

Darkness enveloped Rebecca. Cigarette smoke lingered all around her which was baffling enough, but there was another smell as well. Earthiness. Dank, musty, wet earth. Fear sank its sharp talons deep into her very essence once she realized what it was that she was smelling.

She looked all around her but there was nothing but blackness. She blinked a few times before her eyes adjusted to the darkness enough that she could see. Oddly, once her vision returned so did her other senses.

All around her echoed the sounds of the night. Spring peepers were singing a falsetto concerto with a baritone bullfrog throwing out a note or two on occasion. A yip from a far-off coyote joined in. The mustiness of the swamp assaulted her nose, and she realized her feet were soaking wet.

Her body felt ethereal as if she were walking through a dream, though her feet were freezing cold so it couldn't possibly be a dream. She was about to do the old pinch yourself to see if you are dreaming trick when she realized her forearms were bleeding. There were long, red welts with trickles of blood as if she had run through a briar patch. One does not bleed in dreams, do they? She held her forearm to her lips and tasted, it was blood.

Suddenly the swamp echoed with the cacophonous sounds of splashing. Running. People were running towards her. A beam of light cut a swath across the mire and the footfalls drew closer. Several shadows were rapidly encroaching on her.

Rebecca, no, she was not Rebecca, she was Abigail, Abby Walters. But why did she know this. She did not want to be Rebecca anymore. But she had to keep being Rebecca because they were after Abigail. They were going to kill Abigail.

She found an old stump to hide in and watched with a racing heart as the beam of light stopped near her and scanned the swamp from side to side. Her clothing wicked the dank waters and she began to shiver uncontrollably. The beam of light settled on something in the distance and the pursuer, and their prey continued their journey beyond her through the morass.

Rebecca, no, Abigail felt compelled to follow them through the night. The darkness on either side of her seemed to loom less and less as she traveled, and she soon realized she was leaving the swamp and walking into an open field where she would be dangerously exposed. The flashlight beam stopped moving, and so did she.

Now the beam moved slowly from side to side as the person made their way methodically across the field. They were searching for someone. She moved herself to a position where she was tucked safely out of sight behind an old stump. New growth had grown up around the stump, so she was able to crouch down and blend in with the scrub. This is what a rabbit must feel like when the fox has their scent, and they are too fatigued to continue the chase, just counting the minutes before their slaughter.

The beam of light was on the move again, criss-crossing across the open field. She couldn't see the person being chased but she could hear them. She could hear the person's labored breathing as they drew closer. Suddenly the figure changed directions and headed straight towards her. There was something familiar about the face, but quite unfamiliar as well.

Thunder roared across the open field and she knew it was death's echo. The light beam headed away from her and disappeared into the swamp. Abigail left the safety of her arboreal sanctuary and walked into the field where she had first seen the beam of light.

The night fell deathly still for several minutes. Clouds parted and allowed the full moon to blanket the field with a soft, white glow. My God, she thought, this can't be real. This must be a dream. Melancholy welled up in her and threatened to wash over her like a tidal wave.

She fell to her knees and began to pray. Before her lay shallow, open graves. Dozens of them in a hodge podge arrangement, each with skeletal remains save for one which was still empty. With tears flowing down her face, she moved between the unmarked graves, saying a prayer for each of the departed. She came upon one grave that seemed to be older than the others. There was a certain familiarity about this grave, not the grave itself but the inhabitant. The dress she wore was so memorable, she could almost smell her past. Her mother's remains were lying in the open grave, dressed as she was the day she disappeared.

Abigail was still on her knees when the roar of a truck engine and two headlights broke through the trees and bore down on her. She sprung to her feet to run but was held fast. She begged and pleaded to be left alone, to be let go. Confused, she realized it was not her voice she was hearing but another woman's.

"Do you see now? This is why we had her restrained," the nurse said as she pulled Abigail back into her hospital bed and put the soft restraints back on her wrists and ankles with the assistance of another nurse.

"I'm sorry," Sydney said under her breath as her and Colby turned their backs and left the room without another word.

Sydney walked down the empty corridor toward the lobby for some vending machine coffee. Sun beams broke through the curtains announcing that the morning had come. She was sipping at a scalding hot cup of brown water when the dynamic duo walked in.

"You look like hell," Colby said.

"Exactly what a woman wants to hear first thing in the morning. What have you got there Boy Wonder?" she asked, ignoring Colby and directing her attention toward his deputy.

"The latest photos from that creepy ass camera," Colby said before Shane could open his mouth. "Do you need to stop home before we head to Munising?"

"Munising, for what?"

"We're going to take another little boat ride."

"Hell no, I don't want to spend another four hours with that asshole, Eno."

"No worries there. I had them load the sheriff's boat into the water at Munising. I made sure they put a few loaves of bread onboard as well," he said with a smirk.

Sydney looked over the photos while Colby drove to Munising from Marquette. They stopped at the Holiday to get a couple breakfast sandwiches and hazelnut coffee. Although it was nearly ten in the morning by the time they launched, the morning air was still freezing cold. The sun had been obscured by clouds and the winds had picked up. Sydney was freezing by the time they made it to the Caves of All Colors.

The boat ride had been too choppy to review the photos without getting a headache, so she fanned through them as Colby and Shane were anchoring the boat near the rocks.

"Looking at the angle of the cliffs there is no way that she fell or was pushed and managed to land in that cave," Sydney said.

"I checked reports going back fifty years and there were no reports of any women falling or being pushed from the cliffs at this location. Hell, there weren't any missing person's reports either," Shane called out as he waded through the water to anchor the boat close to the cliffs.

"What do you think Colby, could this just be someone who fell off a boat partying and was washed ashore?"

"Not likely, Sid. This would be a tight fit, too tight for a wave to lodge a body in here. No, if there was a body here, they were put there on purpose," Colby said, after studying the small cave.

Sydney slipped on a set of waders and Shane helped her out of the boat and onto the rocks. This particular section of the cliffs ended in the water so there was no shoreline or beach to speak of. The area was treacherous and moving around was slow and methodical. Sydney inched close enough to peer inside of the small cave. Without warning she pulled herself up inside of the small grotto.

"Hey, what are you doing, Sid, you're going to get yourself stuck in there."

"Careful, you might break a nail," Shane added with a smile which was quickly wiped away by Colby's admonishing grimace.

"Shut up and help me," Sydney said.

The cave was a cave in name only. In reality it was not much more than a hole worn into the sandstone cliff face and was oblong like the eye of a needle. It was just barely wide enough for Sydney to get her shoulders passed the mouth so she stretched out like Supergirl in flight so her arms wouldn't get stuck beneath her. The cave was about twelve feet deep. Less than a minute inside of the dark hole and she was questioning her decision.

"Shine your flashlight in here over my head, I can't see very well, and shove me in a little deeper."

Each one of them shined their lights deep to the back of the cave. Colby tied a rescue rope to her ankles just in case.

"What do you see back there?"

"Not much of anything really," she said.

"Do you want us to pull you out?"

"Can you flip me over?"

They turned her over so she faced the ceiling of the cavern. Sydney liked being in this position even less.

"Are you sure you don't want us to pull you out?" Colby asked.

"No, deeper. I'm just about to the end."

Sydney was deep enough that she was able to see the back wall. She flipped herself over again and went through a small pile of debris that had washed to the back of the cavern.

Without warning claustrophobia gripped her and she screamed.

"Get me out, now!"

It took several minutes to extract her from the cave. The men accidental jerked too hard and pulled her straight out and much too fast causing her to drop face first into the freezing cold lake.

"Shane, I told you not too hard," Colby immediately tried to cover his ass.

"Nice try asshole."

Laughter was on the tip of his tongue, so Colby quickly averted her attention by helping her back up into the boat.

"Did you find anything useful?"

"I'm not sure. Shane, grab me a towel and show me those photos again."

"Sure thing, Sid."

After she dried off as best as she could she went through the photographs one by one. She pulled three out and set them on the deck of the boat.

"Just as I suspected, she wasn't pushed off the cliffs and she didn't get shoved into that cave."

"What are you talking about Sid?" Colby asked.

"Look, at the top edge of the entrance," she pointed to small discolorations in the rocks. "And then there is this," she said, handing Shane a piece of broken fingernail.

"A fake fingernail broken down to the quick. It's a longshot, but there might be some DNA on this thing."

"At the very least we might be able to match the fingernail polish to give us a time frame. It has to be a process similar to matching vehicle paint," she said.

"And those discolorations on the rock, do you think they're blood?" Colby asked.

"Yes, I do. I'm sure there's no longer anything to pull DNA from, but it tells us one very important thing."

"How the hell would that even be possible?" Shane asked.

"How would what be possible?"

"How would it be possible for there to be traces of blood still remaining after all these years?"

"I don't know Shane, but I'm going to have Joyce test it just to satisfy my own curiosity."

"And just what is it you are going to have her test?" Colby asked.

"Whoever this woman was, she managed to escape from someone and pulled herself up into that cave to hide from them. She might very well still be alive and knows who her attacker is."

Sydney wrapped an emergency blanket around her to keep the wind off her while they were driving back to the harbor. She cut arm holes in the blanket turning it into a poncho and was going over the photos one by one. Colby swung wide to pass a tour boat in front of them.

"Hold it. Back off, follow the boat back into the marina."

"Why, Sid? That will take at least another fifteen minutes. I thought you were cold."

"Because I'd like to have a word with Eno," she said.

"I don't like the sounds of that," Colby responded.

"Just follow him, I promise I will play nice."

Sydney had one photo in particular that she was interested in. She continued to gaze back and forth between the photograph and the fantail of the cruise boat. Colby eased the sheriff's Boston whaler into its slip. Sydney didn't wait for it to be tied to the pier before she jumped out and headed over to Eno's tour boat. Shane and Colby quickly followed in case they needed to run interference.

"Eno, I'd like to have a word with you."

"It will have to wait. I have got to get the boat gassed and ready for another cruise. Stop by my office after the last cruise, we can talk then."

"It will have to be now," she said, her tone startled many of the guests who were in the process of disembarking.

"I'm busy, missy, it will have to be later," Eno said and went back to whatever it was he was doing.

Colby grabbed Sydney to keep her from boarding the vessel which only made her angrier.

"Sid, what has gotten you all fired up?" Colby asked.

She jerked her arm free and pulled him to the back of the boat. She held up one of the photos and pointed out an area saturated with multi-colored balls which obscured the upper quadrant.

"What are you trying to show me?"

"Look, it's the same boat."

"How on earth can you tell that? This is so out of focus you can't see anything."

"Look at the very top, leading off the paper."

"Yeah, so, it's a ball of light."

"A ball of light that only shines in one direction. The lens on the light housing is broken. Look there, the one on this boat is broken as well."

"No offense Sid that barely meets the criteria for circumstantial."

"Besides," Shane interjected. "These photographs all seem to be from a different time period other than the present. I doubt that same light has been broken all this time."

"I don't care about the validity of it, and I don't even begin to know what this damned camera is up to. All I care is that now we know Eno is involved somehow, that camera has told us as much," Sydney said.

"No, we don't, Sid, all we know is there may or may not have been a boat with a broken light in the area where we have no body or evidence of a crime. Now come on, let's get to the hospital, I received a text that Oly Walters is there," Colby said, careful not to grab her arm.

"Shane, clean up these damned photographs," was all Sydney said before getting into her patrol car and driving off.

Colby needed to find a prudent way of reminding her that Shane worked for him, not for her.

"Mr. Walters, my name is Sydney Lamppinen, I'm an investigator for the Michigan State Police. How are you?" Sydney asked out of habit, of course he was shitty, the whole damned situation was shitty.

"Good afternoon," he said as he extended a meaty hand. "I'm as well as can be expected under the circumstances. Why do you have my daughter in custody? Did she do something wrong?"

"Oh, no sir, nothing like that at all. In fact, those are not our restraints, they are there at the request of the hospital staff."

"Why on earth would they restrain a comatose patient?"

"She has had, for lack of a better term, episodes."

"What kind of episodes?"

"They are similar to seizures."

"Does that mean she is in discomfort? Pain? Is she suffering?"

"Mr. Walters, those are questions best directed toward her doctors," Sydney said.

Oly Walters nodded and wiped the tears from his eyes with fingers the size of bratwurst. He was a large man, calloused and grizzled from years of hard work. And yet at that moment, he appeared as weak and vulnerable as a newborn kitten.

"It was that bastard Bryant, wasn't it?" he asked under his breath.

"Excuse me?"

"Bryant Musgrave did this to my little girl, didn't he?"

"Mr. Walters, I've studied Mr. Musgraves' file extensively and yes, on the surface it did look like he was the most plausible suspect. However, after interviewing him and checking out his alibi he most definitely did not do this. And to be frank, he is broken up over this. He asked if he could see her and I told him that would be up to you," Sydney said.

"Absolutely not," the man grunted between sobs.

"I understand. I'll relay that message. Let me ask you, what was your daughter doing up here in the Upper Peninsula by herself?"

"She was looking for her mother I would imagine."

"From the information I was given her mother is no longer with us."

"She's not. She has been gone a very long time."

"Then why would Abigail be looking for her?"

"The police never recovered Maren's body. She disappeared one night and I, we, never saw or heard from her again."

"Where did she disappear from?"

"Munising. Pictured Rocks to be precise. We were up here on vacation. Abigail was a very small girl, probably too small to even remember. Maren and I had a small fight while taking one of those cruises that tour the cliffs. When we got back to the motel, she was still angry, so she took a drive to cool off. In the morning she wasn't back to the motel yet, so I called the police. They searched for three days but never found her or the car," Oly explained. "For the life of me I can't even remember what the fight was about."

Sydney felt a surge of energy rush through her. There was no way this was just a coincidence.

"Mr. Walters, I'm sorry to ask this, but would you happen to have a photograph of your wife?"

He dug out his wallet and pulled a battered pictured from one of the dingy plastic sleeves and handed it to her. "This was taken the day Maren disappeared. I'm going to want this back," he said and handed Sydney a photograph of a beautiful woman with flowing red hair and stunning emerald eyes.

"Absolutely. In fact, I'll have a technician make a copy and I'll get the original right back to you."

Shane tapped on the window of the hospital room and beckoned Sydney out into the hallway. She rose to her feet, put a comforting hand on the man's shoulder and started for the door.

"Ma'am," Oly Walters called out to her. "On second thought, tell Bryant I'll talk to him. If I think he is sincere I will let him see Abigail."

"Do you mind my asking why the sudden change of heart?"

"I just remembered how I was treated when Maren disappeared. The police hounded me for nearly two years, my family treated me differently, and her family never forgave me. I was an innocent man the entire time. Abigail here was the only one who never questioned my guilt or innocence and look where she ended up. I should have just lied to her and told her I killed her mother so she would quit looking for her," he said and burst into tears.

Sydney made her exit and joined Shane in the corridor hoping he would not notice the tears staining her eyes. The two of them walked down to the waiting room out of earshot.

"Did you find something important?"

"And quite disturbing. Take a look at these," Shane said and handed her another folder of photos.

"What in the hell are these?" she asked.

"I'm not sure. I went home to see if I could enlarge the photos from the caves and noticed the camera had taken more photos, so I developed them," Shane said.

"When did it take these photographs?" Sydney asked.

"I can't be positive, but it was after you gave me the camera back at Pictured Rocks."

"That would put it somewhere in the time frame when Abigail had her episode. What the hell, Shane?"

She looked through the photos and shuddered. Gruesome, ghastly, words that did not begin to describe what she was seeing.

"Are these mounded areas all graves?" she asked.

"I can't say yes for certain, but that being an open grave in the foreground, I'd wager yes."

"My God, how many are there?"

"I counted eight, not including the open one. But I'm sure there are more."

"What's that shadow, right there by the open grave? Is that Abigail?"

"I can't say for certain, I'll know more after I digitize these and run them through photo editing software to clean and brighten them, but it looks like a person kneeling by the open grave, and she does look a lot like Abigail Walters," Shane said.

Sydney studied the photographs again, slowly going through them one by one. There were not as many as with the others, only twelve in this batch.

"That looks like feet right there, doesn't it?" she asked while pointing at one of the photos. "What do you think that is in the obscured area?"

"I'd say those are truck headlights that those feet are running from it."

Sydney nodded in agreement. "And what do you think is in the open grave?"

"Without being able to zoom in on the area and crop the photo I would have to give it my best educated guess."

"And that would be?"

"It looks like it could be human skeletal remains."

"That is what I see too. But why in an open grave if all the others have been grown over?"

"We would have to see them in person to determine that answer I would imagine," Shane said.

"But we still have no clue where this is or where these graves are."

"No, but I showed them to Colby, and something seemed to register with him. He took one of the photos and hauled ass out the door."

Seventeen

Sydney pulled up into the parking lot of Pine Stump Junction diner next to Colby who was sitting in the sheriff department's four-wheel drive truck designed for off-road use. It was a pretty thing he was quite proud of, so he babied it and only drove it when absolutely necessary. The dirt parking lot was full of police vehicles from several different jurisdictions. Cop after cop spilled out of the diner with containers of coffee to go and boxes of donuts.

"Why the mudder?" she asked, opening the passenger door and looking up at how far she would have to climb to get in. Shane was already hopping up into the back seat and offered her his hand once he was in. "And why the army?"

"I'll tell you when we get to where we are going. Have you ever been out on Pike Lake road?" Colby asked.

"Maybe once or twice cruising as kids. As I recall it can get bad in wet weather, but it has been dry lately," Sydney replied.

"Your car won't make it where we're headed. I'm going to reconnoiter the area for the crime scene units."

"Reconnoiter? That sure is an awfully big word for a redneck from the great white north," she said with a smile as they pulled out of the parking lot, spewing gravel behind them.

The big knobby tires whined rhythmically on the pavement as the trees on both sides of the road whizzed by. Less than a mile up the road they veered to the right onto Pike Lake road. After following the dirt road for several miles, Colby turned off the dirt road onto a two-track heading north. While rutted and filled with mud holes the road was not impassable, so he radioed for the crime scene units to proceed. The two-track lane was so narrow they had to roll the windows up to keep from getting slapped by trees that had overgrown into the pathway. Colby grimaced each time a tree limb scratched down the side of his baby's pristine paint job.

"Where in the hell are we going?"

"Not much farther down and this two-track will open up into a huge field."

"But where?"

"If my hunch is right, it's a killing field. Our killer's dump site."

"Why would you think that?" Sydney asked.

Colby slowed down and crept over a deep rut separating the wooded two-track from an open field. He pulled the truck off to the side and marked the rut with orange cones. He warned the oncoming vehicles to take it very slow. The rut was designed as a trap to stop any trespassers or Curious George's before they proceeded too far into the field.

"How on earth did you find this place?" Sydney asked.

"Look here," Colby said, pointing to one of the photographs of the grave sites.

"It's completely black. What am I looking at?" Sydney asked. "Give me your cheaters. Don't look at me like that, you're older than I am, so I know you need reading glasses."

"Look at that reflection right there," Colby said.

"So, it looks like a red line, maybe a lightning bolt?"

"It's a Kiss S or Z depending on how you interpret it."

"A what?"

"I know you were into ABBA and Elton John in school, so I'll forgive you. Kiss, the rock and roll band."

"Are you talking about that guy with the disgustingly crude tongue? The one who had the television show not too long ago?"

"Yes. One in the same."

"I still don't understand."

"This was my tree stand as a teenager. Peter Conklin and I used to hunt here. We put those reflectors on the stand so we could find it in the dark. The other two sides have a K and an I. KISS," he said, beaming with pride over his detective work.

"Nice work Nancy Drew," Sydney said, impressed, but not enough to pad his already over inflated ego.

Colby directed the crime scene vehicles and other departments to safe parking spots. He dropped the tailgate of his truck, pulled out a large map of the area and spread it out. Joyce Tammi walked over to the sheriff's truck and offered brief greetings. The Upper Peninsula had never enjoyed the benefits of a forensic pathologist, but Joyce was there to change that. She had successfully petitioned the state police and governor's office for the need of an onsite pathologist. Lucky for Sydney Joyce was still in the Upper Peninsula setting up the groundwork to plead her case to the politicians. This case would be a perfect platform for her to pitch her case to the bureaucrats, so Joyce was all in.

"What have you got sheriff?" she asked.

He rolled out a grouping of the photos he had copied and then blown up. He taped them all together and mapped the area into search quadrants.

"This is only an estimation. As soon as I realized what I was into I backed out to preserve the evidence. With that being said, I have no idea how many burial sites there are or if they even have anything buried in them. For all I know we could be looking at a huge local pet cemetery," Colby said.

"Anyone."

"What?"

"Anyone. If there are indeed human remains in those mounds, they are not things, they are people," Joyce said. "This is Professor Madeline Grimes, professor of anthropology at Northern Michigan. She brought a few of her students to assist us."

"Just call me Maddie," she said, extending a hand to Sydney and Colby.

Colby had to make sure he didn't stare at her too long or Sid would notice. Maddie was tall and leggy with long brown hair past her waist. Her eyes were a deep blue and when she smiled the dimples in her cheeks could melt a man. He found it very hard to believe this woman was old enough to be in college let alone a professor.

"The more the merrier at this point. I just hope we haven't wasted your time," Colby said after tearing his gaze away.

Sydney punched him in the arm and shot him a disapproving glance. Colby shot her a cautious smile.

"In all honesty, I really hope you have," Joyce said, sporting what could best be described as a smile.

Joyce and Maddie directed their trainees to start at the furthest quadrant and move through each area marking anything they thought might be a burial site with bright yellow flags. Colby left the scene to make a run into Newberry for more excavating equipment once they realized how many potential sites there were scattered across the open field. The crime scene had quickly evolved into controlled chaos.

Sydney found herself on the far edge of the clearing away from everyone else. Tears streamed down her face as memories flooded her mind. After all these years, was it possible she might finally learn the truth about her mother? It surprised her how much she needed Colby at that very moment. If they were to find her mother's remains, she did not want to be alone. She made her way carefully around the perimeter to where Joyce's crew were working.

"How is it going?" she asked.

"Slower than frog snot in winter, but we will get there. What's on your mind?"

Sydney handed Joyce a copy of the photograph of Maren Walters. "When the time comes, I'm specifically looking for anything or anyone resembling the woman in this photograph."

"I'll keep that in mind. But be aware, finding a specific person will be a longshot until we have definitive DNA results. Most often in cases like this it has been my experience there are no clothes or jewelry in the graves with the victims."

Sydney nodded and walked over to help Colby unload supplies. He brought a couple of folding tables to they set them up and put out more coffee and donuts. He fired up a generator and set one of the tables up as a charging station for phones, camera batteries and laptops. It took them more than four hours, but the potential burial sites had all been marked.

"Hey, Morgan, I didn't expect to see you out here," Sydney said.

"Sid, this is Elmer, he's a retired ranger from this district. He knows the area pretty well," Morgan said.

"Like the back of my hand actually," Elmer said with a crooked smile. "And you can call me Skunk."

Sydney could not shake her first impression of him and struggled to keep from laughing. He looked like a miniature biker trying to act tough by showing off biceps skinnier than Katie's tail. It looked as though he had spent decades trying to grow the dozen or so black hairs she was certain he would call a moustache.

"I'm not sure if we will be needing any outside assistance, we seem to have found what we were looking for," Sydney said, putting some distance between them.

"Suit yourself. I'll be over with the coffee and donuts if you need me," Skunk said and grabbed a bear claw.

"Holy shit, Morgan. If you're going to bring someone along make sure they're not stoned out of their minds."

"Oh that," Morgan laughed. "Skunk isn't stoned, he owns a marijuana farm, he always smells like that. I thought he might be of some help."

"I'm not sure about that. But at least he can't hurt."

Once Colby realized the operation was going to extend well into the night, he made yet another run back into town to get canopy tents and sandbags after checking the weather with the coast guard. According to the forecast there would be at least two days of clear, dry weather with not much wind. Great for excavating, not so great for keeping the black flies and mosquitos at bay. When he got back to the encampment several others had joined. All in all, there were well over a dozen people methodically working the field.

"Sheriff come over here please," Joyce called out. "I think we have something."

The students had been slowly unearthing and sifting the dirt exposing the back of a human skull. Several of them had to be ushered a safe distance away in case they vomited. Sydney ran back to the truck and got them some bottled water. This was the first time the students had been up close and personal with a real skeleton that had been decomposing for years.

"What is your assessment, Joyce," Sydney asked.

"Of course, it's much too soon to tell much of anything. However, I do believe we will find the cause of death will be a gunshot wound to the back of the head."

"How long has she been dead?"

"It's much too early for me to be able to tell you that."

"Can you guesstimate?" Colby asked coming up behind them with three coffees.

"I don't do guesstimations. Once I have everyone working to the point I feel comfortable leaving them I'll go back to the university with the remains. Then and only then will I be able to give you a definitive answer on both approximate time and cause of death," Joyce said.

The sun was only three fingers above the tree line, so Colby started directing the flow of traffic out of the burial site. They had built a makeshift shed for the tools and he posted two deputies on the scene to keep the site secure overnight. Sid and Colby were the last to leave.

"I want to stay at your place tonight," she said.

"That's fine. I'll have to make up the spare room for you, Katie has been trashing the place for some reason."

"No need to bother with that," she said and slid closer to him in the truck seat.

Abigail wandered through the dark field once again, cold, wet, and shivering. Darkness enveloped her in a blanket of fear as tears streaked down her face. She was lost, so helplessly lost. Two shadows made their way across the open field carrying something between them. One of the figures looked straight at her and she froze.

She tried to move but was held fast by her wrists. She turned her head back and forth, trying to catch a glimpse of who was holding her. For a moment she eased her struggling. She smelled something oddly familiar. Warm and comforting, but then she caught the astringent aroma of cigarette smoke.

The two shadows, which by their voices she determined were men, were arguing.

"I wanted this one," one of them said.

"You can have the next one. Now you dig the damned hole while I give her one last ride," the other said, the red glow of a cigarette cherry illuminated his face but not enough for her to see him clearly.

The sounds of the metallic shovel hitting the hard-packed top layer of dirt resounded through the darkness. Each time the shovel bit into the earth it sent a chill up Abigail's spine. The woman was crying out, moaning but she was too weak to scream. She could see the other man had knocked her to the ground and had mounted the woman. Familiarity invaded her senses, and she clenched her fists until her palms hurt. She had to stop this madness.

Without warning the man finished and dragged the woman up from the ground by her hair. He shoved her over to where the other man had dug the hole.

"Do it," he commanded.

"I don't want to. I want to keep this one," the other argued.

"Are you my baby brother? And don't I always look out for you?"

"Yes."

"Well now is your turn to look after me. I tell you what, once you finish her, I'll go over here and have a cigarette. That will give you time enough to get your rocks off."

The man raised his hand and the thunder rolled. The muzzle flash painted the night in death's glow. The woman fell face first into the shallow grave. The younger man mounted her from behind in a frenzy. It was over in less than two minutes. Abigail screamed.

Oly Walters laid across his thrashing daughter and yelled for the nurse. He jammed down on the call button until his thumb radiated an angry red. As soon as the nurse entered the room

Abigail let loose a blood curdling scream and then her thrashing seemed to abate.

"Undo those restraints," Oly said, clutching his daughter to his chest.

"Sir, it is in her best interest to leave them on."

"I said now," he said in such a tone that the nurse complied immediately.

Oly continued to hold and rock his daughter. Tears stained the side of her pillow. He was wiping his daughter's face when the doctor walked in with a somber look on his face.

"Mr. Walters, I'm so sorry you had to witness that."

"What does it mean?"

"What does what mean?"

"Why was she able to scream out like that? I can understand involuntary spasms, but for her to scream out like that, in extreme fear, there must be some level of consciousness," Oly said.

"I'm afraid that all of her tests have come back negative for any form of cognitive brain activity."

"That is bullshit! I just saw her brain activity. I saw the expression on her face, it was sheer panic. You will never convince me that a brain-dead person can experience that level of terror. Now, you do whatever the hell it is you have to do but I want my daughter tested again."

"I understand your frustration Mr. Walters," the doctor started.

"Don't give me that soft shoe bullshit. I want her tested."

"Mr. Walters that will be up to the insurance company and the hospital administrator, not me."

"I don't give a rat's ass about either of them. I will pay cash money. You test her again or I'll take her to someone who will," Oly said and waved a dismissive hand before turning his attention back to his daughter. He caressed her hair and moved it out of her face. He swore he saw her smile.

📷 　　 📷 　　 📷

Eno pulled the tour boat out into the harbor and headed for open water. He unlocked a cabinet, took a burner phone out and dialed a number.

"What is it?"

"It's Eno," he said.

"I know who the fuck it is, you are the only one with this number. Now what is it?"

"Things have gotten out of control. I thought you were going to put a stop to this. That damned state police bitch is riding my ass. I think she knows something."

"How the hell would she know anything if you were doing what you were supposed to be doing?"

"Just fix it before," he paused.

"Before what, Eno?"

"Before I have to," he said and threw the burner phone out into the lake.

Eighteen

Sydney stood in the center of the killing field with tears streaming down her face. She waved off one of the officers several times before he got the hint and left her alone. She looked around her and felt a frustration like she had never felt before in her life. She was so close, yet so, so far away.

Even if her mother were in one of these graves, how would she ever know? How would they ever be able to identify her remains? It was so long ago any evidence would be so degraded it would be useless.

"What in the hell are you doing out here all alone? Do you know it's three in the morning?" Colby said coming up from behind her with a cup of coffee.

"I couldn't sleep."

"I gathered that from the note you left. Breakfast is in the truck," Colby said and snuck a quick peck on her cheek. "Are you thinking about your mother?"

"Yes. Even if she is in this obscene graveyard, how will I ever know? Am I ever going to know what happened to her?" Sydney said and rested her head against his chest.

"DNA testing has come a long way, Sid. They will be able to find a match if she is here."

"A match to what? We don't have anything of hers to compare DNA samples with."

Colby chuckled and hugged her tight. "Oh yes you do Sid, yes you do."

"What do you mean by that? What could I possibly have that Joyce could run DNA on to find a match?"

"You. You will have a familial match which in my eyes is as good as a one hundred percent match given the circumstances."

She pulled away from him, looked him in the eyes and smiled. "I'm such a blonde sometimes."

"Sometimes?"

She swatted him in the arm and went to grab their breakfast. The two of them sat on the tailgate of the truck watching the sun bathe the crime scene in a wash of orange while nibbling on Swedish pancakes and potato sausages. It would have been a perfectly beautiful morning under any other circumstances.

Joyce and her team arrived not much after sunrise and immediately began working at each of the flagged sites. Once they had located the first woman's remains, they were more prepared as to what they were looking for. There were two transports also available to get the remains back to the university as quickly as possible. Sydney was pleased, her boss came through for her this time.

"Good morning, Joyce," Sydney greeted. "I see a lot of new faces."

"Morning. Yes, a few new people had joined in the fun. I called in some favors and talked my colleagues from other universities to join us. To be honest, I barely had to mention what we were up to before the bone geeks were clamoring to sign up. We bone people sure do love our bones and mysteries," she said with an enthusiastic smile and bounded off for a recently unearthed dig site.

By noon, the crew had unearthed three more graves filled with skeletal remains. Sydney put a call in to her boss,

Layton Turner and requested the state police make DNA typing a priority, not because of her and her mother but because of the mounting list of parents, sons, daughters, and husbands looking for long, lost loved ones. Shane came driving into the field a little too fast and hit the rut. As tall as he was his head hit the top of the jeep hard enough that he bit his tongue and lip.

Sydney couldn't help but laugh when he staggered out of his jeep. "Shane, you look like hell."

His uniform was wrinkled and had something left over from breakfast clinging to the right breast pocket. He was about three days away from a clean shave and is hair had not seen a comb in at least that many days.

"Sorry, I was up most of the night thinking."

"About?"

"About our misconception that the boat in the photos at Caves of All Colors was there to drop off a body. Think about it, like you said, you think the woman pulled herself up into the cave. Maybe she was hiding from them. Maybe she survived the fall from the cliff, and they came to finish her off. The boat was there to take her away, not hide her body," Shane said.

"You might be right. I'll see about getting a warrant for Eno's boat," Sydney said.

"Sid don't get your hopes up. That is circumstantial at best not to mention possibly decades ago. Are you prepared to explain to a judge that you need a warrant based on photos taken by a possessed camera and you don't even have a body?"

"Nope, Colby, that will be your job now that I think of it. Don't you attempt to play golf with Judge Gideon once a week?"

"Sid, no. Absolutely not."

She just nodded her head with a smile.

"There's something else. The camera took these last night. I was up all night developing them," Shane said and handed her a folder with photos.

Sydney went through the photos slowly, one by one. The last two photos disgusted her. One showed a shadowy figure putting the muzzle of a gun to the back of a woman's head and firing. The last showed the victim being molested even after she was dead. Again, bokeh obscured a portion of the photograph that seemed to contain relevant information and obscured the identity of the assailant.

"Shane, what is that?" she pointed to an orb in the photograph.

"It looks like another case of these phantom bokeh balls."

"No, I don't think so. This one looks different from the others. Could that be the glow from a cigarette?"

"I think it very well might be," Shane responded.

Joyce came walking up to the group with evidence bags in her hand. She laid the three emblazoned bags on the table.

"I'm no ballistics expert but something looks pretty hokie about these. We removed them from sites one, two and three concurrently," she said.

"They're bullets. But they're different sizes. Was a different caliber of gun used in each case?" Shane asked.

"No, these two are .38 caliber and this one is a .22 caliber," Colby said.

"But why are these two .38's different from each other? Were they dumdum's?" Sydney asked.

"No, these were flat nosed, no hollow point whatsoever. They didn't mushroom on impact. They are different because someone shaved lead off this bullet to change its shape," Colby answered.

"Why on earth would they do that?"

"I have no idea. Or why they would switch to a smaller caliber."

"Maybe they lost the .38?" Shane speculated. "Or there were two shooters."

"Could be. Have the team sweep the area with metal detectors."

The next few hours were slow and tedious. There was not much either Colby or Sydney could do but watch. They had already been warned to stay out of the way on more than one occasion. Sydney was getting lunch together when Colby walked up.

"I just heard something on the scanner. The Coast Guard found a boat adrift by Granite Island."

"Eno?" Sydney asked.

"Sure sounds like it from the description of the boat."

"Well let's go."

"Easy killer, I already called the Coast Guard, and they have a boat waiting for us in Grand Marais. We'll head up through Deer Park and then over to Grand Marais and leave from there first light. The Coast Guard will secure the boat as a crime scene for us even though it's their jurisdiction."

Sydney didn't like it, but the sun was already well past the halfway mark of the day and she knew the boat ride out to the island would take several hours at least.

Sydney woke up cranky. The motel bed was too soft and smelled like old lady perfume, so she didn't get much sleep. Truth be told, her mind continued to wander to thoughts of her mother so often it kept her from being able to sleep.

Colby had hot coffee for them and wisely kept his distance. As soon as they stepped out of the motel room she knew it was going to be a shitty day. The winds were blustery which meant the lake would be choppy, so on the way to the Coast Guard station she stopped at the market to buy a few loaves of bread. She was sure she would need all three loaves by the time the day was done.

The droning of the boat motors made it difficult to talk so she just sat there concentrating on trying not to puke all over the nice shiny boat. The sound was both soothing and annoying at the same time. Like a song stuck in your head you couldn't seem to turn off, but you continued to hum it anyway.

The Coast Guard officer in charge was young, much too young to be the captain of his own vessel in her opinion but he seemed to know what he was doing so she kept her mouth shut. Colby just wore an annoying grin the entire boat ride which widened every time she shoved another slice of Pepperidge Farms dark pumpernickel into her mouth.

Sydney was okay while they were following the coastline but as they neared Marquette the captain veered the vessel out into open water until all sight of land disappeared. This was the furthest out she had ever been on any of the lakes, and it was unnerving to be surrounded by nothing but open water. The wind had started to die down and the water was not as choppy so she moved to an outside seat where she could see better. A female petty officer gave her a warm, friendly smile and eased back into her seat with a cup of coffee.

Not too long after leaving sight of land she spotted a large rock formation on the horizon that reminded her of a breaching whale she had watched on the internet. The island was not much more than a huge rock that the lake somehow neglected to swallow. There was a lighthouse on the very top with a beautiful wooden staircase leading from the water to the lighthouse. The island was privately owned, and the owners did a fantastic job maintaining the place. She found it refreshing to see the American flag flapping in the breeze way out in the middle of nowhere.

The captain slowly backed the engines down until they were almost at a no wake speed. As they edged around the island they came upon a small flotilla. Two Coast Guard vessels flanked either side of Eno's cruise boat, and had it tied off to their boats.

Even though the fires were already extinguished it was clearly evident the boat had been torched.

"Sheriff," the Coast Guard officer greeted with a firm handshake.

"Nice to see you, Ben. I wish it were under different circumstances."

"Like on the golf course?" Sydney said as they helped her onto the cruise boat.

The boat was one of the older vessels with two tier seating with room for passengers inside the boat on the lower deck surrounded by windows and an upper, open air platform on top cordoned off by a safety curtain. The once pristine white boat was charred black inside and out. The windows had all been blown out from the fire.

"Was there an explosion?" Sydney asked.

"Of sorts yes. I'm not the arson investigator, but I have had some arson training," the Coast Guard officer said. "It was more of an incendiary device than it was a bomb."

"What in the hell is that stench?" Colby said.

"Up here, you'll see," Ben guided them to the pilot's cockpit.

Sydney let loose an audible gasp as did the sheriff. The charred remains of a body were slumped over the controls.

"I'll say that whoever did this is one sadistic bastard. Look here, he jammed the captain's face, mouth open, over top of the throttle control and secured it in place. I would imagine he used duct tape. A chemical analysis will tell us what exactly was used. The captain was still alive when the fire was lit," Ben said.

"Can you tell if that is Eno?" Sydney asked.

"No ma'am, not yet. But the reports show him, and one crew member left for a trial run. We're lucky to have even found the boat."

"How so?" Colby asked.

"I think the killer intended for the boat to make it all the way across the lake into Canadian waters. I'm sure we will find traces of a timed detonating device. The Canadians were supposed to find this, and it would have taken weeks to determine where the vessel originated."

"What stopped that from happening?"

"The engine threw a bearing and seized. The killer was probably long gone and didn't realize things did not go as planned," Ben said.

"You mentioned Eno left port with one crew member on board. Dare I ask?" Sydney said.

"This way."

The coast guard officer led them toward the stern of the boat. They saw man's feet, or more accurately, foot, before they saw the entirety of him.

"What the hell?" Colby said.

"The crewman had been checking safety lines and had his back turned to the captain's cabin. By the time he heard the commotion over the sound of the engine it was too late. The killer was on him in mere seconds," Ben said.

"What is that in the man's foot?" Sydney asked.

"It's a marlin spike, used to undo knots."

"Are you telling me he jerked his own foot off to try to escape? How was he killed?"

"Unfortunately, it wasn't easy for him. He didn't jerk his foot off on purpose, it was his thrashing about that separated the foot from the body. He was doused with an accelerant and lit on fire. An extremely hot burning accelerant at that."

"Phosphorus?" Colby asked.

"I can't say for certain, but from my experience, I would have to say yes. It was probably what was used as an accelerant in the incendiary device as well. We will know more once we finish our investigation."

"Please keep us in the loop, Ben," Colby said.

"Absolutely. Hell, I'd much rather just hand it over to your jurisdiction, but I have already been given my marching orders that this one is ours," Ben said. "Maritime law and all."

"I think your boss made a wise decision and I don't plan to argue," Colby said as he helped Sid back onto the Coast Guard boat.

The sun was starting its decent by the time they could see Grand Marais. Sydney stopped at the store and grabbed a bottle of Jim Beam Single Barrel before heading for the backbreaker bed in the motel. They settled in and ordered a pizza which they took a sunset walk along the harbor to go pick up. It would almost seem like a vacation if it were not for the dead bodies piled up around them. They were both asleep before it got completely dark.

"Bloodsucking vampires," Sydney seethed.

Colby laughed. "It's just Amy from the Newberry News and Oren from ABC in Marquette. They're not the enemy."

"Like hell they're not. And look over there, we have got some troll media as well," Sydney said.

She marched over toward them with her arms spread wide to her sides.

"Ladies and gentlemen, this is an active crime scene. You are not welcome here and cameras are to be turned off. Trooper Renkow, please move the crime scene perimeter back another fifty yards and put some of the tents up to block their camera shots," she told one of her troopers.

"Officer Lamppinen is this the work of a serial killer?" the young reporter from Newberry asked.

"Amy, is it? Let me give you the exclusive. No comment!" Sydney said and walked away.

"Remind me to never get on your bad side. You're vicious," Colby said.

"Well now you have gone and done it."

"Done what?"

"Gotten on my bad side."

"They're just doing their jobs."

"No, we are just doing our jobs, they are interfering. They are hoping to catch one of us making a mistake that they can show to the world how bad and incompetent the police are. They aren't interested in news; they only want drama."

"They have an obligation to report the news, Sid, no matter how horrific," Colby said, knowing he was entering dangerous waters.

"No, Colby, they have an obligation to report the facts, all of the facts, not just the facts that will paint the picture they want to paint. The media have become activists, not reporters. Especially the pompous asses who cover national news and Washington DC in particular."

"Sid, calm down, I was just pointing out that these are not the same type of journalists, they're just locals."

"Really? Colby, you of all people should know better. Wasn't it a local who tried to ruin your career by withholding facts and presenting a story that made you look guilty as hell when nothing could be further from the truth?"

"And the reporter was fired for that. It was a one off."

Sydney didn't bother to respond.

"I hate to break up this lovefest but you two need to see this," Joyce said.

She led them to the burial site currently under excavation. Sydney knew immediately something was different.

"Do you think this was deliberate?" she asked Joyce.

"Absolutely deliberate."

"I'm no profiler but that can't be an accident."

"No, this was not accidental. For some reason, the killer started showing remorse," Sydney said.

"Or we have two killers," Colby added.

The remains in the ground were not face down and shot in the back of the head like the others. This body had been gently laid out with her arms folded across her chest. There was a dead rose under the flange bones as if the woman had been clutching it when she was buried. There were decayed rose petals all around the body and she was clothed although most of the clothing had deteriorated.

Joyce held up a small evidence bag and the photograph Sydney had given her. "There was not a lot of fabric left on her upper torso, but I do think this could very well be a match. I will know more once we get her moved up and out of there. There is a good possibility there are some preserved scraps in better condition underneath her."

"Let's hope so, I would love to be able to finally give Oly Walters some closure," Colby said.

"And maybe her daughter too, when she wakes up," Sydney said with confidence.

"And there's this too," Joyce said, pointing to the skull. "She was shot nearer to the front of her skull than the others. Now, mind you, the bullet may have passed from the rear to the front but that doesn't look like an exit wound to me. Again, I will know more once we have her down to the university where I can study her remains more closely. I put a rush on the DNA from any clothing I find as well," she said and turned her attention back to her work.

"Thank you, Joyce," Sydney said.

"You're smiling," Colby said.

"Don't get used to it. I'm just enjoying a bright spot before it all turns to shit."

"Now there is the Sid I know."

"Yep, I'm all kittens and rainbows."

Nineteen

Abigail wandered the empty field alone and so very lonely. A small part of her wished that her shadowy demons would come out and keep her company. The night air was calm and oddly she felt at peace. She knew this was all just one very long nightmare, but it was also so very real at the same time. She could smell, she could taste, and she could feel everything in this frightening dreamworld which meant it just had to be real. The full moon shone big and bright overhead allowing her to see the open field.

There were a dozen or more rectangular holes spread across the open field. Abigail carefully made her way to the first one at the edge of the tree line. Against her better judgment she peered in; she had to see. It was empty. There were little flags on wires stuck in the dirt in numerous places in and around the shallow pit.

She moved on through the field to the next burial site, and the next. Each one was the same. She kept trying to tell herself that these were just holes in the earth and nothing more. But she knew better. She had climbed out of a hole just like this not all that long ago.

Suddenly the taste of earthworms invaded her mouth, and the smell of wet dirt clogged her nostrils. Her fingernails ached from digging at the earth covering her. Why had someone done such an awful thing to her? She tried so hard to remember what had happened, but she could not bring the traumatic event to the forefront of her mind.

She couldn't remember who or what had brought her to this field. Was this just a dream? One long nightmare she refused to awaken from. Something across the field caught her attention. There was another woman in the field with her. She was beckoning her to come to her.

Abigail felt nervous butterflies invade her stomach and wanted to flee the specter, but she also wanted to run straight towards the apparition. The woman was wearing a dress that flowed in the evening breeze, a dress that for some reason or another seemed familiar to Abby. A feeling washed over her, a sensation of a fleeting memory once lost, trying to return.

Once she had closed the gap between herself and the phantasm, the apparition smiled at her. It was a warm and inviting smile, so she returned the gesture. She had found what she had been searching for, yet Abigail could not put her finger on exactly what that was. She just knew that she had found it, and it was the presence which beckoned her.

The wraith spoke to her, not in words, but sentiments echoing within her own mind. The thoughts she passed were comforting but unsettling at the same time. The woman wanted her to leave, but Abigail wanted to stay. She had finally found an inner peace and she was not prepared to relinquish it.

The woman stood near an open grave calling Abigail near with a gentle wave of her hand. The taste of worms and mud once again invaded her senses, and she took a step backward away from the dark abyss. Suddenly a cloud of cigarette smoke enveloped her. It was coming from all around her. She was surrounded.

Her brain echoed with a malevolent laughter and the air around her gripped her in its cold, clammy talons. A face began to materialize in the hazy air, a demonic face she seemed to recognize.

"Do not fear, child. Embrace your destiny," the entity said before filling the air with discordant laughter. "I have a saved a place for you," it said while waving its misty arms over the open grave.

Two headlights broke free of the forest and bore down on her. She was frozen in her tracks and couldn't move.

"Abigail, you have to leave now. You have to leave right now," the woman said.

"No, I want to stay here with you."

"You can't stay here. This is not a good place."

"Then come with me. You have to come with me."

"No child, my place is here. Go in peace, you have found what you were looking for."

"Please, I'm begging you, come with me," she called out as she backed away from the oncoming truck. The engine raced and the truck sped faster toward her through the open field.

"Run my child, run," the woman said as the truck slammed into her, exploding her into a jigsaw puzzle with several pieces missing.

Oly Walters was still clutching his thrashing daughter tightly to his chest when her eyes opened.

"Let me go! Get off me! Get the fuck off me!" Abigail screamed.

The nurse came running into the room followed closely by the doctor. Tears streamed down Oly Walters' face as he slowly relinquished his grip on his daughter.

"Mr. Walters, please," the nurse said with a gentle hand on his shoulder.

The poor girl, his little girl, looked so terrified. Beyond scared. Oly's pleading eyes caught the doctor's and the man nodded. Abigail was trembling and whimpering when the doctor slowly made his way toward her.

"Do you know your name?" the doctor asked.

Abigail didn't respond.

"Do you know where you are?"

Again, she did not respond.

"No one here is going to hurt you, honey," the nurse said while also doing her best to comfort her father.

"Do you understand what I'm saying?" the doctor asked.

She nodded.

"Good, very good. You are in the hospital in Marquette, Michigan. You had a very nasty fall. Do you remember that?"

"Sometimes," she replied.

"Sometimes?"

"I remember parts of it sometimes," she said. A certain familiarity, an aroma, had piqued her curiosity. "Who is that man?"

"I'm your father, Abigail," Oly Walters said, his heart swelling beyond capacity.

"Do you remember your father?" the doctor asked.

"No, but I remember that smell."

"What smell, Abigail?" the doctor asked.

She simply pointed at Oly Walters who smiled and wiped the torrent of tears from his eyes. She remembered his smell and that was good enough for him right now. But then the doctor asked another question that started his blood to boil.

"And does that smell make you afraid? Does it make you angry?" the doctor asked.

"Now you wait just a damned minute," Oly bellowed.

"Mr. Walters, you are here as a courtesy right now. This young woman is a victim, and a victim of an unknown assailant. Please, keep your comments to yourself for the time being."

"No, not afraid. Sad. It makes me sad," she said as tears streamed down her face.

   📷   📷   📷

"We just started on number eight," Joyce said while pouring a cup of Earl Grey from her thermos. She added a generous splash of heavy cream from another container.

"Have you found any remains that were older than the first one you found?" Sydney asked.

"Fortunately, no," she responded. She had no clue why Sydney had asked the question, but Colby did and felt it settle in his stomach. "We think there may be three more. They seem to be progressing chronologically by date. Maybe we'll get lucky and find some evidence with DNA that has not been too degraded."

"Let us hope so," Colby said, pouring Sydney a coffee.

The text alert on his phone went off for the fourth time. He checked it and put the phone back in his pocket.

"Is that your girlfriend?"

"Funny. No, it's Shane."

"So, I was right. What does he want?"

"I don't know. He keeps texting 911 call me."

"Well, shit, Colby, call the man. His water may have broken, and he is having your baby," she laughed.

"Shut the fuck up, Sid," he laughed and pulled his phone back out. He let Shane ramble for a few minutes. "Okay, don't get overheated. We will be there as soon as we wrap things up here."

"Is she on the rag again?" Sydney couldn't hold back her laughter and spewed a mouthful of coffee. "What did he have to say?"

"Not much other than there are some photographs we must see as soon as possible. He said he will meet us at my place and to bring whiskey," Colby said.

Colby and Sydney finished up at the crime scene and drove back into Newberry. They stopped and grabbed a pizza, a bottle of whiskey and just for laughs, Sydney grabbed a bottle of Boone's Farm Fuzzy Navel for Shane. When Colby was not paying attention, she also snagged a bag of dog treats for Katie. The malamute busted her the minute they were out of the truck.

"I told you no treats, Sid."

"Why not? What could they hurt?"

"She gets obsessed and won't leave me alone until she gets one. And she quits eating her food and plays the starving card on me until I feel guilty."

Sydney nodded, reached behind her, and slipped Katie another green biscuit.

"I saw that."

"Shut up and get in the house," she said and grabbed a handful of his butt cheek.

Shane was already in the house when they walked in. The kitchen table was covered with photographs and handwritten notes in a haphazard fashion. Colby cleared a space for the pizza and grabbed some paper plates.

"I know you said you wanted drinks, so I got you something special," Sydney said, handing Shane the bottle of sparkling wine.

"Shut the fuck up, Sid. Colby, pour me a whiskey please," Shane said.

"Damn, would you look at that, he loses the man bun and grows a pair in the process," Sydney laughed.

"Please don't make me tell you to fuck off, Sid," Shane said and downed the whiskey. His hands were still shaking when he laid out the photos in an array.

"What are we looking at, some kind of fog?" Colby asked looking down at four photos that were almost completely black except for a misty haze.

"I don't think it's fog, I think it's smoke."

"Like cigarette smoke?" Sydney asked.

"Why would you ask that, Sid?" Shane asked nervously.

"Because there is no glow in any of these shots. A fire large enough to put off this amount of smoke would have to be large enough to be seen in at least one of the photos," Sydney replied, not wanting to reveal any details of her dreams just yet.

Shane laid out the next four photos in the series. The smoke seemed to be gathering in a central location in the photos and in the last two there was a shrouded figure.

"What in the hell is that?" Sydney pointed.

"Is that Maren Walters?" Colby asked.

Shane shrugged and laid out the next two photos. In these two photos the shrouded figure was close enough to the camera to make out details. It was unquestionably a woman and she was wearing the identical dress and sported the same flaming red hair as the woman in the photograph Oly Walters had given to Sydney. The smoke had gathered into a tighter area and had begun to resemble a face, albeit not a human face.

"Oh, fuck you guys," Sydney said as she got up from the table laughing. She went over to the kitchen counter and poured herself another whiskey. She started moving things, a couple of glasses, the toaster, she even opened the bread box. She moved on to the living room where she flipped down some framed photos and moved some knick knacks.

"What in the hell are you doing, Sid?"

"Screw you Colby. It was funny for a minute, but I'm not about to look like some giant dingbat blonde you can show the guys down at the station for a good laugh."

"Why do you always think you're being pranked?"

"Because you are always screwing with me. Funny, ha, ha, but you are not getting me this time. Nice try though."

"Sid, this is the first I'm seeing these photographs, so if anyone is being pranked, it's the both of us," Colby said.

"I assumed you were going to react this way. Well, not exactly this way, but similar so I created a video of the photos. I used a computer software tool that takes single photographs and creates a rudimentary video from the still images. If you thought I was pranking you a minute ago, just watch this," Shane said and pulled out his laptop.

They watched his short video three times before Sydney finally spoke up. "Did you all see what I was seeing?"

"If you mean, did I see a demonic face form out of thin air with smoke, then yes, I saw what you saw. Shane, if you are punking us I will beat your ass, I'm not joking about that one iota," Colby said.

Colby's phone rang so he answered it. He nodded his head a few times and then hung up.

"What was that all about," Sydney asked.

"Abigail Walters came out of her coma."

"What? Let's get down there right now."

"No reason to. The doctor said she was heavily sedated, and they were running some tests on her. He told us to be there around nine in the morning and we would be able to talk to her."

"Bullshit. One more time, Shane," Sydney said. "Can you run this thing in slow motion?"

Shane pressed play and then opened the settings to slow the playback two times.

"There, stop it. Look at that. Do you all see that?" she asked.

"I'm not sure I'm following you Sid," Colby said.

"Whatever the fuck that thing is, it's looking at us. It's not looking at the woman in the flowered dress, but right straight at us like it knows we are watching."

📷   📷   📷

Abigail scooted herself up in the bed far enough to get her mouth around the straw in her juice box. She took a long drink until she emptied the box with a tell-tale sound. She dabbed at her mouth with a tissue and laid her head back down on the pillow. She was not sure which seemed foggier, her nightmares or her reality.

"How are you feeling, Miss Walters?" a woman's voice broke the silence.

Startled. "Oh, my, I thought I was alone. Are you a doctor?"

"Of sorts. My name is Claudia Inez, I'm a clinical psychologist. I hear you have had some rather unsettling incidents while you were unconscious," the woman said, tucking her long brown hair behind her ears.

"How would anyone know about them? I haven't talked to anyone about that."

"No, honey. The only thing I was told was that you had some very violent outbursts while you were out. You would not even know you had the episodes unless you remembered them. What do you remember?"

"Nightmares, but they felt so real."

"Nightmares about what specifically?"

"I would rather not talk about it."

"It will help you to get passed this ordeal if you open up and talk about it," Claudia prodded, her deep chestnut eyes aflame with compassion. "How are you feeling right now?"

"Sad."

"Why are you sad?"

"Because I had to leave my mother behind," she paused. "With that thing," Abigail said, wiping her tears away with her sleeve.

"What thing?" Claudia asked, sliding closer to the edge of her seat.

"I said, I don't want to talk about it," Abigail said.

"Can you tell me about your mother? Why did you have to leave her? Where did you leave her?"

Abigail pushed the nurse's call button and within seconds her nurse came into the room followed by the charge nurse. Helen Ostrander was young to be overseeing an entire hospital wing, but despite her youth she was a force to be reckoned with.

"Claudia, what in the hell are you doing in here? You need to leave right this instant," Helen ordered.

Claudia Inez got up from her seat, gathered her things and made her way toward the door without putting up any resistance. Abigail was perplexed by the woman's obsequious behavior.

"Wow, you must be pretty high up the food chain. I have never seen a nurse order a doctor out of the room like that," Abigail said as the woman was leaving.

"Oh honey, did she tell you that she was a doctor?"

"Yes. She said she was a clinical psychologist."

"Miss Inez, you should be ashamed of yourself, misleading this poor woman like that. She is no doctor, at least not anymore. She is an ambulance chasing exploitation artist is what she is," Helen said.

Claudia turned back into the room. "I don't exploit people; I try to help them while you simply ignore their real problems."

"Help them to see ghosts that aren't there? You consider that helping them, do you?" Another nurse entering the room added.

"Claudia, you have to leave, this poor woman has been through a very traumatic experience and doesn't have the energy to listen to your cockamamie stories," Helen said while ushering the woman out of the room.

Claudia Inez was almost out the door when she called back, "I saw him too. And my mother just vanished as well. Just answer me one question, did you smell smoke, specifically cigarette smoke?"

Helen had her almost out the door when Abigail stopped her.

"Wait. What did you say?"

"I asked if you smelled cigarette smoke whenever that thing was around."

Abigail swallowed hard. Was this even possible? Could this woman have suffered the same fate as she?

"Please, let her stay," she said to Helen and the other nurse. "Please have a seat. I'm not some naïve little girl so if at any time I think you are trying to play me or work an angle you are out of here."

"Understood. Trust me, my only intention is getting to the bottom of what has happened to the both of us. Let me ask, do you have one of these?" Claudia asked. She turned her head and pulled back her hair to expose a small, dime sized scar at her hairline.

"I don't know. I don't think so," Abigail said.

"Do you mind?"

"No, but I'm not sure if I want to know the answer."

Claudia pulled back Abigail's hair and was both relieved and horrified when she saw both of them shared the same scar on their scalp near their temple. It wasn't anything out of the ordinary as scars go. This was not some horror movie mark of the beast; it was just a scar. But it was the same scar in the same exact location and that was no coincidence.

"Do I have it too?"

Claudia nodded and guided the young woman's fingertips to the scar. "I was in a coma too, just like you. Do you remember what you were doing just before he took you?"

"Before who took me? I was not taken by anyone. At least not that I can remember."

"Do you remember what you were doing?"

"I was looking for my mother."

"I was looking for my mother as well when he took me too. And like you, I did not remember anyone taking me, not for years. But then the nightmares began. He is going to visit you in your sleep," Claudia's voice took a sinister tone.

"If you're trying to scare me, it's working."

"I'm not trying to scare you. I'm trying to warn you."

"For the sake of argument, if he does start visiting me in my sleep, what does he want?"

"I don't know yet. That's what I'm trying to find out."

"So, this thing, this person hasn't tried to harm you?"

"No. Not that I can remember. What I do remember is that I had to make a choice," Claudia said.

"What kind of choice?" Abigail asked, fearing the answer.

"A choice between me staying with him and leaving my mother behind or, quite frankly I don't even know what the other option would have been, my mother made me leave her."

After a long pause Abigail said, "My mother made me leave as well."

"We're on our way up to the hospital right now. Our coma patient regained consciousness last night. Yes, Sid is here with me. Hang on, let me put you on speaker. It's Ben," Colby said to Sydney and handed her his phone.

"We got some of the results back from Eno's boat. Mind you, these are preliminary findings so things may change," Ben said.

"What did you find?" Sydney asked.

Ben paused for long enough Sydney had to check to make sure they had not been disconnected. "Diddly squat."

"What do you mean by that?"

"The lab turned up absolutely nothing other than what you would expect in a fire."

"What are you saying? This wasn't arson?"

"Not that we can prove."

"So, the fire was started with the boat gas already on board? It looked like it burned hotter than a gasoline fire," Colby said.

"It did burn hotter than gas, and no, gasoline was not the accelerant used to start the fire nor burn the bodies."

"Then what was used?" Sydney asked.

"Nothing that we can find any trace of."

"What in the hell do you mean nothing?" Sydney asked.

"There were no traces of any accelerant anywhere on the boat other than the normal fuel tanks that exploded below decks and no traces on the top deck where we found the bodies. The bodies had zero traces of accelerant on them," Ben said.

"That is impossible," Colby said.

"I know it's impossible, but that's what the evidence indicates. What in the hell is going on?" Ben asked.

"Ben, the results just have to be wrong."

"But they're not. The boat has been towed back to the Coast Guard Station and I have called in a federal arson investigator who is with homeland security. Maybe he can find something we missed," Ben said and disconnected the call.

There was not much more discussion about the news from Ben on the drive to Marquette. Colby dropped Sydney off at the front of the hospital and then parked the truck. As soon as Abigail saw Sydney, she got excited.

"I'm detective Sydney Lamppinen, I work for the Michigan State Police."

"Detective, thank goodness you are here. I'm not crazy," she said.

Sydney cocked her head slightly to the side and said, "We haven't even spoken, why would I think you are crazy?"

"Because everyone else does, everyone except for Claudia," Abigail said. "Especially him," she indicated the doctor who had just come into the room.

"Now Abigail, I never said you were crazy. I never even hinted as much. But you have had a significant brain injury. Detective, may we speak in the hall."

"I'm not crazy. We both smelled cigarette smoke and we both have the same scars," Abigail called after them.

Sydney followed the doctor out of the room trying to ignore what the girl had just blurted out.

"Who is she talking about? Is she delusional?" Sydney asked.

"No, she's not delusional. There's a woman, Claudia Inez, who travels the country interviewing coma patients when they come out of their comas, especially in near death cases. She uses pretty sneaky tactics to gain their trust and often claims she's a doctor, a clinical psychologist to be precise," the doctor explained.

"Is this woman not a doctor?"

"Technically yes, she has been educated as a doctor, but she no longer has a license to practice due to her less than orthodox methodology."

"If this woman travels the country, how is it that you seem to know a lot about her?"

"She has been here more than once or twice. We have had to escort her out on several occasions."

"Wait a minute, this is the Upper Peninsula. This place doesn't have a trove of unsolved murders or an abundance of coma patients. Why would she be coming around here?"

"We have had a few coma patients arrive here under similar circumstances as Abigail Walters, Claudia Inez being one of them. But I can assure you, none of the cases are linked in any way," the doctor explained.

"And you didn't think this was worth mentioning to the police?" Sydney barked.

"As I said, the cases were unrelated."

"Unrelated through a doctor's viewpoint, maybe not through a trained police investigator's perspective. Now, what did Abigail mean by they both had the same scars?"

"Both Abigail and Claudia suffered trauma to the same portion of the brain that is where the similarities end. It was nothing more than a coincidence."

"We are not done here, doctor," Sydney said, spinning on heels to march back into the hospital room.

Abigail looked like a scared child lying in the bed with wide, blue eyes staring intently back at Sydney. She couldn't help but think about her own mother and when she did, she felt the same way inside as Abigail appeared on the outside. She pulled a chair from across the room and sat down next to the bed. Colby joined her with two coffees and a fresh juice box for the patient.

"How are you feeling Miss Walters?"

"Please call me Abby," she said. "I'm fine, physically, emotionally I'm a wreck."

"I can certainly understand that. I heard you say you shared a scar with a woman who came to visit you. What was that all about?"

"Right here, see," she said and pulled back her hair.

Both Colby and Sydney looked at the scar near the woman's temple. There was nothing about it that made it stand out. It was not a tattoo, or a brand, it was just a scar. But the location of the scar sent Colby's mind into overdrive.

"And the other woman, the one who claimed to be a doctor had the same scar?" Colby asked.

"Yes. She showed me. I didn't even know I had a scar there until she showed me in a mirror. And we both smelled cigarette smoke too."

As soon as Abby mentioned the cigarette smoke Sydney's stomach did a series of flip flops.

"When did you smell cigarette smoke? Here in your room? Was it on someone's clothing?" Colby asked.

"No, it wasn't like that. You are going to think I'm completely insane," she said and pulled the blanket up around her.

"No, we are not going to think you are insane, not even for a second. We simply want to find out who did this to you."

"Like I told Claudia, I did not smell anything in my room, I smelled it in my dreams. But it was so real. My dreams were so real, they were like reality. I could feel things, I could taste things, not like a dream at all. More like I was alive inside my own head," she said.

The hallway outside of her room was suddenly a lot louder than it had been. Oly Walters seemed to be jubilant. He came bounding into the room.

"See Puddles, this proves I'm your father," he said, holding out a piece of paper.

"No, Mr. Walters, that paper shows that you have familial matches. We are still waiting for definitive results," a nurse added.

"Familial matches are more than good enough for me."

Abigail looked back at Sydney with both fear and relief painted on her face. She and Colby took the opportunity to exit the room. The doctor was still at the nurse's station when they walked by.

"Doctor, can I have a moment of your time?"

"Certainly, detective. What is on your mind?"

"For the sake of argument, if both Claudia and Abigail do have the same scars in the same place on their heads, what might have caused them?"

"That is hard to say without a much more in-depth analysis. I ordered more tests for Abigail Walters, maybe we will learn more from those results."

"Okay. Thank you. Now for more of a hypothetical question. If both women were injured in the same manner, would it have the same effects on each one?"

"That is really hypothetical and really a long shot. You could hit three people in the head with a hammer and get three different results."

"If the injury were to the brain here," Sydney pointed to her own head near the temple. "What might we see as a result?"

"A wide range of possibilities from hearing loss to memory loss. There again, each patient and each injury would net different results I'm afraid. Sorry I couldn't be more help. I wish I had more time, but I've got rounds," he said with a forced smile as he left.

Sydney and Colby walked down the long-polished corridor to the visitors lounge and grabbed some coffee and an Almond Joy to share. The candy cut the bitterness of the stale coffee. Then they made their way down to the lobby and out into the sunshine. An eccentric looking woman adorned in native jewelry more indicative of the southwest than the Upper Peninsula sat on a bus bench across the street. Her long, dark hair flowed in the breeze. Sydney headed straight for her.

"Claudia? Claudia Inez?" she put her hand out which elicited the same response from the woman. And old trick to trip up anyone trying to conceal their identity.

"Do I know you?" she asked while eyeballing Colby. Sydney immediately got the impression the woman didn't like the police.

"I'm Sydney," she started.

"I know who you are. You are with the state police," she said. The woman was wearing dark sunglasses she didn't remove which incensed Sydney as it was a rude and dismissive.

"What is your connection to Abigail Walters?"

"I don't have a connection."

"Then why were you attempting to visit her, and in fact did visit with her?"

"Is there a reason for this interrogation? Do I need to have a lawyer present?" Claudia asked.

"Miss Inez, at the risk of sounding cliché, we can do this the easy way, or the hard way," Colby said, putting his hands on his hips out of habit. He was not trying to take an aggressive stance, but it certainly came across that way.

"Unless you're going to arrest me this conversation is over," she said.

Sydney waved Colby away with a bob of her head and sat down next to the woman. She wanted to rip the sunglasses off the woman's face but mentally checked herself.

"Tell me your story. Why are you so interested in coma patients, and specifically Abigail Walters?"

"I don't have to tell you a damned thing."

"Maybe. But you want to, I can sense it. What is it you are looking for?"

"Answers, damn it. I want answers. I want to know why I spent my entire life missing my mother, searching for my mother and when I finally found her, she was ripped away from me again," Claudia said, a teardrop found its way under the rim of her glasses and streaked down her cheek.

"Ripped away? How was she ripped away?"

"Because I woke up. She made me wake up."

"Who made you wake up?"

"My mother. She told me I couldn't stay and that I had to leave her there with him," Claudia said, tears streaming full on in rivers down her face.

"Who did you leave her with? A man?"

"He looked like a man, but he was no man."

"If he was not a man, then what was he?" Sydney asked, fearing the answer. Fearing what her own mother may be enduring right that very moment.

"You'll think I'm crazy and have me locked up. I'm done talking," Claudia said.

Shane pulled up to the curb next to them and got out of his jeep. He didn't see Colby waving frantically at him to stay away. As a second thought Shane reached back into the jeep and grabbed the camera. He slung it around his neck and walked over to where Sid was talking.

Claudia looked up at Shane and her face turned sour. "Where did you get that camera?" she asked.

"Sid?" Shane said, sensing a trap.

"We found it where Abigail fell off the cliffs at Pictured Rocks," Sydney offered.

"She didn't fall, and you know it. Don't lie to me. Where did you get that camera?"

"I didn't lie, at least not all the way. It was found at the bottom of the cliffs where Abigail was pushed."

"That's impossible."

"Why do you say that?"

"Because that was my mother's camera," Claudia said.

Sydney looked at her sympathetically. "Are you sure it doesn't just look like your mother's camera?"

"No, that *is* my mother's camera."

"How can you tell this camera is your mother's? A lot of cameras look alike," Shane said.

"There is nick on the housing is where I dropped the camera when I was a little girl. And I'll bet there are a set of initials inside the door where you put the film isn't there?"

"I'm not sure. There is film in the camera so I can't open it here without ruining the film."

"Shane, would it ruin all of the film or just the exposed film?" Sydney asked.

"Cover me with your jackets," he said.

The women made a makeshift darkroom and Shane ducked inside with the camera. He opened the back of the camera and looked inside.

"Sid, you need to see this."

Sydney ducked under the hood made of their jackets and investigated the back of the camera with shock. Not only were the initials CI carved into the back of the camera so were several others. Some were almost too small to see. There was AW, JW and most shocking of all, SL. She jerked out from under the coats and was pale as a ghost.

"What's wrong, Sid?" Shane asked.

"Nothing. I need you to find out the history of that camera. Who has owned it and where did it originally come from? Claudia, I will need to speak with you later but for now I have to speak with the sheriff," she said and bolted across the street where Colby stood wearing a perplexed expression.

A cold wind swirled around Abigail's ankles causing her hospital gown to flap in the wind. Her skin was covered in gooseflesh and she trembled. But her tremors were not caused by the drop in temperature, rather the fear coursing through her veins.

Had she dropped back into an endless slumber? Or was this simply a nightmare she couldn't escape. Or had the last forty-eight hours been the dream and she had never awakened from her coma.

Smoke enveloped her, emanating from both the floor and the ceiling at the same time. And the winds changed from bone cracking cold into a searing hot sirocco. She started to cry.

"This is just a dream," Abigail said aloud.

"No, this is my dominion and here you shall stay where you belong. Don't you want to be by your mother's side?"

A man came walking out of the mist in front of her. He beckoned her to him with each step he took and then he stopped. Her mother dropped to her knees at his side and bowed her head in subjugation.

"She is waiting for you, Abigail," he taunted.

"Abby, wake up. Abigail," Oly Walters said, shaking his daughter from her dream. Her eyes opened and for a moment he swore they were filled with an empty blackness.

"You cannot escape me. You bear my mark. You are mine," the voice echoed in her brain as the fog of sleep dissipated. She dropped her head to her father's chest and cried.

Colby stopped at Muldoon's in Munising on the way back to Newberry and picked up some pasties for dinner. He grabbed a cup of gravy to go for Sid, blasphemy in his opinion. Sydney couldn't resist and picked at hers on the way to his place. They had logged more miles on this case than they did in six months of patrolling and it was starting to wear on them. The road from Munising to Newberry was long, flat, and boring as hell, especially if you were a local who knew the route like the back of your hand.

They swung by the crime scene to see how Joyce Tammi and her people were progressing with the dig, but the crew had already knocked off for the day and the only people remaining there were the two deputies, Sims and Conners who had been assigned to guard the site. All was quiet for the moment. Sydney was certain it would be a very brief moment.

The drive from the burial site to Colby's cabin was quiet and peaceful. Each of them was lost in their own train of thought combing over the evidence in their brains. Although there was a long silence between them, it was anything but uncomfortable.

"Katie you know better," Colby said.

"She does, but I don't."

"People food gives her the shits so keep feeding her your pasty and you will be on clean up duty."

"But she loves the gravy."

"Well, she is a dog, so yeah she likes gravy."

Colby grabbed a bottle of Toivo and Eino's sauce and sat down with his pasty. Katie sat in the other room with her front legs splayed out eyeballing him as he ate. Every so often she would slap her paws on the wood floor and give a short, soft whine.

"No, you are not getting any. Now, go eat your food."

Katie slinked away with her tail between her legs, glancing back with sad, neglected eyes.

"Do you see what you have started? She went two whole years without people food and then you start coming around and create a monster."

"But she loves you," Sydney said. "And so do I," she finished under her breath.

"What was that?"

"What was what?"

"What did you just say?"

"I said you better check your phone to see if your girlfriend has texted you."

Colby shot her a sarcastic grin but knew she was right; Shane should have called by now. He dug around in his pockets, then his jacket and finally ran out to the truck.

Matthew F. Winn

"Damn it, I misplaced my phone again. Give it a call would you please."

Sydney dialed his number several times but there was no luck finding it inside or outside.

"I must have dropped my phone at the crime scene. I'll run back over to the scene really quick and take a look for it. Give the phone a call in about an hour or so."

"Real quick? The dig site is over an hour away. If there's something really pressing Shane will call me. I'm sure he knows we are together," Sydney said. "You can just get your phone in the morning."

"I wish I could, but something else might come up and the department has no way of getting in touch with me. No land line remember?"

"Oh, that's right. I forgot I was shacking up with Jeremiah Johnson. Hurry back. And don't wake me when you come in."

Colby grabbed his plate and scarfed the rest of his pasty down in one bite. His cheeks were bulging like a chipmunk's in late fall.

"Was that necessary?" Sydney said.

He just nodded his head and pointed between her, Katie, and his plate before walking out the door. She listened to the truck spewing gravel before giving Katie the rest of her pasty that was stashed in her purse before running herself a nice, hot bath.

Colby was in such a hurry that he forgot about the rut and hit it at a good clip. He flew up in his seat and banged his head on the roof of the truck. He climbed out of the cab cursing and holding the top of his head. Worse yet, the coffee he had picked up for the two deputies was all over the floor.

"Sorry guys, I spilled your coffee."

"No problem boss, how is your head?" Both men couldn't contain their laughter.

"I'll bet that is going to leave a mark," Deputy Conners said, eliciting another round of laughter.

Conners was short and stout with a buzzed crop of straw-colored hair. He had been with Colby for several years and considered themselves not only co-workers but friends as well. He shouldn't have even been out in the field, it was his kid's eighth birthday. Conners had argued he needed the overtime, so Colby relented and let him work a late shift as long as he promised to spend the following day with his son. Family was everything, and to Colby, his deputies were his family.

Colby salvaged what was left in the foam cups and managed to scrounge two large swallows of tepid coffee which Conners and Simms made short work of. The sheriff suddenly felt uneasy at the scene splayed out in front of him. Tiny flags danced in the night breeze while a low hanging fog drifted across the field of dead women. He shuddered and wiped it from his mind.

"Hey Conners, call my cell. I think I accidentally left it out here today."

The deputy hit speed dial and they all listened. It took three tries before Colby caught the faintest sound of his ring tone.

"What the hell is it doing way over there?" he said.

Colby walked to the very furthest northern edge of the field and waved. Deputy Conners called the phone once more but now the sound was coming from the far western side. They both looked at each other and shrugged. He crossed the field to the western edge and Conners dialed again. This time the sound came toward the center of the field.

"Which one of you two is screwing with me? Is it you?" He pointed at Conners. "Or you?" He pointed at Simms who put his hands in the air. "I'll bet it's the both of you. Funny game, but fun time is over. Give me my damned phone."

"Boss, we're not screwing with you. Honestly though, it would have been a funny gag," Simms said with a nervous smile.

"Both of you dial my number. First one, then the other right after," Colby instructed.

The deputies followed their boss's instructions. First Conners dialed and Colby's ring tone echoed from the southern end of the field. The second he hung up Simms dialed, and the phone rang all the way back over to the northern end.

"What in the hell is going on," Colby said.

They tried their little experiment again with the same results.

"Okay, boss, fun time is over. It seems like you're the one pranking us. What, is Sid out there running around with your phone?" Conners said.

"Do you really think Sid can run that fast?"

"Okay, probably not. But Katie could," Simms added.

"You two really think I brought my dog out here in the middle of the night, put my cell phone on her just to screw with you two?"

They both shrugged and nodded.

"Maybe an animal, probably a coyote grabbed it," Simms said.

"That's entirely possible. Good thinking. There are three of us so let's funnel whatever this creature is to the north. I will take the southern end, Simms you take the east and Conners you take the west side. Maybe we can flush this trickster out."

The three of them split up and walked to their respective edges of the field. They were about fifty yards away from one another. Once they were set Colby gave them the signal to dial his number. This time the phone rang in the dead center of the field. Colby looked and there was nothing there. He motioned and Simms dialed his number. Again, the phone rang in the dead center of the field. He motioned them to continue the process as he slowly walked to where the ring tone was coming from.

The three of them stood in the field looking down at a plot of dirt echoing the musings of Macho Man Randy Savage. The two deputies gave him a look before busting out in laughter.

"That is not my ringtone and you know it. Grab that shovel over there," Colby ordered.

📷   📷   📷

Shane was working on developing photos and scanning already processed photos into his laptop when the camera started going haywire. He got up from his desk and went across the room to where the camera was and realized he had left the back open when he was taking photos of the initials with his phone and there was no film in the camera. He grabbed a fresh roll of film and popped it into the camera.

As soon as the film was in the camera it fired off all twenty-four exposures in rapid succession. Having learned from the past Shane went to work developing the photos just as soon as the camera was finished shooting the roll. As the first photo started to emerge from the blank paper, he found himself confused. It was nothing more than a photograph of Simms and Conners on duty watching the crime scene. There was nothing sinister about it in the least.

The first four photos in the batch were of all the same thing, Simms and Conners shooting the shit while patrolling the vacant field of gravesites. Shane put more exposures into to the processing solution. He wished the damned camera were a digital, it sure would have made things much simpler. The next photograph in the series made his blood run cold.

The phone rang at least five times before Sydney answered. "Shane, this had better be good."

"I'm not sure, it might be nothing. May I talk to the sheriff please?"

"Colby isn't here."

"Do you know where he is? He's not answering his cell."

"That is where he is, he's out looking for his phone. He thinks he may have left his cell at the crime scene. He ran back down there to grab it."

"Oh, shit," Shane said and hurried back over to where the photos were developing. In the next photograph the sheriff was bent down looking into one of the gravesites with Simms and Conners. None of them saw the headlights off in the distance.

"Sid, you need to get to the field as quickly as you can. I will meet you there."

"Shane, Colby took the truck, and my car isn't here. What's wrong?" she asked, a knot beginning to form in her throat.

"I'm on my way. Let's just hope I'm not too late," Shane said and hung up the phone leaving Sydney to wallow in panic.

Simms scraped the last layer of dirt from the hole but there was nothing in the grave except for a large wooden box that resembled a small coffin. He raised the shovel to slam it down on the box, but Colby stopped him.

"Take it easy. This might be evidence," he said.

"Evidence? This is just someone playing a prank on you. Get your ass out here, Sid," Conners called out.

As if on cue Colby's phone rang. This time it wasn't a patented Macho Man's *Oh Yeah,* but his normal ring tone coming from inside the coffin. He carefully removed the lid and stepped back with a gasp. Inside the coffin was a doll, a stuffed bear to be exact. A stuffed animal he immediately recognized. It was a bear he had won for Sid at the county fair back when they were in high school decades ago. She had written both hers and Colby's names on the bottom of the paws in black marker.

Trying to ignore what he had just seen he grabbed his phone and answered. "Sheriff Patino."

"Colby, thank God you finally answered."

"Sid? What is wrong? You sound funny."

"Shane and I are on our way out there, you need to be careful," Sydney said.

"Be careful? There are three of us out here, I will be fine. Though I must admit there is some strange shit going on," Colby said.

"Sheriff listen to Sid. You need to hunker down. The camera took more photos, you were in them," Shane yelled over the speaker phone.

The warning came too late. Before the three law enforcement officers could react a pair of headlights burst through the tree line and bore down on them from out of nowhere. Like a deer in the headlights Colby stood frozen in place. Deputy Conners reached for his gun, but the truck was moving too fast for him to be able to draw his weapon. Sheriff Patino was in the direct path of the speeding vehicle which seemed intent on mowing the man down. Conners yelled at the sheriff and dove from the right-side hitting Colby with a flying tackle breaking him free from his bewildered state. At the last second Colby turned his body away from the impact just as the truck made contact deflecting the brunt of the collision away from his body. Deputy Conners was not so lucky. His head impacted the brush guard bumper of the truck full on and exploded like a watermelon besieged by the infamous Sledge-O-Matic. Colby was unconscious before he hit the ground.

Shane slammed into the rut causing him to lose control of his Jeep. He barely managed to keep it from flipping over as the truck headed straight at them broadside. The jeep's tires sank into the loamy soil and became buried, stopping any chance they had to avoid impact. Shane reached over and pushed Sid up against her door. At the last second the truck took a hard right and headed for the woods. The darkness pealed with gunshots as Simms regained his feet and emptied his clip into the burgundy tailgate as the truck sped away.

"Fuck, he has a steel plate against the back window," Simms said, reloading his weapon. "Fuck, fuck, fuck," he glanced over at the mayhem left behind and dropped to his knees.

Sydney was still cradling Colby in her arms when the ambulance arrived. A second unit showed up to collect what was left of Deputy Conners. She glanced out the rear window of the ambulance as it pulled out of the field and swore she saw a macabre smile form within a cloud of mist from the tailpipe before it evaporated into nothingness.

Twenty

It had been more than a week since the incident at the field near Pine Stump Junction. Colby was still in intensive care with two broken legs, a broken pelvis, a ruptured spleen, and a severe concussion among other less major injuries. He was not in a coma but had been asleep nearly the entire time. Sydney had attended Conners' funeral and recorded it for Colby knowing that he would want to have been there. Conners had given his life to save Colby's.

It had also been more than a week since the camera had taken any photos. Shane was running down the camera's history as well as looking into the backgrounds of Claudia Inez, Janet Whitenaur and Abigail Walters. There had to be a connection somewhere.

Sydney sat on the couch at Colby's house with her legs tucked up underneath her. Dinner was cold, her wine was warm and she herself was numb. Katie jumped up on the couch with her and laid her head in Sydney's lap with a whine. She was missing Colby too.

"You know you are not supposed to be up here," she said, holding the dog's face in her hands which earned her a wet, sloppy lick to the lips which brought on her tears.

She looked over at the kitchen table at the stuffed bear wrapped in plastic. It was stained with Conners' blood and quite possibly Colby's as well. The forensics team processed it but came up empty. She was baffled as to how the bear ended up in a field of graves in the middle of nowhere. The last time she had seen the bear was when she packed her things up for storage before shipping off to the Marines. As far as she was concerned it was still in her father's storage room in a box marked *bedroom*. Maybe it was time to pay the old place a visit.

"Oh sorry, I didn't know you were here. I just came over to feed Katie," Shane said, using his key to get in. He looked like he hadn't slept in a week.

"I parked around back. I didn't want anyone to know there was anyone here. I don't think I could handle any more condolences or casseroles right now. How are things at work?"

"Don't know. The undersheriff told me to take another week off."

"Is she busting your balls?"

"Not openly. She's being hard on Simms too. But can you blame her. I mean, three police officers run down by a truck that came out of nowhere, vanished into thin air and left no tire tracks at the scene."

"What did Simms put in his report?"

"Simms spent the better part of the week trying to figure out how to put into words what happened, especially the nonsense with Colby's phone. And I spent the better part of the week convincing him he wasn't crazy."

"I'm still trying to convince myself that I'm not crazy or dreaming. This shit just can't be real."

Shane set all the developed photos on the dining room table and set up his laptop. While he was doing that Sydney took Katie for a walk. It nearly broke her heart when she asked Katie if she wanted to go and instead of her usually hyper-happy self, she hung her head low and trudged to the front door like it was more of a chore than a treat.

Colby cut a small nature trail that ran the perimeter of his property through a sparse stand of trees, so she wandered along the freshly mowed path lined by white pines on either side with the dog by her side hoping to clear her mind. She felt like there was a weighted blanket covering her.

About a mile away from the house Katie snarled uncharacteristically and her hackles bristled. Sydney stopped and scanned the area but didn't see or hear anything. She chalked it up to a coyote or wolf in the area. Hell, maybe even bobcat or prowling cougar. She gave it a few minutes but then just went back to walking the dog when she suddenly smelled the unmistakable stench of cigarette smoke intermingled with the fragrant pines.

Sydney dropped to her haunches and whispered into Katie's ear to *go get em.* Katie took off like a shot into the underbrush chasing after a phantom. Sydney caught up to her another half a mile down the trail. She was just sitting there whining and pawing at something on the ground. Sydney brushed the area free of dead leaves and twigs but when she tried to dig the dirt it was too hard to dig by hand. She looked around the forest floor for a dead wood limb sturdy enough to dig up the dirt that Katie had marked with her claws.

Sydney dug at the earth for several minutes before the malamute joined in. Within fifteen minutes she had unearthed what Katie was after, and she was suddenly gut punched. It was her high school tassel, and she knew it was hers because Colby's class ring was still tied to it. She held it out in front of her and brushed the dirt off. Katie gave it a good sniffing and sat down on her haunches whining as if she was fully aware of the significance.

"What in the hell is going on here, Shane?" she asked as she came through the door still visibly shaken. Her hands trembled and she was on the verge of tears.

"Excuse me? I'm just digitizing these photos," he replied.

"No, not what are you doing, what in the hell is going on? Are we both having the same never-ending nightmare?"

Katie came walking out of the bedroom with one of Colby's favorite t-shirts. She laid it down on the floor and then curled up on it. She looked up at Sydney and Shane with hurt and confusion in her eyes.

"Even she knows there is something very strange going on," Sydney said.

"She probably sensed it long before we did. What have you got there?" Shane asked, indicating the red and white tassel.

"I found this, to be more precise, Katie found this out on the trail."

"What is this?"

"It's my old high school tassel. And that's Colby's class ring. I haven't seen the damned thing in thirty years or more," she said.

"Maybe Colby dropped it out there while walking Katie."

"First, he couldn't have. The last time I saw it was when I packed it away in a box for storage when I left for boot camp. Second, it was not just lying on the trail, it was buried under the hard pack about a foot down," she said.

"This shit is getting weirder by the day. Do you think someone is just screwing with you?"

"I don't see how that would be possible. That dirt was hard pack, not freshly dug. I'm going to jump in the shower and then we can go see how Colby is doing."

Shane continued scanning photos into his laptop while Sid was in the shower. He was not one to believe in ghosts, demons, or other paranormal activity but things were not adding up. This was far too creepy to just be a series of odd coincidences.

Sydney sat down next to him and toweled her hair. "Is that a new laptop?"

"Not new, it's my own personal laptop. It has a touch screen which makes it a lot easier to work with photos. I'm sure the sheriff would grind my ass about using non departmental gear for department use, but what the hell. It's going to be a long time before he will be able to put a boot in my ass," he said. When he looked over, he saw that Sid was crying.

She shrugged and said, "This is a lot to process."

"I can completely understand that. Tell me, what is the significance of this stuffed bear, and your graduation tassel?"

"Shane, I really don't know other than Colby is connected to both items. He gave me the bear in my sophomore year I think it was. He won it at the state fair in Escanaba. A couple of years later he tied his class ring to my tassel before I left for the Marine Corps."

"But how does everything look brand new, as if they have never seen use and especially do not look as though they have both been buried for thirty odd years."

"That's because they haven't been buried for thirty years, nor have they been used. I sealed them up in a box and left them at my father's house when I went away."

"Can you call your dad and have him check the box? Maybe someone has duplicated the items just to screw with us."

Sydney was quiet for several minutes before shaking her head no. "He's been dead for years. He hung himself after I left for the corps. In that house. He hung himself in our house. I have never been able to go back. I pay the taxes every year so that it doesn't get taken by the state and I pay to have it mowed and looked after when it needs it, but I didn't think I would ever set foot in the place again."

"Oh my God, Sid, I'm so sorry. How tragic. Why would your father hang himself?"

"After my mother's disappearance, things just fell apart for him. He was the prime suspect, just like in all the other husbands were in our other disappearance cases. The police hounded him relentlessly. He started to drink heavily and eventually I was removed from the home because of his drinking.

The poor man held on until I shipped out to the Marine Corps before he succumbed to his demons."

"I hate to ask this, but do you think he was guilty? Do you think he had something to do with your mother's disappearance?"

"No, even though the evidence against him was strong, the cop in me knows better. I know guilt when I see it and I know innocence as well. But back then, I didn't believe him like I should have. I distanced myself which made things worse for him. I was such an asshole," Sydney burst into tears.

"You were a child, Sid. Don't put this on yourself. The best thing we can do for your father is to prove who did this because as it looks right now, the same person has been involved in all of the disappearances as well as the murders," Shane said.

There was a long, awkward silence between them. Sydney went into the kitchen to make some coffee and Shane messed around with the photos on his laptop.

"Sid, you know we have to go check," he finally said.

"I know. But can we give it a rest until later when we get back from the hospital?"

Sydney sat with Colby for nearly three hours before she needed to take a walk around the hospital to stretch her legs. She spent more than half an hour in the serenity garden contemplating the lost years she spent blaming her father for her mother's disappearance. She thought back on her rebellious teens and wondered how much different her life would have been had none of that happened. It was breaking her heart the more this thing played out and it looked as though none of the husbands had anything to do their wives' disappearances even though they had shouldered all the blame.

"What are you doing down here?" Sydney asked, shocked to see Terry Simms sitting outside by himself.

He just shrugged. It was obvious he had been crying.

"Have you been up to see Colby?"

"No, not yet. I can't seem to get up the nerve."

"The nerve?" Sydney took him gently by the shoulders and turned him to face her. "You can't possibly be blaming yourself."

"I was right there, I froze. I should have grabbed him. I should have grabbed them both. I should have shot the driver. I should have done anything except stand there and watch them both get run down," Simms said.

Sydney put both her hands on his face and looked him square in the eyes. "This was not your fault, Terry. I read the report, there was absolutely nothing you could have done. I also read in the report something about Colby's phone that just didn't make any sense. Were you on pain killers or something when you wrote the report?"

"No, Sid, I swear I was stone cold sober when I wrote it and stone cold sober when it happened. I was there and it doesn't make any sense to me," Simms said.

"What happened?"

"Hell if I know. The sheriff's phone kept ringing all over the place and then, then it was buried in a damned grave that had not even been dug up yet. How in the hell could that even be possible, Sid?"

"There has got to be some logical explanation. I'll get with Joyce's people in the morning and see if maybe they covered the gravesite up."

"And planted scrub grass on top? No, that grave had not been disturbed for quite some time. I don't think Joyce's team had even found it yet."

"Was there anything in the grave once you dug it up?"

He shrugged. "Beats me. I never bothered to look."

As she got up to leave Sydney put her arms around his neck and said, "It would be very beneficial to you to use the department grief counselors. I know I have on occasion and it helped tremendously," she lied.

Shane was already in Colby's room when she walked in. He was awake but heavily sedated.

"How is he?"

"No change really. He's pretty messed up."

She nodded. "It could have been much worse," she said, thinking about Deputy Conners and his grief-stricken widow agonizing through a closed casket funeral.

"Any idea what our next move is?" Shane asked.

"Yes, and I don't like it."

"Whatever path you choose, I'm right there with you."

"Thanks for all of your help, Shane. You've been a blessing."

Colby rolled to his side a little with a groan. "Have I died?"

"What? Why would you ask that?" Sydney said.

"Because you two are getting along which is just plain weird."

"Shut up and go back to sleep."

"Answer Shane, what is your next move, Sid?"

"Cranberry Lake."

"Why Cranberry Lake. And just where in the hell is Cranberry Lake?" Shane asked.

"You think my place is in the boonies, Cranberry Lake invented the word boonies," Colby struggled to laugh.

"Why would we be going there?"

"That's her pop's place. It was the family vacation house, but Sid and her mom didn't care for it too much, so they never went up there very often. Sid's dad took me fishing there once, man, is it ever remote. It was like a weekend on Gilligan's Island."

"Where is Gilligan's Island? I have never heard of the place. Is it in the Porkies?"

"Shut up, Shane," they both said in unison and he shrugged with indifference.

"Why on earth are you going to your father's cabin? The place holds nothing but bad memories for you," Colby said.

"Because all roads are leading me there."

"What roads?"

"First the bear you gave me from the fair and then I found this," she said, handing him the tassel and class ring.

"Where did you get this? I haven't seen this for thirty years," he asked.

"Me neither. Katie found it on our walk around your place."

"What the hell would it be doing at my place?"

"It gets even more peculiar, it was buried beneath the hard pack," Shane added.

"I know for a fact that I packed both the bear and the tassel up in a box that I stored at my father's cabin when I left for the corps," Sydney said.

"Maybe someone found your things and is trying to throw us off their trail," Colby said.

"That was one of my theories which is why I have to go to my father's place and check that box."

"I don't like it, not one bit. You could be walking straight into a trap."

"I know you don't Colby, but I have to go. And trust me, I will be on high alert."

"Then you are taking Shane with you and that is not a request, it's an order," Colby said and they both nodded.

"Meet me at Colby's place first thing in the morning, I want to leave before daybreak," Sydney said to Shane and left the hospital room. She was emotionally drained and did not want them to see her break down.

Sydney had just poured her third Glenfiddich Fire and Cane when there was a light tapping at the door. Disgusted she slammed the last of the scotch, threw on a shirt and stormed for the front door.

"Damn it, Shane, there had better be damned good reason for bothering me at this time of night," she said, glancing at the clock to see that it was well after midnight.

Sydney swung the door open so hard it almost tore loose from her hand and was close to smacking her in the face. She was surprised to find a stunned young woman standing on the porch instead of Shane.

"Well, if it isn't Amy Taylor. What a pleasant midnight surprise," Sydney greeted.

"Hello, Sid. Can you please drop the hostility and sarcasm long enough for us to have a talk?"

"I'm sorry, Amy, but sarcasm is part of the package deal. Did you really think this was the best time to try and get a story?"

"That is not why I'm here. May I come in?" she asked, her eyes rimmed with the same redness that Sydney's eyes sported. She had been crying.

She paused for a moment before saying, "Sure, where are my manners. Come on in and have a seat. Would you like a scotch?"

Amy hesitated, but then nodded. "Let me start by telling you how sorry I'm about Colby, and especially Deputy Conners. My prayers go out to both."

Sydney nodded and poured two glasses of scotch over ice. She handed one to the young, blonde reporter. The two of them sipped at their drinks without a word, each of them lost in their own thoughts.

When she finally spoke, Amy's voice was weak and mousy. "Sid, what is going on?"

"Amy, you know I can't discuss an ongoing case with any member of the press, including you."

The reporter pulled her phone out of her jacket and turned it off. As an afterthought she also pulled the battery out of the phone and set them both on the coffee table in front of Sydney.

"This is completely off the record, Sid. I won't print or mention anything about a conversation we have here tonight, no matter how sensational it may be," she said, making sure to look Sydney in the eye. "I need to know."

Sydney returned the gesture and looked directly into the woman's eyes and saw something familiar.

"Why Amy? What is it that you think you need to know?" Sydney asked, almost to the brink of tears because she was certain she already knew the answer.

Katie sauntered over to the women and dropped down on her feet with a loud sigh. Amy absent-mindedly reached down and pet the malamute on her head and scratched behind her ears.

"I think there is a good possibility my mother is in one of those graves," she finally blurted out.

"What on earth would make you think that?"

Amy took a long, deep breath before speaking. "I was young, incredibly young when my mother disappeared, and my father was sent to prison for it. In fact, I was so young that I don't remember much of anything about her. One night a few years ago my aunt on my mother's side, began blubbering after hitting the tequila a bit too hard at a Cinco De Mayo party. She kept going on about it being her fault. When I pried her the next day about what she had said she clammed up and refused to talk to me. I tried several times to get her to talk to me, but she quit taking my calls and refused to answer her door. Earlier this year she hung herself."

"Oh, my goodness, how tragic. I'm so sorry Amy. I never knew."

"When I was going through my aunt's belongings after her death, I found some notes she had written. They were letters to my mother apologizing for having had an affair with my father. Letters she never sent but I think the police may have known about them and the affair which helped to convict my father for my mother's disappearance."

"Have you spoken to your father about this?"

"No, he was killed in prison not long after he was incarcerated. The official report listed his death as a suicide, but I know better."

"What makes you think it wasn't a suicide?"

"Nothing I can prove; it's just a gut feeling I have."

"I'm not sure what kind of information I can give you, Amy. I'm sorry to admit that I really do not remember the case at all."

"That is okay, I didn't expect you to. Not many people remember, it happened so long ago. You two looked a lot alike," she said with a weak smile and pulled a tattered photograph out of her purse and handed it to Sydney.

Amy was right, she bore an uncanny resemblance to the woman's mother. There was something oddly familiar about her too, aside from her looking a lot like Sydney.

"She looks so familiar to me," Sydney said.

"The two of you went to high school together."

"Oh God, now you are making me feel old. I'm old enough to be your mother," Sydney said with a groan.

Amy gave a timid laugh. Old memories were chipping away at her outer façade. "Her maiden name was Coopersmith, Elizabeth Coopersmith."

"Ah yes, Lizzy. Now that you mention her name, I do remember her. We weren't friends or anything like that, but we had a few laughs over how many times we were mistaken for one other. Is it safe to assume her body was never found?"

Amy shook her head. "No, the police never found any trace of her or my grandmother."

"What? What about your grandmother?"

"My grandmother went missing before my mother did. In fact, my mother disappeared while looking for her. Of course, I don't remember any of that because I was still just an infant and my family was hush, hush about everything after the fact."

"I think I already know the answer, but I will ask anyway. Where did your mother go missing from?"

"Both her and my grandmother went missing while in the Munising area."

"Pictured Rocks?"

Amy nodded and sipped at the sweet, smokey amber liquid in her glass. Normally she didn't care for whiskey, but the scotch was hitting the spot at the moment. She wiped the tears from her eyes with a tissue she pulled from her purse.

"I need to know, Sid," she said.

"I know you do. And I completely understand. Why don't you head to the university and speak with Joyce Tammi in the morning? Give her a sample of your DNA so she can match it against the remains that have been uncovered so far. I will give her a call and let her know that you will be stopping by."

"Thank you, Sid. You don't know what this means to me."

"Unfortunately, I know exactly what it means to you.

"Did you load the generator in the truck? There's no electricity out there in the boondocks." Sydney asked.

"Yes, and the gas, and the dog food and the rifles, and extra ammo," Shane said.

"Did you double check you didn't forget anything?"

"I know you're just busting my balls, but you're more than welcome to inspect my work," he said while loading Katie into the back seat of the sheriff's truck.

They stopped in Robert's Corners at a last chance convenience market for groceries and gas before heading into the wilderness. While she packed the cooler with beer and ice Shane bought a couple of bags of actual sustenance and a cheap cooler to store it in.

"All we needed was jerky and pretzels to go with the beer," she said. "We're not spending more than a night out here."

"Better to be safe than sorry," Shane said.

"Be prepared."

"What?"

"The Boy Scout motto, I thought for sure you were an eagle scout."

Shane mumbled something incoherent and turned his attention to the dog in the back seat. He gave Katie a treat and a pat on the head as he got into the passenger side. Within a few miles they had left the pavement and a few miles after that the road turned into a two-track. Fifteen more miles of two track at not much more than ten miles per hour before they finally caught a glimpse of the small lake.

"How many people live on this lake? I haven't seen a single cabin," Shane asked.

"Last I knew there were four cabins, and you couldn't see any of them from one another. There are a lot of little lakes back here, many of them only have a single cabin on them. I'm sure you have noticed there are no phone lines or electrical wires disrupting the wilderness."

They turned down an overgrown path and Shane had to get out several times to move deadwood out of their way. Finally, after what felt like a three-hour tour, they arrived at the summer hideaway. Sydney pulled down the long two track driveway and parked.

The cabin was in terrible shape paint wise, faded brown strips of paint dangled from the window trim while many of the side boards were down to dingy gray primer or bare wood. In fact, there was little original color left on the little cabin. But the lawn had been mowed recently and someone had put a blue tarp over a section of the roof. Undoubtedly there was a leak that needed Sydney's attention. She had been neglecting her e-mail and was sure the realty company had sent her more than one notification. The soffit boards had been chewed away by birds, bats and whatever else wanted to set up residence in the dilapidated cabin.

"When you said cabin, I never imagined this. No offense, but this place is worse than most deer camps I've been to," Shane said.

"Want the scary truth, other than the peeling paint it hasn't changed much since I was a kid."

"No wonder you hated coming here."

"That was a bit of an exaggeration. I didn't hate it all the time. When I was young, it scared the crap out of me. And then I got a little older and while mom was still around it wasn't too bad. But then once I reached my rebellious adolescent years and my mom was gone there was nothing for a young girl to do up here. No friends, no place to go and my father was so depressed about my mother he was always two sheets to the wind. It just wore on me. At least at home I could occasionally escape from the dreariness," Sydney said.

Shane found the surrounding area to be eerily quiet, especially given the extremely rural setting. There were none of the sounds of summer drifting in off the lake. No redwing blackbird's shrill warnings, no chipmunks chattering as they scurried through the underbrush and no blue jay's screech echoing through the treetop. Nor were there any horny bullfrogs croaking up and down the banks of the lake. The silence made him uncomfortable, so he unloaded the generator and gassed it up first thing.

Even though the cabin had been maintained regularly by the reality company the ravages of time were apparent. Several screens hung loose from their frames, several porch deck boards were broken, and others were ankle breakers and the place smelled of musty death. They went around and opened all the windows that were not painted shut in the hopes of airing out the place while Katie prowled the perimeter. Shane found a suitable place for the generator, fired it up and plugged it into the cabin's outlet.

"It looks like you outsmarted me again," Sydney said.

"Just a logical deduction really," Shane said and screwed in a new LED lightbulb into the living room lamp. "It was a safe bet that all of the lights would be burned out."

They unloaded the rest of their gear into the dark brown cabin. It was like stepping back in time for Sydney, the place looked almost the same as the last time she had set foot in it. She half expected to smell her father's cooking wafting through the place. Oatmeal with cinnamon and a generous helping of raisins along with rasher bacon and eggs every Sunday for breakfast. He even let her have coffee, though he watered it down quite a bit for her when she was little.

They cleaned up the place as best as they could with the worn-out broom and no running water. It was a single floor dwelling with two small bedrooms to the back facing the lake. The rooms were directly across from one another so they each took a separate room. Shane blew up the air mattresses outside with the truck's auxiliary power and then carried them into the cabin.

"Just like camping, huh Sydney?"

"You sound a little too excited there man-bun. Just wait until the ghost stories come to life around the campfire tonight.

Not to mention the rats that will crawl into your sleeping bag while you are sleeping."

"You sure do have a way of making someone feel welcome," Shane said.

Even though the place was technically a one story, there was a small riser of only four steps leading to a small room back behind the bedrooms centered at the rear of the cabin. Shane tried the door, but it was locked.

"Hey, Sid, what's in this room?"

She was quiet for an exceedingly long time before answering. It dawned on Shane what had happened in there, so he didn't ask again.

"My father referred to it as his breakfast nook. He had a fancy French word for it, but I can't remember for the life of me what it was. It's nothing more than an attic storage room with a small view of the lake. But he put a chair and a small table in there where he could watch the sunrise while mom and I slept in. The box should be in there," Sydney's voice trailed off.

"Do you want me to go in there and get the box?"

She nodded. "Please. The key is hanging on a hook by the door."

Shane reluctantly opened the door. Once inside the small room he immediately felt cramped and claustrophobic. There was a wear mark in the beam above his head and he wondered how long her father had hung there before anyone found him. Suddenly the air became thick, and stale and the walls closed in around him. He struggled to catch his breath and dashed from the room as nonchalant as he possibly could.

"I hate to ask, but I think it's relevant to our trip up here. Where exactly did your mother disappear from?" Shane asked.

"From what my father told me, she disappeared here at the cabin. They were up here for the Fourth of July and were going to head into Naubinway for the fireworks that evening. The next day mom and my dad were going to hike at Pictured Rocks.

She went out for a swim in the lake that afternoon and never came back. Her towel, shorts and shirt were still on the dock," Sydney said.

"Wow. And the police never found a trace?"

"None. They even searched the area with cadaver dogs. It was the main reason they looked at my father so hard for it. They were convinced he killed her and got rid of the body. Trouble with that theory was that I was with him while she was swimming so he couldn't have had anything to do with it, though I convinced myself otherwise as time dragged on," she said and wiped her tears away. "They dragged the lake, even sent divers down and brought a cadaver dog out to the property. All that and they never found a single trace of her."

Shane regretted bringing up such painful memories, but things were not adding up. If her father was innocent, and her mother didn't just up and leave them, then who the hell kidnapped her and why?

"Is this it?" Shane asked as he handed her a cardboard box marked *bedroom* on the side in black marker.

She nodded her head and set the carton down on the kitchen table. They inspected the tape seams top and bottom and although the tape was yellowed from age the box itself showed absolutely no signs of having been opened. She took out her Gerber and made a careful slit down the top and then across the two sides. She opened the flaps of the box and laid the collection of her life carefully out on the table.

"The bear is not in here and neither is the tassel. I know damned well I put them in this box. What in the hell is going on here?"

"Is everything else in there?" Shane asked.

"I don't know, grab me a beer and a chair and let me go through all of this stuff."

"I'll take Katie for a walk around the lake if you're okay with being alone?"

"I don't need a babysitter, Shane. I'm perfectly fine by myself," Sydney said. Under her breath as he was walking out the door. "Just don't disappear on me."

Shane put a few dog treats in his pockets along with a cut up Slim Jim, slipped on Katie's collar and leash before heading out for an investigative stroll. They walked the overgrown trail encircling the weed covered lake around the right side. It was a small kidney shaped lake covered with lily pads and duck weed, clearly it had been neglected for decades. He regretted not bringing a fishing pole as he was sure the lake was full of hungry bass. Maybe even a northern pike or two.

Without warning Katie dropped down flat on the ground and refused to move no matter how hard he tugged on her leash. Shane just chalked it up to her stubbornness and relied on the fact he would be able to coax her to him with a treat or two. That was when he realized he was standing where the dock once stood. The dock where Sydney's mother was last seen. The pilings were still standing upright in the water but the dock itself was gone. There was a shiny little trinket on the ground, so he pocketed it before turning back for the cabin.

Katie was on her haunches and growling with her hackles straight on end. Shane looked up and almost dropped to his knees. There was someone standing in the window of the attic room looking at him. It was Sid. It had to be Sid. But a voice inside of his head told him otherwise.

"Come on, girl, that's just Sid in the window," he said with a nervous chuckle.

Katie refused to move and refused to go near the house. Now, his own hackles were standing on end and he started to run for the house. Whoever had been in the window was no longer there and Sid might be in trouble.

"Sid, were you just up in the window of the storage room?" Shane asked as he burst through the door out of breath.

"No, I've been sitting here the entire time you were walking Katie. Why?"

"I swear someone was in that window looking down at us. Katie refused to move."

"Shane, damn it. You are giving me the willies," she said and let loose a visible shudder.

"You stay there, I'll go check," he said.

Shane eased through the small cabin, his heart beating as though it wanted to escape his chest. He pushed open the door and peeked into the empty room. A noxious smell assaulted him knocking him to his knees. It passed quickly so he got back to his feet and went out into the front room where Sydney was staring back at him with confusion.

"What the hell have you been eating, Shane?"

"What?"

"Well that was just plain rude to crop dust me, although I would have done the same to you," Sydney said with a smile while pinching her nose shut.

"What the hell does crop dust mean?"

"Oh, dear Lord, where have you been living, under a rock? It means you fart when passing by someone."

"I didn't fart."

"Then what in the hell was that disgusting smell?"

"I don't know, I was hoping you could tell me," Shane said. "It came from that room after I opened the door."

"Maybe there's a dead mouse or possum, maybe even a coon in there. I'll take a look around."

"Better you than me. Was everything accounted for in the box?"

"As far as I can tell, yes. Except for the bear, the tassel and Colby's class ring of course. Why do you ask?"

"I found this out by where the dock used to be. Does it look familiar?"

She tossed the bauble in her hand and shook her head. "No, that's not mine."

Sydney put everything back into the box and went outside to get a fire started in the fire pit by the lake. Shane went out to help her, but she shooed him away. Katie still wouldn't go near the house let alone inside of it and was perfectly content hiding under the truck. Shane made a bed for her in the back seat of the truck just in case she refused to go in the house when it was time for bed. Hell, he might even sleep out in the truck with the dog the way things were going.

"What in the hell is all this shit?" Sydney asked, dropping the tailgate.

"Stuff I thought we might need," Shane responded.

"Damn, you take that Eagle Scout thing seriously don't you?"

"I was not a boy scout. I just like being prepared."

"For what, the zombie apocalypse?"

"Funny. I thought we might need chairs and a table."

"And hobo pie makers, and hot dog skewers, and what in the hell is this stuff?"

"That is the camera developing supplies."

"You brought the developer and supplies?"

"Why not, I brought the camera," Shane said.

Sydney shook her head with a smile and carried the two folding chairs to the fire while dragging the cooler of beer behind her. Shane carried the makings for hobo pies and s'mores. The two of them didn't engage in a whole lot of conversation and what they did talk about was just idle chatter. Sydney polished off the better part of a six pack of Bell's Two Hearted Ale and gave Shane the nod that she was headed for bed. He sat out by the fire until it was just coals before turning in himself. Something was off and it was nagging at him.

"Sid, hey Sid," he called out from his air mattress.

"Why are you whispering, we're the only two people for miles? What do you want, Shane?"

"Why is it so quiet?"

"Because it's nighttime and like I said, we are the only two people for miles around. And from my perspective, it could be a lot quieter."

"No, listen, there is no sound outside of this cabin. None at all."

"Pardon my French, but what in the fuck are you talking about?" Sydney said, clearly agitated.

"And there were no mosquitos. I didn't get bit, not even once and they usually tear me up. It's a hot, humid summer night, it just doesn't make sense."

"Maybe they sprayed the lake to kill all the flying vampires."

"Did it kill the crickets, the frogs and the cicadas too?"

"Shane, if you shut up and let me fall asleep, I'll start snoring then you will have all the noise you want. Would you like me to dig my old Garfield nightlight out of the box for you?"

"I get it, I'll shut up."

Shane rolled over and closed his eyes. The silence was still nagging at him when he finally fell asleep. Sydney was in the room across from him and was sitting up in bed. He was right, something was very wrong. One of the things that scared her when she was a little girl was how noisy the cabin got at night. She had to drink the last two beers before she could fall back asleep.

Shane was awakened by a loud thud. He was still groggy from sleep, so he wasn't sure where the sound came from. He listened to the night while trying his best not to move or even breathe. It was still as silent as it had been before he fell asleep.

Except for an odd creaking sound that seemed to undulate pendulously.

He was suddenly overwhelmed by a flashback from his youth. His father had taken him to an old Poe film festival, starring Vincent Price of course. Masque of the Red Death, the Tell-Tale Heart and the Pit and the Pendulum, all of which left a lasting impression on him. The synchronous creaking drilled into his brain like a metronome. The unsettling sound was coming from the attic storage room, so Shane reluctantly crawled out from under his sleeping bag and grabbed his flashlight.

As he neared the room the sound increased in both intensity and momentum. Shane eased the door open and peered inside like a child afraid a monster is lurking in their closet. Slowly he craned his neck to where the sound was coming from and gasped. From the beam dangled a thick, braided rope and at the end of the rope was a putrid, gray corpse swinging slowly back and forth. The body had hung for so long and was so decomposed that the flesh was sagging like congealed gravy and was separating from bone. The cadaver's face was frozen in an eternal expression of torment and staring straight at Shane with condemnatory eyes.

Shane shrieked and fell to his knees. The nauseating stench of death enveloped the room and assaulted his every sense. The room filled with invasive cigarette smoke so thick it choked off his airway. He scrambled to his feet, gagged with the dry heaves, and fell down the steps to his knees.

"What the hell, Shane? Were you sleep walking?" Sydney asked, standing over him after rushing to the clamor. He just pointed up the stairs to the small room.

Sydney didn't want to look, but she was compelled to. She took Shane's flashlight from him and slowly shined it into the foreboding room expecting to see something horrific, but it was empty. The chair that had been in the room was lying on its side and there was a small pile of rope fibers and wood shavings beneath the beam. Tears flowed down her cheeks and she backed out of the room. She sat down on the floor next to Shane and they could do nothing but look at each other. There were no words.

Suddenly a racket invaded the cabin, scaring the hell out of them both.

"What in the hell is that?" Sydney asked.

Shane listened for a moment and then said, "The camera."

They walked out to the living room where the camera was firing off shot after shot which should not even be possible considering the fact the camera was not equipped with an auto winder. A fact that still had Shane quite perplexed from the onset of this fiasco because there was absolutely no mechanical explanation for it. When the camera ran out of film it went silent.

"I'll get the developing equipment from the truck," Shane said after several minutes of silence.

"I think I'll help you," Sydney said still stunned from the events of the past twenty-four hours and didn't care to be alone in that house for even one second.

It took them two trips to bring in the equipment from the truck. Sydney went back outside to coax Katie out of the backseat while Shane set up a makeshift film laboratory. He was reading the manual to a recently purchased toy when Sydney came back into the cabin, without the dog.

"You picked a strange time to read," she said.

"Funny. I just bought this toy and I've yet to use it even once, so I better learn what I'm doing before I screw something up."

"What is it?"

"It's a negative scanner that will allow me to scan the negatives into this device where I can then transfer them to the laptop. It alleviates the need for an enlarger and photograph paper."

"Nifty. How much did that set you back?"

"Me? Nothing, the department paid for it," Shane said with a smile.

"There's hope for you yet, man-bun. Are you hungry?"

"I could eat."

Sydney left Shane with his gadgets and brought in the camp stove and the cooler of food he had wisely bought at the store. She started frying up some Wright's thick sliced cowboy bacon. While the bacon was cooking, she whisked four eggs in a bowl and added just a touch of cream that Shane had bought. There was no toaster, so she toasted the cinnamon raisin bread in the pan with the bacon. She took their plates to the table and opened a couple single serving orange juices from the cooler and set them next to their plates.

Shane soaked the film canister in a film reel tank filled with developer while eating breakfast, stopping to agitate the tank every couple of minutes. When they were finished Sydney cleared the table and took a plate of the scraps to Katie who had been softly whining as soon as the bacon started cooking while Shane continued with the process of developing the film. It took him less than an hour to develop, scan and transfer the materials onto a USB drive. He felt gut punched when he saw the photos as they became available to view.

"What is wrong? You look like you've seen a ghost," Sydney asked as she walked back into the cabin.

"Stay there," Shane said.

"What?"

"You don't want to see these," he said, holding his hand up to stop her.

"Like hell I don't," she said and took a step forward. Shane slammed the lid to the laptop closed before she could see anything on the screen. "What the hell?"

"Sid, trust me, you don't want to see these."

"Shane, trust me, I'm a big girl and I can handle whatever is on that computer. In fact, I'm big enough to whip your ass and take that damned laptop away from you."

"Have it your way. But don't say I didn't warn you," he said and opened the laptop. He opened the folder of the photos he had just scanned.

Sydney felt weak in the knees and sat down. The photographs were a chronical of the day her father hung himself. She cycled through them quickly and then went back to the first one where she moved through them again more slowly.

The first couple of photographs were of the empty storage room. There was a desk and a chair that her father would sit at while having breakfast and watching the sunrise. The next series of shots graphically showed her father going through the motions of throwing the rope over the beam, moving the chair into position then putting the noose around his neck before hanging himself. The very last shot was of her father's putrid, gray corpse with its mouth hanging open in a scream of agony just as Shane had glimpsed that very morning. Two nacreous orbs stared back at her from the laptop screen. Tears streamed down her face until she broke down into heaving sobs.

"Is this what you saw this morning?" she asked.

Shane nodded slowly and wiped away tears of his own.

"Shane, could you give me a few minutes please?" Sydney asked as soon as she had her breath back.

"Absolutely. I'll take Katie for a walk," Shane replied.

"Don't go too far."

Sydney spent the next fifteen minutes going through the photographs one by one and then she went through them again. Something wasn't right but she just couldn't put her finger on what it was that was out of place. At least not until she reached for her coffee mug and then it dawned on her. Her father did not kill himself; he was murdered.

"Shane," she called out, her voice shrill with excitement.

Shane came running back to the cabin with Katie who stopped dead in her tracks at the front door and retreated for the backseat of the truck.

"What's wrong, Sid? Are you okay?" he asked, stepping back inside.

"Better than okay. Look at these photos closely."

Shane looked at everything he could see in the screen of the laptop but didn't see anything she might be getting so overly excited about. The photos took a snapshot of her father moving the chair underneath the load bearing beam where the noose dangled obscenely, climbing up on the chair, slipping a noose over his head, mouthing a prayer, and then kicking the chair away over onto its side. The rest of the photographs were of his bloated corpse in death.

"Do you see it?"

"I see it, I'm just not sure what it is you want me to see."

"Look," she said and reached for her coffee.

"You are losing me, Sid."

"I'm left-handed."

"Yeah, and?"

"So was my father. Everything in these photographs indicate he used his right hand for everything."

"Maybe the photos are a reverse image?" Shane said.

"I thought so too at first. Don't look at me like that, I know about a few things about photography. He never stopped wearing his wedding ring. It's on his left hand, so the other hand has to be his right."

This sparked something in Shane, and he started looking at the photos even closer. He zoomed in to certain area, smiling each time he saw what he was looking for.

"Sid, I can tell you without a doubt, your father was murdered. Granted he did hang himself, but not of his own volition."

"I knew it. I knew he would never do such a thing. He was sending a message to whomever investigated his death that this was not a suicide. Too bad no one ever picked up on his clues."

"See here, the reflection in the shiny tabletop."

"Is that a gun?"

"Yes. A gun in a holster," he said and backed up to a couple of photos earlier. "And here, down here in the very corner of the window is a reflection of the same gun with the barrel pointed at a photograph of you."

"Why is that part of the desk shiny and the rest isn't?" Sydney asked.

Shane opened a photo editing program on his laptop and dragged the photo over. He manipulated it until it revealed the answer.

"There was something sitting on that table. The desk is dusty except for that rectangle area."

"A box?"

"I'm sure of it. There was a box sitting on the desk. Whoever did this to your father took the box."

"Well shit. Then the box was probably evidence of some kind and now it's gone."

They scanned through the photographs several times. After a while, their eyes gave out on them, and their bellies grumbled so they made lunch and sat out by the lake eating sandwiches. Katie nibbled on dog biscuits but would grab one and trot back over to the truck to lay under the back end away from the house.

"Wait a second, go back one," Sydney said. "What is that on my father's fingers? You can barely see it."

Shane dragged that photo to the editor and zoomed in on the fingertips. "It's a white powder. Cocaine maybe? Was your dad into drugs?"

"Shut up. That's not cocaine. That's sugar. Dad used to mix sugar and rat poison and put up in the overhead. I know it doesn't look like a typical drop ceiling, but it is."

"Look at where the bokeh is in this photograph. Who am I to argue with a cursed camera?" he said.

Shane got up and dragged the chair to the corner of the room. A sensation washed over him when he climbed up on the chair a man had used to hang himself with. He wanted nothing more than to be able to get down off the chair, so he hurried to lift the panels out one by one.

"What was that?" Sydney asked.

"What was what?"

"Something fell out from the ceiling."

Sydney dropped down on all fours and found a piece of paper, an old photograph, that had fallen and slid down the wall behind a chair. The photo and a large hashtag with the number four written in black marker on the back. She turned it over.

"Look, that is the same bauble I found out on the trail. Is it part of your mom's shorts that were left behind on the trail when she was taken?"

"No, I don't think so. It doesn't look attached, more like it fell out of her pocket" Sydney said and went down to the kitchen area. She grabbed the bauble from the tabletop and brought it back up.

"It's the same," Shane said, comparing the shiny trinket with the photograph. "But what is it?"

"Damn, why didn't I see this sooner? I have not worn one in a long time, but I think this is a button from a uniform."

"State police? Maybe an officer dropped it during the investigation."

"No, it isn't striking me as from a state police uniform, even one from back then. I don't recognize it, but it's definitely a button of some kind."

"I can always scan it and try to find someone who knows what it is. A historian maybe."

"Funny, jackass," Sydney said.

"What?"

"Just pack the truck, let's get back and see how Colby is doing."

As they pulled away from the cabin, both unbeknownst to the other, fought to shake the feeling they were being watched. Shane had never been so terrified in all his life. How could you protect yourself from something that was already dead? Sydney felt sorrow cloaking her like a weighted blanket, pulling her down into an abyss. How could you learn to love someone who was already dead?

Twenty-One

Darkness surrounded Claudia Inez in a thicket of gloom. Her heart pounded as if it were trying to break free of her chest. And the smell of death surrounded her.

She couldn't see him, but she knew he was there just the same. He was always in her dreams, but like a coward, he refused to show himself. Across the dark expanse she could see others. Did he torment them as well? Was he visiting them all at the same time or had he drawn them all together for one big, happy reunion?

She had seen these women before in her dreams, their long, lonely stares fading into the endless night. Their cheeks stained with a perpetual longing of people and places almost forgotten. Sorrow filled the empty, dark void surrounding her in a cocoon of despair.

Although most of the others stood silent and still, there was one far away from her who seemed to be as perplexed as she. The woman looked familiar. She scoured her brain for any scrap of recognition. And then it came to her, it was Abigail. They were in the void together.

Just as soon as she recognized Abigail, she was gone. Replaced by another. One she also found familiar.

Claudia tried to call out to the woman, but her voice was not there. In fact, there was no sound anywhere. She couldn't even hear her own heartbeat though she knew her chest was pounding.

It was the cop, the blonde woman she had spoken with about Abigail. And he was with her, as was the man who had kidnapped her all those years ago. The portly man turned to smile at Claudia before putting his gun to the woman's head. Claudia screamed a warning, but she was too late. They had captured yet another.

"I hear you and Shane are going to be on Dancing with the Stars," Sydney said, taking a drink of Colby's warm juice box. "Ugh, you know I hate grape."

"That's why I have instructed the nurses to give me grape only, so you won't swipe it. You seem pretty chipper this morning. Did you have a good trip with Shane?"

"Let's just say calling it creepy would be an understatement, but enlightening."

"But did you learn anything?"

"I think we learned that my father didn't commit suicide."

"He's alive?"

"Oh, no, he's as dead as dead can be. But he was murdered," Sydney said. "I can't prove it, nor do I know who killed him, but I don't really care either. As long as I know the truth that's all that matters to me at this point."

"Under the circumstances I guess that's a step in the right direction anyway. Enough of the morbid crap, how is my dog? Did she enjoy the trip?" Colby asked, surprised he was missing Katie so much it was painful.

"She enjoyed the ride, but the cabin, not so much. Here," Sydney said, showing him her phone while she swiped through the photos she took one by one. She sped up her swiping finger several times.

"Wait, back up one. Was she on my couch? She's not supposed to be on the furniture."

"Oh, she neglected to tell me that. I'll have to have a talk with her," Sydney said with a smirk.

"And what in the hell is that? Is she eating a Slim Jim?"

"You'll have to talk to Shane about that one."

"And why is she sleeping in the back seat of the truck?"

"She refused to go into the cabin. I told you the place was creepy."

Sydney's phone rang so she answered it.

"Sid?"

"Yes, Shane it's me. I know it's surprising that you called my phone and that I answered, but miracles do happen. What is up?"

"Hey, I have got something here you really need to see," Shane said.

"Okay, let me say my goodbyes and I will be right there. Speaking of which, where are you?"

"I'm at Colby's feeding Katie."

"Okay, I'll be there as soon as I can."

Sydney finished saying goodbye to Colby with a promise to bring him a cudighi later. She also promised to give Katie a kiss for him, but also keep her off the couch and no Slim Jim's. She walked out of the hospital into a beautiful sunny day.

"Oh, thank God you're still here. Hello, officer, sorry I'm terrible with names."

"Sydney, but you can call me Sid. Miss Inez isn't it."

She nodded and offered a delicate hand. "Claudia."

"What are you doing here?"

"Actually, I was looking for you."

"Oh, and why were you looking for me?"

The woman fidgeted while rocking back and forth on her heels. She was clearly distraught.

"What is on your mind?" Sydney asked, disturbed by the woman's demeanor.

Claudia sighed deeply. "I think you're in danger," she said, feeling the weight of the world lift from her.

"Why would you think that?"

"You're going to think I'm totally nuts. Whackadoodle. Bat shit crazy and everything else in between."

"Try me. I think I've just been down that road the last few days."

"I had a dream. No, more of a nightmare. No, it's not like either of those. It's like being in a dream state, but I'm still in the real world as well. Kind of like being in two planes of existence at once. They started ever since I awakened from my coma."

"And was I in this dream?"

"Yes."

"And I'm in danger in your dream? What did you mean by thank God I'm still here?"

"I think you're in danger in the real world as well. I'm quite sure they are coming for you."

"Who is they?"

"The men, or things that did this to me, and to Abigail. They want you. Don't ask me how, but I can sense they have always wanted you," Claudia said, flames of fear dancing in her eyes.

"But who are they," Sydney asked.

"I don't know. I can never see their faces. But one of them is fatter than the other, it's all I can distinguish. Trust me, I have tried repeatedly to remember them when I awaken but I just can't seem to recall details."

"Here is my personal cell number, call me if you keep having these dreams that involve me or if you can think of anything," Sydney said, jotting her number down.

"Okay. I will. Sid, watch yourself," Claudia said as she darted across the street and out of sight.

When Sydney walked into Colby's house Shane was sitting there with twelve photographs in an array on the kitchen counter. She set a pasty and a soda in front of him and set the same up for herself. The room exploded with tantalizing aromas. She broke open the golden crust, poured some warmed gravy into the meat and vegetable mixture. She stabbed her fork in and took a mouthful of meat, rutabaga, and flaky crust into her mouth.

"Sorry, I was starving. What have you got?" she asked between mouthfuls.

"Thanks, I was too. And I'm not sure what I have."

"Did the camera take more photos?" she asked, a feeling grew in the pit of her stomach as she recalled Claudia's warnings.

"Not exactly. I went to load the camera with film and when I opened the canister, I realized that the last canister of film had already been exposed."

"You used it without realizing it?"

"No. I never paid much attention. I must have overlooked that the roll had already been exposed before we even started this little adventure of ours."

"And of course, you developed it, and these are the photos," she said, feeling a certain sense of relief.

Sydney picked up one of the photos and dropped it almost immediately. She was overcome by emotion and had to sit down.

"What is wrong? You have that look about you again?"

"Like I have seen a ghost?"

"You said it not me," Shane said.

"This woman in the photo, she's my mother. Actually, before she was even my mother."

"Are one of these two men your father?"

"No. I don't know who they are. I have never seen either of them before. Although, this one does look familiar for some reason," she said, pointing at one of the young men in the photo. And come to think of it, so does the background. It looks to be a summer camp, but I just can't place it. I've seen that sign they are sitting on before, but the name of the camp is on the other side of the boards facing away from the camera."

"It looks like it could be in Hiawatha," Shane said, referring to the Hiawatha National Forest, a huge national forest that cut a nine hundred-thousand-acre swath through the Upper Peninsula between Grand Marais and Marquette.

They both took turns examining the photographs one by one until their eyes were worn out. Sydney couldn't shake the feeling she knew the place where the photograph was taken so she took a couple pictures of it with her phone and texted them to Colby hoping he might remember. They were making no progress, so they went out on the porch for a mind clearing beer. Sydney had the Keweenaw Brewing Company Widowmaker while Shane opted for a Lift Bridge Brown. It was a nice day all things considered, and Colby's refrigerator was well stocked so why not take advantage. Sydney sported a dark brown, almost black moustache of foam from the smoky, black ale. In two more swallows she finished her beer and went in to take a shower. She did some of her best thinking in the shower where there were no interruptions.

Shane scanned the rest of the photos into his laptop and started going through the folders in chronological order from when the camera took the photographs. He opened his software editing program and began trying to figure out a way to remove the bokeh. He was convinced that the out of focus balls were not only oddly arranged in a manner that was not conducive to the physics of photography but also felt they were hiding some element that needed to be revealed.

First, he attempted to erase the area of the photo but that didn't work because it erased the background as well. He then desaturated the area hoping that by removing the color he would reveal something important. That was a no go as well. And then, as often happens in life, things took an unexpected turn. Katie nuzzled up to Shane trying to coax him into giving her a treat and in the process stuck her wet nose on the computer screen which happened to be a touch screen laptop. When he shooed her away her nose dragged across the screen, dragging one of the bokeh balls right along with it.

"Good girl," Shane said, excitedly patting her on the head, a gesture the dog interpreted as they were going for a walk. "Sid, I'm going to take Katie for a walk, but I think I found something," he called out.

Sydney was dressed in a pair of Colby's oversized but comfortable gray sweats and sitting at the table when Shane walked in with Katie, who immediately came to her begging for a Slim Jim.

"No, I can't give you any treats. Boss's orders. What did you find?" she asked, trying to ignore Katie's constant pestering.

"I'm not really sure yet. Katie was bugging me, so I had to take her for a walk before I got too involved. She actually found it," Shane said, firing up the laptop.

In less than thirty seconds the photo of Abigail at the cliff side was on the screen. He put his finger on one of the bokeh balls and moved it across the screen.

"What in the hell? Is it supposed to do that?" Sydney asked.

"Not in this universe," he replied and moved another.

After Shane had moved four of the bokeh balls she said, "Well that was pretty useless. All that accomplished was to reveal a blank piece of the sky."

"We're missing something. If this is some sort of magical, or supernatural camera it would not be providing us with specific, linked photographs for no reason. These photos and the bokeh in them would not be defying the physics of photography for no reason. It just doesn't make any sense," Shane said. Out of frustration he put his four fingers on the screen, each one on a different bokeh ball and flicked them off in different directions which caused them to swirl around the screen.

"What in the hell just happened?" Sydney asked.

He tried to move the balls, but they were fixed in place. "They just stopped moving and locked into place."

"Hang on, don't touch anything," she said. Sydney went out to the kitchen and brought back two more Keweenaw Brewing Company beers and set them on the coffee table.

"Coasters," Shane said and pointed to a stack of limestone coasters with Michigan lighthouses painted on them.

She grabbed two and handed him the red brick Seul Choix lighthouse and used the Big Bay lighthouse for herself. It was her favorite because it was haunted.

"It's a puzzle," Sydney said after staring at the screen for ten minutes.

Shane looked it over and said, "You're right, it's like a jigsaw without edges."

Shane started rotating and manipulating the colored balls, trying to match them to the two already locked into place. Sydney was being more of a pain than a help, so he suggested she take Katie for a walk. She knew she was getting on his nerves, partially because she was doing it on purpose, partly out of frustration and partly for her own amusement.

Once Sydney was out of his hair, Shane was able to study the shapes and their every nuance. It was very much like a jigsaw puzzle in which the picture was not only out of focus, but every piece of the puzzle was shaped identically. To make matters worse the finished two pieces would not move out of the way and the others would not connect in small batches either.

Sydney came back into the cabin almost an hour later to see Shane sitting on the couch with his feet on the coffee table enjoying a Jim Beam single barrel on the rocks. All the balls on the screen had been combined into one big ball but still, there was nothing there of any importance.

"What are you so smug about? I still can't see shit except for a larger blurry ball," she said.

"Au contraire, you are only seeing what I want you to see. Say the magic words," Shane said.

"Okay, I will play along. Start making some sense or I will hit you so hard it will hurt your mother. How is that for a magic word? How many of those have you had?"

"Damn, you are no fun at all. It's my second. Look. Voila," he said, bringing up another screen in which the new, melded bokeh ball was much clearer. Shane revealed the photograph post processing. It was still out of focus but there was some semblance of order amongst the chaos.

"So, you have managed to change it from a bunch of little out of focus colored balls into a large blurry ball of smoke?"

Shane used the dodge and burn tool before adding clarity and then added heavy contrast to the image. The auto editing process was running in the background filling in details as it filtered out the bokeh and excessive noise in the photograph.

"You have got to be kidding me? What the hell is that?" Sydney said.

On the screen in front of them was a terrifying creature formed from layer after layer of smoke tendrils twisting and swirling as they took on shape and form. The wisps of smoke rose from the bottom of the screen like strands of seaweed undulating with the flow of the tides. The columns of smoke stretched outward giving the beast what appeared to be arms reaching out toward them.

As the photo processing program continued to work more and more of the image was revealed until there was an ominous face with two glowing red eyes reminiscent of the glow of a lit cigarette. The glow of the eyes increased and decreased in intensity as if the cigarette were being drawn into bestial lungs.

"What does that look like to you?"

"Like a something out of a monster movie. I swear to God Shane, if you are screwing with me, I will bust your ass."

"Sid, I'm not screwing with you."

"But that looks like it could be a Hollywood movie poster. It can't be real."

"I'm not sure if it's real or just some optical illusion and our minds are filling in the blanks," Shane said.

"That sounds as if there is a but in there," Sydney said.

"But I did the same thing on the image of Eno's boat and one of the other photos," he said, opening those two processed photos on the screen. "The results produced the same image."

Sydney's throat tightened up and goosebumps erupted over every square inch of her body. When she moved, the eyes followed her. At first, she thought she was experiencing a mild form of hysteria, so she stood up and walked several steps to her left, the eyes followed her movement.

"What the fuck, Shane. Did you see that?"

He nodded, picked up his whiskey glass and slammed the remaining finger of amber nectar.

"This is nuts. Do you hear me, nuts! I don't even believe in ghosts let alone demons from hell, or wherever the fuck old evil eyes there comes from."

"All three images are still processing, maybe it's just what I said, some sort of optical illusion."

"The same one on all three? Mass hysteria suffered by two people and by different photographs taken in different locations at different times?"

"By a camera operating all by itself, I might add," Shane said, rocking his empty glass back and forth so the ice cubes sang.

Sydney made a pot of coffee while Shane made them some sandwiches. Half an hour later they went back to the laptop and hoped for something more definitive. The images were still a whole lot of nothing other than disturbing.

"There, that area right there, can you clean that up?"

"I'll see what I can do," Shane said and used the unsharp mask tool.

"Do you see that? It looks like an eye to me."

"It is an eye. Let me clean this area up."

Several minutes of manipulating the image and there was a discernible face within the haze demon's face.

"That face looks familiar," Shane said.

"That is because it's right there in that photo with my mother."

"Where? It's not either of those two guys with her."

"No, it's the person who took the photo. Look at the reflection in my mom's mirrored sunglasses hanging from the front of her shirt."

"Holy shit. Let me work on these photos and try and isolate that reflection. Maybe we can get an identification of the person," Shane said.

"You mean, if AFIS just happens to have a demon database." She laughed nervously and poured herself a cup of coffee and as an afterthought a whiskey as well.

Colby picked up his phone and looked at the photo Sydney sent him. He had been staring at it for the last hour and while it looked familiar, he just couldn't place exactly where it had been taken. There just was not enough information in the photograph. The nurse came in, gave him his meds, fluffed his pillow, and adjusted his legs for him.

"Oh hell, I haven't thought about that place in over thirty years," she said, glancing over his shoulder.

"What?"

"I'm sorry, I didn't mean to intrude," the nurse said with embarrassment painted on her face. She was older but still quite attractive with just enough gray to accent her face.

"No, no intrusion at all. I have been wracking my brain all morning trying to figure out where this photo was taken," Colby said.

"Lord, for the life of me I can't remember the real name of the place. It was some Anishinaabe name that no one could pronounce. Us kids just called it Camp Mucky-Muck because of the wild rice bogs surrounding it. Every year some new kid would wander out too far and wind up stuck in the mud. And of course, we would tease them mercilessly about being stuck in quicksand until they cried. Kids are vicious little beasts aren't they," she said with a smile.

"That's right. I still have a shoe buried out there somewhere. Where is it, do you remember?"

"Oh, it's long gone. It sank into the bog back in the mid-eighties, I guess the swamp reclaimed what was hers."

"Okay, I guess I didn't pay much attention. Where was it, I guess I should be asking."

"It was in that no man's land area southeast of Dollar Settlement, by Brimley," she said.

"You appear to be about my age," Colby started.

The woman just gave him a look that said *tread lightly.* "Careful how far down that road you travel mister," she said with a smile. "If you are thirty-nine, then we are indeed close in age, however, you would be older no matter what."

"Anything strange ever happen at that place?" he asked.

"Now that you mention it, the year before it closed down two of the counselors disappeared. Hey, if my memory serves me, I think that girl was one of them," the nurse, Renee, pointed to the screen on his phone. "I remember feeling so bad about it because she had always been so nice to me."

"Thank you, Renee, thank you so very much."

As soon as the nurse left the room Colby called Sid and told her what he had learned. The name *Mucky-Muck* was enough to jog her memory and she remembered exactly where the place was. He didn't even get to talk to her about anything else before she abruptly ended the call.

Abigail struggled against the darkness. It wasn't fair. She didn't belong to him anymore, so he shouldn't have control over her any longer. She willed herself back into the light without result.

Once her eyes had adjusted to the darkness, she could see the woman, Claudia, across the expanse. Her long dark hair trailing behind her. She tried to call out to her, but she had no voice. She tried to walk over to her, but she was held fast.

The stench of smoke hit her long before the mist enveloped her, and she gagged. She felt his cold, ethereal hands roaming across every square inch of her body causing ripples of fear to careen through her. The world was closing in on her, but there was no escape.

"I beat you, you bastard. Leave me alone. You have to leave me alone!" Abigail screamed into the nothingness.

"Sid, the camera was going off all night but there's no film in it," Shane said as soon as she walked through the door of Colby's house.

"Colby will kill you if he sees his place looking like this," she warned.

"It's all Katie's fault. For some reason she's all wound up. I couldn't keep after her and edit photographs at the same time."

"The poor thing doesn't understand why Colby hasn't been home," she said and gave the dog a big hug and kiss.

"Oh, and the camera is still out of film."

"Why is the camera out of film?"

"Like I mentioned earlier, I used the last roll. We are out of film. I've called all around and the nearest place that has any film is at the Wal-Mart in Escanaba."

"Okay. You head to Esky and get the film and then meet me in Brimley. I'll set us up a base of operation at the motel there and we can head out to the camp."

"What in the hell is in Brimley?"

"That's where the photo was taken. Colby recognized the place and then I remembered where it is. While you're screwing around in Esky I'll ask around in Brimley and Bay Mills and see if I can't get an identification on the two men in the photo."

"Sounds like a plan. I'll get all the film I can find just in case," Shane said, ignoring her screwing around comment.

"Take your uniform but don't wear it. We will probably get more answers if we travel incognito as tourists," she said.

"Like a grandmother, grandson outing. Cool," Shane said, returning a dig which earned him a very painful shot to the arm.

They went about the task of packing the truck for another road trip. Shane packed the developing equipment into his Jeep since he would be traveling separately, and she had no clue as to how to use the gear. Each of them checked in with

Colby to let him know what they were doing, that Katie would with them, and that they would see him in a couple of days.

Not wanting to screw around with the back roads Sydney took M-twenty-eight straight to Brimley. She got two rooms at a motel on the banks of the Waiska River, unloaded her gear into the motel room and took a quick cat nap. After a shower she was ready to head into Dollar Settlement to ask around about the old youth camp.

She took lakeshore drive passed the Bay Mills Casino and Point Iroquois lighthouse. She eased into the dirt parking lot of the settlement bingo hall and went inside. She bought ten dollars' worth of cards and an ink blotter before taking a seat near a coven of geriatric women. Sydney asked several of the older women sitting around her table without so much as a peep in response until a brutish grandmother threated to snap her neck if she didn't keep her *lips zipped.* Another of the old women was brandishing a chicken's foot she used to mark her bingo card. Sydney thought it best to seek refuge elsewhere.

Outside she found an old bench and figured she would start asking the people as they left the bingo hall instead of interrupting their quintessential game. She smelled cigarette smoke and her senses went on high alert but relaxed after determining it was a false alarm. The smoke was emanating from an old man sitting on a bench by himself enjoying a Camel while avoiding the petulant mob inside.

"Nice evening isn't it?" she said.

"That will all depend on luck my new friend," he said.

His leathery complexion gave away the fact he had spent most of his life in the sun. Probably a fisherman due to the fact it was the only thing to do in this town other than deal cards and his hands were much too rough for that. His bright white t-shirt contrasted with his dark, reddish skin.

"On my luck? Your luck? Our luck?"

"Oh no, on Sadie's luck. If she don't win I'm going to hear about it until next Thursday because it will somehow be all my fault. If I sit with her in there and she loses it is my fault, if I sit out here and she loses it's my fault and I'm just too plain cowardly to tell her that she loses because both her hearing and eyesight are shit. Not to mention she is a shitty bingo player," he said, laughing up a wet cough.

"Trust me, I feel your pain. I think I may have met Sadie inside. You seem to be familiar with these parts, how long have you been in this area?"

"I'll be giving away my age, but I've lived here since coming back from Viet Nam," the old man said.

"I went to a youth camp up here when I was just a young girl and I would love to have a look at the old place. Just to reminisce, you know," Sydney said.

"There are several camps in this area."

"Us kids used to call it Camp Muck, some called it Camp Mucky-Muck."

"Oh, that place. Hell, that's been gone more than twenty, hell, probably more like thirty years or so."

"Would you happen to know where it is?"

"Yup."

"Would you mind telling me?"

"Won't do you no good. It's private property now. Can't get in."

"Leave the getting in part to me," she said with a wink and an elbow.

"Fair enough. It's off Plantation Road. You can't miss the property, smells like shit and there's an eyesore of a pole barn in the dead center of it. Not to mention high tension wires running right to it."

"It smells like shit. Do you mean literally?"

"Naw, the bastard who owns it grows that marijuana stuff in there. Stinks up the place worse than a manure spreader in summer."

"So, head down to Plantation Road and roll my windows down, got it."

"Hey, you're smarter than you look little lady," he said with a grin and an elbow of his own.

"Tell me something, old timer, any armed guards or dogs on the place?"

"Naw, nobody stupid enough around here to try and break in, the local Johnny Law has a grub stake in the place. But still, better watch yourself out there, I don't much care for the feller who owns the place and I trust him even less than I like him."

"Thanks for the warning."

Sydney went back into Bay Mills for some coffee, snacks, water, and other assorted stakeout supplies. She shot a text to both Colby and Shane to let them know where she was going. She easily found the unsightly building on Plantation Road, so she drove the perimeter of the area several times to get the lay of the land and to see if anyone was moving about. It was on the third pass that she spotted the old campground entrance road. The only reason she even noticed it was because a tree had fallen and uncovered a window on an old camp bus. The sun was on its downward trajectory and glinted off the dingy glass.

Sydney parked and locked the truck a half mile down the road. She checked her pistol and made sure she had an extra clip before cautiously making her way back to the old bus to find it was parked across the old entrance, effectively blocking the way in. She bushwhacked her way around the rear of the bus, earning her a multitude of scratches across her face and arms for her troubles.

The first thing she noticed once she was inside the campground was that there was no sound. Just like at her father's cabin and it set her nerves on alert. An image of the smoke demon invaded her thoughts and she had to stop for a minute to shake the notion from her brain.

Even though the place had sat unused and neglected for decades she was still able to follow the main path until she reached a split that went off into three directions as well as continued straight. She closed her eyes and oriented herself with her memories. Sydney tried to recall the place when it was filled with bustling children running scatter mouse from building to building. The problem was there weren't any buildings left standing, so it was nearly impossible to get her bearings. She followed the first path to her left which led her to a large foundation. There were no traces of plumbing causing her to conclude this was one of the bunk houses as there had been no running water in any of the twelve person cabins.

Although the paths between buildings were overgrown and covered in leaves, with some work Sydney managed to find them. As she walked through the rubble bits and pieces of her youth began to fall into place. She came across another foundation that had some of the wooden wall still standing. It had been the kitchen and the infrastructure was still somewhat intact which kept the wall from collapsing. Copper pipes jutted toward the sky with an old stainless-steel sink sitting on top. She stepped back and peered into the nothingness. She could almost recall the sweet smell of cinnamon permeating the air as breakfast trays were piled high with oatmeal and cinnamon raisin toast slathered in butter.

She continued down the path passing quickly by what must have been the outhouses by the odors permeating the surrounding air. Decades later and shit still smelled like shit.

She came to another bunkhouse foundation with a few of the beams lying nearby. Several sets of initials were carved along the entire expanse of the beam. She searched for S.L. loves C.P. but couldn't find it amongst the scrabble and debris. A pile of dilapidated bunk beds lay scattered on the ground. Remnants of old blankets had deteriorated to the point they were only strands of dull colored fabric. For some reason the sight of the debris caused a melancholy mood to invade her psyche, so Sydney thought about Colby and Katie until the feeling passed. She was certain this was the girl's bunkhouse so if her memory served her correctly there should be a trail leading to the lake toward the east.

Before entering the densely overgrown area, she grabbed a pink piece of ribbon she had cut earlier and tied it to the first tree with the bow facing the way toward the exit. As soon as she entered the canopy of the forest the temperature dropped at least ten degrees, and the sunlight faded considerably. She tied another piece of ribbon every ten or fifteen yards.

Lady ferns blanketed the whole of the forest floor and were almost waist high making it impossible for her to see if anyone was lurking in the weeds waiting to pounce. Her Spidey-sense was on high alert. A musty, dead odor started reaching her nose alerting her that the lake must be near.

The path opened a little to reveal a lake, or what was once a lake and was now nothing more than a giant bed of muck. Pilings from old docks broke the surface like drowning swimmers trying to capture that very last sip of oxygen before going under. Having succumb to decades of neglect the skeleton of an old wooden rowboat sat chained to a tree. The bow was the only part of the boat that had not returned to whence it came.

Sydney caught sight of something in the muck so she baby stepped her way out on the only dock with deck boards still intact. She had to long step over several missing slats but was soon out to the edge a good fifteen feet from shore. An eerie sensation washed over her, and she realized how absolutely still the forest was. This was not natural. The surrounding forest was as dead as the mucky pond.

Sydney was turning around to go back when she spotted a glimmer of white in the black muck a few feet from the dock. She pulled out a pair of binoculars from her backpack and scanned the surface. It was a bone. She was stunned at first but then realized there had to be a lot of dead things in that black water so of course bones were going to surface on occasion. She was laughing off her trepidation when she caught sight of something much larger, and round.

She made her way back off the dock and into the forest. Looking around she found a long, dead limb that would reach out to what she had discovered. She carried the limb back out to the edge of the dock and used it to draw the object closer to her. The object was within a couple of feet from her when the limb broke. Sydney dropped to her belly and scooted out as far as she dared until she was able to get her hands on the object in the muck. She freed it from the ooze and lifted it up. It was a human skull with empty, accusatory eyes staring back at her.

Without warning the air around her became cold and foreboding. A darkness spread across the mucky lake, bringing with it the stench of death. Sydney willed herself away, but this was not a dream from which she could awaken. The only sound she had heard since entering this swamp was the crack of the dock giving way and dumping her into the sludge with a splat. She quickly sank until her nose was just above the surface. The smell of death surrounded her, invaded her, and she screamed.

The first thirty seconds were spent in sheer panic as she felt herself sinking deeper and deeper into the muck. She thought of all the old Hollywood movies in which the hero became trapped in quicksand. She knew from her military coaching that she had to stop struggling. Her training kicked in and she spread her legs wide and her arms out to her sides to maximize her surface area. She extended her toes to see if she could touch bottom but there was nothing solid below her.

She finally relaxed enough to think her quandary through. She should be able to swim the breaststroke through the viscous slime. She was about ready to laugh at herself over her predicament when she smelled the smoke; cigarette smoke and she iced over.

"Once or twice a year we get some damned fool stuck in the old pond. I have tried to fill it in, but the DNR won't let me. Wetland conservation and all that jazz. Here, grab this," the man said, tossing Sydney a rope.

Her hackles were still up but she grabbed the rope anyway. She recognized this man, more by his smell than his looks. He was the forest ranger that Morgan had brought to the crime scene. Sydney opted to play it close to the vest and not let him know she recognized him and hoped he didn't recognize her.

"Thank you, I wasn't quite sure what I was going to do there for a minute," she said using her best damsel in distress intonation.

"You looked like you knew what you were doing. My name is Skunk, I own the place. What in the world were you doing out here?" he asked while handing her a clean towel.

"Curiosity I supposed. I was driving by and recognized the place. I went here a few summers as a kid. I think my mother was a counselor here in her youth a summer or two as well."

"Oh, way back in the heyday. I never understood the human need for reminiscing about bridges already crossed, especially when they were also burned like this one. I always look forward, never back. How did you happen to notice the place? It's pretty well hidden on purpose to keep this sort of thing from happening."

"I remembered the road. I haven't been through this way in decades."

"Hope you brought some clean clothes with you," Skunk said.

"I have a bag in my car. I can't thank you enough for saving my life," she said, still trying to pull off the damsel in distress routine. There was a reason she never got into acting.

"I hardly saved your life. I'm certain you would have managed on your own."

"Well thank you either way," Sydney said and started walking back towards the path. She hoped the bulge of her gun wasn't too obvious.

"Let me take you up to the front. I have a quad around the corner. But you're going to have to sit on that towel," he said with a wink.

Sydney was expecting the worst with every second that ticked off the clock. There was something about this person that just didn't sit right with her. He had taken so many different turns that she had lost her bearings. At least she had sent Shane the GPS coordinates so he would know where to search for her body. A sense of relief washed over her once she spotted the rear of the bus peeking through the overgrowth.

"Here we are. I can't go any further so you're on your own from here," he said with a sinister smile.

Still playing the woman in peril card Sydney asked, "Would it be alright to get a selfie with my knight in shining armor?"

Skunk nodded and she lined up to get a selfie of the two of them together. She felt an ominous energy while standing that close to the man. A malevolent tasting energy that she wanted nothing more than to be away from.

"Thanks again," she said and started to slip out behind the parked bus.

"Oh, one more thing officer, detective, inspector, or whatever it is you call yourself. Take this as a warning and not a threat. If you ever show up to this property without a warrant, there is a very good chance of getting yourself shot," he said and drove away before she could respond. So much for being incognito.

Once she was back at the truck Sydney started to strip down out of her wet clothes. Luckily, she had been smart enough to bring a change of clothes, although she did forget clean underwear. She was down to her soggy, mud encrusted panties and bra when she heard a noise behind her. When she spun around there was an old man on a bicycle behind her.

"No need to cover up missy, my eyesight ain't what it used to be," he said.

"You're the man I spoke to outside of the bingo hall, aren't you?"

"One in the same."

"What are you doing way out here?"

"I collect bottles and cans for drinking money on account of my wife being a tightwad. And I gather up trash as well. People got no respect anymore. Hell, they never did have much, but they seem to have a lot less nowadays. I fill this basket up pretty near every day," he rambled. "Find what you were looking for?"

"I'm not really sure what I found."

"You a cop?"

"Why would you ask that?" Sydney asked, surprised by the old man's comment.

"Your gun sitting there in the seat. Looks to me like a police issue."

Still standing there in her underwear she suddenly felt self-conscious. "I though your eyesight was for shit," she said, hurriedly slipping on a pair of sweatpants.

"Well, I lied. Don't get much opportunity to gander at such a beauty," he said with a sneer.

"I should arrest you, you old pervert."

"Which one of us is the pervert? The one getting naked by the side of the road or the one who just happened by to witness it?"

"Point taken. How would you know that was a police issue?"

"Not really by the gun itself, but the way you handled it. Like military or police."

"First-hand experience?"

"Yes ma'am, on both accounts. After Nam I did a stint as a tribal police officer back before you were even born, I imagine."

"Thank you for your service," Sydney said out of habit. "Let me ask you something," she said, reaching into the truck and pulling out an evidence bag. "Would you happen to know what this is?" she asked and handed him the bag.

"It looks like a button," he said.

She nodded. "It looks like a uniform button to me. But not any uniform I have ever seen. Go ahead and take it out of the bag if you'd like."

The old man took the button out of the bag and rolled it around in the palm of his hand with his index finger. "Yep, I sure do know what this is. Had one of them myself years, hell, decades ago."

"So, you do recognize it?"

"Sure do. It's a button from a tribal police uniform. Old though. Not used anymore."

"Do you know where it might have come from?"

"No clue. But you could always ask that prick, Joe."

"Joe?"

"He's the chief of tribal police in Bay Mills. But be careful around him. I trust him even less than I trust the prick who runs this place," he said, nodding toward the ugly pole barn.

Sydney finished getting dressed while the old man rode away on his ancient bicycle. She texted Shane the selfie photo she took with Skunk and headed back to Brimley. It had been a long day and she needed a long, hot shower followed by whiskey and sleep.

Twenty-Two

Escanaba is the closest thing to a big city in the Upper Peninsula outside of the college town of Marquette which has grown over the years. Most cities and towns could be driven through in less than five minutes with mostly mom and pop shops to choose from. Shane grabbed the only four rolls of film at the Wal-Mart before heading over to Meijer and then Walgreen's. In all he was able to get eight rolls of film. He grabbed a gyro at Bobaloons and headed for Sand Island.

While eating his lunch Shane tried to look at the texts and photos that Sydney had sent him, but Katie was pestering him for a walk. She had been cooped up in the truck for hours and probably had to use the facilities. He finished his sandwich and gulped the last of his soda before tossing everything into the trash bin. The island and park were not a large one, but there was a nice little system of walking trails, so he grabbed a poop bag and away they went.

They were back on the road heading north within the hour which meant they were on schedule to be in Brimley by nightfall. Before leaving the park, Shane had loaded a film canister into the camera, and it went through the entire roll of film before he was even a mile out of town. He had to stop and move the camera to the back seat in order to get Katie to ride up front with him. She acted as though she wanted no part of the infernal contraption and would have preferred Shane just left it behind with the rest of the lunch garbage.

He took the longer, but more scenic route along the lakeshore through the town of Manistique. He knew he was coming up on Naubinway long before reaching the little fishing village. The powerful aroma of smoked whitefish drifted in through the Jeep windows making him hungry, so he stopped in the little town of Epoufette to grab a couple of smoked chubs and an iced tea. Katie whined until he moved the camera back to the front so she could lie down in the back seat, away from the pugnacious smell of smoked fish.

Shane pulled into the parking lot of the motel and went into the office to check in. Sydney had already paid for his room and the key was waiting for him. He unloaded his gear and then went next door to her room, but she didn't answer the door. There was a note telling him that she had gone into Bay Mills to follow up on a lead. He unloaded the Jeep and took a much-needed shower.

Sydney read the text from Shane and responded by assuring him she was alright by herself. She told him to hang tight and she would be back to the motel in an hour. She grabbed a coffee from the rustically ornate Dancing Crane coffee shop and walked over to the small police station which was essentially a rectangle box of red bricks. Her senses were on high alert, nothing was as it seemed and she knew she could trust no one, not even the local constabulary. After the fiasco at the campground, she thought she had better operate above board.

"Good evening. My name is Sydney Lamppinen, I'm a detective with the Michigan State Police. I'm looking for your chief of police. A man named Joe from what I understand," she asked of the young deputy at the desk.

"Oh, Joe has been long gone," a young girl at the front desk said.

"Oh, did he retire?"

The deputy giggled in a girlish sort of way. She twirled her tri-colored hair around her fingers while chewing on at least three sticks of gum. Sydney didn't think she was old enough to work the local ice cream stand let alone be a cop. Her multi-colored eye shadow matched her hair.

"I'm sorry, no. He's still the chief. What I meant was that he's gone home for the evening."

"Okay, when can I expect him to be back?" Sydney asked, resisting the urge to tell the young lady to go wash her face.

"Is there a problem, detective?" a large, burly officer said as he came out of an office down the hall.

He sported a deep, ruddy complexion and his long black hair hung past the middle of his back but was also held in place with an ornate tribal hair band. He was a rugged man, and yet his face was delicate, almost feminine. His deep, dark eyes were piercing, in a friendly sort of way. Sydney quickly decided she wouldn't make any disparaging remarks about his hair.

"No, no problem."

"Are you here investigating someone in particular? I know most of the troublemakers in this neck of the woods. Most are just misguided youths," he said and offered a beefy hand that bore the scars of hard labor.

She shook his hand and said, "No, nothing like that. Just following up on some leads from an unfortunate incident in Pictured Rocks."

"Okay. I'll let Joe know you are looking to speak with him," he said and turned away.

"Hang on a second if you please. I see you have a lot of artifacts around here. In fact, the place looks almost like a museum."

"It is a museum in a manner of speaking. It houses a lot of our tribal history, at least as it pertains to our law enforcement department."

"Would you happen to know what this is?" she said and handed him the evidence bag.

"That's a uniform button. But it's old, incredibly old."

"How old?"

"We change designs every few years or so. Local artists design them for a contest and then the winning design gets used for that year's uniforms. It's a pride thing. This one dates back way before my time, but I think I recognize the button from somewhere. Let me take a picture of it and I'll look around here. We keep a lot of the old uniforms in storage," he said and pulled out his cell phone.

"Thank you for your time. And yours as well," Sydney said to the young woman as she left the building.

She walked around to Bay Mills Point to enjoy the sunset. The lake was calm, and the waves gently licked the sands like a toddler with an ice cream cone. Canada lay off in the distance, its once pristine beauty now dotted endlessly with gaudy windmills. So much for progress.

From the point she could see Shane's Jeep in the motel parking lot, so she started ambling back towards the motel. It was a such a nice night for a walk she took her time and gathered in the sights. Once she could see her car in the coffee shop parking lot, she got a strange premonition that someone was following her. She thought about ducking back into the police station across the street but then chided herself for being foolish. She texted Shane and told him she was on her way back to the motel.

First thing Sydney did when she walked through the door was to pour two fingers worth of bourbon over ice, swirl it around for thirty seconds before downing the glass. She banged on the wall between rooms to let Shane know that she was back. Old habits die hard, she could have just used the less intrusive method of shooting him a text.

"Did you find what you were looking for?" Shane asked with a smile as he and Katie entered the motel room.

"What is that grin for?"

"I saw the selfie. Did you decide to go for a swim?"

"Shut up. That place and that dude are creepier than hell. In a roundabout way he threatened to shoot me," Sydney said.

"He what?"

"He warned me that if I were to come on his property without a warrant I might be shot."

"You told him you were a cop?"

"I didn't have to, he already knew. He goes by the name Skunk. He was the consultant that Morgan brought out to the Pine Stump Junction crime scene."

"Quite the coincidence, eh?"

"I don't believe there are any coincidences when it comes to this freak show of a case. Speaking of which, what photos did you get from the camera?

He got up and poured them each a bourbon over ice. "I have the film canister soaking. It won't be too much longer. I glanced at that selfie you sent, there was something odd about the man's eyes. Let me go get my laptop and finish with the film."

"I'll take Katie for a walk while you're busy with the technical stuff. Do you need anything while I am out?" she asked.

"Grab me a burger from Jack's if you would please," he called out as they both went separate directions.

Sydney walked up Fourth Street alongside the Waiska River. Oddly, there was no river walk on the banks of the river as it was all private property so the road would have to do. Katie didn't seem to mind the lack of wilderness and spent the entire walk with her nose in the air instead of on the ground. The restaurant was spewing some intense aromas out into the night air. Her phone rang and thinking it was Colby she answered it without looking.

"Well, hey there handsome, I thought you would be sleeping."

"Oh, I'm sorry I must have the wrong number," an unfamiliar voice said.

"My apologies, I was expecting a call from someone. This is Sydney Lamppinen, and you are?"

"Junior, from down at the police station."

"Junior?"

"Sorry, ma'am, everyone just calls me Junior. Kind of like calling a fat man Tiny or Slim I suppose. I'm the deputy you spoke to earlier at the station."

"What can I do for you? Did the chief show up?"

"About that. I got to thinking after you left and went down to check the uniforms in storage. That button came from a uniform from sometime in the nineteen eighties as best as I can figure."

Sydney got a little excited. "Would it be possible to get a list of names of the officers working at the time? Maybe I can find out whose uniform it belongs to."

"No need for that. I'm pretty sure the button came from one of the uniforms we have here in storage."

"Is there any possible way to know whose uniform that belonged to."

"Absolutely. It will be easy in fact. All of the older uniforms were donated to the museum by Joe himself."

"The chief?"

"Yes ma'am."

"Interesting. Thank you so very much for the information. Maybe we should have coffee tomorrow," Sydney said.

"That could be arranged. And ma'am, you watch yourself around the chief," he said just above a whisper.

After a long silence she said, "Was that a threat?"

"No, ma'am, on the contrary. That was a legitimate warning."

"Huh, that makes two in one day. I'll take that to mean I'm on the right track. I take it you're not a fan?"

"Not in the least. I've only been here for six months, I transferred up from Mt. Pleasant. I'd rather not discuss delicate matters over the phone, not even my personal phone."

"Fair enough. I'm over in Brimley at the motel on the river. Stop by if you feel inclined."

"Will do," he said and hung up.

Sydney grabbed a pint of Founder's Red's Rye while waiting on her food. She picked up a bacon cheeseburger for Shane who had suddenly abandoned his veganism and got herself the whitefish. Katie tried to mug her several times on the way back to the motel which was just across the parking lot. She set the food down on the table inside the room and poured some of Katie's food out into a bowl and hid pieces of broken Slim Jim in the bottom which was about as effective as hiding an elephant under a washcloth.

"I'm glad you're back," Shane said.

"Are you that hungry?"

"Famished, but that is not why. Look at this."

"What am I looking at? Or looking for?" she asked, looking at the selfie photo she took earlier in the day on his laptop screen.

"Watch," Shane said and zoomed in on Skunk's eye. "I told you something didn't look right."

"Are those the same bokeh balls that were in the other photos?"

"One in the same. And they move as well."

"What is the image they make?" she asked.

"I don't know, I've been waiting for you."

"You didn't want to spoil the surprise?"

"No, I didn't want to be alone when I monkeyed with this thing. I don't know about you, but I have been terrified ever since the night at your father's cabin."

Shane poured the liquid out of the film canister and hung the celluloid strips from the shower curtain with clothes pins. He turned on the hair dryer on the low, cold setting and left the bathroom. He sat back down at the small table and started working on the photograph.

"This is a pain in the ass."

"What is wrong?"

"They pixilate if I enlarge it too much and they are too small to see if I don't enlarge them," Shane said.

"Here," she said, handing him a magnifying glass she dug out of her purse. "No wisecracks."

Shane bit his tongue and refused to spout any Sherlock Holmes references for his own good. He had already been at work manipulating the bokeh for an hour without much result.

"Would you like me to try?" Sydney asked.

"Be my guest," Shane said and went out to the motel vending machine for some stale peanuts.

Sydney blew the selfie up on her phone and used as she would the box from a jigsaw puzzle. Half an hour and two cups of shitty coffee later and she had arranged them in such a manner that they clicked together to create one, single image. When Shane came back in the room tears were rolling down her cheeks.

"What is wrong Sid?"

"That image in Skunk's eye is my mother and the child at her feet is me. Somehow, that bastard either has my mother or he damn sure knows where she is."

"I'm not kidding, Sid, this is creeping me out. Can we just go home?" Shane said with a tremble in his voice.

Sydney just shook her head. "I'm afraid it's much too late for that."

"Good morning, sunshine," Colby's voice chimed.

"What time is it?" Sydney asked, still groggy from the night before.

She looked at the table of empty mini bottles and didn't have to wonder why. She didn't remember falling asleep let alone getting into bed. She was still wearing the same clothes from the previous day.

Colby grunted. "I don't know. I have no concept of time in here. There's no clock in my room, and I dropped the television remote. Maybe there is a clock, but I can't figure out which one of these numbers is my blood pressure, my temperature, or the time. The U.S. Farm Report just ended so that should give you a time frame."

"Damn, why are you calling me so early. Is the sun even up?"

"Quit your bellyaching. So, what is this about finding your mother?"

"Who told you that?"

"Shane sent me a text last night, but I think he was pretty shitfaced."

"Yeah, I guess we both were. It was a long, strange night."

"And?"

"And this shit is starting to make me see boogeymen around every corner. I have never believed much in ghosts, or the supernatural, but damn, there is some freaky shit going on here, Colby."

"What did you find at the camp?"

"That the camp is deserted, hell it has pretty much disappeared without a trace. Even the lake has dried up into a pond of thick muck."

Colby laughed. "I saw the picture."

"Did you see the selfie I took with that weird old man?"

"He looked familiar."

"He was that retired forest ranger who Morgan brought to the crime scene out at Pine Stump Junction. He has a marijuana plantation in a pole barn on the old camp site. Just a little coincidental don't you think?"

"A little maybe. But he seems harmless."

"He threatened me, Colby. And then later, I don't want to give details over the phone, someone else warned me about him."

"Threatened you? How?"

"He *warned* me that if I were to go nosing around on his property without a warrant that I might just get myself shot."

"He has a point. Growing weed can be lucrative which also means dangerous as well."

"Don't you dare," she said.

"I'm not. I'm just playing devil's advocate here."

"And then there's this," she said, sending him the photo of Skunk's eye with her and her mother's reflection that she took of Shane's laptop screen with her phone.

Colby looked at the photograph when it came across on his phone. A chill washed over him once he realized what he was looking at.

"That has got to be some kind of trick," he said.

"I wish it were a trick. I wish this were all one giant nightmare that I will wake up from eventually and we can all have a laugh, but it's far from being just a bad dream."

"What does Shane think about it?"

"Honestly, he's even more freaked out about it than I'm. I keep trying to rationalize this as just some sort of hysteria playing tricks on the both of us. There's something going on here that's just impossible to explain in rational terms. And then to make things even more cloudy, there seems to be a human element at work here as well," Sydney said.

"Dare I ask?"

"For the sake of argument let us say that there is a ghost, or demon or something else unexplainable at work here, there's also a human element. A human being killed these women, or at least buried them. It was a human being who shoved poor Abigail off that cliff. It makes me wonder, are there two components at work, or are they both one in the same?"

"Like a vampire's familiar?" he asked, unable to stifle his chuckle.

"Yes, exactly like that. And I'm busting your ass the minute I see you again."

"Have you mentioned anything about this to Layton or your superiors?"

"Are you fucking nuts?"

"I figured as much, but I had to ask. What's your next play?"

"I'm not sure yet. Shane developed some more photos last night and they showed something disturbing. They were photos of Camp Muck, but it didn't look the same as when I was there yesterday afternoon. I think it's a burial site, but I didn't see any grave sites while I was out there. Granted, I didn't get a chance to look around much, the compound is huge if you remember."

"What are your chances of getting a warrant?"

"Slim to none. If I could have gotten my hands on the skull, I might have been able to talk the right judge into signing a warrant."

"Wait, what? You found a skull? A human skull?"

"I think so. It was suspended in the muck. That's how I fell into the sludge."

"A judge should take your word for it right?"

"No, I was trespassing when I found it so I can't take that to a judge. I'm sure Skunk, the landowner, will claim it was an old

Halloween gag or something. On another note, how are you feeling?" she asked.

"Like I got hit by a truck."

"Cute."

"How's my baby?"

"I'm fine, just a little tired."

"Cute. I meant Katie."

"She is sleeping off that box of Slim Jim's she ate last night," she said. "Actually, she is pestering me for a walk, so I had better let you go before she messes up this fine motel carpeting."

"Sid, you watch your ass. These guys, or whatever they may be, have already shown they have no problem killing cops."

"I know, Colby, trust me, I know," she said and disconnected the call.

Sydney banged on the wall to let Shane know she was awake. She took a quick shower and then the two of them headed out for coffee at the Dancing Crane. The barista, a good-looking local woman, slyly handed her a note written on the side of her double shot Americano. She read it and then handed it to Shane.

"What do you think? Can we trust this person?" Shane asked.

"It doesn't look like we have much of a choice. Put together all of the information we have on this case and bring it with us."

"We could be walking into an ambush."

"Could be, but I doubt it. Besides, we will be taking our equalizer with us just in case."

They picked up Katie and the case files and loaded them into Shane's Jeep. Sydney spotted who she thought might be the chief, an overweight fellow dressed in uniform at the tribal center. He had his back turned to them, so Sydney didn't think he spotted them passing through town. Outside of town Shane took a left turn and drove up a huge hill to a cemetery overlooking

Spectacle Lake and Lake Superior. They parked the Jeep and followed a trail marked with yellow ribbon just as instructed.

"Sorry about all the cloak and dagger stuff but from up here I'm able see if you were being followed," Junior said, giving a head nod hello to Shane.

"Why are you so on edge?" Sydney asked.

"I didn't know it when I transferred up here from Mount Pleasant that the reason there was an opening was because the previous officer went missing. And the man he replaced before him went missing as well. I mean, look around you, does this look like a place where cops are in danger of just disappearing?"

They both just shook their heads.

"I started to do some digging and then things got pretty weird."

"How so?" Sydney asked.

"Things out of place in my house. Photographs left in my mailbox. Even once, my truck was turned completely around in my driveway. It was still locked and there was nothing to indicate a tow truck had hooked up to it."

"Photographs? Of what?"

"Photographs of family members from downstate. But older photos, not anything recent."

"So, someone went into your house, took photos out of a photo album and put them in your mailbox? Maybe as a warning?" Shane said.

"No, that's the disturbing thing, these were not in an album in my house. They were downstate, in Mount Pleasant, at a relative's house," Junior replied. "I'm not faint of heart, but this has me spooked. I keep having the sensation I'm being watched."

"May I be the first to point out that you wanted to meet us in a cemetery of all places," Sydney said.

Junior laughed long and hard. "I never even thought of that, I just wanted an eagle-eye view of the road coming up here. I guess I trust the dead more than I do the living right now. What's going on? Do I have a reason to be worried or am I just being paranoid?"

"I can't really explain what is going on, mainly because it's all circumstantial and guesswork. But to answer your question, no, I don't think you are being foolish or paranoid."

Shane sorted through some of the photos and handed one to the officer. "Have you seen this truck before?"

"I have seen it around here. It was outside of my house a few times."

"Do you know who it belongs to?"

"No, I have never even seen the driver now that I think about it. What's the deal with the truck?"

"We have very good reason to believe that this truck was used to run down a sheriff and two deputies outside of Newberry, killing one of them," Sydney said.

"My sheriff and my deputies. My friends," Shane said. Sydney reached over and patted his arm.

"I'm terribly sorry for your loss. And you think someone in Bay Mills or Brimley had something to do with it?"

"All circumstantial. But all the circumstantial evidence leads us back to here," Sydney said.

Sydney and Shane stepped away to discuss the situation. Shane was more reluctant than she, but in the end, they decided Junior should be read into the situation. They showed him all the photographs including her selfie with Skunk.

"I know that dude. He's always bending the chief's ear. I don't like him much, hell, I don't like him one bit," Junior said.

Once the man revealed this, Sydney continued with the story. She told him about finding the camera at the cliffs, and about Abigail's story. She even told him about her father's murder. He took the photos from her and went through them as she told their tall tale.

"You don't seem to be phased too much," she said.

"I grew up in a household full of old women, ripe with superstition and old tales. Quite often I found there to be a bit of truth in each of the legends," he said as he sighed deeply. "I think I can trust you, so I had better be completely honest with you."

"I told you we shouldn't trust him," Shane said.

"Easy killer, nothing like that. I wasn't completely forthcoming is all. I just didn't realize I wasn't the only one."

"Please elaborate," Sydney said.

"My mother went missing when I was just a toddler. My sister was a bit older and when she was in her late teens, she started looking for her. I mean really looking for her. She disappeared as well. The two officers who went missing from here, they were cousins of ours and they were helping me. So no, I don't find your story strange in the least because your story is my story as well," Junior said and went back to scanning through the photographs.

After a long silence Sydney said, "So I'm not crazy? We're not crazy?"

"Not unless all of us are." He stopped and looked at the photograph of Sydney's father swinging from the rafter. "Look there, in his hand," he said.

Shane looked closer. "I missed that," he said. "Do you know what that is?"

"Just a guess, but it looks like a badge to me. A tribal police badge to be precise."

Twenty-Three

There was a light tapping on her motel room door, so Sydney closed the laptop, put Katie in the bathroom and cautiously answered the door. To her surprise there was a corpulent man dressed in blue jeans, a dungaree shirt, and a cowboy hat rimmed with she thought was rattlesnake skin. His ensemble was completed with a silver bolo tie sporting a turquoise thunderbird. He looked like he might be more at home in the southwestern desert than on the Lake Superior coast.

Before she could say a single word, he started in. "Good morning, ma'am. I hear you were looking to have a few words with me," Joe said.

"Good morning, chief, yes I do have a few questions if I could have a moment of your time," Sydney said while holding the door open for him.

"We don't get many state police investigators up here, especially not on tribal lands," he said, the tone of his voice made it clear he was already challenging jurisdiction. "I didn't realize we had a problem that required the big guns."

"This has nothing to do with Bay Mills or tribal lands," she lied. "We recently uncovered some old missing person's information that warrants looking into. I just have a few questions if you don't mind."

"Fire away, I'm all yours," he said with a toothy grin that made Sydney uncomfortable. There was something very disturbing about this man. There was something in his eyes she had seen before. He had the vigilant gaze of a predator on the prowl.

"Have you ever seen either of these two women?" she asked, showing him a photo of Abigail Walters and another of Claudia Inez.

"Can't say that I have. They sure are lookers though, I'm sure I would have remembered them if I ever had the pleasure of making their acquaintance," Joe said in a manner that made Sydney's skin crawl.

"And what about this truck?" she asked, showing him the photograph of the black pickup with the burgundy tailgate.

"I've seen it around here once or twice, mainly on the backroads and two tracks. I don't know who it belongs to though. Lot of beat-up old Chevys in these parts, Fords too," he replied.

Completely off topic she asked, "Chief, by any chance, do you smoke?"

"Cigarettes?"

"Yes."

"That is an odd question, but no, I don't smoke, cigarettes," he said, leaving the innuendo to hang in the air.

"And what about this photo, do you recognize anyone?" she asked, showing him the photograph of her mother and what appeared to Sydney to be the chief himself many years ago.

"Nope, can't say that I do."

"Isn't that you standing next to the woman?"

"I guess it could be, in another life. Even if it was me, I still don't recognize anyone," he said with a sideways laugh.

"Isn't this the camp the kids called Camp Muck?"

"I think they actually referred to it as Camp Mucky Muck. That place was named Camp Waabanoowiwin, most likely by rich white folks wanting it to sound authentic after reading

Longfellow, when in fact the name could be looked upon by some as blasphemous."

"How so?"

"I will let you learn that little secret on your own," he replied cryptically.

"What are the chances of me getting in to have a look around the old campground on Plantation Road?"

"Slim to none. Besides, I've heard from a reliable source you already enjoyed a dip in the pond," he said with a sneer.

"Is this funny to you, chief?" Sydney asked, immediately furious at herself for falling prey to his goading.

His cell phone rang, and he answered it. He got up from his seat, put a finger in the air and walked toward the door. "This is important," he said and stepped out of the motel room.

"This is not over chief, I have a lot more questions," she called after him while he just nodded and walked away.

She went back into her room and slammed the door behind her. It was such a rookie mistake to let him push her buttons like that.

Shane walked in thirty seconds later. "Who was that?"

"That was the illustrious Joe LeBlanc, chief of the tribal police.

"Did you have any luck with him?"

"No, and I let him get under my skin. I think I may have tipped our hand a bit. I think Junior was right when he said we need to watch our asses. He sure is a smug bastard and I know he's more than aware of what is going on around here," Sydney said.

"What's the game plan for today?"

"I think I'll run over to Jack's and get us some breakfast while you take Katie for a walk. Maybe one of us will think of something by then."

"Sounds like a plan, or maybe not," Shane smiled.

"Shane, thanks a lot for everything. Your help means a lot to me," Sydney said and started her jaunt across the parking lot toward the smell of bacon.

Shane grabbed a quick shower, put Katie's leash on her and started for the door but Katie refused to budge. He tugged her leash a little harder and she simply dropped to her haunches in defiance. He grabbed a treat from a bag and held it up to her nose. When that didn't work, he walked to the motel room door, opened it, and tossed the treat out onto the sidewalk. Katie still wouldn't budge.

Suddenly he was enveloped in a cloud of cigarette smoke. Katie darted off to the bathroom and jumped into the bathtub. The bathroom door slammed shut behind her. Shane turned around to see a man silhouetted in the doorway.

"Who are you?" he asked. There was a familiarity about the man, but he couldn't place it.

"You have done well. You brought her here just as I instructed."

Shane opened his mouth to say something, but his voice was gone. His mouth was filled with a horrendous taste that forced him to gag. Moistened earth spilled forth from his agape orifice onto the motel room floor. Still unable to breathe he used his tongue to push out more of the foreign substance until it became a thick, soupy sludge that tasted of decay.

As he gagged, earthworms, beetles and other assorted hexapoda spilled forth onto the carpet. His eyes filled with confusion as he tried to speak. The more he tried to speak the more he spewed forth a multitude of multi-legged creatures.

"It's time for the reward I promised you. You will live forever," the man vanished into the same cloud from which he had appeared.

Shane felt a clamminess surrounding him. He tried to touch his face, but his arms oozed a viscous fluid that pooled at his feet and his limbs were no longer at his sides.

He sensed his core body temperature was falling rapidly until he reached a state of near hypothermia. He shivered and shuddered as his body mass melted into thick strands of slime saturating the carpet.

Cohesive thoughts no longer formed in his brain, he only acted out of instinct. His skin itched in the dry air, so he began to move toward the source of moisture he detected. He slithered as best he could on the dry, rough carpeting, through the open door and across the small grassy knoll. Without a sound he slipped beneath the waters of the Waiska River and made his way out into the depths of Lake Superior.

Sydney was crossing the parking lot of Jack's on her way back to the motel when she caught the faintest hint of cigarette smoke in the air and stopped dead in her tracks. She cocked her head sideways like a dog who just heard a cheese wrapper and tried to remember if she had left the motel door open. Then she realized it was Shane's room door that was open, and there was a thick black streak of sludge leading away from the room. Her eyes tracked the black streak until she spotted the source. She had to convince herself of what she was seeing.

On the riverbank, not more than twenty-five yards away from her was a lamprey the size of a python. The creature appeared to look over at Sydney before opening it gaping maw filled with dozens of razor-sharp teeth. Its beady black eye glistened at her just before the grotesque eel slipped into the depths of the Waiska.

She dropped the bags in her hands and took off on a dead run. Just as she came around the side of the motel and onto the walkway a beat up, black pickup with a burgundy tailgate sped out of the parking lot and down the road. Katie was howling as loudly as she could from the motel room bathroom. Not wanting to contaminate the scene Sydney walked across the furniture to get to the bathroom door. She led Katie around the puddle on the floor without much coaxing at all and put her in the truck.

Sydney had been around too many crime scenes not to know how this was going to play out. She went back into the motel room and loaded the files, the camera and developing equipment and everything else she thought might be damning evidence into Colby's truck. She then moved the truck over into the restaurant parking lot out of the way in case she had to make a quick break for it. She was not worried about getting rid of any fingerprints, she would have to tell them she was there so reluctantly she made the call.

Sydney was still sitting on the banks of the Waiska River next to a black, sludge trail when the crime scene unit as well as her boss, Captain Layton Turner, showed up on scene. She wiped her tears away as Layton walked up to her. He was a tall, lanky man who towered over her, even more so while she was sitting in the grass.

"Lamppinen, what in the fuck is going on around here?" Turner asked, straightening his tie.

She shrugged.

"Do you not have anything more than that to offer?"

"I don't know what the fuck is going on around here, okay?"

"Why are you mixed up with a county sheriff's deputy? What were you two doing in a motel together?"

"I'm not mixed up with anybody. Just what are you trying to insinuate?"

"I'm not insinuating anything. Were you fucking him, and the relationship took a shit?" Turner barked.

Sydney knew Layton was a hot head, but this was the worst she had ever seen him. Usually, his bark was worse than his bite, she wasn't so sure if that were the case now.

"No, I was not fucking him, Layton. We had separate rooms if you would have bothered to check."

"I didn't need to bother. I'm asking you outright. Did you shoot him?"

"Is there a body? Is there even any blood? Have I discharged a weapon?"

"Then what the fuck happened to him? It's a mess in there. Where is he?"

"The best I can figure, boss, is he's in there," Sydney said and pointed to where the creature had slithered into the river.

"Okay, if you are not going to be straight with me, I'm going to have to involve the FBI," Turner said, his face red and criss-crossed with throbbing veins.

"Please do! I beg you, get the FBI in here because I have no clue what is going on," Sydney burst into heaving sobs and walked away from the river. Her boss didn't follow her but instead walked over to Shane's motel room where Joyce and the rest of the crime scene unit were working.

The vanishing man's clothes were splayed out on the floor like a macabre chalk line. The smell was more atrocious than the smell of old death and many of the technicians were having a difficult time processing the scene. Layton stood at the threshold with his arms crossed absorbing the scene. The more he digested the more he wanted to regurgitate. This just didn't make any sense. Men didn't just vanish into thin air leaving behind bucket's full of slop and slurry. And as much as he didn't want to believe Sid's far-fetched tale, he had to. The evidence spoke for itself. There had been no struggle, no gunshots, and no evidence of a murder.

Sydney watched Layton from a distance. He seemed to have aged ten years in mere minutes. She wanted answers but was afraid there were none to give. She wanted to tell her boss about the black pickup truck, but then what. What about the truck? What if they managed to find it with the driver what in the hell would she tell them to arrest them for? Her hands were trembling when she dialed the phone.

"What in the hell is going on, Sid? I just caught the news. They are saying you killed Shane?"

"Who is saying that?"

"Mostly the media, but you know story, "unnamed sources" which means that information was leaked to them by someone, so at the very least there is one person at that crime scene who claims you murdered a sheriff's deputy."

"There's no body."

"What?"

"There is no body at the scene."

"Then what happened to Shane?"

"I don't know."

"Did he kill someone and leave you with the mess? Help me out here, Sid, this is making my head hurt."

Her voice trailed off. "It looks like he just slithered off into the river."

Twenty-Four

Layton Turner read the crime scene analysis report while waiting for Joyce to show up and explain it to him in person. There was no way what he was reading was even remotely possible. Hell, it wasn't even plausible. No fucking way did Deputy Shane Crane just disappear into thin air! He poured himself half a shot of Johnny Walker blue label and slammed it back.

"You wanted to see me, sir?" Joyce said. Normally she could dish out any gruff given to her, but this situation was atypical to say the least. The captain had every right to question her findings because she questioned them herself.

"Can you explain this this report to me in such a manner I may understand your findings?"

"Probably not. It says what it says because that was the story the evidence told us, sir."

"So, a man, a police officer was reduced to primordial sludge leaving only bones behind and there was no trace of any acid used?"

"None. No acid, lye, lime, nothing. There were no traces of any corrosive chemicals at the scene."

"How is that even possible?"

"I haven't a single clue, sir. I'm having all of the remains run again at an independent lab just to be on the safe side, but this will be the third time," Joyce said.

"And am I reading this correctly, there was lamprey DNA in this sludge but there were no lampreys or lamprey eggs found?"

"Correct."

"I'm not a biologist, is lamprey juice, goo, secretion, whatever in the hell you want to call it acidic or corrosive?" Turner asked.

"No sir, not in this universe."

"And this says you tested the trail from the motel room to the river and it had traces of lamprey DNA as well?"

"Yes, sir."

"Could you please respond to me with more than simple one-word answers? How about providing me with some details."

"Captain, if I had any details, I would gladly share them with you."

"And the bones found in the sludge, were they Deputy Crane's?"

"We are still waiting on those results. It will be a while before I can answer that."

Layton Turner sighed deeply and rubbed his temples. He took a long drink of his coffee and rubbed his temples again.

"Tell me, Joyce, what's your take on Lamppinen?"

"She's rough around the edges, but a straight shooter."

"She and the deputy have a thing going?"

"Not a chance, sir. Sid and Sheriff Patino have been in a strange sort of relationship dating back to high school. But it has been an exclusive relationship, so there's not a chance in hell she was stepping out with Deputy Crane."

"Has she gone absolutely bat shit crazy on us?"

"I saw no indication of that over the past few weeks of working with her. Like I said, she can be a bit abrasive, but aren't we all?"

"Then what in the hell is going on? What was she doing here?"

"The evidence led her here. As strange as it seems, she is on to something, something big and it's centered in Bay Mills. Talk to her, not as her boss, but as an outsider looking in. Go over her evidence with her."

"I wish I could, Joyce, but unfortunately Sid is in the wind.

Sydney Lamppinen sat on the edge of an open field watching the comings and goings on Plantation Road. Junior had given her a map to an old tree stand that was just under a quarter of a mile away from the pole barn which gave her an optimal vantage point while also providing good cover as long as she didn't move around too much. The tree stand, used for deer hunting, was sturdy with four enclosed walls and shooting ports so she was well concealed.

Having cried herself out the first day or so, anger was now the predominant emotion coursing through her veins. She had begun to consider Shane a friend and losing a friend was always difficult, but in this case, it was damned near impossible to cope with. So far, over the past few days Chief Joe had spent more time at the pot farm than away from it.

She scouted the area thoroughly and found no security cameras so either they were very well hidden, or they simply didn't exist. She had been camped out in the tree stand for three days coming down only to squat in the woods. On Colby's advice she had ditched her phone and purchased several burner phones which she destroyed after a single use.

"Hey, it's me," she said.

"Where are you?"

"It's best if you didn't know. How are you holding up?"

"I'm fine. Moving around is still a bitch but I have an in-home nurse who helps quite a bit, especially with Katie. Speaking of which, how did you manage to get her back here and why didn't you just stay when you dropped her off?" Colby asked.

"I didn't get her back there; she must have found her own way home. Thank God, I was so worried about her. She split from the motel on a dead run while I was loading the truck and I couldn't find her. I can't blame her though; I wish I could have done the same. I'm so sorry, Colby," Sydney said, it was obvious she was holding back tears.

"Sid, it wasn't your fault. None of this was your fault. I checked again when I got home and there has been no warrant issued for your arrest and there haven't been any more media releases about Shane, or whatever the hell he was. Other than that initial report which Layton seemed to get quashed with little fanfare."

"This just doesn't seem real."

"No, it doesn't that's for sure. I wish I could be there for you."

She laughed nervously. "Whatever you do, don't send me another one of your lizard people deputies."

"About that, I've done some digging and you were right, Shane wasn't from Bay Mills just as you suspected."

"No shit, a town as Podunk as this one and not one single person recognized him."

"I thought maybe we had heard him wrong, but no, it was right there in his file. He graduated from Brimley High."

"So, is she cute?"

There was a long silence. "Is who cute?"

"The nurse who is giving you sponge baths," Sydney said with a laugh.

"It's a guy, but yea, he is kind of cute. Hey, I checked out this Officer Proudman for you and what you have told me seems legit. He seems legit, so I think you can trust him. I took the liberty of mailing him some pre-paid debit cards for you to use until this thing blows over."

"You didn't have to do that."

"Sid, I have to be able to help you and this is the only way. No matter how much I want to be there for you, physically I just can't. I sent Deputy Simms up there tonight to see if Proudman needs any help. Hopefully, no one is watching him," Colby said with tears in his eyes. The urge to take her into his arms and hold her until the end of time was overwhelming him.

"Colby, Shane turned into a pile of sludge and slithered out into the river, nothing is going to fix that," Sydney said.

"Maybe Shane was eaten by whatever and it slithered back out into the river when it was finished," he said, regretting it immediately.

"Oh great, thanks for putting that disturbing image in my head. Now I've got to try and get some sleep while dreaming about land walking, man-eating lampreys. I love you," she said and hung up the phone before he even realized what she had said.

Colby poured some food into Katie's bowl and hobbled back to the kitchen table where he sat down to enjoy a cold cup of coffee. He was getting tired of constant pestering by the nurse, so he had sent him home early. The man's intentions were good, but he was much too motherly, especially given the fact the man was a large, hirsute beast of a man.

Katie picked at her food and then plopped down next to his feet. She hadn't had a decent walk in close to a week. Colby trusted her to run the property on her own, but she was having none of it. He couldn't go to the bathroom without having to squeeze her into the small cubicle with him. He still didn't know exactly what it was that happened in that motel room, but it sure the hell scared her to her core.

"Colby Patino," he answered his phone without checking to see who it was. He was hoping Sid would call, but it had been two days.

"Sheriff, it's Layton Turner. I'm Sydney Lamppinen's boss. I think we have met a time or two."

"Good morning, sir, how are things?"

"About as fucked up as they have ever been."

"I'm sorry to hear that."

"Listen, I know you and Lamppinen go way back, I'm not calling to make trouble for her. In fact, just the opposite."

"How so?"

"I'm looking at a comprehensive evidence report from more than one reputable source that makes absolutely no logical sense whatsoever. None. What in the hell kind of manure pile have you two stumbled into?"

"Honestly, I wish I could tell you. I've spent a large part of it sidelined. I would say talk with my deputy but we both know how that turned out."

"How much do you know about that?" Turner asked.

"Only the little bit Sid managed to spit out."

"Okay, I'm going to say this out loud, but it's against my better judgment. The slime, for lack of a better term, we tested had both DNA from Deputy Crane and that of a lamprey eel. Joyce Tammi assures me that there was no way possible that the evidence was contaminated or for Deputy Crane to have been in the advanced state of putrefaction under the given circumstances."

Colby was silent for several moments. "I'm not sure what to say to that."

"Oh, it gets better. Two days ago, the coast guard was called out into Whitefish Bay to a report of a fishing vessel being attacked by what the fisherman called a sea monster. The coast guard shot and killed a lamprey eel. A fucking six-foot long lamprey."

"That sounds pretty hard to believe, sir."

"You're damned right it's hard to believe. Impossible in fact. If you think I'm going to my superiors with these bizarre circumstances you are crazy, at least not until I have some answers."

"I wish I had some to give you, but I'm just as lost as you are."

"I'm not finished yet. To top things off, Joyce tested that damned lamprey the Coast Guard killed and though her findings are preliminary, the damned thing shares DNA with your deputy. How is that even possible?"

"Layton, nothing about this entire ordeal was physically possible, and yet, everything happened just the same," Colby said, a lot more scared for Sid now that the facts had been laid out on the table in front of him.

He spent the next fifteen minutes giving Turner the Cliffs Notes version on the camera, about the mother-daughter connection, about Sydney's father and everything else they had experienced.

"How am I supposed to respond to what you are telling me?" Layton said, wearing a sore spot in his temples from his constant rubbing.

"I don't expect you to be able to sir, in your shoes I don't think I would be able to."

"Listen, I like Lamppinen, she is a good trooper. If you say she had nothing to do with what happened to your deputy then I'm obliged to believe you."

"Absolutely nothing, sir. If anything, she's the victim in all of this," Colby said.

"Do you have a way of communicating with her?"

"In a limited capacity and only when she contacts me. I can send her texts but that is about it."

"I haven't mentioned any of this to anyone above my paygrade so it's just between us and I would like to keep it that way. I had administration put Sid on FMLA paid leave due to a serious illness in her family. That will buy her thirty days from now before anyone in payroll starts asking questions. Finish whatever the hell it is you two have started," Layton said, still rubbing his temples.

"Understood."

Layton Turner sighed deeply. The cop in him began to override the bureaucrat. "What is her threat level?"

"Sir?"

"She's out there all alone, isn't she? How much danger is she in? Is her life in danger?"

"For the most part, yes, she is in extreme danger. I can't physically help her no matter if I wanted to or not and she won't trust another of my deputies."

"That is completely understandable. I tell you what I can do. I will put together a small contingent of people I trust to keep things quiet. It's an elite assault unit who knows how to be discreet. You let her know that if the shit starts to hit the fan, we will be there for her," he said.

"Thanks, Layton that means the world to me. Hell, I might even hit that panic button myself before we get off the phone."

Sydney had been observing the pole barn for nearly a week and there had been no movement. It wasn't that there was not any suspicious movement, there was no movement whatsoever other than Skunk coming and going. How could Skunk be running an operation of that magnitude without a single worker? No suppliers coming to the property to deliver fertilizer, soil, even just plastic bags to package the finished products in. And even more perplexing was the fact there had been no shipments leaving the facility. Nothing. It just wasn't possible to run a business without shipments or deliveries.

She was cold, tired, and reeking worse than a polecat, so she decided to break off surveillance and head into the Sault to sleep in a bed for the night. Colby had sent her a text to let her know what Layton had said so she wasn't too concerned with being arrested if seen. But just the same, she took extra care to obey all the traffic laws on the way. There was no sense in tempting fate.

Colby also made it clear that she was okay to keep using his truck and to not feel guilty. It would be quite some time before he would be able to drive. She pulled into the Comfort Inn on the outskirts of town and unloaded her gear. It wasn't until after her long, hot shower that she realized the camera had taken more photos.

Sydney made sure to get a crash course in film developing from Shane in the motel room should the need ever arise. She soaked the film in the developing chemicals and went across to Applebee's to grab a bite of real food. The beef jerky, canned beans, and malted milk balls she had been living off while in the tree stand were doing a number on her colon.

She picked at her Bourbon Street Steak while scanning photos into the laptop when she realized the battery was getting low. She felt like an idiot for leaving the charging cord behind. There was still a little over an hour of battery life remaining, so she crossed her fingers. The first series of photographs simply took her breath away and made the field at Pine Stump Junction look like child's play.

The first several photographs were of the muck lake with the docks still intact and water in the lake instead of the current sludge. Orange buoys marked the safe swimming areas and there were two long strings of blue and white buoys dividing the lake into swimming lanes. Sydney recalled the swim team would practice there during the summers.

In the next series of photos all but two of the docks were missing and the other one was jutting out of the mud. The lake was gone. In the next two photos there were dozens of white lines just off the distant shore of the lake. She zoomed in but the image pixelated so badly she couldn't make out what the objects were. In her heart of hearts, she prayed her first impression would prove to be wrong.

The next four photographs confirmed her suspicions. They were human remains. Bones. From the angle they must have been resting on the bottom of the lake. She advanced to the next four photographs. In these she could see dozens of sets of remains, each shackled in chains and half buried in the silt.

Once she was able to stop crying, she called Colby. "I have to get in there. We have to get in there," she said.

"Slow down. What are you talking about, Sid?"

"The camera took more photographs. There are dozens of bodies at the bottom of the lake."

"What lake?" he asked, groggy from her having woken him up.

"The lake at the camp."

"Are you sure?"

"No. I'm only sure of what the photographs are showing. But the camera has not been wrong yet. I have to go out there," she said.

"No, Sid. You leave this to Layton. Just call him, tell him of your suspicions and let him do the rest."

"What is he going to do? You know he would never be able to get a warrant without any evidence of a crime. I need to go get him some proof."

"And then what? If you go in there without a warrant any evidence you might uncover will be inadmissible. You will lose your career and these killers will walk."

"Then I just have to find another way."

"What in the hell are you planning?"

"I'm planning to find my mother."

Twenty-Five

The more Sydney looked over the most recent photographs the more incensed she became. She was convinced that one of the bodies at the bottom of the bog belonged to her mother. Either way, she had to know.

She gathered up all the photographs that had been amassed over the course of the investigation and marked them on the backs with dates, locations and other information she thought might be pertinent. She put them into chronological order the best she could and put everything into folders and then into a mailing carton. Before leaving the Sault, she stopped and faxed the information she had gathered to both Colby and Layton.

There was a certain blanket of comfort wrapped around her. She had arrived at a point where she didn't care what other people thought about her. She didn't care if they thought she was bat shit crazy, hell even if they deemed her clinically insane. Sydney came to the realization she didn't care because she wasn't expecting to get out of this alive. If she couldn't bring these monsters to justice for all their past crimes, at least they would go down for her murder.

She checked her voicemail at work remotely and found a message from Layton Turner.

Sid, Layton here. Let me start out by apologizing for my behavior in Brimley the other day. I was completely out of line. I had a chat with Sheriff Patino and whatever it is you are planning; you don't have to do this alone. Also, I'm deeply sorry to hear about your dear, sweet aunt. Your thirty-day FMLA has been approved. Please call me when you get this message.

Sydney wished she could trust him, but she just couldn't. This was going to have to play out on her terms, her way, with her on her own. The last sequence of photos had told her as much. When she manipulated the bokeh it had revealed her destiny. She would be with her mother again.

Before leaving Sault Ste. Marie Sydney bought a cheap wig, some dark sunglasses, and an ugly hat. She knew it would prove to be a useless disguise, but that was the point. She may be able to blend in with the locals, but she would stand out to the people whose attention she wanted to attract. She also picked up extra ammunition for her service piece as well as her backup piece. This didn't bring her much solace as a part of her was certain bullets were not going to be of any use.

She found herself missing Katie's cold nose nudges on the drive back to Bay Mills. The malamute's scent was imbedded into every square inch of Colby's truck. An overwhelming sense of despondency invaded her, and Sydney had to pull over to the side of the road where she cried for a solid ten minutes. She wasn't sure if she were more angry, confused, or frightened. She hadn't heard from Junior for two days and found she was starting to worry about his well-being. If he was correct, more than one police officer had already disappeared while investigating the goings on in the reticent community so a third was not a preposterous conclusion to jump to.

She blatantly drove through town five miles per hour slower than the already snail's pace speed limit. The chief tried to play nonchalant as she cruised by, but she knew he was eyeballing her. It was a pleasant drive along the shore out past the Point Iroquois lighthouse and down to the motel overlooking Nadoway Point. The smell of frying whitefish and onion rings drifted on the breeze from a small restaurant down the street from her motel.

Sydney unpacked her store-bought menagerie and took a quick shower. After drying off she donned her disguise and headed for the marijuana warehouse on Plantation Road certain that old Chief Joe would be lurking somewhere in the weeds. It would be hard not to recognize the Luce County Sheriff's truck passing through town at a turtle's pace. She stopped in the middle of Plantation Road, right in front of the entrance to old Camp Mucky-Muck and got out of the truck. She walked up and down the road taking photographs from every angle. Half of the time she was not even firing off the shutter, just making the motions for appearances sake. She stopped just short of screaming out, "Hey you bastards, here I'm, come and get me."

After she was sure she had gotten their dander up Sydney returned to the small eight room motel and then walked over to the nondescript restaurant across the street. There were only two cars in the dirt parking lot which made her breathe a little easier. Sydney took seat in a red Naugahyde covered booth to the rear corner where she could see anyone or anything coming toward her. Her back was against the wall in more ways than one.

A manila folder sat on the table in front of her as she fanned through the photographs one by one. The lone waitress announced with glee that the cook had just taken a batch of cinnamon rolls out of the oven, so Sydney ordered one with a tall glass of milk and a cup of coffee. She was shocked to see that the pastry was as large as a dinner plate with more frosting than is on most cakes. The waitress assured her they were famous for their cinnamon rolls which seemed to be a common claim of many an eatery across the Upper Peninsula.

Sydney felt eyes on her so she readjusted herself in the booth seat so she could watch the watcher without being seen. It was the bubbly young officer with tri-colored hair she met the first night in Bay Mills. She made a discreet motion with her finger and the woman came bounding into the restaurant. So much for being clandestine.

The young woman slid into the booth across from Sydney. Her eyes immediately fell upon the gargantuan dessert, so Sid motioned for the waitress to bring another plate and another glass of milk as well. She cut the young woman off a very generous piece of the cinnamon roll.

"Hi, you're that cop that came into the department a while back, aren't you?"

"What gave me away?"

The woman gave Sydney an awkward, sideways glance and then laughed. "Sarcasm, that's funny. My name is Cali, like the state."

"Good morning, Cali. is there something I can do for you?" Sydney resisted the urge to test whether or not the woman knew California was the name of the state and not just Cali, but she was too afraid of what that answer might be.

She was sheepish and continued to glance around her like a meth head waiting on their dealer. Sydney was getting more nervous by the minute. She rested her hand on her weapon under the table.

"I saw you talking with Junior the other day when you were here, and I just wondered if you had seen him lately."

"No, why would I have seen him?"

"I overheard him and the chief arguing. I think it was about you. That was three days ago, and he hasn't been to work since. He doesn't answer his phone and Joe won't tell me anything. In fact, he yells at me if I even mention Junior," she started to cry.

"Sorry, I wish I could help you, but I haven't spoken with Officer Proudman or Chief LeBlanc since the last time I was in town," Sydney lied. She did not trust this woman, at this point she did not trust much of anyone.

"I'm just worried about him is all. He's a really nice guy," she said.

The woman got up from the booth, shot Sydney a forced smile and wiped a trickling tear from her eye. She watched her leaving the diner and had to wonder if the chief had sent her in there like a lamb to the slaughter. The waitress set a patty melt down in front of her distracting Sydney for just a moment during which Cali disappeared around the corner of the building. Sydney never saw her fingering the scar on the side of her head.

The motel room was eerily quiet and lonely. Sydney's entire world was spinning out of control with no way she could see of stopping it. She had not wanted to part with the camera, but she didn't want it to disappear forever either, so she packed everything up and mailed it to Colby while she was still in Sault Ste. Marie. She was lost deep in her thoughts so when her cell phone chimed alerting her to a new text, she almost screamed out loud.

Sid, are you there?

When she didn't recognize the number she cautiously responded with a generic, "Who is this?"

Junior.

"What did you find out about that button I gave you?"

Didn't I already tell you about that? It came from Chief LeBlanc's uniform from back in the eighties.

"You told me. That was a test. I can't trust anyone right now."

No, no you can't!

"That young girl, Cali, from the station ran into me, rather tracked me down. She claimed you are missing and that she is concerned about you."

Do not trust her!

"I don't. Are you in trouble?"

We are both in trouble, but I don't think we are in any immediate danger. I found some information pertaining to those two missing officers. I think I know what happened to them. It's all connected.

"Where are you?" Sydney asked, not wanting to have the conversation via text. She wanted to see who she was conversing with face to face.

Do you remember where you found the button? It is the center of it all. I think your mother is here. Hurry.

Everything about the conversation screamed trap but she had already admitted to herself she was doomed if she were to go at this alone. She had no other choice but to trust Officer Proudman, but that didn't mean she was going to walk into a trap either. She pulled out the photographs that were taken the night her father's ghost dangled from the rafter.

From the window, the dock where her mother was last see was visible off in the distance. The path led north to the edge of the lake before bending off to the west to follow the far shore. But there was something else there was well. The reeds and sawgrass were spaced just a little bit further apart in one area no bigger than a deer trail. She brought up a map of the area in her web browser and scanned the area. The trail led across the northeastern edge, across the dirt road and into Cranberry Lake Bog. She shuddered at the memory of her father admonishing her for exploring the marshland when she was still quite young. She would never forget the ghostly white look on his face. She understood now her father must have known what lurked out in the swamp.

The phone rang as she was getting out of the shower. She was not in the mood to speak with Colby but when she didn't recognize the number she answered.

"Lamppinen."

"Sid, it's Joyce."

"What can I do for you?" she asked with apprehension thick in her voice.

"I'm afraid it's what I can do for you," she said. "I have some information you are going to want to hear."

"Shoot," Sydney said.

"You may want to use different terminology. I finished my preliminaries of the remains in the graves at Pine Stump Junction. So far, half of them were not only older when they died, but their bodies had also been in the ground much longer."

"Mothers and their daughters," Sydney said, having already figured out the pattern. A pattern of which she was somehow a part.

"You would be correct. While I didn't find any wounds that would point to a cause of death in the older victims, each of the younger victims died from a bullet wound to the head. However, in each case the wound was slightly different," Joyce explained.

"Different how?"

"The angle and positioning were just a little different each time."

"The victims flinched?"

"No, I don't think so. This got me to thinking, so I went up to Abigail Walters' room and examined her. The wound on the side of her head was similar to the skeletal remains but different. It was not a bullet wound. A woman named Claudia Inez was there visiting her and had the same scarring."

"I'm not sure I like where you are going with this. Was this a Dahmer kind of thing?"

"Bingo, give the lady a cigar. I don't think this psychopath ever meant to kill any of his victims. I'm positive he was perfecting his methods over time. Sid, he was creating slaves."

"And he was successful more than once."

"The quandary for this bastard was that the women eventually recovered from their wounds and their brains healed over time. While they didn't regain all their memory, they recouped enough to question whatever line of bullshit he was feeding them and more than likely tried to leave him which ultimately cost them their lives."

"At least now I know what I am up against," Sydney said.

"Where are you?"

"Bay Mills."

"You need to be incredibly careful. The chief of the tribal police is knee deep in this bullshit. With a therapist's help I was able to extract from Abigail what happened during her ordeal. It was a man named Joe, the chief of police, who rescued her or so went the line of bullshit he fed to her. He kept her hidden away for over a year. I figure she started getting antsy to leave and he shoved the poor girl over the cliff to start all over again with a new victim. From what I have gathered Eno would pick up the bodies with his boat from the base of the cliffs and they would dispose of them later. With the increase in recreational activity out there on the lake I guess Abigail was found before they could get rid of her body," Joyce said, her voice heavy with contempt.

"Jesus Christ. How long has this been going on?"

"Decades."

"And what about older victims? How did they die?"

"I can't determine that by the remains. There's no sign of trauma on any of the older remains. Just what is it you are up to?" Joyce asked in a gruff, accusing tone.

"Excuse me?"

"Sheriff says you won't answer his calls. Layton Turner has been pacing like a caged tiger and no one will tell me a damned thing."

"Joyce, I have to stop these bastards at all costs. Make sure you take good care of me," Sydney said as she hung up and then turned off her phone. She needed time to think.

The road leading out to her father's cabin was deserted and more forlorn than usual. She stopped a mile or two away from the cabin and stood next to the truck to get a lay of the land in the daylight before proceeding any further. Shane was right about the area being so quiet it was unnerving. She was surrounded by swamps and lakes, yet not one single frog croaked. Not one lone night bird zipped past her in the shadows hot on the tail of an unsuspecting mosquito. Not one cricket chirped, or bat squeaked, there was nothing but silence. Even the breeze didn't blow gentle whispers through the treetops. It occurred to Sydney that it was because she was surrounded by death.

She pulled the truck off the road and onto a two track where she parked and started walking toward the cabin. She stayed off the road and hidden in the reeds that surrounded the perimeter of Cranberry Lake. As far as she could tell, there were no signs of anyone else having come this way. There was no movement near the house, nor any voices carrying on the wind, absolutely no sound whatsoever.

Suddenly a hint of smoke reached her nostrils, not cigarette smoke, something much more astringent. She crouched in the weeds and studied the back of the cabin. Wisps of smoke reached like boney fingers towards the sky, several shades of gray blending into one.

After fifteen minutes without so much as a blade of grass moving, she felt it was safe enough to proceed. There were traces of fabric still smoldering in the campfire ring. The remnants of a police uniform from what she could gather. The collar had dried blood imbedded in the fabric. She looked up into the window of the breakfast nook overlooking the lake and saw something reflecting off the glass.

Against every shred of common sense she had remaining, she went into the cabin and up to the breakfast nook. Her hands were trembling as she opened the door to the small room. Sydney sighed in relief when it turned out to be empty. There was no bloated, gray corpse swinging from the rafter, but something had been reflecting off the glass. There was an object dangling in the far corner. It was a tribal officer's badge. Junior's badge, and it was covered in blood.

Every instinct Sydney possessed screamed at her to call it in and wait for the cavalry to arrive. She had almost convinced herself to do just that when the first scream echoed across the marshland. Because the night was so silent the man's torment rang out as if it were right there in the room with her. With her stomach twisted in knots she ran out of the house and down the edge of the lake until she came to the small deer trail that led through the reeds out into the bog. There was a short distance where she would have to cross the road and would be exposed so Sydney took several minutes to gather her nerve before darting out into the open to cross the road.

She entered the bog on a dead run but was immediately slowed down by the peaty soil. She was out of breath and had not heard Junior scream for quite some time, so she squatted and listened. Another scream echoed from the north. She paused to think, she was certain the first scream she heard had come from the south, but sounds could play tricks on a person's ears out here in the swamps.

There was a loud metallic sound followed by a terrifying scream from the eastern side of the bog. She darted off in that direction but stopped after fifty yards and hunkered behind a large silver maple. For some reason, the leaves were showing their backsides, an indicator of rain but there wasn't a cloud in the sky.

Another scream split the stillness, this one emanating from a completely different direction. She was ready to run but then Sydney remembered the story Colby told her about the night the truck ran him down and how the ringing of his cell phone kept coming at them from all different directions. She ran toward the sound but quickly doubled back and hunkered down in the brush. Sure enough, the sound came from the opposite direction, and she realized she was being toyed with.

When looking at aerial shots of the place for surveillance she noticed an out of place formation of trees near the center of the marsh. There was a long, tree–lined path leading toward a circular grove with a single large tree in the center of a clearing. She waited until nightfall completely settled in before making her move. Hopefully, the sky would remain cloudless and allow her to navigate the swamp by the stars.

The depth of the water was nearly mid-thigh and her feet sunk into the freezing cold muck above her ankle. This put the water in an extremely uncomfortable place on her body, especially being as cold as it was. With each step the cold water lapped at her crotch and caused her skin to burst into gooseflesh. And of course, each time the water passed through her legs with a tickle her overactive imagination screamed lamprey. Eventually she found the trail leading to the small grove and was able to extract herself from the murky depths.

Once she was out of the blackness of the swamp she was exposed under the glowing moonlight. She heard another loud metallic sound followed by yet another horrific scream. She was certain now that Junior was being tortured, whether it be to extract information or simply as a tool to lure her to her demise she didn't know.

The orange glow of a bonfire illuminated the circular grove, and she could see Chief LeBlanc standing over Junior who was staked out by his arms and legs. For some reason she envisioned some sort of satanic ritual complete with resplendent robes and demonic looking scepters adorned with goat's heads but instead found Joe standing there in mud caked khakis and a dingy, tattered wife beater.

Sydney leapfrogged the trees staying to the shadows, inching ever closer to the two men. Another metallic sound echoed through the night and Junior screamed. She was close enough to see what was happening and tears burst forth in rivers down her cheeks.

Junior was been staked out, naked, by his arms and legs forming a large X in the dirt. Each wrist and each ankle were held in place by bear traps that were spiked into the earth. Joe was spreading the jaws apart on the traps until they clicked open. He would then tap the release mechanism with a dead limb causing it to snap shut with a violent bite on the man's already broken and mangled limbs.

"Well, my friend, this is not working like I had hoped. I guess she is just going to let you suffer," Joe taunted.

Sydney eased herself back out into the water so she could maneuver into a better position without being seen. Once she could see what Joe was up to, she knew she had to do something, but she also was quite aware of the fact Junior was already as good as dead. There would be nothing she could do to save his life even if she managed to get to him before he bled out. By the time emergency services would be able to get to him, he would most assuredly have succumbed to his wounds.

"Maybe this will get her attention," Joe said as he walked over to the fire and pulled a glowing red cattle brand from the coals. "I know you are out there Sid, I can smell you," he said while sniffing at the air and grunting like a wild pig.

Sydney maneuvered herself into such a position she felt confident she could rush the man while firing and be able to hit him at least once.

Joe let the red-hot brand hover over Junior's eye. The man's eyebrows and lashes singed and his skin smoldered. He was too broken to even scream but managed an animalistic moan that broke Sydney's heart.

"You son of a bitch put it down," Sydney screamed as she ran toward him. She got off two shots but they both went wide before the ground suddenly gave way beneath her feet and she plummeted into a chasm in the earth.

Twenty-Six

Clarity inched along Sydney's cerebral cortex at a funeral's pace. The clearer her mind edged back into view the more she was acutely aware she was being crushed. She heard a metallic "ching" and then more weight being added on top of her, and she understood she was being buried alive. The air around her was infused with the earthy smell of worms, dirt, and decay.

Another load of dirt added weight down toward her ankles. She tried to draw her legs toward her, but they were completely buried so she couldn't retrieve her back up piece from her ankle holster. She felt the cool night air on her face but didn't dare open her eyes and tip her hand that she wasn't dead. She felt Joe climb down on top of her in the shallow grave just before she felt a punch to her head near the temple. The left side of her head was on fire deep down into her brain and she struggled to focus.

So, was this his ritual? This creep lured women out into the woods, shot them in the side of the head and then buried them alive only to dig them up later? Why? What was the purpose of this charade? Why not just abduct the women, or simply kill them?

Between shovels full of dirt, she eased her hand up to her head. Armed with the knowledge gleaned from her discussion with Joyce, Sydney had taken precautions before entering the fray. The prosthetic device she fashioned was still in place though the pseudo flesh was torn, and the interior metal panel had a decent sized dent. The fake blood must have looked real enough in the dark that it fooled Chief LeBlanc. Although, she was suffering from a monster of a headache despite the protection from the prosthetic device.

She felt a warm dampness seeping through her clothes to her skin. She opened her eyes just a slit, enough to see Junior's mangled corpse was the brunt of the weight baring down on her, and his blood was oozing down all around her. She almost screamed when she realized the objects poking her in the back, arms and legs were not stones as she had first thought, but bones. Human bones.

She managed to turn her body just enough that she was able to get a better assessment of the damage to Junior's body. He was in bad shape. In fact, it was only by the grace of God he was not already dead. His once dark, ruddy complexion was ashen, and his breathing was slow and shallow. Another shovel of dirt landed in the poor man's breadbasket causing Junior to let out a loud grunt.

"Holy shit, you're still alive down there? You are one tough son of a bitch, Proudman, I'll give you that," Joe's voice carried down into the pit.

She heard the hammer of a revolver cock back. "I'm sorry about this, Junior," Sydney said, rolling the man over so she could free her arms but also roll him out of the way of the two shots Joe fired into the open pit. Luckily neither bullet found flesh. She clamped her hand over his mouth to keep him from screaming. "I promise you, I'm going to get us out of this," she breathed into his ear.

Shovels full of dirt continued to rain down on her but she was able to steal glances between each one. When she rolled Junior over, she realized she was laying on Joe's discarded uniform shirt. She pulled the brown shirt up over her face to keep the dirt from covering it. She then folded her arms to her sides with her palms facing up. When the time came, she should be able to push through the loose, wet dirt.

Her mind raced at a mile a minute settling on a plan that just might work. She convinced herself Joe was not trying to bury her alive, well at least not with the intentions of killing her. Each of the women she interviewed, Abigail and Claudia remembered bits and pieces of being buried but then this stranger, came along and saved them. Piecing that together with what Joyce had told her she figured out Joe's game, or so she hoped.

She heard metal tools being tossed into the back of a steel truck bed. The truck engine fired up and the tires spit gravel as the truck pulled away. A black truck with a burgundy tailgate she imagined. Once the rumble of the truck disappeared into the night, silence settled in around her. She had never been claustrophobic but being buried alive with a dying man on top of her and a scattering of human bones beneath her was putting that phobia to the test.

The broken man lying next to her was still breathing, albeit labored and shallow. The dirt held him firmly in place but her turning him to his side saved him from added pressure on his chest and allowed him to breathe. In his condition she wasn't sure if that was a good thing or not.

Sydney sang songs in her head for what she estimated to be an hour before making her next move. After running through the entire ABBA catalog of hits three times, she felt it was safe enough to make her egress. She turned her hands so they were touching backs together and used a breast stroke motion to pull at the dirt above her up and away from face. She held her hands in position which funneled the dirt down into the gaps she created by turning slightly sideways. She didn't think Joe had buried them very deep, he was fat and lazy and surely didn't want to work too hard at digging up his buried treasure.

The more she dug away at the loose soil the harder it became for her to move and the more pressure it applied to the dying man. Her heart ached every time he moaned in pain and there was not one single thing she could do to comfort him. She worked at uncovering herself for hours and finally felt the cool, night air filtering in from above. She pulled the covering off her face and gazed up through the fist sized hole at a crescent moon dangling overhead.

Her first attempt to sit up or even outstretch her arms was futile. The more she moved the more Junior cried out in pain. Guilt ate away at her every time she wished he would just shut the hell up. She managed to work enough of the dirt away and push it underneath herself to elevate her until she was able to get an elbow out onto the firm ground. She scooted her butt until she was almost sitting upright and wrenched herself painfully to the side. Using both arms she was able to break free of the grave.

Once free she jumped back down into the pit and tenderly brushed the dirt away from Junior's face. She used the same scrap of cloth and covered his face before piling the dirt strategically around his head. A few more shovels of dirt to fill in the gap she created when she freed herself and she felt the grave looked damned close to what it was when Joe left.

Sydney found a big tree and scooted her back up against it and relaxed as best as she could. She needed some rest. Her mouth was dry, chalky and she would have sold her soul for a bottle of water. Dew from the wet grass was going to have to suffice. Off in the distance the "who cooks for you," call of a barred owl soothed her as she drifted off to sleep.

Sam Jenkins rolled over for the third time in less than fifteen minutes thanks to a pair of barred owls courting each other from a limb directly above his tent. Even though it was still well before sunrise he unzipped his tent and crawled out to face the day. He poured a lukewarm cup of coffee from his Stanley and put a pot of water on the camp stove to boil for a fresh brew.

Rain spit down in a gentle drizzle, just hard enough to make it annoying. Once the coffee was done brewing, he sat in his camp chair in the rain just to spite nature and the weatherman who forecasted a rain free night. So much for following the science. Ten hours of constant rain throughout the night left Sam feeling thankful his tent hadn't leaked.

The rain finally relented, and the sun started to peek out. It was threatening to be a scorcher of a day. Sam gathered up his gear and began his hike into the bogs on the outskirts of a secluded nature preserve. He was on a mission to get a few photographs of a reclusive bull moose he knew to be in the area.

Sam spied a fresh trail leading deep into the bog, so he opted to take the new trail instead of the well-worn path he usually used. He knew it was a risk and he might be forced to double back if the animal had bushwhacked into the thick scrub which would waste the better part of his day. As luck would have it, his moose was not too adventurous and stuck to the lowlands. Most likely because the animal wasn't pressured or threatened by human presence as this was some of the most desolated landscape in Michigan, if not the country.

A rusty blackbird was thoroughly engaged in bathing in a small creek, so Sam plopped his tripod down and fired off a few shots of the bland, yet unique looking bird with its haunting golden eyes. While he took a little respite from hiking, he scoured the surrounding area for tracks, droppings, and other signs of his moose's presence. As he wandered, he waxed philosophical about his photography and how he cherished being able to freeze a particular moment in time, capturing it forever as it was and never will be again. One day when he became too old, or too feeble to hike these harsh environments he would be able to look back on his life's travels with reverence.

Sam rounded a wide arcing hairpin in the trail with his head down and eyes to the ground when he heard loud rustling straight ahead of him. When he glanced up his heart skipped a beat, there was a moose calf just off the trail in a small patch of swamp. With deliberate, slow movements Sam set the tripod down and readied his Canon. He took the cable release in his hand and fired off several shots without overthinking which he had a tendency of doing.

He shifted his weight and a twig snapped underfoot causing the calf to raise its head and issue a warning which was half bellow, half bleat as if the creature had not mastered either. From behind him Sam heard splashing followed by the mother's grunt and realized he had somehow managed to maneuver himself precariously between a mother and her young. Her hackles were raised, and her ears were sloping to the rear which was not a good sign. With no other option available Sam began to creep backwards one methodical step at a time with his tripod in front of him as a last line of defense. The cow took a half step toward him but then held her position, feigning an attack.

Sam fought the urge to turn and run while slowly backing away from the mother and child. Sharp limbs gouged into his calves and lower back as he pressed against a patch of bearberry that argued against his intrusion. The moose charged and Sam stumbled backward into the shrubbery which gave way against his weight and dropped him into a small clearing. Inexplicably the cow stopped her charge and held fast on the other side of the glade. She gave a couple of snorts, paced back and forth but refused to cross the boundary between the bearberry bushes and the clearing. Finally, she abandoned the confrontation and returned to her calf.

Sam gathered his spilled gear, dusted himself off and began to look for an alternate route out of the clearing in the opposite direction from the mother and child. His attention was focused on the perimeter of the small clearing, and he wasn't paying attention to where he was walking. Something grabbed at his ankle, tripped him up and sent him sprawling to the ground in a flurry of vulgarities that made him blush even though he was alone in the vast wilderness.

After rubbing his angry knees, Sam looked around for what tripped him up and let loose a scream once he saw a human hand attached to a severed arm. He then saw he was surrounded by at least a dozen bloody, human arms protruding from the soil with old, wrinkled hands contorted into grotesque claws. He doubled over and vomited his meager breakfast of oatmeal and coffee. After rinsing his mouth, he dialed 911 and started running for his car on Pond Road.

"What in the hell were you doing by yourself in Jinny Palms without telling anyone where you were going?" Sheriff Blake Jenkins barked through his open window before even getting out of his patrol car. Dust trailed the sheriff's cruiser as he came to an abrupt stop. He was in a sour mood after spilling his coffee during the long trip down bad roads to get out to the remote nature preserve.

Sam simply shook his head in response.

"Sam, what has you so spooked? Aimee claims you wouldn't give her any details other than you needed to see me out here. Are you injured?"

Again, Sam just shook his head. He was afraid that if he started talking, he would then have to accept what he had witnessed as being real and that was a situation he didn't think he could handle.

"Come on, Sam, give me a little help here," the sheriff, and incidentally, Sam's brother-in-law prodded.

Sam tried several times to talk but the words wouldn't come out. Finally, he said, "I found something terrible back there, in the bog."

"Come on and show me what you found," Blake said. He knew his brother-in-law could sometimes been an overly dramatic drama queen, but he had never seen him this distraught, not even when Trump won the presidency.

"No, I am not going back there, ever," Sam said.

"Sam, what the fuck has gotten into you?" the sheriff blurted out, his patience having worn thin.

"Blake, call me a coward, call me a pussy, call me whatever you like, but I am not going back into that swamp, ever."

"Fine, have it your way," Blake said, giving a whistle and a hand wave beckoning his deputy to join him.

Sam showed the law enforcement officers the trail back to the clearing and went to his car without another word. Blake always considered the man a whiney ass, but this was taking things a bit too far. Had the man run into a poacher's gut pile? Maybe an illegal dump site knowing Sam. But there was nothing back in that swamp that should have shaken the man up as much as it had.

"What do you think is back here, Sheriff?" Chippewa County Sheriff's Deputy Brad Larkin asked.

"I don't have a clue. Sam wasn't too forthcoming with the details."

The deputy laughed. "Maybe he ran across a group of hunters wearing MAGA hats."

Sheriff Jenkins shot his deputy a disapproving glance while suppressing a smile. He pointed to fresh tracks in the sand heading straight towards them indicating this was the direction Sam had exited the swamp.

"Looks like Sam wasn't bullshitting us, he was on a dead run according to the distance between his footprints," Deputy Larkin said.

That last two dozen donuts or so were taking a toll on Sheriff Jenkins as he plodded though the loose sand and scrub patches carrying twenty or so pounds too many. He stopped to catch his breath and waved his deputy on. Larkin took his cue and trotted on ahead until he busted through the scrub and into the clearing.

"Sheriff," he screamed as loud as he possibly could while holding back dry heaves.

Blake picked up the pace, his body screaming at him with very step that he should have retired ten years ago. Sweat was pouring down his brow from under the brim of his hat when he finally made it to his deputy. He took several moments to gather himself before bushwhacking through the scrub and into the clearing. The sight before him took his breath away.

Rimming the edge of the glade were at least a dozen human arms jutting grotesquely out of the ground. He took a moment to gather in the licentious spectacle laid out before him before walking over to the nearest blood-soaked appendage. Shaking his head in disgust he dropped to his knees and began to pull the ground away from the arm to uncover the body.

"Sheriff, I don't think there's a body buried there, just the arm," Larkin commented between breaths.

"What makes you say that?"

"Over there by where the bearberry was disturbed, one of the arms are lying flat. Sam must have tripped over it and that's what spooked him."

The sheriff nodded, struggled back to his feet and walked over to the prone arm. He surmised that at one time it had belonged to a woman in her sixties or seventies. He moved the appendage gently with a stick, trying to preserve any evidence while still being able to examine it. Larkin's observation was indeed correct, the arm had been hacked off at the elbow joint and there was no matching body buried in the ground. The earth around each of the arms was hard packed, undisturbed for years if not decades except for just enough soil to bury the arms standing upright.

"Just what in the hell is this?" Blake Jenkins commented aloud to himself.

Both men stood in the center of the clearing absorbing the atrocity laid out before them. Larkin was further disturbed by the unnerving silence. Not a single songbird chirped out a song. Not a single buzzard circled overhead even with a smorgasbord of flesh splayed out for the taking. Whatever happened in this clearing, it just wasn't natural. As he turned in a slow, tight circle something struck him as odd and he walked from arm to arm looking at the hands and jotting letters into his notebook.

"What is it Larkin?"

"Sir, I think you need to get in touch with Layton Turner right away."

"Layton? The state police commander?"

"Yes, sir."

"Why would we need the state police?"

"How many people named Sydney do you know of sheriff?"

"Larkin, spit it the fuck out before I bust your ass."

"You know my middle daughter was born deaf."

"Yes, but what does that have to do with anything going on here?"

"These hands are all arranged in ASL, American Sign Language."

"Oh, fuck a duck. What do they say?" he asked, gripping his forehead and squeezing tightly to ward off the monster headache that threatened to invade his brain.

"They spell out, *Sydney is mine.* Sir, that's a pretty unique name, especially for the Upper Peninsula. It just can't be a coincidence."

The sheriff nodded with his eyes closed. "Go back to the car, get in touch with dispatch and have them send the crime scene unit. Also, have them look into any recent missing persons reports. While you're there grab the crime scene tape from the trunk of the patrol car and come back here to tape off the area."

Larkin nodded and took off on a slow trot away from the clearing back to the sheriff's patrol car. Blake Jenkins circled the assemblage of human debris strewn out in front of him. Right away he observed several of the hands were adorned with what appeared to be rather expensive wedding rings and other jewelry indicating that wasn't simply a thief disposing of his victims. And while he was not versed in sign language, it was apparent from the florist's wire arranging the fingers these gestures were deliberate and were arranged in this manner to send a message. He sighed and dialed a number with reluctance.

"Layton Turner," the man answered his private line.

"Layton, Blake here."

"Good morning, Blake. I've been meaning to call you. I'm really sorry about missing Ketchum's retirement party," Layton started.

"That's not why I called. We can catch up on the chit chat some other time. I've got a mess out here in Jinny Palms."

Considering recent events this was the last thing Layton wanted to hear. He braced himself for the worst. "What have you got, Sheriff?" he asked, putting the conversation back on a professional level.

"I know this is going to sound strange, but trust me, I wouldn't be asking if I didn't think it was necessary. Your trooper, Lamppinen, is she into something or in trouble of some kind?"

The line was silent so long Blake thought the call had dropped.

Layton took a deep breath. "What have you found? Please tell me you haven't found her body."

"Not in so many words, and yet, we found several bodies. Or at least parts of bodies."

📷   📷   📷

"Any word from Sid?" Colby asked.

"Nothing so far, I'm afraid," Layton Turner replied, handing Colby a take-out coffee.

"I don't like this one bit. I know she told us to trust her, but this has been way too long without any word from her."

"It gets worse. She left word she was staying at a motel just outside of Bay Mills. I called this morning, and they haven't seen her for days."

"Maybe she checked out."

"No, I had the desk clerk check out her room. Some of her belongings are still there. I checked with a diner across the street from the motel and the waitress remembered seeing her two days ago, but not since."

"And the chief?"

"I spoke with a woman at the Bay Mills Police Department, she said the chief was not there but would be back soon. I asked about Deputy Proudman, and she got a little snippy with me. I got a very strange vibe from the way she talked, almost robotic like her answers were rehearsed. There's something else," Layton said, handing Colby his phone with a photograph of the scene at Jinny Palms.

"What in the hell is this?" Colby asked.

"The sheriff's deputy assures me that those hands are arranged to spell out *Sydney is mine*. I also received a call from the Canadian authorities. They found a charter boat washed ashore at Pointe Louise. It looks like it was a bingo cruise filled with blue hairs from Bay Mills."

"Is it safe to assume they were missing their arms?"

"Yes, but even worse, most of them were still alive."

Colby's stomach lurched. "What is your gut instinct telling you?"

"That Joe LeBlanc is up to his elbows in this," Layton said, immediately regretting the turn of expression.

"Something doesn't add up though. How would Chief LeBlanc know we would find the hands out in the middle of nowhere?"

Layton's phone rang, interrupting the conversation. He stepped a few paces away and answered in case it was bad news regarding Lamppinen. There was a long pause, during which Colby could hear some excited commotion echoing over the speaker but couldn't make out what anyone was saying.

"Good news. Sid turned her phone on, and our techs were able to triangulate her location. She's at her place in Cranberry Lake," Layton said.

"We have to go," Colby said.

"You are in no condition to travel, sheriff."

"I sure as hell am not going to just sit here. I will be fine, just as long as you don't expect me to chase anyone."

Layton Turner made a few phone calls and within twenty minutes he was able to assemble a small elite team of Michigan State Police resources and had them meet up at the Luce County Sheriff's office. He kept the team small with only a handful of officers but had the forensics team on standby with Joyce taking the lead at her insistence. As soon as everyone was together, they headed out for Cranberry Lake.

Sydney trembled as she huddled against the rough bark of the ancient oak. It was the second night since climbing out of the shallow grave. This sick son of a bitch buried these poor women and left them for days. Guilt ate at her for not trying to go get help for Junior, but she just didn't have the energy. Furthermore, even though she had protected herself from Joe's shot to her head, she realized it had still done some damage to her brain. She was out of sorts but couldn't put her finger on why. At the very least she had suffered a severe concussion.

Rain started coming down, little misty droplets at first but was now pelting her in sheets of cold wetness. The clouds darkened the sky to the point she couldn't tell if it were the darkest of night or if it were nearing daybreak. The smell of ozone hung thickly in the air from the numerous bolts of lightning flashing across the sky.

She was nodding off for the umpteenth time when she heard him coming long before she saw the headlights of the truck breaking through the trees. She found herself hoping and praying it was Colby coming to rescue her, but she knew better. Besides, she had to see this through to the finish, she already convinced herself there was no rescuing her from this one.

Joe's bladder was about to burst so he backed off the accelerator. He was having a hard time containing his excitement. He had waited a long time for this one. Granted she was much older than he preferred, but he had also lusted after her since she was a little girl, so he hoped the wait would be worth it. Maybe she was finally the one. He hoped his dear old brother Frank would be able to watch what he was going to do to his little princess from beyond the grave.

The headlights of the truck glared over the open grave glistening with rain. Something looked off about the shallow grave, but Joe dismissed it as settling due to the unforeseen deluge. His stomach took a sour turn. What if she had drowned in there? He hadn't counted on the rain, so he didn't dig her up the previous night as planned. He was so giddy about capturing his white whale that he drank a whole fifth of Jack and was too hungover the next day to come and retrieve her.

He quickly turned the truck around and backed up to the grave. Joe slipped on a dark green poncho and pulled the hood up tight around his head which obscured his peripheral vision, an oversight not wasted on Sydney who was standing tense in the shadows. He cursed himself as he dug into the wet mud with his spade, his timeworn back screamed out in defiance with every heavy shovel full he pulled out. He wiped off his glasses and took a long, hard look at the muddy pit. The dead cop was still in there, but she wasn't.

He turned to swing with the shovel, but he was too late. Sydney landed a solid shot with a tree branch that put him on his back. He reached for his sidearm, but she stomped on his hand with enough force to break bones. A flash of lightning streaked across the sky and illuminated the field along with Joe's frightened grimace, bringing a satisfied smile to her face. The sick bastard was afraid of her, terrified in fact.

"You are nothing but a cowardly piece of shit," she said, planting a solid boot to his face.

Sydney grabbed the man's handcuffs and cuffed him to the brush guard bumper on the front of his truck. Shards of Deputy Conners still clung to crevices of the steel bumper. She grabbed the shovel and carefully removed the mud from Junior's face. She grabbed blankets from the cab of the truck that had been intended for her and covered Junior as quickly as she could before ripping the poncho off Joe and tucking it around the man in the grave as well. Before covering his head, she checked his pulse and was amazed to find he was still alive.

"Why you sneaky little bitch," Joe said, regaining consciousness.

Sydney realized the prosthetic she had used to protect herself was dangling loose away from her shaved scalp. She ripped it the rest of the way off with a scowl and tossed it on the ground next to him. She strode over and kicked the man square in the teeth.

"Don't ever call me bitch," she said and picked up his service revolver and slipped it into the front of her pants. "And just what in the hell are you smiling about?" she asked.

"You're in deep shit now, bitch," he sneered, earning himself another boot to the face.

The wind shifted ever so slightly, and Sydney caught the faintest hint of cigarette smoke. She spun on her heels and was face to face with Skunk, or whatever the hell he was. The man was standing twenty-five yards or so away from her. She started to pull the revolver from her waistband.

"Put that away, it will be of no use to you," he said with a dismissive wave of his hand.

She ignored him and drew the revolver. She fired and missed. She assumed a shooter's stance and fired another two rounds. The entity before her turned into a smoky mist and neither bullet found its mark. She pulled the hammer back and fired once more and once more the man appeared before her with a sinister smile greasing his face but unharmed.

"That's four," Joe laughed, and she back kicked him in the forehead.

"Oh, you are so going to pay for that. The things I am going to do to you," he said and jerked at the handcuffs with a metallic rattle.

Sydney popped open the cylinder of the revolver and checked the spent cartridges. Each one was missing the bullet and had a dimple mark in the primer. She turned, closed the cylinder, and fired a bullet into Joe's upper thigh near his crotch just missing his femoral artery.

"And that is five. Well shit, I guess they aren't blanks," Sydney said as a pool of blood immediately began to form while Joe screamed in agony.

She spun and fired and once again the bullet merely passed through a cloud of mist.

"What in the hell?" Sydney said, looking down at the gun. "What kind of creature are you? A demon? A ghost?" she asked.

He stood there for a moment with a perplexed look washing over his face. "You know, I never really thought about it much. I suppose I am what I am, nothing more, nothing less," Skunk replied.

"You forgot to save the last one for yourself, bitch!" Joe cried out.

"Where are your manners, Joe. That is no way to treat my new guest," Skunk said.

"Your new guest? But she's mine. You promised."

"Well, I lied. And you are starting to bore me, Joe."

"You are doing a lot more than boring me," Sydney said, planting a fist across the man's jaw so hard her knuckles screamed in protest. "You killed my mother you sick son of a bitch."

Joe laughed until he coughed and spat a chunk of bloody phlegm onto the ground. "You don't even have a clue, do you? You think you have this all figured out, but you don't know shit!"

She punched him again even though her better judgment told her not to. "Shut up, I'm sick and tired of hearing your voice."

"Oh, but I know you want to hear what I have to say," Joe said. "Didn't you ever wonder what drove your father to kill himself?"

"You lying bastard, he did not kill himself, you murdered him."

"Okay, you got me there. But only because he was too much of a coward to do it himself."

"Why did you kill my father?"

"For the same reason I killed your mother. He told me to," Joe said with a nod in Skunk's direction.

"You know you're not being entirely truthful, Joe. I didn't care if you killed her father or not, guilt was killing him slowly anyway, and that was more delectable in my humble opinion," Skunk said.

"What would my father have done to feel guilty about?" Sydney asked, her voice wavering with nervous anticipation.

"Let's just say, your father made a bargain with me, but once he found out the cost of the bargain, he felt the price was too high and reneged on our deal. For that betrayal, I took the things which he loved the most."

"You killed my mother?"

"In a manner of speaking. I took her from your world and brought her into mine."

"Why?"

"Why not? It's what I do. From the very second I laid eyes on her I knew I had to add her to my collection."

"Then why him?" Sydney asked, jabbing an accusatory finger at Joe.

"To keep to the short answer, there are rules, certain boundaries that I cannot physically cross."

"Certain rules? You make it sound like this is all just one big game to you."

Skunk, or whatever the hell his real name was let loose a deep belly laugh. "You might be even smarter than what I have given you credit for. Your kind has entertained the gods since the dawn of time."

"Gods?" Sydney laughed. "You consider yourself a god, you are nothing more than a pathetic little man, a psychopathic coward who can't even kill on his own."

At that precise moment, the entity standing before her metamorphosed into an acrid column of thick, black smoke that darted straight for her and swirled around her body from her ankles to her head. She felt dozens of anomalous hands groping at her womanhood, her breasts and anything else this creature desired. She felt him probing her very soul. Repulsion overcame her and she vomited. When she regained her composure, Skunk was standing before her once more as though nothing out of the ordinary had just happened.

"Can a pathetic little man do that? And I must say, you have some genuinely nice assets."

Sydney didn't want to tip her hand she was absolutely terrified of this being, though she suspected it knew. She was now quite aware of the fact whatever this was she was dealing with, it was not human by any stretch of the imagination. But she refused to accept such a monstrous creature could be a god either.

"So, you see humans as nothing more than mere playthings?"

"I don't see them that way, it is the reality of your pathetic lives. You serve no other purpose than to amuse us. After all, it is what you were created for. For a time, it was Atum-Ra, then Zeus, Jupiter, even Odin had a go at it, but you were never anything more than mere curios. I mean really, for dust thou art, and unto dust shalt thou return, does that not exemplify a pitiful existence without any meaningful purpose whatsoever?"

"Those are gods of mythology, fiction passed down from generation to generation and nothing more," Sydney argued.

"And what makes you so certain that the god you worship now is not exactly the same thing, mere mythology? Jesus Christ had twelve apostles just as Zeus and Jupiter had councils of twelve did he not? That certainly sounds like a case of plagiarism to me."

"The God we worship is not a malevolent god and would never murder his own creations," Sydney argued.

"You forget the plagues of Egypt. The Great Flood. Human sacrifice and everything in between. You speak as a foolish woman speaks, one who only wants to see her own truth," he told her. "Should you accept from God only good and not adversity when he has clearly told you he is all things?"

"Do not try and twist His words. Who does that make you? Hephaestus? Vulcan? I would be more inclined to believe you are some perverted incarnation of that little prickster Loki," Sydney said.

"Or quite possibly I'm something altogether different. Something new. A new player to this game of the Gods as you will."

"There is only one true God," Sydney said, confidence lacking in her voice.

"And every pawn has claimed the exact same thing throughout the ages. There was only Ra, only Zeus, and now there is only Yahweh, Jehovah, Allah or whatever else you wish to call him. But remember, an opposing force must also exist."

"You mean Satan."

"Satan, the Devil, Mephistopheles and my all-time favorite, Beelzebub, all one in the same with a different name."

"And just what is your name then?" Sydney asked.

"We don't come to you with names, you must provide them for us, and your species has been lax in that department as of late. How about Mixcoatl, I really liked that one."

"Is that Incan, maybe Mayan?"

"What you called the Aztecs. Don't you find it very odd that you humans, especially in this current carnation, wave off the existence of gods and demons as mere myths? And yet, every single civilization on the face of this worn-out planet has worshipped and feared the gods of earth, water, fire, and everything else in between. If we are merely allegorical then why has every civilization believed in us since the dawn of time and beyond?"

Sydney found herself listening to this reprobate with a logical ear. What he said made sense, but it also begged more questions than it answered. Suddenly, cigarette smoke permeated the air and caused her to gag.

"I have to ask, why the cigarette smoke? It seems a tad bit juvenile if you ask me," she said.

"Again, that is something you pathetic puppets created. It was your ancestors who used tobacco in their religious ceremonies when worshipping us gods. So, who am I to disappoint by not playing along with the ruse? Besides, it is a very pungent, easily recognizable stench making it a perfect accoutrement to the diversions."

"If this is all but a game, then I will take great pride in beating you. I will trust in my God and forsake every one of yours. You underestimate both me and my God," she said, standing in defiance of this creature before her.

"Funny thing about this game, Sydney, we always win, and you always lose."

Suddenly the bog was filled with the sounds of racing engines as headlight beams split the darkness of the pre-dawn hour. The cavalry had arrived, sort of. From the racing engines and spinning tires Sydney deduced they had driven headlong into the bog and were now stuck. Joe cackled and spat a chunk of phlegm into the wet earth.

"Uncuff me bitch and I'll take it easy on you," Joe said and jerked at the handcuffs.

Sydney started to step forward for one more kick to the bastard's face, but she stopped when she saw flashlight beams breaking through the trees. The sounds of men slugging through the murky water echoed across the mire.

"No, you prick, killing you would do you a favor, so I'm going to let you rot in a prison cell."

Three officers she didn't recognize burst through the darkness into the clearing first, followed closely by Layton Turner who was helping Colby to struggle through the swamp. They were close enough to witness what was going on but not close enough to stop anything that might happen.

"Five men, that's all the backup you brought?" Joe laughed. "Show them what you've got," he said, turning his attention to Skunk.

Emanating from where Skunk stood a tiny tendril of gray smoke began to form. It forked and licked at the air like a snake tasting its surroundings as it hunted for prey. Layton Turner cocked his head toward Colby in disbelief as the tendril snaked through the air. Joe was laughing, gloating at what was about to be unleashed upon these interlopers. But then his laughter caught in his throat when he realized he was the object of its desire.

The tentacle of vapor swirled around the handcuffed man who tried to scream but only mounds of dirt and worms escaped his gaping maw. His fingers began falling away into piles of clotted soil on the ground beside him. His eyes were wide with panic as his toes and feet filled his boots with wet, earthen clay. Sydney recoiled and darted away not wanting to be near another lamprey.

A disembodied voice chuckled, "Joe is not afraid of sea creatures. But ironically, he does have deep rooted fear of being buried alive. So, he shall remain interred alive for all eternity."

Joe's body continued to fall way into clumps of earth until there was nothing but a small pile of loam where he stood only a moment ago. His pathetic screams dissipated into the cold, night air. The police officers had taken a shooter's stance and were dropped down to one knee as the cyclone of mist returned to form and the diminutive Skunk stood before them. Three laser sights dotted the man's chest where his heart should be and again, he swirled around them in a miasmatic pirouette. Layton

Turner stood in disbelief. There was no way in hell that he just witnessed one man turn to mud and another into a puff of smoke right in front of him.

"What in the fuck was that?" he said.

Colby shrugged and cried out, "Sydney, get over here."

She started to turn but something held her in place.

"I'm afraid I can't let you do that. While you have earned your freedom in my book, you are far too dangerous for me to let you walk amongst the living. You will have to spend your days as part of my collection," he said, materializing back into his human form.

"I believe that is an empty threat. If you wanted me dead, you would have killed me long ago. I don't know what in the hell kind of creature you are, but I'm certain you don't possess the ability to harm a living person or you wouldn't have had that slime ball Joe doing your bidding," Sydney said.

Skunk stood stalwart in defiance of the guns trained on him. He smiled at the grouping of armed men, turned his gaze back to Sydney and sent her a playful shrug. His eyes took on a metallic hue and fear rippled through her. One of the officers turned to the man beside him and put a bullet in his brain. The other officers unleashed a volley of shots at Skunk believing that was where the shot had come from that killed their colleague.

A hail of bullets ripped through Skunk until his body exploded into a multitude of prismatic orbs hanging in the air. With an audience of stunned police officers, the blurred balls spun and rotated until they connected together and slowly fell back into place. Once more the petite man was standing in front of them unharmed.

"Disarm, damn it, disarm," Colby cried out.

Layton Turner could not believe what he was witnessing. Even though Sheriff Patino had told him everything about the case, he had only listened half-heartedly. What the man had been saying was hogwash and there was a simple, logical explanation for everything. The current situation had no simple nor logical answer. He ran over to the remaining officers, ripped their weapons free from their hands and tossed them away. He quickly handcuffed each of the officer's hands behind their backs before running back over to where Colby was.

"Cuff me," Layton said, turning his back to Colby. "This bastard has somehow hypnotized the lot of us and is controlling our actions. I'll be damned if another officer will die."

Skunk stood in the center of it all with a smug grin eating away at his face. He may have held all the cards, but Sydney held an ace up her own sleeve and had formulated a plan, no matter how ill-conceived it was. She ran to the truck and grabbed the device Joe had use on countless other women including herself. She put the modified nail gun over the sore spot Joe's first attempt had caused. She had no idea if what she was about to do would work and if it did work, what that would entail other than simply committing suicide.

Sydney looked back at Skunk with her own smug grin. "I will see you on Olympus." She turned her head to Colby and said, "I'm so sorry. I truly love you." And then she pulled the trigger.

Her brain exploded into a fury of white light. Searing pain raced through her and she dropped to the rain-soaked earth. Colby looked up and through tear-stained eyes saw that Skunk, or whatever the hell he was, no longer stood in the field. He smelled a wisp of smoke pass by them before dissipating into the sodden, pre-dawn air.

Twenty-Seven

Sydney wandered down an empty trail overlooking Lake Superior. She couldn't have been more contented. But that was not reality, it was a scenario her mind was creating for her. A coping mechanism of sorts. No, her reality was as skewed as it could possibly get. Only miniscule tatters of her remained intact, but they were enough to remind her of where she was and how she came about being there.

She felt a weight around her neck and glanced down. The device returned another snippet of remembrance to her and a triumphant smile creased her lips. The camera hung around her neck. She was in his world now and he had no idea how dangerous that was for him. Her first order of business was twofold, find her boundaries and limitations in this altered state and find a way to communicate with Colby. And she had a theory about how she might go about accomplishing those tasks.

Miles and miles were behind her and yet she was able to continue forward without even the slightest hint of exhaustion. She had walked the entire length of Pictured Rocks National Shoreline and before she knew it, she was passing through Grand Marais where she spotted other people for the first time since awakening in this realm.

A gentle wave of her hand elicited no response from the passersby. She was like a ghost, but when she checked her own pulse it kept a rhythm as it should. She thought back in time and for the life of her couldn't recall one single moment of her journey across the cliffs. She had a hypothesis and decided to test it out.

As she walked, she started humming an old Gordon Lightfoot tune and before she knew it, she was standing on the shores of Whitefish Bay. The winds blew cold, and she half expected the Edmund Fitzgerald to break apart and be swallowed by the sea witch right in front of her. But that didn't happen. What did happen was she had a realization of how this strange plane of existence functioned. She merely had to think of a location, and she would then be transported to the location within her own mind.

While on the surface this seemed quite positive, but deep down she knew there must be something she had not learned about the technique yet. With every bit of give there had to be some take as well. Whatever this creature was, they certainly were clever enough to not give her an advantage. She did learn that traveling in this manner left her mind clouded for a time after. Once she arrived at her destination she couldn't remember where she was or why she was there. How much of this world was reality and how much was nothing more than a holographic or mental projection remained to be learned.

One thing she found once she reentered civilization was that while the world appeared as it had, she couldn't interact with all of it. She couldn't drive a car, she couldn't pick up food and eat it, and she couldn't even enter a building unless the door was already open. Sydney caught herself wondering more than once if she had died and was but a ghost.

There were moments when she felt as though she were slipping away from this magical milieu, that the plane of existence was fading from beneath her. It was during those times when she had to fight to stay grounded which proved to be exhausting. She feared what would happen if she lost the will to fight. Would she simply vanish into nothingness?

Her thoughts turned to Colby and her need to send him a message. The plan she formulated within her mind intrigued her. After all these years could it still be here? But she knew, if she could find the object she was searching for it would certainly send a clear message to him.

Camp Mucky Muck's lake of sludge spread out before her like a blanket covering the dead. She was thankful there were no skulls suspended in the mire staring back at her with empty, hollow eyes. She spent what felt like hours searching through the ghastly slurry but the object she had hoped to find was nowhere to be found. It had succumbed to the ravages of time or it was never in this world in which she now resided. She held the camera up and focused on the lake hoping it might send a message to Colby. She fired off a roll of film and sat down to wait, for what, she hadn't the slightest clue.

Colby drifted in and out of sleep. His hips continued to scream out in agony, but he refused to leave Sid's side. It had been several days, and her prognosis was not good as far as the doctors were concerned. But he knew better. He knew Sid. She would fight until the bitter end and she wasn't even close to that point yet. Junior groaned from across the room bringing Colby out of his semi-hypnotic state.

"How are you feeling?" Colby asked.

"Like I got hit by a truck."

"That's my line."

"How's she doing?" Junior asked.

Colby had demanded the nurses bring Junior's bed into the same room with Sydney so he could keep an eye on them both. He refused to take no for an answer and when they caught him trying to drag the bed down the hallway himself, they finally capitulated.

"About the same, I'm afraid."

"It looks like you could use some sleep," Junior moaned in pain.

"I need a month of Sundays to catch up. Are you okay? Do you need a nurse in here?" Colby asked.

"It only hurts when I laugh as the old saying goes."

"I hate to say it, but I'm amazed you survived. You are one tough son of a bitch."

"Not really. I'm only alive because of Sid. She kept me from drowning and somehow, she made me feel like everything was going to be okay. I wish I could say the same for her."

The nurse came into the room and set trays of food down for each of them. She carefully raised Junior's head and changed out his pillow. His head was about the only part of his body not in a cast or wrapped in bandages. Both men picked at their lunch trays without any further conversation. After lunch, Junior pressed the button on his pain medication dispenser and drifted off to sleep. Colby took a walk down the hall and got some vending machine coffee. Claudia Inez was waiting in the room for him when he got back.

"Good news I hope," he said.

He had solicited her help when she came to visit Sid after hearing the news. Small town, news travels fast. She let on that she knew how to develop film, so he gave her the camera and all the developing equipment. It was a long shot at best, but Colby had to hold on to at least a shred of hope.

"I'm not sure what kind of news it is actually."

"Did the camera take photographs?"

"Yes, but I'm not sure what they mean," she said and handed Colby a folder filled with photographs.

He set them on the floor one by one. They were of the lake at Camp Muck, but there was water in the lake. In fact, the lake was just as he remembered it. He saw something on the dock across the water. Quickly he laid out the next few photos until he stopped, picked one of them up and looked it over more closely. Tears immediately began to flow down his cheeks. There was a single, mud encrusted shoe sitting on the dock. It was his shoe sitting atop an old wooden beam with the initials S.L. loves C.P scratched into the side.

"Sid is in there," he said, stabbing a finger at the photograph.

Sydney made her way from the lake to the large building by the road. She was still trying to assimilate to the myriad of sensations enveloping her. She had been instilled with a sense of indestructability, but extremely vulnerable at the same time. She felt in control and yet chaotic. She felt as innocent as a newborn yet imparted with the wisdom of the ancients.

She could feel another presence, his presence, in the air surrounding her, yet there also seemed to be a barrier between the two of them. She could also sense that her being in this plane of existence threatened him and she intended to use that to her advantage. Oddly, as scared as she had been of the entity outside in the waking world, she barely feared him at all in his domain. Maybe this was not his domain after all.

She walked around the large nondescript building. It was built with four walls of corrugated steel painted forest green to match the surrounding woodland. It was tall, at least three stories with no windows and not a single door that she could find. She had walked around the place several times but found no way to gain entrance. Look as she may, there was not a door.

Sydney stepped back onto the center line of the road to get a wide angle shot and took several photos of the front of the building. She did the same to the east side and then the rear of the building without any results that she could see. It was on the western end of the building that her efforts proved fruitful. As soon as she pressed the shutter button on the camera, she could see there was something peculiar about the wall. It was shrouded in bokeh balls.

Cautiously she approached the building and as soon as she touched the area of the wall obscured by bokeh she found herself inside of the building. She couldn't believe what she was seeing. She expected to find marijuana plants, but these were huge. Sydney had to wonder whether all of this was real or if she was just experiencing a major contact buzz. The plants were only three rows deep around the entire perimeter of the building but then opened into a clearing. Once in the open an enormous graveyard was revealed, and she immediately realized this was what he had meant by *his collection*.

The scene laid out before her took her breath away. Dozens upon dozens of pillars of light extended from the soil to the ceiling of the building. The myriad of lights flickered in rhythm, pulsating as if they were alive. As if they were breathing. When she looked at them more closely, she could see there was a fluidity about them like water flowing upstream. Tiny bubbles spiraled upward, disappearing into nothingness, and then repeated the cycle. Sydney put her face as close as she dared to the mysterious stream of bubbles and realized they were not air bubbles at all, but tiny shards of bokeh. Was this stream, in essence, pieces of a person's soul trapped within the molten hues?

Nervously she reached her hand out, index finger first and as lightly as she could she touched the edge of the rivulet. All at once the room resounded with the echoes of an inhuman scream and the stream stopped its movement. The bokeh orbs rotated and looked directly at her. Sydney was wracked with an overwhelming sense of grief. This column of colorful luminosity was nothing wondrous, this was an enslaved human soul who was fully cognizant of what was happening to them.

Dozens of streams around her stopped their motion. The room fell deathly quiet as tears streamed down her face. Without warning the stream she was nearest to screamed out for help which awakened the others and they all cried out in unison. Within seconds the interior of the building echoed with the screams of helpless souls crying out for salvation. Sydney dropped to her knees and wept.

"How are you holding up, son?" Layton asked Junior with a sympathetic eye.

"I would be much better if I could scratch my own ass," Junior responded with a crooked smile.

"Don't expect any help out of me on that one," Layton said with his hands held high in the air. "And how about you?"

"I plan on playing some hockey this weekend," Colby added.

"I see you two have been hitting the morphine button," Layton said with a soft laugh.

"What brings you here?" Colby asked.

"I wanted to check on Sid and give you an update."

"An update on what?"

"Catching the man who did this to her."

"Layton, you were there in that field with me. You saw what happened. That was no man, and you can't possibly think we can apprehend whatever the hell that thing was," Colby said.

"Joe LeBlanc somehow drugged us, and we were hallucinating," Layton argued.

"You can't be serious. And then turned himself into a pile of mud?"

Layton Turner knew Sheriff Patino was right, there was no catching the thing that did this. But there was no way he could relate the true facts of this case as he witnessed them to his superiors, not if he wanted to keep his job. He knew what he had witnessed and while it was the furthest from reality he had ever wandered, the events had truly transpired exactly the way he experienced it.

The nurse came in and adjusted Junior's bed so he wasn't lying completely flat. And even though it was agonizing, he didn't have the nerve to ask her to scratch his ass. He was ignoring the other two bickering when he noticed something across the room.

"Hey, is she coming to?" he asked, nodding a head toward Sydney.

"Why would you say that?" Colby asked.

"Look at her hand, her finger is moving."

The three of them watched as her index finger raised and lowered in a tapping motion. Up and down, up, and down repeatedly. But the tempo seemed to change every once in a while.

"Holy shit!" Colby shouted.

"What?" Layton said.

"She is communicating with us, specifically with me."

"How on earth is she doing that?"

"Morse code. She is sending me Morse code."

"Well, what in the hell is she saying?" Layton asked.

"How in the hell should I know? The last time I used Morse code was back at Camp Mucky-Muck with Sid more than thirty years ago. We would use it to talk to each other after lights out by tapping on the walls of our bunkhouses."

"There has to be an app for translating Morse Code, there's an app for everything," Junior said.

They got on their phones and started searching the internet for an app that would help them. Each of them found numerous programs that translated text into Morse code and vice versa but nothing that would suit their needs.

"Try this," Layton said, handing his phone to Colby who then slid it under Sydney's finger.

Once she started tapping on the screen the phone emitted a tone with each tap. They listened to the Morse code being transmitted by the phone and after a couple of minutes Colby pulled it away from her hand and looked at the screen.

"Does it say anything or is it just gibberish?"

"No, Layton, it's as clear as day."

"What does it say?"

"She says, *there are hundreds of them!*"

"Hundreds of who?"

"Or hundreds of what?" Colby added.

Just like everything else in the universe Skunk was bound by laws of nature. Not human nature, but nature none the less. There were certain actions he could not take, one of which was interfering with humans in their earthly realm, or physically harming humans trapped within his own domain. The dead, he could screw with the dead all day long. But the living, they were off limits.

He knew this plaything was smarter than most. He knew enough to stay away from her. He also knew he should have severed his relationship with Joe long before the man was able to cause this much irreparable damage.

Skunk watched Sydney as she moved about his cherished collection. With every new step, every new inspecting glance he shuddered. While he was omnipotent, he was only able to be so with his collection in place as he drew his power from his horde of deprivation. If she were to find a way to negate his triumphs, then she would undo his power as well.

While he did not answer directly to a higher deity, he also did not have any entity who could step in and save him from destruction. He was not a demon from hell, but fabric that legends were fashioned from. He was all things, and yet, nothing at all. And his entire existence was but a mere thread pull from being unraveled.

Twenty-Eight

Sydney wandered among the incarnate pillars and wondered what it all meant. What was the demon's purpose for all of this? Each one she passed emitted a certain energy she could sense, almost like an emotion. But not a single emotion like happiness or sadness, no, this was a conglomeration of emotions that bourgeoned in intensity the closer she moved to each of the columns.

A sorrow gripped her like none other she had ever suffered before in life, not even after her mother's disappearance. Grief and despair hung thick in the air like an endless fog of deprivation. These women had not only been murdered but then their souls harvested by some demonic entity for nothing more than its own amusement. Sydney was certain there was more to it than that, but it was enough of an explanation for her to know she had to destroy it. She had to destroy this *collection*. Somehow, she had to find a way to release these poor beings from their endless persecution.

Sydney noticed one of the pillars were emitting a different light than the others. It was pulsating, strobing, as if beckoning her to it. She walked over to the pulsating column and watched the orbs spin upward out of sight. A sensation seized her, and she dropped to her knees. She was filled with a profound sorrow that emptied out from her very core. Tears flowed from her for reasons unknown. She was not sad, but she couldn't stop weeping. And then she was filled with a sensation she had never really felt before, at least not for an exceptionally long time.

She was overcome with a sense of pure unadulterated love. She gathered herself and managed to get back to her feet. She reached out with two trembling hands to caress the living stream.

"Mother?" she said.

I have waited for this moment for so long, my little princess. But it also fills me with great sadness.

Sydney did not hear her mother's words in her ear, rather, she felt them like a warm embrace that solidified into understanding.

"Why are you sad?"

I knew one day this would come, but I had hoped it would be much further away. You are much too young to be dead.

"But I'm not dead, mother."

But you are here amongst us? He must have found you and killed you as well.

"Who found me? Who killed me?"

Your father.

"Father is dead. Why do you think he killed me?"

Because he killed me.

"No, a man named Joe murdered you. Daddy tried to stop him."

No child, your father killed me.

"How do I set you free? And all these others as well?"

I do not know.

With tears flowing down her cheeks Sydney did the only thing that seemed to work. She stepped back, focused the camera, and took several shots of her mother's cylindrical form. The orbs inside of her mother's stream began to rotate and turn, spinning faster and faster until they organized into an image she recognized. Sydney could see her mother's face as she remembered it.

Sydney found herself suffering with a blinding headache. She had tried several times to send messages to Colby, but it was just too taxing. She prayed he would understand whatever manner of communication she was able to convey but she had no way of knowing if her efforts were fruitful. She simply had to put her faith in him to comprehend whatever method she was able to come up with.

Once her headache subsided and she was able to see again she found herself sitting on the floor of her childhood living room. The house was still decorated for Easter, *Schlemiel! Schlimazel! Hasenpfeffer Incorporated* echoed from a television in the corner of an adjacent room Tom Jones was crooning his latest from the speakers on a console Hi-Fi. On the floor in the middle of the room she, as a small child, gnawed at the ears of a chocolate rabbit with one yellow, sugary eye missing and its pink bow half gone. Sydney was enveloped with the familiar fragrance of her mother's Charlie and tears flowed down her cheeks.

"I've got a surprise for you," Frank Lamppinen said, coming up from behind her and kissing his wife Gloria on the back of the neck.

When her mother turned, Sydney saw the scar on the side of her mother's head and her far away stare. Her heart ached as she came to the sudden realization her father was just like Joe. Her mother had been abducted and buried in a shallow grave to create a love slave for her father. She had to struggle to keep from vomiting. This meant that she had never even known her mother and she herself was an abomination that should never have happened. Had her mother been torn away from a loving family who never knew what had happened to their loved one?

Did she have children who spent the rest of their lives without their mother?

"What?" Gloria asked, with a smile that was awkward and seemed forced.

"We are going to take a trip. I bought you a camera to take pictures like you wanted. I thought we might head to the cliffs in Munising."

"That sounds fantastic. I need to pack. I need to pack Sydney's things too," she said, more excited than a person should have been when presented with an offer of a simple weekend getaway.

"Oh, there is no need for that. We only have time to make it a day trip. I thought Elmer and Joe could watch her. Besides, she is too young, the cliffs are a dangerous place for young children," Frank said.

Gloria's nose crinkled as she tried to hide a scowl. Sydney studied her mother's mannerisms and found them to be somewhat odd. She seemed to be apprehensive and second guessing herself about everything.

"I don't like that man and you know it. And he smokes in the house even though I have asked him more than once not to," Gloria said. Under her breath she finished. "And I don't like your bother Joe any better."

"I know, Gloria, but he's my boss, and he's great with Sydney. He really does love her like she's his own. Besides, her Uncle Joe will be here as well."

"You haven't told him about my dreams, have you?"

"No, I thought it best to keep that just between us," Frank lied.

"When are we going?"

"We'll leave tonight so we can get an early start at hiking first thing in the morning," he said, glancing down at his watch.

Sydney stood in her living room watching herself as a small child while living out a scene from a Dickens' novel, except she was being visited by all three ghosts at the same time. The doorbell rang and younger versions of Joe and Skunk were greeted and ushered inside with a smile. She swore Skunk looked straight at her, not the toddler her, but the ghostly vestige of her as she watched her past unfolding.

The toddler began to cry as her parents scooted out the door. Sydney watched as Skunk knelt to whisper in the child's ear. Immediately she stopped crying but the look on her face was not that of contentment rather, it was fear. What had he said to her all those years ago?

Sydney found herself on a trail overlooking Lake Superior watching as her parents hiked ahead of her but there was something wrong. Every time her mother would step close to the edge to take a photograph her father would hang back behind her. She realized this was akin to the first photographs she had seen, the ones from Abigail's assault at the cliffs. She checked her camera for film, the same camera her mother was using, and began snapping off pictures of them as they walked.

Butterflies fluttered about inside of her each time her mother inched closer to the edge. She could see a look in her father's eyes that was beyond disturbing. But every time he had the opportunity and Sydney thought this would be the moment, he pulled back. This went on for miles and the longer it went on the less she thought it would come to fruition. But it must, because her mother was dead.

Sydney smelled cigarette smoke drifting through the air and tensed up. Even if there had been someone smoking at the cliffs it would have been in this macabre vision and not within her own mind where she was being held captive. And then she saw Skunk. She eased closer to where he and her father were talking.

"What are you doing, Frank? You know what has to be done."

"But I can't, I just can't kill her. I love her."

"But you must," Skunk said, glancing down at the toddler nestled between his feet. "She is ready to become part of my collection which means she is no longer yours to play with," Skunk said. "You know how this works. I warned you about falling in love with them."

Frank Lamppinen stiffened and puffed out his chest. "No, I won't do it," he said.

"Very well, then I no longer have any use for you, Frank. Joe," he said, craning his neck towards the forest. A young, much less rotund Joe emerged from the bushes like the weasel Sydney knew him to be.

Sydney knew her mother was perched dangerously on the edge of the cliffs but there was nothing she could do to warn her. Joe took off running toward Gloria with Frank not far behind trying to catch him. Both men's arms were outstretched in front of them, each with a different intention. Just as Joe reached Gloria he sidestepped, letting Frank blow right past him. At that precise moment Gloria turned around to say something to her husband only to see him charging straight for her. Frank tried to stop himself but couldn't and ran right into her, catapulting her from the cliffs and down into Lake Superior. A faint humming rose from the water below, a boat motor idling at the bottom of the cliffs.

Sydney couldn't help herself and she screamed. Skunk turned and looked at her, straight at her and smiled the most devious smile she had ever seen. And then, all was gone, and she was back in the warehouse, alone with the tortured ghosts.

"Mother, daddy didn't kill you."

I know that now child. You must leave this place now. You must leave me and go back.

"No, this is where I belong. This is where I need to be. I think I know what needs to be done. You can rest now mother. Your child is safe. He did not get me. In fact, I'm going to get him. I'm going to put an end to his reign of torment and suffering. I must know, why are you here mother? How does he have you imprisoned?"

I'm not imprisoned; I'm here waiting for my little girl.

"Mother, your little girl is fine. I'm right here with you."

But she is all alone. She is the one who is trapped in here with him.

"No mother, I'm not trapped. I'm right where I need to be. You need to go. You need to be at peace," Sydney said with tears rolling down her cheeks.

Sydney apprehensively eased a finger toward the radiant column she believed to be her mother's essence. Even before she made contact an electrical charge jumped to meet her finger and she was flooded with a memory so vivid it was as if she were reliving it again that very moment.

She was young, so young in fact she had all but erased this moment from her memory. It was one of the last bonding moments she had ever spent with her mother, so she was clueless as to why she had repressed it all these years. But now that it was flooding back her heart swelled with such love and affection she could barely stand.

Coyotes had raided a rabbit den near their house early one spring, even before the trees had begun to bud. The varmint managed to kill the mother and all but one of the baby bunnies. Maybe it hadn't seen this one or maybe it had already eaten its fill, but this little rabbit had been spared.

Perhaps it was all part of the grand scheme of things that Sydney was destined to find this helpless baby rabbit. It was so tiny it fit in the palm of her own little cherubic hand. So young in fact, its eyes were not even opened yet.

Even though her mother thought the poor creature wouldn't survive more than a day or two she relented to Sydney's pleas to rescue it from certain death. Miraculously the baby not only survived that first night but began to thrive within the next couple of days and over the course of the next few weeks it had grown into a healthy baby rabbit.

Sydney recalled her profound sadness when the bunny finally grew into a rabbit and her mother convinced her it was best for the animal to be released back into the wild. Her mother told her that it did not belong being cooped up in a house meant for humans and not rabbits. She remembered the certain sense of peace that washed over her the day she let the bunny go in their backyard and it had stopped long enough to look at her just before disappearing into the underbrush. It was clear now what she must do. She must let go.

She caressed the pillar of light and felt something spectacular, an overwhelming sense of happiness and relief. Her mother's energy began to wane, and the column began to flicker. The bokeh inside of the pillar began to assemble into an image of her mother with outstretched arms. Sydney could feel her mother's embrace as she drifted away to finally be at peace.

For a moment, the room was eerily quiet with only the sparkle of the other pillars emitting any sound. Then all at once the room exploded with a discordance of noise so intense, she was forced to cover her ears and drop her knees. Dozens upon dozens of voices pleading for help echoed in her skull until she finally had to scream out.

"Shut up! I can't possibly listen to you all at once, it will drive me insane." She was immediately wracked with guilt over her outburst.

Slowly the volume in the room leveled down until the voices were just a murmur. The cries for help turned into sobs and moans of despair which were even more horrendous than their boisterous pleas. Sydney wracked her brain for what to do next. When she felt her mother leaving this realm, she felt something else as well. Something that was not tangible, yet she could feel it inhabiting this realm. She could only describe it as a weakening, like a small tear in the fabric of the demesne that was this place. She understood what it was going to take for her to beat him. She realized how to steal his life's energy from him and there was not a damn thing he could do to stop her, demon from hell or a god from some unholy realm, he was powerless against her.

"Listen up, this is very taxing for me and there are a lot of you, so I'm going to try and start with the easiest first. Who is Maren Walters? Which one of you is Abigail's mother?"

As if signaling her, the multitude of glowing columns began to diminish in intensity until there was only one shining more brightly than the others. Sydney made her way through the warehouse over to where the pillar of light was pulsating. It struck her as being like a person's chest heaving as they sobbed. She cupped her hands around the beam and smiled.

"Abigail is safe. She is alive and doing well the last time I saw her," she said while caressing the stream of consciousness before her.

Sydney felt something odd and swooned. She could feel her mind being probed, not mechanically, but somehow through the transference of her touch. She felt Maren's emotions cascading over her. Everything from sadness to elation and finally relief. And then just as her mother had done, Maren's light flickered, faded, and then disappeared. As soon as the light vanished, she also felt other emotions wash over her that were not emanating from the room but rather from the atmosphere itself. Anger, frustration, contempt and finally fear.

Tears rolled down Colby's face as he caressed Sid's hand. Her doctor stood over her with a stern, yet compassionate expression.

"Doctor, there must be something you can do?"

"I'm afraid there is nothing more we can do. She's brain dead. We are going to have to take her off life support."

"But she sent me messages. How could she do that if she is brain dead?"

"She couldn't."

"Then how do you explain this?" Colby said and handed the doctor his phone with the Morse code message from Sydney.

"Grief," the doctor responded rather nonchalantly.

"What's that supposed to mean?"

"It means that there's nothing there. Your grief created this, not my patient."

"But then what about me?" Junior interjected. "I barely know the woman and definitely not well enough to have been overcome with grief. I watched her send that message myself. Now, I'm no doctor, but I'm pretty certain that a brain-dead person would not be able to communicate."

"You're right, you are not a doctor," he said and started to leave the room, but Colby blocked him.

"I'll get a court order."

"Then you do just that, but you may want to expedite the process. I will give you until eight o'clock tomorrow morning," he said and left the room.

Sydney was careening about in her mind which sent her meandering off in every direction within this fantasy realm she had imprisoned herself in. She knew she had to focus, take one thing at a time or else she would simply be spinning her wheels in the mud. Every time she looked across the expanse of entombed souls pleading for her to release them, she became overwhelmed.

With her mother now at peace she was so utterly alone in this domain that it physically ached. She opened her eyes and found she had somehow been transported to the rocky coast of what he assumed was Lake Superior. Still unsure of the mechanics of this place she left nothing to chance. Sydney bent down and brought a cupped hand of water to her mouth. It was fresh water, so this was not the ocean. But where on earth was she?

She walked up the dome of the smooth rock formation jutting out into the lake. Suddenly its dark surface reminded her of where she was. This was Black Rocks at Presque Isle Point in Marquette. She searched her memory for a reason that may have brought her to this place.

Standing on the very edge of the rocks she dove into the frigid waters and swam into the rising sun toward another rock formation a little more than half a mile offshore. The water was sapping her strength and within a hundred yards she was chopping at the water with fatigued arms. Her lungs burned and ached from exhaustion and fear was forcing her to realize what a stupid mistake she had made.

Luckily, her lifeguard training kicked in and Sydney turned over on her back. She let the current between the land masses pull her to the archipelago while she rested. Seagulls swooped above her, contrasting against the cloudless blue sky. She could hear a group of boys on the rocks cheering her on. She could hear all but one.

It seemed like an eternity, but she finally found the rocky outcropping under the water with her extended toes and used them to propel her to shallow waters. Exhausted she dropped onto her back on the dry rock of the middle island of Presque Isle Point Rocks. She screamed out in triumphant laughter.

She recalled the surprised look on Colby's face that quickly morphed into anger. He was furious with her for swimming that far out by herself. He was the captain of the swim team and he wouldn't make that swim alone. After a few taunting elbows and giggles his teammates dove back into the water and headed for the biggest of the rocks to give the couple some privacy.

Tears ran down her cheeks as she thought back on that day. The tough high school junior chewing out the bothersome freshman who followed him everywhere. She looked at her reflection in the water and saw the tomboy she used to be and laughed. She had endured just about enough of his shit so she stepped up the rocks until she was face to face with him, planted both hands on his cheeks and gave him the biggest Hollywood movie kiss she could muster. That was their first kiss.

Sydney broke away from her reverie and choked back her tears. That was in another life. A life that was over and long behind her.

She turned to start her swim back to the mainland still wondering what had brought her out here. She looked down at her feet and saw the camera was sitting there. But how in the hell was that even possible? It hadn't been around her neck when she started the swim. She picked the camera up and fired off shot after shot of the rock while sobbing uncontrollably.

Junior awoke to find himself standing in a long corridor in a basement. How did he get down to the basement of the hospital? Down the end of the corridor a man stood in the darkness, illuminated only the single red glow of his cigarette. He tried to walk but it was much too painful, and he dropped down onto his buttocks. His thumb jammed down on a button in his hand. Immediately his brain was cloudy, and he was giddy.

"What are you doing in my dream?" he laughed.

"Silly boy, I'm not in your dream, you are in mine," the man said and disappeared into a cloud of smoke.

Junior staggered back to his feet, but it was easy and there was no pain. Something felt strange. He saw a reflection of light down the corridor, so he made his way to where there was a stainless-steel panel on the wall. He was shocked to see a small, long haired little boy looking back at him.

Behind the boy was a beautiful woman coming toward him in a fluid motion as if gliding rather than walking. At first Junior was afraid until he saw the specter's face, it was his mother's face in the reflection. She used her hands as a blindfold to cover the little boy's eyes and whispered, "Guess who?" into his little ear before giving him a tender kiss on his neck. Tears flowed down Junior's cheeks and formed a pool on the cold concrete floor at his feet.

"She is going to kill her you know," a familiar voice said in his ear with hot, fetid breath.

"Who, who is going to kill her?"

"That cop. That woman cop. She killed me, now she is going to kill your mother."

Junior spun around and was immediately overcome with pain. He was no longer a healthy young boy; he was a broken man staring up at his tormentor.

"You know what you must do."

The warehouse erupted into a horrific scream that while inhuman on the surface Sydney knew it was a mother's sorrow. She walked through the pillars of light, a forest of lost souls, moving from column to column trying to sense the source of the shriek. A breeze blew all around her but there was no wind to speak of and she understood this was a tangible wave of emotion.

Sydney stopped and closed her eyes. She stood in the very center of the huge expanse with her arms held out at her sides. Slowly she pivoted in a circle until she was finally able to get a bearing on where this wave of emotion was coming from.

She ran through the columns sliding and dodging between them. She ran until she thought her heart would simply give up and stop beating. She was doubled over in pain gasping for breath when she saw the pulsating light. The bokeh within the pillar of light streamed like tears.

She arranged the bokeh until she saw the beautiful face of a woman with long dark, flowing hair whose sorrow was etched in her bokeh. Sydney braced herself before reaching her hands into the stream and allowing the woman's essence to cascade over her. The anguish was indescribable and cut her to the marrow.

The woman forced a smile and tilted her head slightly to the right. She captured Sydney's gaze with her own while reaching a bronze toned hand out to her. She was immediately transported to somewhere else. To the field at Stump Junction.

A young woman stood in the field with her back to Sydney. She couldn't hear the woman's sobbing, but she sensed it just the same. And icy chill crept across her skin as the silhouette of a man appeared from the tree line moving toward the woman. She wanted to scream at her to run but she was silenced. The outline of the man's hat revealed it was Joe who was sneaking up behind the unaware victim.

Sydney noticed the woman was looking at something on the ground keeping her distracted from her surroundings. Sydney had never felt so helpless as she did at that very moment watching that evil bastard shoot the poor woman in the back of the head. He dumped her body onto the ground like a sack of potatoes.

Shovel after shovel of dirt piled up next to the shallow grave until the hole was about two feet deep. The poor woman must have been witnessing this as well as Sydney could feel the mother's sorrow surrounding her as they shared this tragic moment. The bastard was done digging and climbed out of the hole. He rolled the unconscious woman into the hole and snatched a yellow shawl off the ground. It was the same shawl the woman in the pillar of light was wearing.

She turned her attention back to the grave and stared at the poor girl lying there so all alone. So unaware of what her world was about to become. But something was not right, there was something oddly familiar about the young woman. She was not a young woman, he was a young teenager with long, black hair. It was Junior.

"So how much do you think it would cost me?" Colby asked, glancing over at Joyce who was grimacing over the cup of hospital coffee.

"To do what?"

"Weren't you listening?"

"Nope, you tend to ramble. You lost me at give me your opinion," she said with a crooked grin.

"How much would it cost me to move Sid from the hospital to my house with the same set up and an on-site nurse?"

"Do you know how to get your hands on a time machine and go back in time so you can invest in Microsoft or Apple?"

Colby just looked back at her with an innocent expression.

"Are you shitting me? How much?"

"I don't know. In all honesty I put it in the back of my mind and never really thought about it much. I live a very comfortable life right now, money has never been an issue or a priority for me. I'm certain it would have only complicated my life."

"How much?" Joyce persisted.

"When I was in college my grandfather gave me ten thousand dollars towards my college education. I told him repeatedly that I was given a scholarship and didn't need that much money. He insisted I take it, so I deposited the money into a money market account at the bank."

"And?"

"And a year or so later a college roommate who was a tech geek talked me into buying into Apple in nineteen eighty."

"How much?" Joyce asked, her growing impatience obvious.

"To make a long story short I bought into Apple for five thousand dollars and then when Microsoft came around, I did the same," Colby said.

"So, you are worth," Joyce started.

"Millions."

"A podunk UP sheriff worth millions, whodathunk," she said with a raspy laugh. "So, you're expecting me to believe all this time you didn't know how much your stock was worth?"

"I had an idea, but I wasn't really paying attention after the first couple of years," Colby said.

"You're buying the coffee from now on, and this good stuff, not this swill," Joyce said and tossed her nearly full cup of putrid, cold coffee in the trash.

"So how much?" Colby asked.

"I think you'll be able to afford it Scrooge McDuck."

Wanting to change the subject Colby asked, "Have you been out to the warehouse yet?"

"Layton and I just moseyed about the place, but we haven't gone inside yet."

"Why not?"

"He still hasn't decided on a way to ask a judge for a warrant."

"Always the politician."

"It's no skin off my ass, that place is creepy as hell."

"I thought you said you didn't go inside," Colby said.

"We didn't. I'm telling you Colby, I don't spook easily but there was a vibe about that place even before we got out of the car. I was covered in goosebumps."

"And Sid is inside there somewhere," he said under his breath.

"Come on, let's get back down to the room and see how the old girl is doing."

Colby laughed. "Say something like that in the room and she might come out of her coma just to kick your ass."

Joyce helped Colby back to his hospital room. Walking was getting easier by the day. He was no longer suffering in excruciating pain, but he was not ready to dance a tango either. A strange noise caught their attention as they neared the room. Something was being scraped across the floor.

The two of them were dumbfounded and frozen in shock when they came around the corner into the room to see that Junior had somehow dragged his bed over to where Sydney lay helpless in a coma. He was laying across her body using his body to force a pillow down over her face.

"She is killing my mother," he said, looking back at them with remorse saturating his eyes.

Without hesitation Joyce Tammi pulled a pistol from an ankle holster and fired one round. Junior fell limp and immediately the room exploded into chaos.

Twenty-Nine

Sydney sat at the kitchen table in her own house with her face buried in her hands. She had spent hours talking with Junior's mother, or what she thought were hours without gaining much traction. She needed to put the poor soul to rest and the only way to accomplish that would be to convince her that her son was safe. That he was no longer in the monster's evil clutches. And the only way she could think to do that was to free Junior from this demon. Therein lay the conundrum.

There was a certain amount of solace for her now that she had learned how to manipulate this realm to suit her, but it was still shaky. She imagined Skunk was working just as hard to disrupt her by any means necessary. One thing she knew for certain, she was weakening his grip on them which in turn weakened his grip on her. As he weakened, she gained more control.

Suddenly the camera started taking photographs by itself causing her to startle. She had been poring over how she could communicate with the other side, with Colby, Layton, Joyce, or whoever the hell would listen. Could it really be this simple? But the more she thought about it, the more sense it made. It was not that the cameras were similar, that they were the same brand, make and model. No, they were the exact same camera, the one she had in her plane of existence and the one Colby had in the real world. If his world was even the real world.

She found it very unnerving that not only was her house in the same place it had always been, but everything inside was unchanged. Except for things she wanted such as developing equipment that had never been there prior to this charade. Was this illusion being created by her damaged brain, or was this created by her tormentors simply as a means to amuse themselves? Was she just another pawn moving from space to space, a willing idiot participating in their pious game?

"Bullshit," she said aloud, the sound reverberating off the walls.

This was no game, at least not from her perspective. And she was a willing participant only because she wanted to be. She was going to beat this bastard no matter the cost. She would not allow him to spread his seeds of despair any longer.

She stepped out of her front door with a packet of photographs and a smile. It was not until she was back inside the warehouse walking amongst the forest of the damned that she had an answer to something that had been nagging her from the beginning. Each of the columns resembled the strips of negatives hanging in Shane's makeshift darkroom.

Sydney felt a gut punch at the thought of the poor man's transfiguration. If he were ever even a man at all.

As she made her way through the pillars, she felt energy licking out at her as she passed each one as if they were trying to touch her. With each flicker of essence, she was invaded with a sense of sorrow that was numbing. But intermingled was a sense of hope and Sydney knew she was doing the right thing.

Once more she found herself in front of Junior's mother. The woman's deep, chestnut eyes were glossed over with tears and her brown orbs reflected her deep despair. Sydney sensed the woman's energy flowing away from her and into the room itself as if it were feeding some unseen entity. She was about to throw a monkey wrench into Skunk's dinner plans.

Opening the folder Sydney held the first photograph of Junior up to his mother. It wasn't a family portrait by any stretch of the imagination, but it was all she had to work with.

"He is a little worse for wear, but he is safe. You have to let him go."

I cannot leave him to that monster!

"He is not with that monster, not now. But as long as you remain here in his control, your son's life remains in danger."

There was another surge of energy in the room and the woman bent over at the waist before throwing her head back in anguish. The bastard was tormenting her somehow.

"Listen, your son and I have become friends and he is with another friend of mine who I promise is taking very good care of him. But you have to let him go."

He says if I let him go, he will die a horrible death. I must stay.

"He is lying to you to manipulate you as he has done with every single mother in this room. I promise you, when this beast no longer has any control over you, he no longer has any control over your son," Sydney said, holding another photograph of Junior up to the column.

How can I trust you?

"How can you not trust me?" Sydney said with a smile. "I promise, no harm will come to him, but you must go. You must allow yourself to be at peace."

Suddenly the room appeared to breathe, as if alive. The shadows flickered and came to life. The woman had begun chanting something rhythmic, something that seemed to be putting her at peace. The louder she chanted the more her appearance faded. She reached out with outstretched arms and Sydney returned the gesture. The woman blew a tender kiss and was gone.

The energy in the room surged in what only could be described as a spasm. Sydney had an epiphany; she was in the belly of the beast. All these cylinders of lights, all these souls fed this evil creature and for each one that disappeared it took his life's essence with it. But she also absorbed a portion of that energy. As she felt him weaken, she felt herself grow stronger.

She moved to the center of the room and sat down cross legged on the floor.

"To all of you, each and every one. I'm not going anywhere until I'm finished. Until this game is finished, and we are going to win this time!"

Sydney felt a wave of emotion crash over her as the pillars of light called out to her in unison. It was heartfelt gratitude on a level she couldn't even imagine existed. Tears saturated her cheeks and for once in her life she felt her existence had a purpose.

"And you Skunk, Loki, Mixcoatl or whatever the hell your name is, I have figured you out. You are no god; you are nothing but a mere pawn just like me. And pawns were meant to be sacrificed."

Using her finger Sydney scrawled something in the sand and then stood up to take a photograph of her artwork.

"Colby, I sure hope you're smarter than you look," she said before wiping a tear from her eye. She knew she was exactly where she was meant to be, and she was fine with that.

Chapter Thirty

"What are we going to do with him?" Layton nodded his head over at Junior who was just coming around from a drug induced slumber.

"Water under the bridge, Layton."

"But he almost killed Sid."

"But he didn't."

"But he wanted to."

"And now he doesn't. Listen, Layton, there were extenuating circumstances. I'll keep my eye on him, but I trust he won't try that again."

"Especially not if I'm around," Joyce added dryly.

Claudia Inez came bursting into the room with a folder clutched in her hands.

"What do you have there?" Colby asked.

"The camera took some more photos," she said and handed Colby the folder.

The first photo in the group made his skin prickle with energy. His eyes let loose a torrent of tears.

Joyce looked over at him and asked, "Where is that?"

He dried his eyes with his shirt sleeve and said, "Presque Isle Point Rocks."

"And?"

"And what?"

"Don't play coy, mister. Why did that photograph have such in impact on you?" Joyce asked.

"It's the place where I first kissed Sid. Well, more specifically where she first kissed me," Colby said.

The room fell into an uncomfortable silence. Claudia was not expecting that kind of reaction from Colby. After a couple of minutes, she took the lead and handed him a couple more photographs.

"What is this all about? These are just pictures of Junior. Why would the camera take these?"

"I think this is a way to communicate with Sid."

"How so? These are just photographs of Junior and then some of some native woman," Layton said.

"No, it isn't. Look here, this photograph of Junior. This is one that was accidentally taken when the camera was knocked over during the struggle," Claudia said, purposefully avoiding calling the fracas a murder attempt.

"I'm not following you," Colby said.

"It's not the same photo that was taken in this room, it's a photo that Sid must have taken."

"What in the hell are you driving at?" Layton asked.

"Hear me out," Claudia started. "This camera that we have here, I think Sid has it too. Not just any camera, but this very same camera. She must have gotten the photograph that this camera took of Junior by accident."

"Okay, assuming that is all true, why is this photograph so significant?"

"Because it's not just a photograph of Junior, it's a photograph of the photograph that was taken in this room. Meaning, Sid somehow got the photograph in her camera, developed it and then took her own photograph which I then developed here."

"Are you saying that if we want to communicate with her, we simply take a photograph of what we want her to see?"

"In theory."

"We need to test that theory," Layton Turner said.

"These are the last photographs in the batch, but I have no idea what they mean," Claudia said and handed Colby a photograph of nothing more than a name scrawled in the sand.

"Lizzy Coopersmith?"

"Who is Lizzy Coopersmith?" Layton asked.

"I don't have a clue," Colby said.

"She's my mother," Amy Taylor said as she walked into the hospital room. "Sid promised me she would find her."

"There were two more photographs, but I am not sure what they mean. Do they mean something to you?" Claudia asked, handing the photographs to Amy.

"Despair, and fondest memory, both written in the sand. I don't have a clue what they mean," Amy said.

"I'm not sure about the despair but I have my suspicions about the fondest memory aspect. I think what Sid is telling you is to recall your fondest memory of your mother," Joyce said.

Amy nodded hesitantly and closed her eyes. After a few moments a slight smile creased her face as she recalled the last Christmas spent with her mother. They were in the kitchen making Christmas cookies. Cinnamon and vanilla permeated the air as did molasses from the gingerbread men. Amy didn't like the spicy confections, but she loved to decorate them, so her mother always made a batch of them as well. Suddenly her tongue was coated with the taste of buttery vanilla frosting and her eyes darted open to confront a sea of gawking faces.

"What?" she asked.

"Take a sniff of the air," Colby said.

Amy reluctantly smelled the air. No longer did the hospital room smell of antiseptic, rather it hinted of freshly baked gingerbread and sugar cookies. There was something else as well, a slight hint of the lavender from her mother's clothes left by a sachet hanger in her closet.

"Do you all smell cookies too?" she asked. "And perfume?"

The small group nodded in unison.

"How is this even possible?" Layton said, glancing around the room at the faces just as bewildered as his and was responded to with a conglomeration of shrugs.

A smile forced its way onto Amy's face as a feeling of euphoria washed over her. She swooned, her knees buckled and without warning she dropped to the hospital floor. Tears gushed from her eyes, but they were not tears of sadness, they were tears of pure joy. Tears of freedom. Sid had kept her promise

A tandem of nurses came into the room, tended to both Junior and Sydney and checked their vitals. They eyeballed the small crowd gathered around Amy with displeasure but had already been told to leave them be, so they left without saying a word.

"Are you okay?" Joyce asked, helping Amy to her feet.

"I'm better than okay, I'm unburdened.

Colby struggled to keep his emotions at bay lest he end up bawling like a baby in front of everyone. Not only was he now convinced that Sid was somehow okay, living in another dimension, he was also certain it was exactly where she wanted to be. Which also allowed him to believe that when the time came and she no longer wanted to be where she was, she would return to him.

"May I see that photograph of the native woman, please?" Junior asked after taking a long drink of water.

Joyce helped Colby over to Junior's bedside and he handed the man the photographs. Junior was looking the pictures over when something happened that amazed everyone. The woman of the photograph smiled, turned her head slightly to the side and blew Junior a kiss before she began to fade. Not a single person in the room wanted to be the first to say what they had just witnessed so they all just let it go.

Junior felt a surge of energy rush though him like a warm bath, cleansing him of everything unholy. Tears streamed down his face as he understood his mother was finally at peace. That he was finally at peace.

"Eighteen down, only a few more hundred to go," Colby said, shutting the door on a file cabinet.

"Don't forget, four sadistic bastards in prison and two in their graves," Junior added.

Claudia came in with another folder of photographs and picked up a batch of film for the camera. Layton sat in the corner at his desk arguing with someone on the telephone about yet another missing person cold case.

Joyce was in the back room talking to Sydney while the private nurse tended to her patient. She broke off a piece of Slim Jim and tucked it under Sydney's leg. Less than a minute later Katie came padding in from the other room, nose in the air, sniffing frantically until she found the priceless nugget. She shoved her cold, wet nose under the blanket and came out victorious. Colby watched the whole scene with a smile and had to wonder if Katie was smart enough to know what was going on or if she thought Sid was magically crapping bite sized nuggets of spicy sausage.

"Sid, you would be proud of these guys. We miss you and hope to see you soon," she said with a tear in her eye while caressing Sydney's hair. Joyce swore the comatose woman smiled back at her.